EDITH'S
DIARY

EDITH'S DIARY

Patricia Highsmith

THE ATLANTIC MONTHLY PRESS
NEW YORK

Copyright © 1977 by Patricia Highsmith

First published in Great Britain in 1977 by William Heinemann Ltd.
First Atlantic Monthly Press edition, December 1989
Printed in the United States of America

Library of Congress Cataloging-in-Publication Data

Highsmith, Patricia, 1921–
    Edith's diary / Patricia Highsmith—1st Atlantic Monthly Press ed.
    "First published in Great Britain in 1977 by William Heinemann Ltd."—T.p. verso.
    ISBN 0-87113-296-6
    I. Title.
[PS3558.I366E35   1989]   813'.54—dc20   89-37489

The Atlantic Monthly Press
19 Union Square West
New York, NY 10003

FIRST   PRINTING

To Marion

EDITH'S DIARY

1

Edith had left her diary among the last things to pack, mainly because she didn't know where to put it. In a crate among the blankets and sheets? In one of her own suitcases? Now it lay naked, thick and dark brown, on an otherwise clear coffee table in the living room. The moving men weren't coming till tomorrow morning. The walls were stripped of pictures, the bookcases of books, and the rugs had been rolled up. Edith had been sweeping sporadically, amazed at how much dust could stay under things, even with a good cleaning woman like Priscilla, who had been helping Edith this morning. Now it was nearly 5 p.m. Brett should be back soon. He'd telephoned an hour ago, saying he wouldn't be back as soon as he'd thought, because he hadn't been able to find the right drill for his Black and Decker and was going to try Bloomingdale's.

And now, Edith thought, today, this evening, was the last evening and night the Howland family would spend on Grove Street. They were moving tomorrow morning to Brunswick Corner, Pennsylvania, into a two-story house surrounded by a lawn with two willows in front and a couple of elms and apple trees on the back lawn. *That* was worth an entry in her diary, Edith thought, and she realized she hadn't even noted the day when she and Brett and Cliffie had found the Brunswick Corner house. They'd been looking for some time, maybe six months. Brett was in favor of the move, with Cliffie ten years old now. A country environment would be a blessed thing for a child, something he deserved, space to ride a bicycle, a chance to see what America really was, or at least where the same families had been for more generations than most families had been in New York. Or was that true? Edith thought for a few seconds and decided that it wasn't necessarily true.

'Cliffie?' Edith called. 'Have you got those drawers emptied yet?' A long wait as usual before he answered.

'Yes.'

His tone was feeble. Edith knew he hadn't emptied the chest of drawers, though he had said he wanted to do it himself, so she went into his room – whose door was open – and with a cheerful air began to do it for him. Cliffie was upset about the move, Edith knew, though he'd seen the house and loved it and in a way was looking forward.

'Can't get much done if you sit reading comic books,' Edith said.

She knew from his wide, dreamy eyes that he wasn't even reading, simply trying to lose himself in the fantasy world of talking animals, spacemen, or whatever it was.

'There's no hurry, is there?' Cliffie asked, hitching himself back on his bed. He wore levis and a T-shirt which had University of California printed on it.

'No, darling, but we may as well do as much as we can today, because there'll be odds and ends tomorrow morning, and the moving men are coming at eight, you know.'

Cliffie didn't answer, didn't move, and Edith went on loading a crate with Cliffie's sweaters, folding them carelessly, dropping them. Then his pajamas, then shirts.

'You ought to be *happy*, Cliffie. Aren't you happy, going to live in a real house – with land – all your own?'

'Sure.'

'Didn't any of your friends say –' Edith tried to shake out a crumpled shirt from a bottom drawer and found that it was hopelessly stuck. With glue, apparently. Plainly it was tan-colored glue, couldn't be anything else. 'What happened to this?'

'Oh, I don't know.' Cliffie stuck his hands in the front pockets of his levis and walked from the room, head hanging.

Edith straightened and smiled. 'It's not so serious, Cliffie. Let's be cheerful! We're going to the Chinese restaurant to-night!'

It was a good white shirt, however, and otherwise clean. Had

Cliffie done it deliberately? What took out glue? Hot water? Edith dropped it into the crate-in-progress, and went on with her work.

'Cliffie? Is Mildew all right?' Her voice sounded sharp in the rugless apartment.

'Yes,' said Cliffie in the same toneless way.

Edith had last seen the cat sitting on the radiator cover in the living room, gazing out the window as if taking a last look at her three-story view of Grove Street. To make sure, Edith went into the living room, and saw Mildew on the floor by the sofa, her paws tucked in. Not a usual place for Mildew.

'Mildew,' Edith said softly, 'you're going to a much nicer house!' She touched the top of Mildew's head. The cat purred, half-asleep.

Mildew was a little over a year old. Edith and Brett had acquired her from the local grocery store, which hadn't been able to find a home for her. They'd named her Mildred, but Cliffie had arrived at Mildew, which they called her more often than Mildred. She reminded Edith of the cats in Hogarth's paintings with her white breast and feet, the rest of her brindle with a patch or two of black. A hearth-loving cat, Edith thought, and in Brunswick Corner she'd have a real hearth.

Cliffie at that moment was gazing out the window of his parents' bedroom. He realized that his heart was beating faster. The move was real, not something he had imagined, otherwise the carpets wouldn't be up, the refrigerator wouldn't be nearly empty. Cliffie often imagined much more violent things, like a bomb going off under their apartment building, even under all of New York, the whole city going up sky-high with no survivors. But suddenly this, their moving to another state, was somehow like a real bomb going off under his own feet. He looked around the neatly stripped bedroom, noticed the small leatherbound travel clock on his parents' nighttable, and at once thought of hurling it out the window. Cliffie imagined it hitting the pavement, maybe not breaking because of its leather cover, and imagined a stranger – delighted at having found something valuable – picking it up and pocketing it quickly, before anyone could notice him. Cliffie felt like breaking something, felt like hitting back at his parents.

Edith's big diary finally went between the second and third folded sheets in one of the crates. She must record this day, and tomorrow, right away in Pennsylvania, she thought, no matter how busy she was in the new house. She was rather glad she hadn't filled the diary with trivia all these years, because it meant that more than half the diary was still empty. The diary had been a present when she was twenty, still at Bryn Mawr, given her by a man called Rudolf Mallikin, who'd been about thirty (to her an older man), and she remembered with a slight embarrassment that she'd asked him for a Bible – when he'd said, around Christmas time, that he wanted to give her something nice, something she really wanted. That had been Edith's metaphysical period, Jakob Boehme, Swedenborg, Mary Baker Eddy and all that. Not that she hadn't a Bible, in a way, in her family's bookshelf, but she had wanted a nice leatherbound one all her own. But since Rudolf's objective had been to get her to go to bed with him, he had declared with a laugh that he simply couldn't give her a Bible, anything else but that, a fact which Edith later understood. So he had found a beautiful blank book, not even lines in it, so that she could make little sketches or draw maps, if she wished. Its brown leather was grainy and tooled with a gold Florentine design. The gold had flaked off to a great extent, but Edith had kept the leather oiled, and considering it was fifteen years old, the book showed only moderate signs of wear. To Edith it looked more handsome now than when it was new. She kept the diary always among her own things, her typewriter paper, dictionary, World Almanac, if she had a spare room to work in, as she had had here in Grove Street, or at least among her own things if she had to work in a corner of the living room. But Brett wasn't the type to pry, that was one of the nice things about him, and as for Cliff, Edith simply couldn't imagine him being interested in her diary.

And – Edith smiled to herself as she tackled more of Cliffie's possessions – she seldom looked back at what she'd written in her diary. It was simply *there*, and an entry helped her sometimes to organize and analyse her life-in-progress. She remembered she had opened the diary at random about a year ago, and had winced at something written when she was twenty-two. The more recent entries were apt to be about moods and thoughts. Such as one she remembered quite well written at least eight years ago:

'Isn't it safer, even wiser, to believe that life has no meaning at all?'

She'd felt better after getting that down on paper. Such an attitude wasn't phony armor, she thought, it was a fact that life had no meaning. One simply went on and on, worked on, and did one's best. The joy of life was in movement, in action itself.

If she had any problem, it was Cliffie, she admitted. He wasn't doing well in school. He didn't try, he had no initiative. He liked best to sit in front of the television set, not even paying much attention to it, just day-dreaming and nibbling at his fingernails. Worse and maybe more significant than the school failure was that he didn't or wouldn't or couldn't make any friends among kids his own age. He didn't passionately like anything or any person.

Edith's futile and familiar thought path was interrupted by a muscular effort – heaving up a stack of magazines, some of them curling at the corners with age. *New Republics, Commentarys.* She realized with a pang of guilt that her last article had been printed three years ago in 1952, a lance hurled against McCarthy.

The doorbell rang.

Edith pushed the door-buzzer blithely, not knowing or caring who it was. She went out on the landing and looked down the stairwell. 'Marion?' Edith called, thinking she recognized a coat sleeve.

'Me no less!' said Marion. 'How y'doin', kid?'

'Coming along, thanks!'

Marion emerged, onto the landing. 'Brought you a pie,' she said, smiling, a little out of breath.

'A pie! Aren't you a darling! Come in and see our progress!'

Marion Zylstra lived on Perry Street. Her husband Ed was a radio engineer. She was just a bit older than Edith, thirty-six.

Marion refused to let Edith cut the lemon meringue or make any tea or coffee for her, because she was sure Edith couldn't afford the time, but Marion did sit down on the edge of the sofa.

'We're going to miss you,' Marion said. 'Where's Brett?'

'Oh, Brett's looking for a gadget for his Black and Decker. He'll be here any minute.' Edith had lit a cigarette, but she didn't sit, only leaned against the heavy oval table in the living room, the table on which they dined when they had guests. 'Don't forget we're just two hours by bus from Manhattan. We want you to see the place as soon as you can. A real guest room. Imagine!'

Marion laughed. 'Plutocrats. I envy you. Ed's so stuck with his job in New York. Every family ought to have a certain amount of time in a country atmosphere, *I* think.'

Marion had no children. She was a registered nurse, worked irregular hours, and earned good money. Edith and Brett had taken a mortgage on their Pennsylvania house, they were anything but rich, but Marion knew that.

'I'm free for a little while now, Edie, if there's anything I can do. Ed's working midnight to eight, so he's sleeping now.'

'You're an angel but – Brett and I can manage the rest. Brett says most people wouldn't do nearly as much as we've done already, they'd leave it to the moving men, you know? Even the fragile things. But I like to do as much as I can. – Want to come to dinner with us tonight, Marion? We're going to the Chinese joint on Fourth.'

'Oh –' Marion begged out. She had to write to her mother, and there was a possibility that a patient might telephone if another nurse couldn't go on tonight.

Just then a key was fitted into the lock, and Brett came in, slender, alert, smiling. He wore an old tweed jacket, a turtle-neck sweater, baggy gray flannels. He had short-cut, straight black hair, and gave a boyish impression until one noticed crow's feet in the dryish skin under his eyes. His glasses had round black rims.

'Well, Marion! Greetings!'

'Hello, Brett! Just stuck my nose in to bring you a pie and wish you well.'

'A pie,' said Brett, advancing toward Edith, kissing her cheek as he usually did on coming home. He turned back to Marion. 'That's very samaritan of you. Why aren't you both diving in? Into the pie, I mean.'

'Marion hasn't the time,' Edith said.

Marion stood up.

'You and Ed better find the time to visit us,' Brett said.

Marion promised that they would, and Edith assured her that she'd make them come, even if the house wasn't completely fixed up. The Zylstras hadn't even seen the house, just a couple of photographs Brett had taken of it.

'And I hope your new job works out, Brett.'

'Oh. *Trenton Standard*,' Brett said, a bit uneasily. 'Less money, I'll tell you that right now.'

'Yes, *I* know.' Marion laughed, then she was gone.

'What's *that*?' Edith said in a whisper, having heard an ominous growl from the cat, from somewhere.

Brett followed her across the hall into the bedroom.

'Cliffie?' Edith said. 'What's happening?'

Cliffie wriggled off the double bed and stood up. From a heap of blue-and-white eiderdown the cat emerged, staggering, coughing, and jumped limply to the floor.

'Were you trying to smother her?' Edith said quickly, and anger suddenly burned her cheeks. 'You were!'

'All right, Edith, I'll –' Brett, just as grim as Edith, checked himself, however. He had long ago decided to let Edith handle Cliff, in case of crises. Brett didn't want Cliffie scarred by paternal sternness, and Brett realized he did lose his patience, had since quite a while lost it in regard to Cliff, beyond the degree to which a parent should lose it.

Speechless, Edith stared at the cat long enough to see that she wasn't seriously hurt, then looked at her son.

Cliffie's face was expressionless, as usual in such circumstances, neutral, rather calm, as if he were saying inwardly, 'What've I done, after all?'

Edith knew quite well that if not for the brief silence after Marion closed the door, she and Brett might not have heard the cat's growl under the comforter. Mildew might've been dead, if Marion had stayed two minutes longer.

'She was sleeping under the comforter,' Cliffie said with a shrug. '*I* didn't know it.'

Edith exchanged a dismal glance with Brett.

Brett passed a hand across his forehead, as if to indicate that they had enough to deal with just now without going further into this.

When Cliffie walked out of the room, Edith's shoulders relaxed, and she called after him, 'Go and wash your hands and face, Cliffie. We'll be going out to dinner soon.' Then to Brett she said softly, 'He's upset about the move, you know.'

'Yeah-m-m. And he seemed to be crazy about the house.'

'Did you find what you wanted today?'

Brett smiled. 'Oh, sure.'

They walked to the Chinese restaurant. It was a lovely September evening, just growing dusk, the air just cool enough to promise autumn. Edith felt happy at the thought of the work ahead, which meant writing too of course, in the new house. She and Brett had talked of starting a newspaper which they might call the *Brunswick Corner Bugle* or *Voice* or some such, a four-pager to begin with, with a letters column, an editorial column by her or Brett, local advertisements to keep it going. The healthy American liberal outlook, a bit left-wing. Edith had hopes. Brunswick Corner wasn't stuffy, wasn't mainly peopled by the rich and elderly. It was pretty enough to be a tourist attraction, however, had some historical houses – manses they were called – built around 1720 and 1740, had its share of gift shops, but lots of people commuted to New York and Philadelphia to their jobs.

And maybe it was the last time, Edith thought, they'd be having dinner at Wah Chum's. The food was good and reasonably priced. They could gorge on fried rice and soy sauce, butterfly shrimp, rice cakes, plus free fortune cookies which Cliffie adored.

14

'You're not sorry about the move, Brett, I mean – doubtful?' Edith asked, because it had been her idea.

'Gosh, no! I'm all for it. Even –' Brett paused to spoon more bean sprouts onto his plate.

Edith waited.

'Went by to see Uncle George this afternoon. Just a little ways from Bloomingdale's, you know. He said he envied us. Asked how many rooms we had. As if I hadn't told him.'

'I suppose he'd like to live with us,' Edith said.

Cliffie groaned, the first sound from him since he had attacked his food.

'There were hints in that direction,' Brett said.

Edith said nothing. Brett's old uncle – he was seventy at least – was a bit of a worry to Brett. He had something wrong with his back, just what no doctor had been able to find out, but he had pains, and he subsisted on his hospitalization money in an old people's resthome-*cum*-nursing-service in the East Sixties. Edith suspected him of malingering, though of course people of seventy had the right to retire and even malinger, if they could afford it. George seemed to be practically bedridden, though he still got up to go to the bathroom, Edith had been told by Brett. George Howland had been a successful lawyer in Chicago and New York, had never married, and was well-to-do, with a sum of money which he had said – though this wasn't definite as far as Edith knew – would go to Brett.

'And what did you say?' Edith asked finally. She was smiling a little.

'Oh, I was suitably evasive, I think. He was complaining about expenses where he is. Boredom et cetera.'

'If he's got enough tucked away, why doesn't he use it?' Edith said. 'Put himself up in a better –'

'Yeah!' Cliffie interrupted. 'Starting with a bicycle for me. I wouldn't mind a *bicycle*!'

'You'll get a bike and not from Uncle George,' Brett said, wiping his lips on a napkin stretched between his hands. Suddenly Brett grinned and slapped his son on the back. 'Cheer up, Cliffie. We're going to have a great life in Pennsylvania.

Maybe some fishing. Maybe a little boat of our own to sail on the Delaware! How about that?'

That night, just as Edith was walking toward the bed in her nightgown, she remembered a dream she had had. In the dream, she had closed the refrigerator door, into which Mildew had been poking her head, and cut the cat's head off. Either she had fainted in the dream or not realized what had happened, because later she had seen the cat walking around the house headless, and when she had rushed to the refrigerator and opened it, the cat's head had been in there, eating the remains of a chicken, eating everything. Often Mildew stuck her head into the fridge, and Edith had to push her away with her foot before closing the door. Would Cliffie some day slam the fridge door on Mildew's neck and say it was an accident? Edith found herself clenching her teeth. It hadn't happened. It wasn't true. But in her dream, *she* had done it.

2

Edith sat at her worktable (a flush door on trestles) which was pleasantly set to catch the maximum light from a north bay window. The curving window, some fourteen feet in width, was framed by white curtains, transparent enough for the willows, the green of the box hedges to be visible, and now a light breeze stirred the hems of the curtains. It was a fine November afternoon. They had been in the house nearly two months.

Beyond her worktable, on the wall facing her and above the bench seat hung a framed quotation from Tom Paine which Edith loved.

... These are the times that try men's souls. The summer soldier and the sunshine patriot will in this crisis shrink from the service of his country; but he that stands it NOW, deserves the thanks of man and woman. Tyranny, like hell, is not easily conquered.

The Crisis

She had told Cliffie about Tom Paine, the English-born corset-maker who had become a journalist, whose words had rallied the not always enthusiastic volunteer soldiers of Washington's army — which had brought their nation into being. She and Brett had taken Cliffie to see the cracked Liberty Bell in Philadelphia, and had in general tried to introduce him to his new Home State, which also included the battlefield of Gettysburg.

Now her diary lay open before her on the table. Last month she had written:

Our Brunswick Corner house — I would like to call it Peace — is as wonderful as I had hoped. Late tomatoes given by Johnsons still yielding in garden. Every day a little improvement on the house. B. arranging for a printer in Trenton for our newspaper which we think to call *The Bugle*. People here quite friendly, esp. the Johnsons who are one of us politically. Gert J. gives me gardening tips, comes to have a drink around 5:30 now and then.

B. likes his job. Less pressure, less money, but it is time B. began to enjoy life, existence.

A hasty entry, that was. A few days before, in the first weeks of Cliffie's starting at Brunswick School, Edith had written:

C. today accused of having stolen a football from gym. Teacher called up, asked if I'd seen it in the house. I said no, but would search the house. Did not find it. Have no doubt C. did steal it, maybe passed it on to some boy who doesn't even go to Brunswick School. This evening C. was evasive, angrily says he is being falsely accused. B. and I on the fence whether we should offer to pay for football. B. ashamed, says let it ride till we know something definite. Too bad C. starts out so soon on wrong foot.

Edith stared at the remaining half page, which was blank, on the right side of her diary, and rubbed her forehead. She and Brett now made Cliffie take a swat at his arithmetic, still his worst subject, two or three evenings a week. She or Brett would sit with him, trying to make it amusing, never making the session a full hour, so that half an hour or forty-five minutes would seem a treat. His English teacher and geography teacher, a woman and man respectively, had written them courteous notes saying that Cliffie was turning up without his written home-work done, though Cliffie professed to have had no homework assignments, when Edith had asked him about it. Edith was pleased that the school troubled to write her, after two months. Certainly no New York school would have troubled. Confronted by Cliffie's obvious lying, Brett had drawn a hand back as if to hit Cliffie. But Brett hadn't.

She sighed and picked up her pen. She didn't want to make the entry she was about to make, that she thought she ought to make to keep an honest record. Still balking, she turned back some eight or ten of the sturdy white pages and read:

18

7/Nov./54. In New York people say politics don't interest them. 'What can I do about it anyway?' This is the attitude government powers in America want to foster and do. News is brief, filtered and slanted. The Guatemalan 'uprising' would have been far more interesting if social conditions there had been described and if United Fruit Company's activities had been exposed – by radio and TV. Discussion clubs should be set up all over America to talk about forces *behind* things. We have been brainwashed for decades (since 1917) to hate Communism. *Reader's Digest* has never failed to print one article per issue about the inefficiency of anything socialized, such as medicine. From the American news media we have snippets without scenery, character or background. How could it be 'interesting'? People attempting to start discussion clubs, such as B. and I envisage, are labeled Communist. When a Russian is quoted on radio or TV, I find myself thinking in advance, 'This probably isn't going to be true, so why listen?' and if I feel that way already, how about the others? It is still true from 1936 to 1939 the Communists (Russians) were the only people giving the correct interpretation of the Spanish Civil War, giving reasons for the behavior of USA, Germany, France and so on, and the proof was the further rise and enhancement of Hitler and Mussolini and the Second World War.

Since then, of course, she'd read Orwell's *Homage to Catalonia* and *1984*. Betrayal, betrayal.

That thought did not make Edith feel any better, but she took a firmer grip on her pen – she preferred her lever-filling Esterbrook to a Parker Brett had given her last October for her birthday – and wrote:

9/Nov./55. Awaiting B.'s return from NY with Uncle George. He is coming to stay with us, for a while anyway. I wonder what I'll be writing a year from now about him? Because I don't see any end to it, and don't think G. is anywhere near dying. He's 73 or 74 and the family lives a long time. I'm quite sure he's going to need some waiting on. C. already grimly resentful (no milk of human kindness in him!) saying, 'Does he think we're an old folks' home or something?' If G. does turn out to be insufferable, surely I've got the right to say so to B. G. has plenty of money to live in a proper nursing home somewhere. He wants to pay us something, B. says, exactly what I don't know. When I

She stopped. Through the gentle hum of a car passing on the street, the distant shout of a child, she had heard the closer, more meaningful crackle of the Chrysler climbing the graveled driveway. She made sure the ink was dry on what she'd just written, closed her pen, closed her diary, and pushed it toward a corner of her worktable. She checked her appearance in a mirror on the wall. Hardly any lipstick, but it didn't matter. Her hair would do, and she ran her fingers upward through the loose, reddish brown curls.

At thirty-six, Edith was trim and athletic, in the sense that her shoulders were strong, her waist rather flat. Once in a while she thought she had put on too much weight, but she could take it off in days with a minimum of effort. She had light brown eyes, much the color of her hair, and eyelashes that seemed to be pointed artificially, which gave her a bright, alert look, she thought, a fact she was grateful for, because she did not always feel bright and alert, and it was nice to think she looked it. Her face was rather square, unlike her mother's or father's, and was perhaps a throwback to her Irish great-grandmother whose daguerreotype Edith possessed. Brett had once said she looked like a girl one could come up to and talk to, and Edith remembered he had said this in regard to the first time they met, Brett among a contingent of left-wingers from Columbia visiting Bryn Mawr in the spring of 1942. Brett had been then a postgraduate student at the School of Journalism. How full of energy and enthusiasm he had been then! Why should she think of all that – now? Edith gave her hair a final touch, and turned from the mirror.

A cheerful welcome was what counted now, and Edith intended to give George that. Plus tea or a drink of whatever he wanted. She had seen the old boy three or four times, she remembered, a couple of times in his New York apartment, then once in the nursing home more than a year ago. It was not quite 5 p.m.

Edith went out on the front porch, which had side steps onto the driveway as well as front steps. George, in the front seat beside Brett, seemed to be wearing a plaid bathrobe, and Edith felt a twinge of pity which was at once counteracted by the thought that he might be putting on an act. 'Hello, George!' she called as Brett opened the passenger door for him. 'Welcome!'

'Hi, honey,' Brett said. 'Give me a hand with a couple of these things? Is Cliff around?'

'He went for a walk with some boys – or to get a soda, I don't know. – How're you, George?' There were two or three carry-alls besides a big suitcase on the back seat.

'Not too bad, thank you, Edith. And it's kind of you to have me – indeed.' He coughed, and had barely squeezed out the last words. His face was pale and flat, his head bald with a fringe of gray. He was a tallish man, and by no means slender but rather solid.

Brett assisted George in getting out of the car and walking up the steps. George stooped, as if he hurt. Edith hovered, ready to take an elbow, but Brett seemed to be doing all right. George wore black shoes with no socks, and had pajamas on under his robe. There was something indecent-looking to Edith about his bare, blue-veined ankles.

'That's it. Thank you, Brett, old boy,' said George.

They got George seated on the living room sofa, and then brought all the luggage into the front hall. Edith announced that she would make some tea, and Brett took the suitcase and one carry-all up the stairs. Edith had decided to give George the small bedroom, not the main guestroom which had a double bed and which Edith knew Brett had thought to give him. They had occasional weekend guests like the Zylstras, and Edith wanted the big guestroom for them. As it was, she was giving up her sewing-and-ironing room.

They had tea in the living room with cinnamon buns and lemon cookies from the shop in town called the Cookie Jar, which was first-rate and used old-fashioned ingredients like butter. George praised the cinnamon buns and ate heartily.

'How is your back now?' Edith asked, thinking it a permissible question, and that George might even like to talk about his ailments.

'My dear, if I only *knew*,' replied George. 'The X-rays don't

21

show anything, doctors can't – put their fingers on anything, though they poke enough. Ha-ha! Damned back hurts, that's all.'

'You didn't fall – I've forgotten –'

'No, no. I remember lifting someone's suitcase, friend I was seeing off at Grand Central – *years* ago, maybe nineteen-fifty, and *bang* – a day later, crick in the back and I went from bad to worse.'

'But – you can walk, at least,' said Edith, speaking clearly, because George was a little deaf.

'With a cane sometimes. Yes. But I manage.' George had large, dark brown eyes, shiny as eyes in a varnished picture, and intelligent.

But George didn't come down for dinner. Edith had seen that his clothes, sweaters and so forth were stowed away in a small chest of drawers which she had cleared for him, and that his trousers and jackets were hung in the closet. There was a closet in every room in the house, which Edith considered a godsend, as one had no right to expect closets everywhere in a house a hundred years old. Brett had gone up to ask George to come down to dinner, but George had been in bed and asked if they minded if he had a tray. Brett carried the tray up, complete with Jello dessert and a cup of coffee.

'Is he going to want all his meals in bed, do you think?' Edith asked when Brett returned.

'Gosh! An invalid! Bedpans too?' Cliffie asked, and shrieked with appreciation of his own wit.

'Hush, Cliffie!' Edith said.

'I dunno,' Brett said. 'Can't tell any more than you can.'

Edith sighed, thinking Brett might have asked or somehow found out about a thing as important as this. Cliffie was listening sharply. It was not the time to ask about George's finances. Edith was ashamed of her own hardness suddenly. Was she tired today? Maybe. The curse to boot. 'Cliffie?'

'Yes?' His brown eyes, hardly darker than her own eyes, looked at her steadily, though sideways.

'I want you to be polite to your Uncle George, do you understand? Your great-uncle George.'

Cliffie nodded. 'Yes, mum.'

After dinner, Brett helped Edith in the kitchen, as he often did. It was a good time to talk, amid the clatter of dishes, and when Cliffie had drifted off to the television.

'He's offered – well, he wants to pay us sixty dollars a month,' Brett said, drying plates one behind the other, making a brisker clatter than usual.

That would just about take care of food, Edith calculated. 'Well – that's nice.'

'I really don't think he's stingy.'

What had he been paying at the place he left, Edith wanted to ask, but she didn't want to seem petty. There was his bedlinen, laundry to consider if he wanted his shirts done. But above all Edith was going to miss those hours Monday to Friday when Cliffie and Brett were out of the house. She liked being alone. Her thoughts flowed better.

'Look, if it doesn't work out, honey, we'll give him a gentle hint, all right?' Brett kissed Edith below her left ear. 'I promise.'

Edith didn't want to say bluntly that it appeared a permanent move. 'Yes. If he's got enough money to live somewhere else – and it appears he has.'

'Sure.'

'What's his money in? Stocks?'

'Some kind of trust, I think. He gets a certain income.'

Edith wanted to have a bath and go to bed and read, but George was in the bathroom. She could see the light under the door. The bathroom was absolutely silent. Edith seized the moment to see if all was well in George's room, and noticed that Brett had not taken down the tray, though he had come up to chat with George after the dishwashing. Edith picked it up from the floor. George had eaten everything.

A firm, assertive belch came suddenly from the bathroom, and Edith smiled, even shook with laughter for an instant.

In the days that followed, it became evident that George could come down for his meals, but he came down or not, according to whim. Anyway on the days (or noons or evenings) when he wanted a tray brought up, he didn't say that his back was any worse than on the days when he came down for two or three meals. He never dressed for breakfast, just wore bathrobe and pajamas, and didn't always get dressed for dinner.

When the Johnsons came for dinner one Saturday night, George did get dressed, and though stooped and stiff as ever, talked a lot and plainly enjoyed the company. George had worked as Paris representative for his law firm in his late twenties, and he had amusing anecdotes to relate. Gert and Norman Johnson lived in Washington Crossing about ten miles away. Norman was a free-lance interior decorator, Gert a painter as well as commercial artist, and she had also been a journalist for a while in Philadelphia. They had three children, the oldest twelve, and they hadn't much money. Edith rather liked them for their bohemianism (their house was a mess), their sense of humor, and left-wing politics. Edith's idea of starting a discussion club that would meet once a week at Edith's house, or at the house of anybody else who was willing, had brought a quick response from Gert. Gert had offered her own house at once, and Edith had gone, bringing one recruit, Ruby Maynell, whom Edith had met in the Brunswick Corner grocery store, where she had met Gert also. And Gert had invited a youthful widow from Washington Crossing, plus another woman who hadn't come. Edith had had some ideas for topics, and they had discussed them for twenty minutes or so, then the conversation had wandered. Such meetings needed a chairman, Edith knew. One could always try again, and she meant to. The same Trenton printer whom she and Brett intended to engage for the *Bugle* had said he could also print throw-away notices in regard to meetings. That was what they needed, real meetings of twenty or more, men and women, and if they got a discussion group going with at least twelve attending every time, the Brunswick Corner Town Hall could be lent to them, Gert had said. The Town Hall had heating and plenty of folding seats.

The Johnsons had brought their oldest, Derek, along at Edith's request. Derek went to a different school from Cliffie and was doing well, especially in math and physics, much to his parents' surprise. He was a slender, blondish boy with slightly wavy hair, a long nose and intense eyes. Now he stared at George

Howland, opposite him at the table, like a painter memorizing a face for future use, until finally George said:

'You've got photographic eyes, my boy, as well as a photographic memory?' George chuckled and glanced at Edith. 'I think he's taking a slow daguerreotype.'

George was sensitive about some things, insensitive about others, Edith had noticed.

Gert heard this and looked at her son.

Derek blushed. 'Sorry.'

'That's more like it.' Gert's pudgy face broke into a warm grin as she looked at Edith.

They were dining on rather good spare ribs with barbecue sauce. Norm's fingers were greasy to the second joints. He had shaved, but the rest of him looked as sloppy as ever: plaid lumberjack shirt, unpressed trousers, no jacket. Only Derek and Gert had made an effort, and Gert looked quite splendid in an East Indian skirt and white blouse and filigree earrings two inches long.

'Naa-aow, what were we saying?' Norm asked, still chewing on a bone. He had a Pennsylvania accent that Edith had learned was typical.

'About Eisenhower – how he did *nothing* about McCarthy,' Gert said with the same drawl and flatness as Norm. 'It was Senator Ralph Flanders of Vermont who had the guts to make a move against that bastard. "If Eisenhower won't, *I will*," Flanders said. If you remember, Norm.'

'Hear, hear!' said Norm, putting down a clean rib. 'You're right, dee-eerie, you're always right.'

Edith felt comfortable in the conversation, though it was only what she and Gert had said weeks ago. Edith had had almost three martinis, and a warm buzz had risen to her ears. She thought Derek handsome this evening. Doing well in school! If only Cliffie would pull himself together like Derek. Hardly two years' difference in their ages. Maybe puberty ...

'I was wondering, Edith, could you and Brett lend us a hundred dollars for a month?' Now Gert was in the kitchen, helping to put things away and stack the dishes for washing.

They'd had coffee. The men were in the living room. Edith didn't like to say yes without consulting Brett. Or was that a dodge? They hadn't any extra money now, however.

'It's the dentist's bill for Norm,' Gert went on. 'His father's promised to pay it and he will, but the dentist in Trenton is dunning us. We owe more than a hundred,' Gert said with a frank laugh, 'but a hundred will shut him up, and we ought to get a couple of hundred from Norm's father in *less* than a month.'

'Mind if I ask Brett?' Edith said in a pleasantly conspiratorial tone, which she was at once ashamed of.

' 'Course not!' said Gert. 'I know how it is. Specially now with – Brett's uncle on your hands.'

'Oh, he's contributing to his upkeep.'

When Edith got Brett in the kitchen alone, she told him what Gert had asked.

'Absolutely not. Don't start that,' Brett said.

'All right.' And it would be up to her to tell Gert, of course.

'It's the way to lose friends,' Brett said. 'An old saying, but true. – Sorry, darling. Tell her we've got extra expenses now too.'

Edith prepared herself to do it.

'Frankly,' Brett threw over his shoulder in a soft voice as he left the kitchen, 'I bet they've got debts all over the countryside. They're that type.'

Edith thought that was very likely true. But alone, she'd have lent the hundred, and maybe regretted it a little when she never got it back.

In the downstairs hall, where Edith encountered Gert getting something from her coat in the hall, Edith said with a wincing expression, 'Brett says no. We can't do it just now, Gert. I'm really very sorry.'

'Oh, that's all right.' Gert's relaxed smile made it seem as if nothing had happened. 'Where'd the boys go? To Cliffie's room?'

'Probably. If they're not around.' Edith imagined Derek taken aback by Cliffie's room, which looked like that of a six-year-old: comic books everywhere, a field of toy soldiers on the floor. Edith lifted her head and followed Gert into the living room.

Along with Gert, Edith took an unaccustomed nightcap of Chartreuse (expensive, and the bottle must have been with them for a year now), and lit a cigarette.

'How long you staying, George?' asked Norm from an easy chair, hands behind his head.

Edith listened with some interest.

'Oh – I dunno. Not as long as my welcome lasts, I trust. Ha-ha! It's pleasant here – with my nephew and wife – long as I'm not too much in the way.'

Edith offered people more coffee, served tonight from her silver pot, a present from her great-aunt Melanie.

The boys came back from Cliffie's room. Edith hoped they had made a date. They both had bicycles. The boys Cliffie went around with were younger than he, and it was absurd: It wasn't that Cliffie wanted to be a leader, a big shot, just that his contemporaries found him boringly young himself. Just as Edith was about to ask Derek if he could come for lunch next Saturday, Gert said:

'Oh Edie, Derek's taking clarinet lessons now. Isn't that something?' She spoke as if Derek had started the lessons on his own, and he probably had.

'How nice!' Edith said. 'Where?'

'Oh-h.' Derek waggled his head in embarrassment. 'Washington Crossing. It's a group lesson, three of us. But it's – interesting.'

'Got your own clarinet?' Edith asked.

'I'm buying it on the instalment plan.'

'With his allowance,' Norm said.

'And that's not very regular,' Derek put in.

'No comments,' Norm said, 'or we'll make you take a summer job. Like the rich kids.'

George got up creakily. 'Edith – must be retiring. Tired. Excellent dinner.' George relied upon his cane to begin walking.

Derek, the nearest, got up from the floor where he had been sitting. 'Help you, sir?'

Cliffie, also on the floor, didn't move, but watched George as if he were an animal in the zoo, remote, of mild interest.

'No, no. Night, everybody,' said George.

Brett at least perfunctorily helped George out of the room, started him on the stairs.

George did rather all right on his own, if he did things slowly. His cheeks weren't as pink as when he had arrived, but then he hadn't acted on Edith's and Brett's suggestion to sit out on the lawn in a deckchair, and he certainly didn't take any walks.

The atmosphere was decidedly more relaxed after George was upstairs.

'Really – he's living with you folks now, huh?' Norm asked.

'You could call it that,' said Brett.

'What does he do all day?' Gert asked.

'Reads a lot,' Edith said. 'I get books out of the library for him all the time. Then there're our books. He even reads some of Cliffie's encyclopaedias. Then he sleeps a lot.'

'Well, is he – going to a doctor at all?' This from Gert.

'No, his main doctor's in New York, and it seems - well, I have to take him once a week to Trenton, Saturdays, because the New York doctor sent his reports there. Records, I mean.' Brett took a breath. 'They take a look –'

'It's his back, isn't it?' asked Gert.

'Yes, they do pal – palpation,' Brett said in his earnest way, and for some reason they all laughed. Cliffie the loudest.

3

It was a morning blighted by the return of a self-addressed, stamped manila envelope, formerly folded in half, containing Edith's article 'Why Not Recognize Red China?' which she had sent to the *New Republic*. They wrote:

We remember your earlier two articles and we liked them, but this isn't for us right now, mainly because your main argument is covered in an article already scheduled. However we thank you for your submission.

Edith had once had an agent, Irene Dougal on West 23rd Street. But she felt she didn't write enough to warrant an agent, and had Irene really done her much good? Edith had sold just as much on her own, four things, so the score was 4–4, and the agent took ten percent. She had had no correspondence with Irene Dougal in a long time.

It was mid-December, and it seemed ages since the weekend in November when they had taken the car and rambled over Pennsylvania. Edith had asked the Quickmans, who lived next door, if they could look in on George and see that he was managing to get his own meals – which Edith had prepared as best she could in advance and put into the fridge. Frances Quickman had also fed Mildew. Edith and Brett and Cliffie had stayed a night in a motel near New Holland, another night in Lancaster, Amish country. Edith had bought half a dozen Pennsylvania Dutch pie plates of pale green glass, oven-proof, for fifty cents each at a dusty old roadside antique shop. She had also found a hand-painted chest of drawers for a mere eight dollars, and the man had been kind enough to deliver it the following week. Edith had installed it in the guestroom. It was beige with dainty blue and white painted flowers – delightful!

As Edith went about her chores that morning, hanging T-shirts and levis and pajamas on the back lawn line to dry, she reminded herself that she had vowed to change her attitude toward George. If he was going to become a fixture, it was destructive to fret – inwardly. It had occurred to her that George might be an asset, if she 'held a thought,' as Mary Baker Eddy would put it. George could be a good influence on Cliffie, if they got to know each other better. George had made a success of his career as a lawyer, and certainly passed exams in his time, and had been capable of organizing his life. Even now there was a method in his reading: nineteenth-century history for the past three weeks. Cliffie needed organization. Brett didn't spend nearly enough time with him. Edith decided to have a talk with George about Cliffie.

Her other equally important thought was that she ought to take it easier in regard to Cliffie. Nothing was going to be accomplished by reminding him that if he didn't pull himself together he'd never get to college. Cliffie wanted to go to college, Princeton indeed. Edith had had this same thought before, she had to admit, and she'd never stuck with it long. Anger and impatience would rise again, she'd feel like shaking him (only two or three times had she), and the old round of nagging would begin again. But this time with George in the house, things just might be different. Hope springs eternal, she thought, and smiled wryly at herself.

'George?' she called gaily from halfway up the stairs. 'Like a tray for lunch?'

'If you wouldn't mind, Edith – yes.'

'Right you are! Ten minutes.'

She made chicken sandwiches with lettuce, a touch of mayonnaise and sliced stuffed olives, put a couple of slices of tomato on each plate, and carried the tray up. She had also brought glasses and a quart container of milk.

'Thought I might join you,' she said, 'if you've no objection.'

'Of course not, why should I? A pleasure.' George heaved himself up a little against his pillows, and laid his book aside.

Edith put the tray on his lap, and managed for herself by

dragging up a second chair to put in front of her as a table. They were silent for a few moments as they ate, then Edith came out with it directly. 'It occurred to me, George, that you might be a good influence on Cliffie.'

'How so?'

'Well – because you're outside the family. I mean – of course you're Brett's uncle, but you're new to Cliffie. You're a man who's had a successful career, you know how to organize yourself – how to *work*, I mean, when you do work.'

George laughed dryly, 'Ha-ha!' with his mouth wide for an instant, then asked pleasantly, 'What do you mean by being a good influence? I never was a saint, you know.'

'But you can see, I think, that Cliffie doesn't buckle down to anything. He's got no drive, he doesn't see any reason for doing anything, not even for getting dressed sometimes in the morning, even finishing a model airplane once he's started.' Edith stopped, because she could go on and on about Cliffie.

But George seemed to be waiting for her to say more.

'I don't know if Brett's said anything to you, but Cliffie's been a worry since he was two and three years old. He's not stupid, really there's nothing wrong with his I.Q., I've been told. But all during his childhood, he seemed to take a pleasure in not doing what we wanted him to do like – make progress in reading before he even started school. He's like a person only half alive – except that's not really summing it up either.'

'Hum-m,' George said, pushing his head comfortably back into the pillows and gazing at the ceiling. 'I consider him simply a modern boy. He's a product of the television age. He's become passive, and like all of us now, he's bombarded by information, baffled and amused by events over which he knows he has no control – and he never expects to have any. A fit candidate for the Welfare State or whatever they call it in England.'

Edith remembered that a few years ago, she'd written much the same thing, using different phrases, about Cliffie in her diary. 'We even tried to budget the TV once,' Edith said. 'It didn't work. Cliffie can sulk.'

George coughed and reached for a wadded handkerchief. He

had Kleenexes, but preferred handkerchiefs. He was making no reply.

'I wonder where we went wrong?' Edith laughed a little. She realized she was goading George to make a remark in Cliffie's favor, to mention any smallest positive, praiseworthy thing.

'The time is out of joint,' George said. 'This is not an age for heroes.'

'Gumption I'm talking about. Maybe with puberty – You know –' She was launched now, for better or worse baring her mind to selfish, pain-in-the-neck George because at least he was a new ear and was listening quite as attentively as Brett ever did. 'You know with puberty, there's often an impetus, life takes on a meaning, and there's a drive toward something, even if it's only – butterfly collecting or making model ships.'

George looked at her condescendingly. 'Puberty means what puberty means. There's an increased awareness of the opposite sex, perhaps.'

'I mean,' Edith said, pushing the second straight chair farther from her and wishing she had a cigarette, 'you know what they say about artists, that every child is an artist till puberty, then with puberty he drops it, while the real artist derives strength and a sense of purpose and goes *on*.'

'Is Cliffie showing any interest in art?'

'No.' Edith smiled.

There was a silence then. Was George about to doze off? But his dark brown eyes, which were not looking at her, had not quite closed. Their lower lids sagged a bit, showing pink, reminding Edith of an ageing hound. She looked away.

'I just sometimes wonder if he'll ever pull out – wake up,' Edith said. 'So does Brett.'

George still said nothing. Edith felt his silence, felt his eyes which were on her now. It was as if George might not want to hurt her by commenting further. Then he said:

'Is Brett really liking his job in Trenton, liking the life here?'

Edith felt a swift shock of insult. 'Oh, the life, yes. He says the atmosphere isn't as lively as in New York with the *Trib*. Most of the material the *Standard* prints is syndicated. But the pay's not too bad. – Brett and I are starting a newspaper here, maybe he told you. *The Brunswick Corner Bugle*. We're aiming for Christmas for our first issue – aided financially by some ads the local shops have given us.' Edith smiled. 'That's why the phone rings more often lately. Advertisers. Or Gert informing me –' But Edith wasn't sure George was able to hear the telephone. Edith knew George didn't care for her or Brett's politics, thought they were babes-in-the-wood, doomed to failure. But after all Tom Paine's *Crisis* had been a small paper, and with what results!

'Is it cheaper living here than in New York? I suppose so.'

'Oh, it would be now, if we hadn't so many expenses on the house. You know how it is at first, the extras –' Edith was not thinking about what she was saying. She felt embarrassed, somehow almost humiliated, and stood up, saying, 'I'll take off. Things to do below stairs.' She collected plates.

'Dear Edith, I wonder if you'd mind terribly bringing me a cup of hot Ovaltine?'

'Now?'

'Yes, please. I think it's just the thing to get me off to sleep. Had a bad night last night. My back – right side this time, usually it's in the middle.'

Edith went down with the tray, vowing to herself that she'd get an electric kettle for George's room so he could make his own odd cups. She could perhaps get one with the Green Stamps she already had. She had been saving stamps for a new steam iron, but an electric kettle was clearly more urgent. She put the tray down a little hard on the kitchen table, and poured what was left of the milk into a pan to heat.

Her thoughts flew off at angry tangents as she snatched down the Ovaltine jar and reached for a spoon. Since when was George God, even if he had made some rather astute comments on Cliffie? Edith didn't believe Cliffie was hopeless, but George had implied as much. Why hadn't George ever married, for instance? What was the matter with *his* make-up? Edith couldn't imagine a man thirty-five or so not getting married, if he could afford to, because it was so convenient to have a wife, they performed so many services. If George had a wife, he wouldn't be here now, for instance. George was better looking than the average man, he must have been earning pretty well all his life, so Edith concluded that he was selfish, or had made mistakes in handling women, or was perhaps incapable of love or affection for another person. As she carried the Ovaltine up on yet another tray, a smaller one, she felt miserable, felt she had revealed too much to George. She felt vulnerable to him now, more cut down in his eyes. And yet here he was in *her* house, and it was she who was his servant.

However, some ten minutes later, she was feeling decidedly better. Marion and Ed Zylstra were coming for Christmas, staying at least three days. Friday, day after tomorrow, Brett was bringing the first copies of the *Bugle* in his car, a homely way of distributing a newspaper, Edith supposed, leaving copies at the grocery store, the hardware, the drugstore – four hundred copies. The first issue was a give-away, though the four-pager was supposed to cost fifteen cents. She had tried hard to strike the right note in the editorial, and had gone over it with Gert Johnson. It was mainly about a bill in Harrisburg about upping school taxes, a big concern in the area at the moment. After some asterisks, the last paragraph ran:

Two refugees from New York, Brett and Edith Howland, send Christmas greetings to new friends and neighbors and all readers of the *Bugle*, and wish everyone a most Happy Season!

Edith put some Brahms waltzes (Opus 39) on the record player, and closed the living room door which went into the hall, so the music would not awaken George. She had lit a cigarette, and was relaxing in an armchair. The piano music delighted her, transported her to a world of beauty and brilliance – with a beginning and an end. It was odd to feel for a few seconds at a time – the sensation came and went – completely *like* the music, quite at home with it, familiar with every note, yet to realize that the music was not her home, was not the main part of her life. Sometimes she thought music that she especially liked was a drug for her, magical and unreal, and yet necessary.

34

Unreal, and yet for many seconds the inspired waltzes made her love her house more, made her remember that the house and the semi-rural life she had now was after all what she had wanted for years. The interior of the house, walls and doors, were of a creamy color, like the exterior which had been originally more white but was now weathering. The front porch pillars could be called doric, but were certainly not pretentious. And Brett was happy enough with his job. George wasn't *such* an old bore, after all. He'd given Brett money to buy blue jeans and a sweater for Cliffie for his birthday in November.

When the first side of the record was finished, the silence began to attack Edith like a live thing, eating away at her brief contentment. This was life, she thought, back to the ironing which she now did in the kitchen, back to thinking of where next she might send the article on recognizing Red China. A vague depression crept through her, crepuscular, paralysing. She knew the feeling well. Sometimes it was incontrollable, so much stronger than herself that she had wondered, even in the first weeks she had been in the house, if it weren't due to a vitamin deficiency or something physical. But the report of Dr Carstairs, a local doctor recommended by Gert, just last month, had been good. She was not anaemic, her weight was normal if not a trifle under normal, which the doctor thought preferable, and there was nothing wrong with her heart.

It was a mental attitude, Edith thought, nothing else. She often consoled herself by thinking that probably everyone in the world, who was at all sensitive, suffered the same low moments and for the same reasons. Edith had constantly to bolster herself by remembering that she didn't believe life had any purpose, anyway. To be happy, one had to work at whatever one had to work at, and without asking why, and without looking back for results. This plainly demanded good health for a start, and she had that. So why was she discontented, periodically (for a few hours at a time) unhappy? Edith couldn't answer that.

4

On Christmas Eve day, just after 4 p.m., Ed and Marion Zylstra arrived on the bus, bearing gifts, bottles, and a lightweight suitcase. Edith had met them with the car.

'Hello, darling! Isn't it perfect weather!' Marion said, embracing Edith.

Snow had fallen during the night, some eight inches of it, and now the sun shone brightly. Everything looked clear and white, and the Delaware River was a noble gray-blue between its rocky, snow-covered banks.

'And how are you, Ed?' Edith asked. They were storing things in the back of the car.

'Pretty well, thanks. Looking forward to three days without duty. Not that we have to camp on you that long!'

'But we hope you will. We really do.' Edith remembered that Ed always called his work duty, like a soldier. He was about forty, blond and blue-eyed, with a muscular, not very tall figure which Edith had always thought rather sexy. It was only the second time the Zylstras had come to Brunswick Corner.

'I suppose you've been working wonders in the house since we saw you?' Marion said.

'Well, you'll see. Here we are.' The bus stop was hardly a quarter of a mile from the house.

Marion and Ed exclaimed at the changes in the living room. The curtains were all hung now, the windowsills graced with a potted plant here and there, the bookcase loaded – just as in New York. A six-foot Christmas tree stood by the back window, far enough from the fireplace that its needles had a chance of lasting ten days.

Edith made old-fashioneds in the kitchen.

'And where's Brett?' Marion asked. 'Working today?'

'Just this morning. He'll be home any minute – from Trenton. He's bringing the first issue of the *Bugle* so we can christen it.'

'I'm longing to see it!'

Edith went into the larder off the kitchen, and had just lifted a jar of maraschino cherries from a shelf, when she noticed the turkey – the turkey's breast. A great gouge had been taken or eaten out of each side of the raw breast, and Edith at once thought of Mildew, because it looked as if a cat's teeth had been at it, then thought of Cliffie, because the larder door had been firmly closed. Edith glanced at the floor. The cat was not in the larder. Cliffie might have put Mildew at the turkey, Edith thought, because Mildew on her own wasn't a thief, well fed as she was. No, these gouges were man-made. No time to stew over it, and no time to buy another turkey either, though the appearance of this one was ruined.

Brett arrived, bearing a stack of *Bugles* which he had to carry in both arms with interlocked fingers. Norm Johnson had just dropped him in front of the house, Brett said, but he hadn't time to come in. The Johnsons were due to look in later, around midnight.

'Tooty-toot-toot, the *Bugle*! Let's see it!' Marion said.

Brett lowered the stack to the floor. 'Just distributed about three hundred with Norm's help. Local stores. These I have to distribute tomorrow. Well, some tonight, shops nearby. Things are open late tonight.'

Edith refrained from seizing a copy, went into the kitchen and made a drink for Brett. It promised to be a beautiful Christmas time. She wasn't even dismayed by the turkey. They'd laugh at it tomorrow.

'Thanks, darling. Cheers!' Brett said, lifting his glass. They all drank to the *Bugle*. Brett had on his padded army jacket with its belt hanging at the sides now, chino trousers under which, however, Edith knew he wore long underwear. Pennsylvania was often eight below zero in winter. 'Where's Cliffie?' Brett asked.

'Don't know. Maybe out somewhere,' Edith said.

She had baked a ham for that evening, and it was now almost done in a low oven. Somehow it was already after 6, and Edith went into the kitchen to get the dinner moving, while the Zylstras took off with Brett to help with the *Bugle* deliveries. It had grown dark, which Edith thought dramatic tonight, with the white snow everywhere outside. And it was nice to think of the earth (since yesterday) tipping toward the sun again, and to know that the days would start to become longer.

Cliffie strolled into the kitchen.

'Well, where were you?'

'In my room.'

Edith suddenly thought, *My God, I didn't ask George down for a drink.* But George often slept from 5 until dinnertime. 'I don't suppose you know anything about the turkey,' Edith said as she shook the lettuce swinger over the sink.

'The turkey? I haven't seen it.'

'Of course not. You don't go into the larder usually, do you, because your Coca-Cola's in the fridge, but –'

'I don't know what you're *talking* about.'

Edith had had enough to drink to pursue it. 'Who opened the larder door? I didn't. Didn't you know the turkey was there – naked?'

'Naked? Naked turkey!' said Cliffie, and laughed.

Edith could have slapped him. She forced herself to be calm. 'You didn't possibly show Mildew the turkey?'

'No!' Cliffie protested, all innocence.

'You're a liar,' Edith said, and went about her work.

Cliffie lingered, a wishy-washy vertical object which Edith avoided looking at directly.

'Or did you just poke at the turkey yourself with a knife?'

'I don't know anything *about* the turkey!' Cliffie said, his face reddening, tears starting. Then he went aggressively to the fridge and extracted a bottle of Coca-Cola.

Dinner was merrier. George had come down, dressed. Edith was feeling mellow with the wine, and it didn't seem of earth-shaking importance if the dishes weren't done till tomorrow morning. *The Bugle* had been thoroughly examined. The paper was slightly glazed, the print dark, the lay-out pleasant, Edith thought.

'Want to see some before and after snaps?' Edith asked, dragging an album from the coffee table shelf. 'Very *few*, so you won't get bored.'

They were of the house, of course, and this led Marion to look back in the album to earlier pictures of Edith and Brett and Cliffie when he was in diapers. Edith laughed loudly at some of them.

'Here's Poughkeepsie,' Edith said, 'versus Virginia. You have to admit Virginia is prettier.'

On opposite pages, Brett's family's redbrick house in a city street confronted Edith's family's house with its grounds and trees. A fact, Edith thought, of geography, not money, because Brett's family wasn't any poorer than hers was rich, which was to say they were both medium. Only great-aunt Melanie was rich in Edith's family, and that because of her husband, now deceased, who had inherited part of a tobacco firm. There was a fine color picture of Aunt Melanie serving tea on her sunlit lawn near Wilmington.

'You trust Brett in the kitchen?' Marion asked. 'Ed's hopeless.'

'Oh, Brett's a gem. But don't think he's *washing*, he's just stacking. – Brett?' Edith called. 'How's the coffee?'

'Coming!' And just then Brett appeared in the doorway with a tray.

Edith poured.

'Cliffie gone to bed already?' Brett asked.

'Haven't seen him,' said George, who was nearest Brett. 'Coffee smells so good, I think I might indulge myself tonight.'

Edith went to get another cup and saucer, and when she came back, Marion was asking:

'Are you enjoying your life here, George?'

'Oh, yes, indeed! Healthful climate. I ought to get out more. But it's difficult for me to walk.'

The telephone rang.

'Bet that's the Johnsons,' Edith said. Brett went to answer it. 'You'll like the Johnsons, Marion. I don't think you met them the first time you were here, did you?'

'*What?*' Brett said in a horrified tone. 'When? Are you s –' The sibilant sound turned into a slow whistle.

Edith got up and walked toward the hall. 'Brett, what's up?'

'Oh, he's all right. Good. – Sure we'll be up. We could also –' Brett looked at the telephone, then put it down slowly, and walked toward the living room. 'Cliffie just jumped in the river.'

'The *river*?' said Marion.

'That was the hospital in Doylestown,' Brett said. His face was paler in the last seconds.

'Is he hurt?' Edith asked.

'They said no,' Brett answered hoarsely, and sank into his chair. 'Holy Christ! Right *here*! Three blocks from home! Jumped in the river this time of year!'

'Or did he fall?' asked Ed, frowning.

'No, they said he jumped, because someone saw him jump.'

'How'd he get out?' George asked.

'They had to go get a guy with a rope. And then another man jumped in,' Brett said. 'Had to, because there's a current, you know.'

George leaned forward. 'Who was it saved him?'

'We'll have to find out tomorrow.' Brett wiped his forehead, and poured more coffee for himself. 'Yes. We ought to be grateful – for good neighbors tonight. Somebody jumped in and pulled him out.' He glanced at Edith.

Just then the fire gave a loud *pop!*

'Hark! the herald angels sing ...'

This came from beyond the front door, and the singing swelled as a group of kids climbed the front steps.

'We ought to give them something, Brett,' Edith said.

Ed was getting up, reaching in his trousers pocket. So was Brett. The two men went to the door.

Edith had a glimpse of five or six small children, a couple of them bearing candlesticks, standing on the doorstep.

'Thank you! Merry Christmas!' one said, and there was no pause in the music.

'... Glory to the newborn king!'

'So Cliffie's not hurt at all?' George asked as Brett came back.

'They're treating him for shock – or exposure or something,' Brett said. 'They're bringing him any minute. What the hell happened, Edie? Something happened after dinner that I didn't notice?'

'It was no doubt the turkey,' Edith said, feeling embarrassed and yet not embarrassed, as everyone listened, because she'd had just enough to drink that the whole thing seemed unreal, untrue. 'Someone gouged the turkey breast. Turkey's in the larder. I may as well tell you now, because we'll have to face it for tomorrow's dinner.' Edith felt like giggling.

'Oh, the turkey!' Marion said. 'Who cares about the *turkey?* We don't have to have –'

'The turkey's *there,*' Edith interrupted, 'it just looks like the cat's been at the top of it, and the larder door's always shut *firmly,* unless Cliffie opened it deliberately.'

'And of course you told him he did,' said Brett precisely, without mercy toward Cliffie, and without resentment against Edith.

'I did because I –' Edith had started out boldly, but suddenly she collapsed inwardly. 'Because I know he did open the door on purpose. And I don't even think it was Mildew, I think he poked at it with a knife to ruin it.' She was finished. She put her face in her hands.

Marion held her in one arm, rocked her on the sofa.

And suddenly it was over. Edith lifted her head, smiled, and said, 'I'm sorry. It's the shock of it.' It struck Edith that Ed was strangely silent, sober, that he perhaps didn't like them, that he thought the atmosphere crazy, unnatural.

Edith heard the stomp of a foot on the porch, then their bell rang with a loud peal.

'Maybe the hospital,' Marion said.

Brett opened the door.

'Hello! Merry Christmas!'

Gert and Norm Johnson and Derek stomped the snow off their boots on the doorstep, removed boots, and entered in stocking feet, carrying presents in red and white striped paper.

'Merry Christmas, everybody!' Gert repeated, smiling broadly.

'Merry Christmas!' Edith replied, and got up smiling. 'This is Marion Zylstra – and her husband Ed. Our neighbors the Johnsons.'

'How do you do?' said Gert.

'Howdy do?' from Norman.

'Heard a lot about you,' Marion said.

'And Derek,' Edith continued.

'Evening,' said Derek.

'Boy's just had three glasses of punch and he's as oiled as we are,' Norm said. His tasseled scarf hung nearly to the floor, and there was a hole in the toe of one of his socks. 'Hee-*yappy* Christmas!'

'Same to you!' Brett replied, and at that moment he and the rest heard the drone of an ambulance siren.

'Jesus, what a time for a car accident,' Norm said. 'Or maybe somebody's reenacting Washington crossing the Delaware –' Norm broke off, stifled by laughter.

'You know some of these idiots around here,' Gert began cheerfully to Marion, 'get into a rowboat Christmas Eve and fall in. Our town's called Washington Crossing, where he crossed on Christmas Eve to surprise the British at Trenton. Maybe –'

'Let's have the date, mom!' said Derek. 'Seventeen –'

The doorbell rang.

Gert set her two packages down on the floor under the tree. 'God bless!'

'Cliffie just jumped in the river,' Brett said, more or less to Gert.

'Huh?' said Norm.

Brett went to the door.

Gert was listening, and Edith said, 'It's true, Cliffie jumped off the bridge – and the hospital's just bringing him home.'

Norm looked at her blankly.

Derek took it in, Edith saw from his face.

'I hope he didn't hit any rocks,' Derek said.

'Come in,' Brett said to someone at the door.

A tall redheaded young man came in with Cliffie in his arms. Cliffie was swathed in blankets. A second intern followed, ready to lend assistance. Marion got up from the sofa.

'He's all right. They thought since it's Christmas Eve –' said the man carrying Cliffie.

'Put him on the sofa,' Brett said. 'Or does he have to –'

'How you doing, Cliffie?' asked George, who was still seated on the sofa.

Cliffie looked quite alert, was even smiling, but he didn't say anything. The intern installed him in a corner of the sofa, setting Cliffie upright.

'You're all right, Cliffie?' Edith asked, bending over him. 'Where's your hand?' She had extended her hand. Cliffie was wrapped like a papoose. As soon as she thought this, she heard Gert saying:

'... like a *papoose*!'

'Oh, he's warm enough now. That was the main thing,' one of the interns was saying to Brett. 'He's not in danger, or we wouldn't have brought him home.'

'Can I offer you a drink?' Brett asked the interns.

'Well, I – We shouldn't, because we're on duty tonight,' said the redheaded intern, looking as if he wanted to stay for a drink. 'Your boy jumped, they said.' He glanced quickly at Cliffie. 'You should look into that. We're just a hospital, you know.' He was almost whispering.

Brett nodded. 'You'll send us the bill, I trust.'

'Not sure there'll be any. Not for something like this.'

The two men took their leave, Brett thanked them again, and all three exchanged wishes for a happy Christmas.

Gert had her hand on Cliffie's shoulder, a mound of blankets. 'How're you feeling, Cliffie? You'll want to go to sleep soon, won't you? Are you hungry?'

Cliffie shook his head. 'No.'

'Why'd you jump, Cliffie?' Brett asked. 'You jumped, didn't you? You didn't fall.'

'Oh, Brett, don't question him now,' Marion said.

'If I don't now, I may never get the answer – or the right answer,' Brett replied.

Edith knew Brett was tired after a long day, that he was more ashamed of Cliffie than concerned about his state.

'Do you know who pulled you out?' Brett asked Cliffie.

'We'll find out, Brett,' Edith said. 'The whole town'll know tomorrow.'

> '... Good King Wenceslas ...
> ... on the feast of ...'

They were back. No, passing by, Edith thought. No, *back*, because here it came louder. However, these were men's voices. One singer broke off in a tipsy guffaw.

'Nobody's going to ask for alms, so we're *not* ringing the bell!' a man said, and his voice came clearly from the snowbound street, because no one in the living room was talking just then.

Gert had just lit a cigarette, and she shook the match out with a jerk of her wrist and said, grinning, 'Bet that's Malc and Harry from the Stud Box, Norm. Sounds like 'em. They're always clowning.' She laughed a merry laugh.

The Stud Box was a men's shop in the town.

'Faggots,' said Norm good-naturedly. 'Can I have a re-fill, Brett?'

'Help yourself, Norm!' Edith said. She had put rye, whisky, rum, gin, and the ice bucket on a card table, in easier reach than the bar cart.

'I think Santa Claus or a friend of yours brought you an interesting present from New York, Cliffie,' Marion said, bending toward him. 'Want to see it now?'

'Oh – he can wait till tomorrow,' Edith said. Cliffie looked all right, but was in a trance, Edith thought. She was familiar with his trances. 'Want to go to bed, Cliffie?'

Cliffie didn't answer, though he looked at his mother. He

44

was not quite smiling, but he was enjoying perhaps the happiest moment of his life. He loved being wrapped up like a mummy, so that he couldn't even lift an arm or a hand, loved being warm and cozy and fussed over, because he really had jumped off the bridge. He could hardly believe it himself, that a couple of hours ago he'd climbed over the metal parapet which was nearly as high as his shoulders, looked down for a few seconds, then jumped – into the darkness, into the water. Even at camp, he hadn't had the courage to jump off a diving board, even when the distance had been much less and he could see what he was jumping into. Cliffie was also amazed that he'd been rescued, and pretty quickly. The seconds when he'd thought to jump, and had jumped, had been brief and magical. Had it been *he*? Of course! Here he was, and he knew quite well that he'd just been in the hospital in Doylestown, with people hovering around him, giving him hot tea, putting hot water bottles at his feet. Cliffie felt that he was a changed boy, that he might sprout wings, that he might have stupendous powers from now on. He was *happy*.

Cliffie's dream of glory was jolted, slightly, by a clatter on the staircase, a little shriek from his mother in the hall, a yell from somebody else. George was groaning, mumbling something.

'You all right, George?' said Marion in the hall.

Cliffie giggled, shivering and shaking at the same time under his blankets. Old Uncle George had fallen on the stairs! Ha-ha! Maybe fallen on his ass, or his nose!

Brett and Edith were getting George to his feet. He had fallen forward, thank goodness, and had only a nosebleed, or so it seemed, because Marion, the nurse, busied herself with Kleenexes and soothing words.

'What *else* tonight?' asked Marion, laughing.

Edith was in a mood to laugh also, but part of it was hysteria, she knew. They got George up to his bed, made sure he was all right, didn't want Ovaltine or anything else.

The present-opening took place Christmas morning, as was the Howlands' custom, and with this went eggnog in silver mugs, and spice cookies. The Zylstras gave them a portable barbecue grill with battery lighter and a bag of charcoal. Cliffie got a transistor radio from George. Brett and Edith gave the Zylstras a turquoise towel set to match their bathroom in New York. The cat romped noisily amid discarded wrappings. Edith opened Melanie's present the last, a pretty Mexican box with a rooster design, and she thought at first it contained nothing but tissue paper until she found an envelope which held a check for a thousand dollars and a note: 'Am not very imaginative this year, so will give you this for you to use your imagination on – with love always from your Aunt Melanie.'

'A check,' Edith said to Brett with a grateful sigh. 'Isn't she a darling?'

And Cliffie also was happy. He loved getting presents, loved the transistor radio that was shiny and new and all his own, and loved equally his gift from the Zylstras, a Superman suit of black tights and cape (yellow-lined), and a kind of metal trumpet to yell through, which apparently came with the suit. Plus a black mask. The suit fitted perfectly, and clung to him. Cliffie, feeling better than new that Christmas morning, donned the suit at once in his own room in the back downstairs corner of the house. He leapt up so he could get a view of hips and legs in his mirror. *Superman!* And he felt worthy of wearing it, because he had jumped off the Delaware River bridge the night before. Not for him the Washington Crossing silliness in a rowboat! He swilled Coca-Cola while the adults drank their eggnogs. Cliffie stalked about the living room in great strides, glancing at himself in the big rectangular mirror over the blanket chest. Then he slipped out the door, knowing his parents wouldn't have let him go out without a coat and snow boots.

Cliffie walked in more or less stockinged feet (though they had some kind of stiffening on the bottom) through snow that had been swept off the sidewalk but was still a few inches thick. He had the black mask over his eyes, and therefore had to turn his head sharply in various directions to see where he was going. He hailed people he didn't know at all, saying, 'Merry Christmas from Superman!' and was rewarded by laughter and returns of the same.

He walked – by now wet up to his ankles – to the bridge from which he'd jumped last night. There the bridge was, solid and gray in the sunlight.

'Hey!' said a small boy who was with his parents.

Cliffie recognized him, a fellow called Vinnie or Vincent who went to his school.

'Cliffie?' said Vinnie.

Cliffie ignored him, and strode on toward the bridge, but suddenly turned and said, 'Superman greets you!' raising his right arm.

Vinnie looked stunned.

'You're going to freeze!' said the woman.

Cliffie leapt up and hunched himself over the rail of the bridge, bracing his shivering body on his forearms.

'What're you up to?' said a man in galoshes, clumping past on the bridge.

Cliffie ignored him. The river's edges, both sides, were prettily adorned with clumps of snow on rocks and bushes. Some rocks were visible, gray and sharp. Amazing he hadn't a scratch on himself from the rocks, Cliffie thought, but then – he was Superman! Cliffie ran swiftly across the bridge, dodging a car, to have a look from the other side, and just then became aware of a running beige figure over his right shoulder.

His father!

'Cliffie! *Dammit!*' Brett said. 'You going to do it again?'

'No-o!' Cliffie yelled, suddenly hating his father who was putting an end to everything.

'Dammit, you caused enough trouble last night! Come on!' Brett took Cliffie by the hand, fairly yanking him, and seeing that Cliffie's feet were wet, Brett picked him up by the waist and carried him in one arm like a sack of wheat, turned the boy slightly so he could breathe. 'Honestly, Cliffie – Do you want pneumonia next?'

Cliffie erased his thoughts, and endured the short walk home. He stomped his feet on the doormat, entered the warm house calmly, but even so his mother was hovering, telling him not to wet the waxed floor. Someone spread wrappings from Christmas packages under his feet.

Tea again. A sweater over his Superman outfit, the pants of which they had compelled him to take off, because they were attached to the wet feet. The hospital blanket again over his legs as he sat on the sofa. 'I'm still Superman!' Cliffie said to the whole room.

Cliffie was pleased by the way the adults stood around wordless, looking at him.

5

2/Feb./57. *Bugle* still tootles along, though barely breaking even now. I refrained from noting its initial success, thinking it bad luck to do so. People (advertisers) simply don't need it, and that's the crunch. Gert's (and I must say my own if I do say so myself) editorials are damned good, and dear old Gert writes extra letters under another name sometimes. Not enough people seem to care enough.

The hopes Edith had had for Brett's taking Cliffie fishing or rowing – some people did row a bit on the Delaware, some even ventured out in small sailing craft in summer – simply hadn't materialized. Brett didn't enjoy taking a walk with Cliffie in the woods because Cliffie (according to Brett) announced after fifteen minutes that he was bored and wanted to go home. Of course Brett wasn't much of an outdoor man himself. He liked to do jobs like insulating the roof, or putting up shelves in his basement workroom. But Cliffie didn't like such tasks, and had always been clumsy with his hands. He didn't grip even a Coca-Cola bottle properly, much less a hammer. It was an everyday thing for him to drop a knife or fork on the edge of his plate. The articulated thumb, praised by anthropologists as man's blessing (along with the monkeys of course) was in Cliffie short and stiff, and of about as much help as another little finger. His ineffective hands seemed to proclaim that his grip on life or reality was nil.

Edith's great-aunt Melanie visited every six months or so, and stayed about five days. Edith adored her visits. They talked of a variety of things – old family stories that Melanie might have heard from her own grandmother's knee, Thomas Mann's essay on Nietsche and The Will, school integration (the South would do better than the North, Melanie predicted), and the proper way to make dill pickles. Melanie's visits brought an extra treat in that Cliffie put on his best behavior. But Edith knew that Melanie was not fooled. She always had a gift or two for Cliffie, always talked with him as if he were a human being worthy of respect and love, but Edith knew that Melanie simply didn't like Cliffie, didn't or perhaps couldn't understand him. 'There's nothing to hang onto in him, is there?' Melanie had said once. Or had she really said it? But Edith knew that was Melanie's feeling. 'Is he showing any interest in girls as yet?' Melanie asked when Cliffie was fourteen or so. It was for Aunt Melanie a rather bold question. Edith said not as far as she could see. Cliffie was unsure of himself, Edith had added quite unnecessarily, and the subject had been dropped.

These days, Edith knew, kids twelve, maybe younger, were attempting intercourse. There was something bizarre, even depressing about it, Edith thought. Cliffie perhaps had a fantasy world as definitely peopled as that of – the Marquis de Sade came first to her mind. She was under no illusion that Cliffie was innocent, naïve in heart and mind. Was he still a male virgin? Edith smiled to herself at the thought. Very likely not. Whom did he meet, hanging around Mickey's, a popular seedy bar on Main Street, where kids Cliffie's age could have soft drinks but weren't supposed to be sold beer? Gert fairly boasted about Derek's conquest of an eighteen-year-old assistant of the family dentist in Trenton. Had Brett ever had a talk with Cliffie about the facts of life?

'But – what'm I supposed to tell him? At his age,' said Brett, looking nearly as blank as Cliffie did sometimes. 'After all, his voice has already changed. Fourteen –'

'Well – don't you think it's a little funny he's never had a girl friend, not even a crush –'

'He wouldn't necessarily *tell* you,' Brett interrupted.

'Oh, Brett! Kids phone. They write letters. It –'

'Kids these days are illiterate.'

'It even crossed my mind he might be queer, I swear.'

Brett laughed heartily. 'I doubt it from the way he borrows

my razor. Trying to scrape up a beard.' Brett shook his head, still grinning. 'Honey, did you manage to pick up my shoes today? That heel job?'

Edith had.

'All right, Edie, I'll take him out camping – this next Saturday. I promise.'

Edith imagined an overnight camping trip, the two of them talking across a bonfire. Man to man. Edith smiled at the triteness of it, but it must work sometimes, or people wouldn't keep trying it, or talking about it. She knew Brett considered it a sacrifice of his weekend time. Brett liked his own little projects, liked reading and making notes for a book he intended to write on the origins of war.

'But if it's self-confidence you're talking about again, I'm afraid I can't inject him with that,' Brett said.

So Brett and Cliffie went off the following Saturday after lunch, equipped with sleeping bags, tarpaulin, flashlights, the Winchester ·22, sandwiches, alcohol stove, instant coffee, a thermos of soup, a big jug of fresh water. Edith relished her hours alone (except for George), even declined an invitation from the Quickmans next door for Saturday dinner. Brett and Cliffie were back Sunday evening around 8, dinnerless, but Edith had not eaten as yet. Cliffie looked as usual, grinning, taciturn, as he switched on the television before even removing his nylon jacket. Only Brett was – somehow – not his usual self, a little tense, maybe a little angry. Edith knew something had happened. Had Cliffie recounted a saga of erotic conquests, all fantasy, Edith wondered.

Brett was close-mouthed until he and Edith were ready for bed, their bedroom door closed.

'I woke up this morning and found him standing over me with the gun,' Brett said. 'Funny – isn't it?'

The gun. The ·22, Edith thought. She could imagine Cliffie pointing it. Smiling? 'Joking, you mean.'

'Oh, I dunno.' Brett threw off his bathrobe. 'I didn't like it. Sure, I tried to smile. Sure. Had his finger on the trigger!' Brett was whispering, though Cliffie was downstairs in his back corner room. Suddenly Brett laughed. 'Anyway, I'm safe. I think.'

Was it real, Edith wondered. Of course it was real, what Brett had said, the gesture, the lightweight gun which could kill at short range. Edith was not sure Brett had got around to discussing the facts of life. She was not going to ask him about that.

Somewhat to Edith's surprise, Brett wanted to caress her, to make love. That was real, that night.

6

When Edith put the telephone down, she climbed the stairs slowly, walked down the hall to her workroom, and after a few seconds, realized that she was staring at her diary. It lay atop some stacked magazines at the lower left end of the bookshelf under the bay window seat. Today was a day to make an entry, she thought. When had the last entry been? Four or five months ago, perhaps, and she couldn't even remember what had prompted it. Something happy? What?

She had just received a phone call from a Mr Coleman or Colson in Trenton, saying that Cliffie had been caught with an answer paper in the room where he had been taking his college entrance exams. The man said they wanted to talk to Cliffie after the exams were over at 4 p.m., therefore Cliffie might be a little late. The man had sounded rather annoyed, curt. Cliffie's being late was of no importance, as he was supposed to wait for Brett to pick him up at the high school just after 5. But the cheating! The answer paper (where had he got it from?), after the private tutors they had paid for in the last year! Cliffie's math tutor, a boy going to Princeton and no older than Cliffie, had said last week that he thought Cliffie could make it on his intermediate algebra exam. Cliffie's English was all right, if he bothered to use half his brain. And Cliffie had said just a couple of days ago that he *wanted* to pass this batch of exams so he could get into college (some college, because Princeton was out), so Edith and Brett had thought, this time, surely, Cliffie would come through.

Brett was going to be livid, the atmosphere in the house awful for the next days. How many days? Would Brett be so angry, he'd tell Cliffie to get out of the house and fend for himself?

Brett might want to, but he'd be afraid to, Edith thought, afraid Cliffie would get himself into worse trouble. Cliffie could strike up an acquaintance in a bar, for instance, go with someone on a robbery and – Cliffie would be the fall guy. It hadn't happened, but it might.

Edith forced herself to stop thinking about that. Cliffie was going to stay home. There was nothing stronger than Cliffie's will to stay home. Home was comfortable, safe, cheap – in fact he didn't pay anything except five dollars a week now and then when he had a temporary job. Home provided meals, laundry service, television, heat in winter and air-conditioning in summer.

'We asked your son if he didn't want to call you himself, Mrs Howland, but he didn't, so we're doing it,' Mr Colson or Coleman had said on the telephone.

That meant Cliffie was in a funk of shame. Cliffie could lash out at his father verbally, and had once even swung a fist at him, but the blow hadn't landed. Cliffie must've been in a muddle not to have told them that his father was picking him up after 5. Or did they mean to keep Cliffie longer than 5?

It was nearly 4 now. She'd have to ring Brett. Edith took a deep breath, left the comfortable atmosphere of her workroom, went downstairs, and picked up the telephone. She dialed the *Standard*'s number.

'Hello, Mike,' she said, recognizing the voice. 'Could I speak to Brett, do you think?'

'Why, I think that's quite permissible, Edith,' Mike drawled, and connected her.

'Yep?' said Brett.

'Hello, Brett, it's me. Listen – Cliffie might be a bit late, I'm not sure. They telephoned me and said there's some delay with everything.'

'Something happen?' Brett sounded on the scent already.

'I don't think so. Just that he might not be on the steps when you get to the school. You might have to ask where he is.'

Brett laughed a little. 'You mean he fainted and they're still trying to bring him to?'

54

'Maybe. See you later, dear.' She hung up.

Now it was time for George's tea. Today Edith almost enjoyed the chore, though most days it annoyed her, interrupting her writing, or gardening, or something else. She made Twining tea in the blue and white pot, and put two ginger cookies on a saucer. She carried the tray up.

George was asleep, wheezing a little, propped up on his back. His right hand, big and bony, lay limp on a library book which was open on his abdomen. The room smelt musty, despite the partly open window. The room had a paleness, a whiteness that depressed Edith. It was due to the expanse of bedsheets, she thought.

'George?' Edith called. 'Teatime.' She had to repeat it, more loudly. Edith disliked waking people up, even waking George who liked being awakened because it was evidently for a meal.

'Wha – Oh! 'Course, dear. Thank you – kindly.'

She settled him, made sure the pillows could keep him upright, that the tray was reasonably balanced.

George's bald head shone like something polished, pink alabaster, perhaps. In the last years his lower lids had sagged farther. Edith couldn't bear to look at them. And now he was never up for meals, only got up (thank God) to use the bathroom.

'Cliffie – isn't he taking his exams for college today?'

Had she said something to George? If so, she was surprised George had retained it. 'Yes, this afternoon in Trenton. He's not back yet.' What was she doing, standing here? Edith retreated and slipped out, leaving the door ajar, as George liked it.

The dinner was simple that evening, a corn casserole with leftover roast beef in it, garnished with green pepper. Edith had half cooked it, and would put the oven on again when Brett arrived, as they always liked a drink and a look at the *Standard* before dinner. Now it was twenty to 6, ten minutes later than Brett's usual time of arrival – though that varied, Edith reminded herself.

The telephone rang. Edith had a feeling it was Brett.

'Hi, Edith,' said Gert Johnson. 'Just wanted to ask how Cliffie made out. Or how he thinks he made out.'

'Well –' Edith began, trying to make herself sound just as cheery, because she could tell Gert the truth at some other time. 'I dunno. They're both a little late. Brett was going to pick Cliffie up afterward.'

'Tell Cliffie we send him our best wishes. Those exams aren't really stiff, you know, Edie. I'll bet he'll pass if he wants to.'

'Wait and see. Cliffie's full of surprises.'

'Y'know, Edie, there's a junk sale at the antique place near Flemington Saturday? Feel like going? ... Well, call me if you do. I'm going and I can pick you up.'

They hung up. Edith wanted to make a drink for herself, but lit a cigarette instead. The living room looked handsome, she thought. The big sofa acquired three years ago was second-hand, but in good condition, upholstered in green leather which Edith took the trouble to polish reasonably often. Two oil paintings of her nineteenth-century great-grandparents hung on one wall, and over the mantel was a large mirror not exactly clear and in a fine frame whose gold-leaf was just worn enough, Edith thought, to look right. They had been in the house almost ten years now. Yes, George had come during the first weeks of their moving here, when Cliffie had been ten, his voice still a boy's voice, his body still slender. She remembered Cliffie well, his likes and dislikes then. The amazing thing was that Cliffie had not changed much. He still liked comic books, though they were not now his exclusive reading. He liked James Bond and science fiction too, but Edith felt sure if she looked thoroughly in the bookshelves in his room, she would find some yellowing comic books dating back to the 1950s. He was now a little more sure of himself, or pretended to be. His tantrums had metamorphosed into touchiness, a downing of tools, a huff if his employer (a grocery store manager just now, as Cliffie worked at the Cracker Barrel lately) tried to bring him into line about something. He had barely scraped through high school, and now at nineteen was trying half-heartedly, for the second time, to make college entrance exams. Of course it didn't matter at what age one entered college, but one had to *want* to go. Failing to make it, Edith thought, might be one more thing Cliffie had thought of to disappoint her and Brett. In fact, what could have been worse than what he had done today?

Mildew's jumping onto her lap cut off Edith's daydreaming. Mildew was nearly twelve. She jumped in an arthritic way, sparing her left hind foot.

'Old Millie –' Edith made kissing noises, and fondled the cat's black ear. Mildew sensed when Edith was upset. Many a cold night, too, Mildew crawled into bed on Edith's side and made her way down to rest like a fur-covered hot water bottle at Edith's feet. Edith thought of something and grew tense: she remembered their last day in New York, when Cliffie had tried to smother Mildew under the eiderdown – and had nearly succeeded. Horrid!

Edith sprang up, lifting Mildew with her, as she heard the crackle of car tires climbing the driveway.

They came in, Brett first, and he gave Edith a brief look. 'So – here's our genius,' Brett said.

Cliffie followed his father into the living room, swinging his feet a little, hands in his back pockets, and Edith saw he was going to assume a 'So what?' attitude.

'Come on,' Edith said, 'I'll give us all a drink and we'll talk it over.'

'Talk what over?' Cliffie said, and burst out in a laugh. He was not quite as tall as Brett, and inclined to plumpness. Brett was always saying a boot camp would get Cliffie into shape, but the Army had rejected Cliffie – for no reason that Edith or Brett knew except silliness and maybe an air of ineradicable contempt. Cliffie bent and rubbed the cat quickly on the ribs with both hands, causing Mildew to shrink backward. 'Don't know what miseries you've missed today, Mildew, staying home.'

Brett went to rinse his hands, as he nearly always did, in the room off the hall which had a basin and a toilet. Edith made a pitcher of martinis in the kitchen.

'Beer, Cliffie?'

'Yes, mom!'

'Well, it seems the school called you up and told you,' Brett said when she came back. 'I had to face the news cold. Why the

57

hell, Cliffie, when you had a good chance of passing, did you take the damned answer papers in with you? And last year's at that. Didn't it occur to you they might change the exams a little?'

'What exam was it?' Edith asked.

'All of 'em! Imagine sitting there looking at the answer papers! And Cliffie isn't telling us where he got them from,' Brett said.

'So they're not –' Edith began again, 'Are they giving him any credit at all for –'

'He's *out*,' Brett said, lifted his glass and drank almost half of it, and winced. 'That tastes good,' he said to Edith.

Edith did not exactly look at Cliffie, but she was aware of him looking at both of them, waiting eagerly for their remarks, as if he had done something praiseworthy rather than shameful. And she was aware that there was nothing to say, nothing that would do any 'good' for the future, no scolding that would be of any value. Years ago he had talked of going to Princeton as if it were a *fait accompli*. These exams today had been minimum requirements to enter *any* college, however low its standards.

'Oughta paint my face black,' Cliffie said, 'then they'd let me in anywhere!' He guffawed, showing excellent teeth.

'No, they wouldn't,' Brett said calmly, and Edith knew his drink was already having effect. 'You have a disrespect for education, and people can smell it a mile away. Well and good, but why do you waste the time of the rest of us? Why, above all, do you trouble to cheat – and even if you hadn't been caught, I bet you'd have managed to fail.' Brett glanced at Edith.

If Cliffie were only doing something else, Edith thought, as she'd thought a hundred times before, like writing or painting, then a college degree wouldn't have been important. But Cliffie wasn't doing anything except loafing around the house.

'Just what did they say at the school, Brett?' Edith asked, trying to appear relaxed, leaning back in the armchair. Mildew was again in her lap.

'A Mr Coleman,' Brett said, 'was brief – and to the point.'

Edith suddenly found unbearable Cliffie's just sitting there, waiting for them to go on. 'How'd you make out with Clark today?' she asked. That was an office matter of Brett's writing original material for their editorial page more often than he did, which was now hardly once a month. Edith barely listened, but Brett said he had made progress, had nailed Clark down to four items a month, though the number of lines wasn't specified. 'Dinner's almost ready,' Edith said, getting up. 'Want to finish the dregs, Brett? I'll call you in a couple of minutes.'

She went into the kitchen, where Cliffie at once joined her in quest of another beer from the fridge.

'I'll just live like George,' Cliffie said, flinging the fridge door shut. 'Just hang around waiting for meals. Ha-ha!'

Did he want them to throw him out, Edith wondered, or at least threaten to? She wasn't going to reply, wasn't going to ruin dinner – hers not Cliffie's – by exchanging any words at all with him.

A year ago, when Cliffie hadn't had the grades for college, she and Brett had thought he might join a group of young people, all of whom Cliffie knew, who had rented a house in Lambertville, New Jersey, just four miles away. All the young people had jobs or were going to schools, their parents lived near enough to keep an eye on them, and Edith was sure the kids frequently went home for meals or weekends. The communal hostelry was a stepping stone to independence as adults. The group hadn't wanted Cliffie, however. Cliffie had made an effort, maybe a half-hearted effort, as was his wont, but he hadn't been accepted. 'They need a plumber now,' Cliffie had told Edith when he came home. 'They want people who can do things like carpentering – electricity.'

'Naturally you can't just sit around and do nothing. I suppose they could use a cook too,' Edith had said.

'That's for girls,' Cliffie had replied promptly. In some ways, Cliffie was quite conventional.

Cliffie now drifted out of the kitchen with his beer can, and a minute later, as Edith was about to serve the meal, Brett came in.

'I'm not going to say a damned thing tonight,' Brett said softly and grimly. 'I've absolutely had it.'

Edith carried the casserole into the dining room and set it on the cork mat in the center of the table. She wondered if Brett was wondering, as she was, if she or he were the more responsible for Cliffie's spinelessness? Wasn't it sometimes a matter of genes? It was Edith's opinion that environment wasn't as important as heredity, though years ago she had thought it fifty-fifty. Wonderful people could come from awful backgrounds. And lots of the kids in gangs now, the drug-takers, the house-robbers, came from middle-class families.

Give it up for a few minutes! Edith told herself. She served four plates, the fourth for George. Brett had brought a tray with napkin, knife, fork and spoon, a glass of milk, as George drank no coffee at night. Brett took the tray up. Cliffie was ravenous as usual, had two helpings of everything, and was finished his second bowl of sliced peaches with cream before Edith and Brett had eaten their first. Cliffie stood up and asked to be excused, in that order.

'Indeed, yes,' said Brett.

Cliffie went into the hall to his room, and Edith knew he would switch on his transistor at once, then close his door.

Brett seemed to remain silent deliberately, so Edith did the same. She might have reminded Brett that the Zylstras were coming on the weekend, or said something about the letter she had received from Aunt Melanie that morning, saying she was going to the hospital again in regard to her hip – broken some eight years ago, and giving her pain occasionally. Edith's thoughts drifted for a few seconds to the memory of the trip to Europe with Aunt Melanie the summer Edith had been seventeen. They had sailed on the *Queen Mary* – first class – to Southampton, and Edith had seen London, Paris, Rome, Florence and Venice. Those had been the most wonderful two months of Edith's life, still vivid, fresh with bursts of beauty. Details of the trip were in her diary – the sight of rain on Michelangelo's David in Florence, for instance – though Edith remembered that she had been a bit intimidated by the big diary then, since she had received it just six months or so before her trip.

Suddenly Brett got up and gently but firmly closed the door on the hall. 'Let's get down to brass tacks. I think he'd better find himself a regular job P.D.Q. and even his own lodgings. Trenton has jobs open now, unskilled labor, construction jobs. God knows he's strong enough. Room and board offered with some of 'em too, right there in the *Standard* ads tonight.'

Edith didn't know what to say, though she wasn't uncomfortable. If Cliffie did get into trouble, or failed for some reason, home was only twenty miles away. 'Well – are you going to ask him or shall I?'

'I'll tell him.' Brett's rather sallow face had gone pinkish in the last minute. 'Ask him, my foot!'

'Maybe not tonight, Brett.'

'Then when?'

'When you're calmer. Tomorrow morning, tomorrow evening. Cliffie's upset too, you know.'

'Up-*set*, eating like a horse as usual.'

Edith shrugged involuntarily and disliked herself for shrugging. 'You know how he is.'

'Yes, indeed I do.'

Edith was thinking of the time capsules, or whatever they called them, that they were storing in some atom-bombproof containers in New York now. They held samples of plastics, books of mathematics, physics, tape recordings, everything that illustrated achievement at the present time, plus a book which would enable people of the future, even if English had been lost, to make sense of what was in the capsules. She was thinking, of what importance was Cliffie, his life, even her own existence, compared to the capsules? Compared to the whole human race and its achievements up to the year 1965? And here they sat, discussing a minor human failure called Cliffie.

'You know, Brett darling, college isn't the be-all and the end-all.'

'It's that he cheated,' Brett said softly, and his jaw shook. 'Oh, I'll shut up, for God's sake. What's on TV tonight? Hottening up in Viet Nam, but they're not going to make news out of *that*, I'll bet. Small item today, LBJ sending more "advisors" over.'

And wait till we get what the French got, Edith was thinking, because Brett said it so often, but he said no more.

It was after 11 p.m. when Edith went into her workroom by herself. She wore her nightdress with a seersucker bathrobe over it. A pleasantly cool breeze came through one of the three curved windows. Brett had gone to bed with a book, and the monotonous beat of Cliffie's pop music came faintly from downstairs. Edith opened her diary and wrote with her old Esterbrook pen:

10 June 65. Cliffie took collectively several exams today in Trenton re college entrance & thinks he did pretty well. These were Int. Alg., English, French, geography, history, chemistry. If he gets an 80 average, he'll go to – maybe Princeton. We are all very pleased tonight, George too, poor old thing.

Aunt Melanie visits end of this month. What a sweetie! And considering her age, no trouble at all. In fact she loves to cook, make cornbread & spice cake & do any mending I might have around the house. She and C. get on well.

Edith squirmed in her straight chair, then closed her pen and diary and stood up.

The entry was a lie. But after all who was going to see it? And she felt better, having written it, felt less melancholic, almost cheerful, in fact.

7

Edith's great-aunt Melanie Cobb arrived at the Trenton railway station one noon, having spent the preceding three days in New York, and both Edith and Brett came in the car to pick her up. Tall and narrow, she wore an eye-catching, wide-brimmed summer hat of dark blue delicately adorned with a veil which covered the hat brim rather than Melanie's face, and a crisp, navy blue linen top coat with white buttons. Walking toward her on the platform, Edith felt a lift of her own spirits, a surge of admiration and love for her old aunt who still kept up appearances so well, still cared so much how she looked. And she was eighty-six!

'Hello, dear Melanie!' Edith cried, embracing her.

'Hello, darlings! Isn't it a lovely day? I'm so glad to be in Pennsylvania! *Almost* in Pennsylvania.'

Brett was ready to carry suitcases, but Melanie had engaged a porter, who walked with them to the car.

'Never mind, I've paid him nicely, I think,' Melanie said as Brett fished for his wallet.

From the smile on the porter's face, Melanie had.

'Now tell me all about life. How are things going?' Melanie asked in the car. She rode in the front seat with Brett, Edith sat in the back. 'How is Cliffie?'

Brett wasn't answering, so Edith said, 'Oh, all right. The same.'

'Did he pass those exams? Weren't there some exams he was taking?'

'No-o, he didn't pass,' Edith replied. 'Yes, they –'

'They were for college,' Brett said. 'Just about the last chance for him. Wasn't the first try, you know. He took a stab at 'em

63

last summer. Same story.' Brett gave her a dry laugh. 'I think he likes letting us down, you know, Melanie? You'd think we'd pushed him too hard in the past, but I don't think that's so.'

'Well – I daresay he's not too depressed by the outcome,' Melanie remarked with a glance over her shoulder at Edith. 'Can't see him buckling down to four years in any college.'

Edith knew Brett was not going to say a word more, and that he was displeased with himself for having said as much as he had.

'Has Cliffie got some kind of a job now?'

Now it was Edith's turn to reply. 'Nothing steady. He's on hand Saturdays to help the Cracker Barrel deliver groceries. That's our swanky grocery store. Cliffie gets good tips. He likes money, all right!' Edith forced a laugh.

'Oh-h, this scenery!' Melanie said, gazing out at the trees in full foliage along the Delaware, at the pale willows brilliant in the sunlight. 'You can believe there's no pollution in America when you see this! – And how's George?'

'About the same,' Brett said. 'Needs a little more waiting on all the time, I'm sorry to say.'

Yes, and he carped at the books Edith took out for him at the town library. He had exhausted the history and philosophy books long ago, read some of them twice without apparently noticing, and sometimes declared rotten a book he had praised a year before.

Melanie asked about the *Bugle*, knowing it had failed, but she asked if there was any hope of revival. 'So much is happening these days. In my part of the country the young people are so vociferous about the Viet Nam involvement, and so they should be! Anyone who takes the trouble to read the history of that poor country! Girls and boys of – the stodgiest families around Wilmington,' Melanie went on, turning to look at Edith, 'are out in the streets with banners and pamphlets.'

Was there a hope, if they tried the *Bugle* again as a monthly? Melanie always gave Edith hope. Lots of people told Edith they missed the *Bugle*.

They were home. Melanie praised their freshly cut (by Brett) front lawn, their climbing red roses at the house pillars. Edith regretted that Cliffie's pop music, not even good music like the Beatles, now boomed especially loudly.

'I hear *someone's* home,' said Melanie.

'And don't forget George!' Brett grinned broadly. In the sunlight his big front teeth looked yellowish.

Edith had bought fresh lobster from the Cracker Barrel, a grand luxury, but Melanie was a grand guest. There was even champagne in the fridge. After Melanie was installed in the guestroom and had said hello to bed-ridden George, they went downstairs to crack the champagne. Edith had set the table before she and Brett left for Trenton. Three creamy roses stood in a vase.

Cliffie joined them, wearing soiled beige corduroys, swinging his hands and feet. 'Hello, Aunt Melanie.'

'Hello, my boy! Come and give your old – great-great aunt a kiss.'

Cliffie did so, with surprising grace, on Melanie's cheek. 'You're looking fine. And I – I suppose you heard about my latest disgrace?'

Melanie hesitated only a second. 'You mean the exams, I suppose. Yes, I did. But maybe you're anti-college.'

'I don't think I care very much one way or the other,' Cliffie replied, flinging himself at the other end of the sofa from Melanie, picking up his stemmed glass of champagne. 'Cheers!'

He had cut off his radio at Edith's request, when she called him in for champagne.

'You're looking well. You've gained some weight,' Melanie said to Cliffie.

Cliffie only sighed, as if his weight were a problem.

He'd snared a couple of beers from the fridge before their arrival, Edith could see from looking at him. Edith knew he did not like putting on weight, but wasn't enough concerned to curb his eating, or the beer.

Aunt Melanie had somehow smuggled down her presents under her arm. These were a sports shirt for Brett, another for Cliffie, and a bottle of Chanel Number Five cologne for Edith. It was like Christmas again.

They drank good white wine with the lobster. Melted butter ran down Cliffie's badly shaven chin before the meal was over. And dear Mildew hovered, riveted by the smell of lobster, accepting gratefully morsels Melanie gave her from her own plate, an indulgence Edith usually didn't like, but now Edith smiled.

'Getting old like me,' Melanie said. 'She deserves it.'

'Now do we *have* to go up and see George?' asked Cliffie, slumping back and lighting a cigarette.

'No – we – don't,' Edith replied gently. She'd already taken George a tray with lobster, wine and potato salad. Edith looked at Melanie and saw that Melanie had observed, not for the first time surely, that Cliffie resented George's presence. Cliffie however, never bestirred himself to carry trays up. *Bone lazy* Cliffie was, Edith thought suddenly, and narrowed her eyes.

Melanie was looking at Edith. Then she said, 'You're not working this afternoon, Brett?'

'I brought some work home. I arranged this afternoon off to welcome you.' Brett's dark eyes smiled at Melanie, then at Edith.

'I'm going to take a nap,' Melanie announced, 'which will leave you all in peace for a while. Edith, this was a sensational lunch.'

Edith was pleased. They had talked about Melanie's New York stay at the St Regis Hotel, the plays she had seen, the art exhibits on Fifty-seventh and elsewhere. Edith knew her aunt needed a rest. Cliffie's eyes were sharply on them both as Edith walked into the hall with Melanie. They began to climb the stairs.

'Look, Mildew's coming with us,' Edith said.

'She always liked me, if you remember. I'm very flattered, Mildew.'

Edith tackled the washing up. It was a pleasure. She was happy to have Melanie in the house. Edith wondered if she would ever reach such a ripe old age, and be in such a well-preserved state if she did? Melanie had always had plenty of money. Did it help not to work too much, Edith wondered? Or did it depend on the constitution of the person? Her great-aunt seemed to have both advantages.

She caught Cliffie with a jigger of scotch in his hand, as she was fetching the last coffee cups from the table. 'So,' Edith said mildly. She had suspected him of tippling, but thought it best not to mention it.

'It's an occasion today. Isn't it?' Cliffie asked.

When Melanie woke up and came downstairs, she and Edith went for a walk along the canal. Brett was working in the bedroom, and Cliffie (Edith thought but was not sure) had gone out. The sunlight was warm on their faces. Melanie wore white tennis shoes with perforations like white polkadots, which she laughed about.

'Doesn't George give you all quite a lot of work?' Melanie asked.

'No. Well – it's trays and such like. But Brett gives me a hand with the trays quite often. At least it isn't bedpans!' Edith added and burst out laughing. She could remember when Cliffie had said 'bedpans' at the age of ten and she'd felt like scolding him. 'He's eighty-three now,' Edith said, anticipating a question about his age.

'And the doctors still can't say what's the real trouble?'

'Oh, they never could! You know these back ailments. As Brett and George say, you can't see anything wrong, it just hurts.'

'Well, if I can ask you a straight question, dear, has he ever offered in all these years to take himself off somewhere?'

'No.' Edith looked down at a tiny frog that had been squashed by someone's foot, then lifted her eyes toward the sun again.

'Are you happy?' Melanie asked.

'Oh – reasonably, I think. Yes. Brett's a dear. Very dependable.' Edith laughed at herself. Maybe she had used the word dependable before in regard to Brett, she wasn't sure. 'I should be working more on my book idea, I suppose, instead of on articles that don't always get published. I have a title, *Madmen's Chess*. About war. Now we're in another, you know, undeclared. Brett's already writing the first part of his book in longhand –

also about war, but mine is more an attempt at – psychological causes. His is more historic – so different we don't even discuss our ideas – maybe just in case they *are* similar.'

'My dear, I'll rest myself on this bench for a minute.' Melanie lowered herself to a weathered green bench at the edge of the path.

Edith didn't feel like sitting. She felt that Melanie had been thinking more about Cliffie than Brett when she asked if she was happy. Cliffie would be twenty in November. It seemed not so long ago that he was eleven – in 1956, a year Edith associated with the Hungarian uprising against Moscow rule and the crushing of the rebellion with tanks.

'Getting a bit of gray in your hair,' Melanie remarked.

Edith shrugged. 'Once in a while I have a rinse. But it washes out.'

They began to walk back. Now the sun was behind them. Edith could see Melanie's blue eyes, her rather pointed nose. She could have been Edith's grandmother, and Edith wished she were. There was a resemblance to Edith's mother in her features, a certain fineness which Edith had not.

'I have another present for you in one of my suitcases,' Melanie said. 'That's for after dinner tonight.'

The present was a cotton quilt made by Melanie herself, of many hexagons of variously colored pieces. Melanie said she'd learned how to do it as a child, and was the last of the family who had bothered.

'Isn't that something!' Brett said when he saw the quilt. 'Melanie, I'm going to have a photographer from the *Standard* come, and we'll do a color picture for our Sunday edition. No!' he protested over Melanie's protest. 'The women love that kind of thing around here!'

Edith was worried about Mildew. Mildew looked stiffer than usual, and had not eaten her dinner. But Edith didn't want to sound a sad note by mentioning the cat. Cliffie had not been home for dinner, and had said nothing to Brett. Edith told Melanie that Cliffie was his own man now and didn't always come home for dinner. Edith suspected that he had drunk too much scotch in the house, or something else like beer outside, and had thought it best not to let his great-aunt see him. If so, it was something to his credit that he was keeping out of sight. Edith was always looking for something to say or think to Cliffie's credit.

8

Breakfast time was chores, George's tray with boiled egg and tea and orange juice before Edith could get at the more serious business of breakfast for four downstairs with the toaster popping up as often as possible, and Cliffie, thank goodness, being quite helpful. More soft boiled eggs and excellent cherry preserves. Edith's mind was on Mildew, who had spent the night, Edith supposed, in Melanie's room. The cat had declined her breakfast, and was now hunched on the kitchen floor.

Brett had left for the office, and Edith and Melanie were in the kitchen tidying up, before Edith said, 'I want to take Mildew to the vet. She might've caught a poisoned mouse. It's happened once before.'

'I noticed she was awfully quiet last night,' Melanie said. 'Where is your vet?'

'Doylestown. We've got a second car now, you know. Half Cliffie's –' Edith dwindled off. Cliffie had paid about a hundred dollars toward the second-hand Fiat 600. It was useful for Edith, with Brett having to take the Impala to Trenton workdays. Cliffie could use the Fiat whenever he wished, but in fact he didn't use it much.

Just before 10 a.m., Edith and Melanie got into the Fiat with Mildew in her basket.

The vet was Dr Speck. One didn't make appointments, just turned up between 10 and 12, and waited one's turn. They had not long to wait.

'I think it's another bad mouse,' said Edith, though she feared something worse.

Dr Speck, a graying man with muscular forearms, pushed his fingers deeply into Mildew's sides as the cat stood docilely on his white table. The doctor had a puzzled expression. Then he looked directly at Edith.

'Cat has a liver tumor – I'm sorry to say.'

'You're sure?' Edith asked.

'I can feel it,' said Dr Speck.

'Well – can you operate?'

Dr Speck shook his head and smiled quickly, regretfully. 'Not at this age, you know. With a thing like this – Poor old Mildew,' he said, pressing the cat's sides gently, bending over her, because he knew the cat since years. 'It's a matter of old age, you know, Mrs Howland. There's nothing one can do.'

Melanie was standing with them, and she said, 'Oh, Edith, I *am* sorry.'

Edith was shocked. The next seconds passed, the next minute, and she talked, replied to the vet's statements and questions, but she felt miles away, as if she were going to faint. The vet was suggesting that she should have Mildew put away now, painlessly with a needle. And Edith had to acquiesce. There was nothing else she could do. She didn't want Mildew to suffer. Yet the verdict had been so sudden.

Then Edith was sitting with Melanie in the waiting room, along with another woman who had a squirming beagle puppy, and Edith smoked a cigarette. She got up with Melanie when the vet summoned them. Mildew was wrapped in a white paper, tucked in at the ends like a package, and Edith watched him deposit the still limp body gently in the basket.

'I am sorry, Mrs Howland. But your cat had a long life and a happy one. You must think of that.'

On the street, Melanie said, 'Do you feel all right to drive home, dear? I'm sure we could get a taxi and arrange to get the car home some other way.'

'No, I'm all right.' Edith pulled herself together and drove. Melanie was wonderfully comforting, saying just the right things. Melanie made tea in the kitchen and insisted on Edith's drinking a cup before they buried the cat in the garden, as Edith had said she wanted to do.

Cliffie was home, his radio was on, and he came into the

kitchen while Edith was drinking her tea. 'What's up?' he asked.

'Poor Mildew just had to be put away,' Melanie said.

The cat's basket was on the floor.

Cliffie looked at it. 'Really? She's in there – dead, you mean?'

'Maybe you can help us,' Melanie said. 'We're going to bury her in the garden.'

'Oh.' Cliffie glanced at his mother and their eyes met.

Cliffie went back to his room, and Edith knew Melanie supposed he would come back in a minute, but Edith knew he wouldn't. Edith picked up the basket and said:

'Let's go ahead. The sooner the better.' With her free hand, Edith took a clean white dishtowel from a kitchen shelf, jiggling it free from the stack, an old linen cloth from a Pennsylvania antique sale.

Edith dug with the fork, Melanie helped with the spade, and they lowered the paper-wrapped, towel-wrapped form into a grave more than two feet deep.

'I'll put a stone over it,' Edith said, and went off to get a stone – she'd get several – from a border in the garden. She got the wheelbarrow so she could take the stones at the same time.

'Funny Cliffie wouldn't help us,' Melanie said.

'Oh, death frightens him, I think,' Edith said. When she had placed the stones, she added, 'Besides he's always been jealous of Mildew – knew I loved the cat, you know.'

'But still –' Melanie was plainly surprised.

At lunch, Cliffie said rather boldly, 'I don't see why it should mean so much to me – that cat. I mean, once she's dead anyway – once *anything's dead* –'

Neither Edith nor Melanie replied to that. Edith had rung Brett up that morning to tell him, after debating whether to ring him or not. But she felt better having told him, rather than waiting until he got home that evening.

George was awake when Edith went up after lunch to get his tray. He again said how sorry he was to hear about Mildew. 'I'm sure it was a shock, dear Edith,' he said in a soft, husky voice,

72

and his pink eyelids hung down, full of their usual water, not tears.

'Well – that's life,' Edith said.

She knew George meant well, but she detested George at that moment, more than she had detested him on bringing the lunch tray, when she had told him about her cat, though George had been equally nice then. She detested the vaguely gray-looking sheets (though she changed them often enough), the inevitable sloppiness of the room, the fact that she and Brett were stuck with George, that this room would be occupied, apparently, forever – while nice things that she loved like Mildew would die, disappear, be taken from her.

Brett was a darling, put his arm around Edith and comforted her that evening, long after dinner when the others had gone to bed. They had a nightcap, sitting on the leather sofa.

'Old Mildew did have a happy life – with her back garden,' Brett said. 'The thing to do is get another kitten, don't you think?'

'Of course. Of course.'

On the third day of Melanie's stay, Cliffie invited her for a drive in the Fiat. Edith was a little surprised by his attention, or politeness, but pleased also.

'Take her toward Centerbridge – the waterfall's so pretty,' Edith whispered in the kitchen, as Cliffie fortified himself with a mid-morning beer. 'And you might invite her for a Cinzano or something at Cross-Keys. Have you got some money?'

'I could use a fiver. Might have to buy some gas.'

Edith gave it to him.

Around noon, Cliffie rang up and said Melanie had invited him for lunch.

It was a Friday. Edith relaxed, prepared lunch for George, made a sandwich for herself. She took a last glance at Sunday's papers so they could be got out of the way, tidied a little in the living room, cut some fresh roses for Melanie's room, and in her workroom made sure she could put her hands on two articles she wanted to show Melanie which she had written in the last weeks. One was on the need for socialized medicine and its eventual advantages to the public and the whole economy, which – if *Harper's* declined – Edith was optimistic that she could sell somewhere.

In the silent house, George's snores came with unusual clarity down the hall. Edith went and gently closed his door, getting a glimpse as she did so of the framed photograph of the young-looking dark-haired man called Paul, who was another nephew of George's and who lived in San Francisco, an engineer of some kind, with wife and a couple of kids. Why didn't that one take George on for a while, Edith thought to herself.

Edith also found a good color photograph of dear old Mildew, white-breasted, brindle-nosed, dozing with her feet tucked in on a pillow under a back garden apple tree. Mildew was in dappling sunlight, her eyes half-closed. Edith smiled, and felt better for smiling.

She was taking a swat at the garden when Cliffie and Melanie got back a little after 3.

'Had a marvelous time,' Melanie said. 'I was really squired around in fine style. But now I'm ready for my post-prandial nap.'

'I'm very pleased.' She had the feeling Melanie wanted to talk to her, but perhaps not now, and maybe Melanie really was tired. At any rate, Melanie went upstairs.

That evening, the Johnsons were coming to dinner, though not with either of their teen-aged kids. Derek had been drafted, much to Gert's and Norm's fury, a few months after he had graduated from Penn State, and had been in Viet Nam now more than six months. Edith started organizing her dinner. Melanie knew the Johnsons quite well by now, and they had got on from the start. Edith looked forward to a happy evening.

And it did go well. Edith had rung Gert up that morning to tell her about Mildew, so the only talk of that was a word of sympathy from them both when they arrived. They talked about Viet Nam. It had become a din in Edith's ears, or a drone, a record repeated, and yet she knew it was important, because it seemed that the Pentagon, which Edith considered a war-making and war-loving machine, had greater influence than Congress on the President. *We are reaping the fruit,* Edith thought, *of blind anti-Communist, anti-social brainwashing.* But since she had said it before, and would be preaching to the converted ·anyway, she said next to nothing.

'You're so lucky, playing it like a clown, Cliffie ol' boy,' Gert said in her slightly rowdy way. Gert loved her drink and had had three generous ryes before dinner.

Cliffie didn't rise to the remark, but looked a bit affronted, and glanced at Melanie to see how she was taking it.

Melanie let it pass, having heard about Cliffie's interview with the military examiner in Harrisburg.

'Our boy Derek's in Viet Nam,' Norm explained to Melanie. 'We tried to get him into the Navy instead of the Army, because – you serve four year-rs in the Navy instead of two in the Army, but at least the Navy's safer.'

'People say, thank goodness Derek isn't wounded yet,' Gert added, leaning forward over her fruit plate on which she was eating tangerines, 'but they're not wounded there so often as they're just blown up by – by –'

'Booby traps,' Norm said. 'Oh, honey, talking won't do any good. – He's got a year more. Well, a little more than a year,' Norman informed Melanie.

Gert smiled and shook her head. 'And there's old clever Cliffie –'

'Oh, Gertie,' Norm said. 'Come on!'

Late that night, when Edith and Melanie were stacking dishes in the kitchen, putting things away in the larder and fridge, Melanie said:

'Cliffie invited me to lunch today, insisted on paying. I thought that was really sweet of him.'

Had Melanie said it to make her feel better after the remarks at dinner? Was it true? But Edith knew it was true, if Melanie said it. 'It does surprise me,' Edith said.

Cliffie's transistor was on, playing pop music on the other side of the kitchen, music interspersed by voices now and then, interviews with pop stars. Sometimes Cliffie fell asleep with his radio on.

'Has he got a girl friend now?' Melanie asked.

'We wish he had,' Edith said. 'It might pull him together.'

'He's quite a good-looking boy. He's just not interested?'

'Oh-h,' Edith began, 'he hangs around a couple of successful boys here. Successful with the girls, I mean. In the bar called Mickey's – up Main Street. But it doesn't mean their girls go for Cliffie.' It sounded as if the other boys had harems, which was perhaps true, Edith thought. 'Yes, well.' Edith turned, smiling, from the sink, and dropped a squeezed out sponge on the drainboard. 'God knows Brett and I would make his girl friends welcome, but he doesn't bring any home. I don't think he sees them anywhere else, or they'd be telephoning – or he would.'

9

Cliffie just then had an ear to the door in the hall, not far from the kitchen. A finger of his right hand pushed against his right ear, cutting out much of the noise from his radio. So his mother was yacketing about girls again, and even his old great-great aunt! Cliffie had decided he could take girls or leave them, so what was the problem? Vulgar prying, Cliffie considered it. Cliffie thought he had done pretty handsomely by Aunt Melanie that day.

He slipped back into his room and left his door open a little, so he could see when the light went out in the kitchen.

And that yack tonight about his not being drafted for Viet Nam! Who wanted to be drafted for that place? As his parents would be the first to say, some of the best brains in the country were against fellows going there, advised fellows to resort to any kind of trick to keep out, so Cliffie considered himself a bit cleverer than Derek, because Derek certainly hadn't wanted to go.

When the kitchen light was out and various doors had shut upstairs, Cliffie tiptoed down the hall and out the front door. He simply had to get some fresh air and stretch his legs after a day like today. Cliffie whistled a tune in the June moonlight, and walked with a slightly rolling gait, heading for Mickey's which didn't close till around 3. He recognized Billy Watts coming toward him on the sidewalk. Billy lived beyond the Howlands on Main.

'Hi, Cliffie,' said Billy, passing.

'Hi,' Cliffie replied. He had waited for Billy to greet him, not being sure he would, because they'd had a slight argument – Cliffie had forgotten about what, maybe juke box tunes and who had played what – at Mickey's not long ago.

Cliffie got to Mickey's, walked up the sidewalk and the couple of steps to the door, under the little pink sign saying *Budweiser*, and into the familiar, dimly lit room with its counter on the left where Mickey sold take-away beer, and the long bar beyond. The juke box was playing Elvis Presley now. Cliffie knew at least three of the fellows hunched over their drinks at the bar, but went to an empty space, said hello to Mickey – a skinny guy about forty-five – and gave his order for a rum and coke.

'How you doin', boy?' Mickey asked, as he set the jigger down for Cliffie to pour.

'Pretty good, and you?' Cliffie replied, fixed his drink and straightened up before he tasted it. He was feeling good tonight, thinking he'd behaved in exemplary fashion today, taking his old aunt out on his own money, not a cheap lunch, either. Cliffie had a vague – extremely vague – idea that he might inherit something from her one day, something not too big, but solid, like ten thousand dollars. Therefore he cared about the impression he made on Melanie. He peered at himself in the mirror behind the bar, not that Cliffie cared how he looked now, but he liked to feel he was *here*, real, his longish and rather wavy hair making his head look bigger, he thought, covering the top part of his ears lately. At thirteen or fourteen, Cliffie remembered, he had pilfered Melanie's handbag in her room – twice during her same visit, and the second time she had unfortunately walked in and caught him in the act. Cliffie recalled this with embarrassment, remembered the hot shame in his face, but Melanie had spoken softly to him (not like his father would have done!) and had given him a couple of dollars from her handbag, and said she would not say a word to his mother, if he promised not to do it again. 'Always *ask* if you want money,' Melanie had said.

At the bar, Cliffie laughed with sudden nervousness, and tried to hide it by ducking his head and coughing. His heart beat faster than usual.

Joey Costello came in, preceded by a giggling girl. What was her name? Joey was laying her these days, Cliffie knew. Cliffie felt a swift envy, very passing.

'Hi, Joey! Ginger!' Cliffie said, remembering the girl's name suddenly. She was about sixteen, and Cliffie didn't know where she lived, but it wasn't Brunswick Corner.

Joey put in an order for two rums and cokes, and he and the girl went to a table.

Cliffie ordered more rum, a double. On top of the wine and stuff he'd had at dinner, the rum was making him feel fine and mellow, as the song said. He stood up straighter and slapped his solid ribs once or twice. He had pulled off his sweater, tied its arms around his neck, and rolled up the sleeves of his striped shirt. It was a warm night. He wanted to glance over his shoulder at Joey and Ginger, but didn't.

Now as to girls, Cliffie thought, feeling philosophical as he began on his double rum, he took the attitude that it was safer for the time being to hold himself aloof. He could always jerk himself off and did, if he felt so inclined. No complications there. He used his socks to come in, which caused him to wash them rather often, which earned him a word of praise from his mother! Cliffie had to laugh again. Girls, for instance, had no sense of humor. They only laughed 'Hee-hee-hee!' or shrieked like police sirens to flatter the fellows they might be with, make them think they'd said something witty. Girls were also expensive. Then, suppose you got a girl pregnant? You had to pay for it or be labeled a cad, or blame somebody else which maybe wouldn't be possible. Then the nice girls (Cliffie couldn't imagine anything more boring than one of these) were traps, saying, 'You've got to marry me before I will,' just as they said in a lot of books and articles Cliffie was always reading about 'the sexes' or 'the sex war'. Thank God the type was dying out with the Pill, but Cliffie knew some of the girls around B.C. couldn't get the Pill, and so didn't do it with anyone. Cliffie had heard fellows like Joey laughing about it. Why bother with girls like that, Cliffie thought, since he was only twenty? There was time.

'*Yee-hoo-oo!*'

'*Yee-ow!*'

A tipsy trio had burst through the door.

'You people keep it quiet!' Mickey warned them. 'I don't want the cops here tonight!' Mickey was half joking, half not.

Cliffie had seen Mickey refuse to serve drinks to people already tight. But Cliffie was in a dream world of his own, not interested in the three whom Mickey might not serve and might eject.

Girls, he'd been thinking about. Well, as with the Viet Nam thing, it was best to stay out of the rat-race as long as one could. A job, a wife, the inevitable kids – a wife who'd yell if he spent too much time out at night with chums – who wanted that?

One of the trio jolted Cliffie in the right elbow by accident, causing Cliffie to spill a bit of his drink. 'Hey!' Cliffie said, his eyes flashing sudden anger.

' 'Scuse us,' said the tight guy, his arm around the girl's waist.

'Don't do it again,' Cliffie said.

'Take it easy, all of you,' said Mickey. He was rinsing out glasses in the aluminum sink.

Within seconds, Cliffie's mind had drifted to another subject, George, that pain in the ass, that sponger, that mealy-mouthed hypocrite, simply *using* his parents, occupying a room for years that Cliffie would have preferred as his own, and which should have been his by right, instead of the stinking maid's room or whatever it was that he had next to the kitchen. Cliffie knew George didn't like him either, called him lazy and stupid. *That* parasite calling anybody lazy! And stupid? Just because he considered, he *knew* college was a bore? Why bother starting college, if you knew you were going to be flunked out in a year, incurring further disgrace, criticism, Cliffie supposed. Why let yourself in for one month after another of 'failing' something? *That* was what he hated, being criticized constantly, when he was at least honest enough to say he didn't give a damn about passing or doing well or whatever they were talking about. As for success in life, or making money, Cliffie was pleased to say, 'Look at all the rich people who *never* went to college, oil millionaires who started as roustabouts and ditch-diggers.' Even New York had big-shots who'd just walked into some dead-on-its-ass firm and told them how to run things, how to cut the crap and be efficient, and they'd had their salaries upped, until finally they'd owned the fucking business, just ordinary guys like himself.

80

Cliffie wished Mel Linnell would come in. It was not even 2 a.m., so he might. Mel lived in Lambertville. He had a powerful motorcycle. He also had pot and booze and beer and usually a girl in his one-room apartment which was over a dry cleaning shop. Sometimes there were poker games, but Cliffie stayed out of those, because he always lost. Cliffie liked Mel, because Mel let him hang around. Mel was about twenty-three. Cliffie liked to imagine himself Mel, living on nothing but luck, maybe picking up money by playing cards or selling pot or harder stuff. Mel had no regular job, anyway, and he did fine, even beautifully.

After another survey of himself in the mirror, Cliffie ordered a beer. The drink calmed him, he felt. He drank a couple of inches of the beer, then went to the john, and was back in less than a minute. Yes, and he had muscle-power too, and wasn't bad looking if he bothered to dress up. And if he ever made love to a girl – like this girl Ginger – she wouldn't forget it, Cliffie thought. He didn't enjoy being a trifle overweight, but he told himself that with a slight effort, a matter of five days' exercise, he could strip off those few extra pounds.

When did guys like George ever die? Was George going to be around another ten years? Till he himself died aged thirty? That would be funny: when he was thirty, George would be into his *nineties*!

The fellow on Cliffie's right lurched backward against Cliffie's right shoulder, and Cliffie instantly mustered strength and returned the fellow to his chums with a mighty shove which nearly knocked the girl in the middle down.

'*Hey* there!' Mickey yelled.

'*Up your ass!*' Cliffie retorted to everybody, hot in the face with rage.

'Cliffie, you've – Calm down, Cliffie,' said Mickey.

'What the fuck did *I* do?' Cliffie asked.

'Don't get hot under the collar. And watch your language. The man says he's sorry,' Mickey said with a glance and a nod at the man Cliffie had shoved.

Cliffie could see the man wasn't about to say he was sorry. He was in his mid-twenties, taller than Cliffie, glaring at Cliffie now, and Cliffie glared back. Stepping back to relax a bit, Cliffie nearly fell, because his left foot was inside the bar rail, and he hadn't realized it. Cliffie thought it best to depart, which he did with as much dignity as possible, even leaving part of his beer. 'Night, Mickey,' he said mechanically, and realized he was a little drunk as he got the door open and made his way to the pavement.

By the time he got home, he wasn't feeling too bad. A glow was visible in the narrow upstairs hall window, meaning George was on his way to or from the john. It was 2:22 a.m., Cliffie saw by his radium dial watch. Old George had to pee at least once a night, and there were a couple of floorboards that squeaked, so often Cliffie heard him. Cliffie went on tiptoe, careful as a burglar, through the front door which he'd put on the latch and which he now latched, down the hall to his room.

In no time he was in bed, doing the usual, this time with a fantasy of making it with Ginger. Cliffie made her scream, first with shock and pain, then with delight. Afterwards, he removed his sock, dropped it on the floor between bed and bedtable. Another sock was handy, its mate. Cliffie preferred dirty socks, they were somehow more sexy. Thirsty, he went into the kitchen with the aid of his pocket flashlight, and drank two big glasses of water.

How often did his parents make love, Cliffie wondered, or had they stopped it? It was difficult to imagine, and Cliffie didn't like to imagine it, had never wanted to imagine it. He could remember when he'd had quite a crush on his mother, maybe when he was around ten, but now if she so much as put an arm around him when somebody was taking a snapshot of them, Cliffie hated it and squirmed away as soon as possible. Brett, in Cliffie's opinion, looked like a quietly sexy man, even yet.

Now – Cliffie's thoughts had found a vigorous new stream – who was this new secretary of Brett's called Carol? Carol sounded like a promising name. His father had mentioned her nearly a month ago, a blonde, Cliffie recalled his father saying, surely in her early twenties, because his father had said, 'She's a good worker, because she hasn't been working long enough to get lazy.'

Cliffie went to bed again and tried to make it with the imaginary Carol, failed, and felt quite tired suddenly.

What did he have to do tomorrow, really? Nothing. That was nice. Was Melanie leaving tomorrow or the next day? *Carol.* Cliffie liked the name, somehow. Probably his mother hadn't even registered the fact his father had a new secretary, instead of ugly Miss McLain, who'd retired this year, and who'd looked like a female prison warden. Often his mother seemed to be in a daydream, although Cliffie realized she ran the house quite efficiently. She worked so hard on her articles, looking up things in reference books and all that, and so little came of it. His mother was fighting a losing battle, Cliffie thought, because she was trying to fight the majority. The majority wasn't even fighting back, it was just indifferent. Cliffie felt like smiling at that piece of wisdom, and smiling, he dozed off.

A highly unpleasant dream awakened him, and Cliffie sat up in bed, glad to find himself back in reality. He gripped his own shoulder for solace. He had dreamed he was twelve years old, standing on the diving board at summer camp, being asked to dive for the end-of-summer test, and he refused. He had refused when he was twelve, although he had with an awful effort forced himself to dive twice before off the same board into the lake, and Cliffie admitted to himself that the board wasn't very high. But in the dream just now, when he had stood at the end of the board with his hands together and looked down at the water, he had seen a lot of little men struggling like fighting and drowning soldiers down there, and he had said to the P.T. teacher, 'I can't, because there're a lot of little *men* down there!' and the other boys had laughed at him, and the teacher, furious, had been heading toward him to push him off, when Cliffie had awakened. Cliffie remembered jumping off a much higher thing – the bridge – into the Delaware, however, when he was barely eleven. And hadn't that taken guts? How many guys who had laughed at him in the dream had the guts to do that? It had happened, it wasn't one of his fantasies, because once in a while his parents mentioned it, told people about it. Cliffie considered it the most courageous thing he had ever done, maybe the act he was most proud of in his life, up to now. Purposeless? Sure. What had any purpose in life, anyway? Purpose? Life was a joke.

Cliffie remained on his elbow, blinking, glad to see the pale rectangle of his window. His mother was obsessed by politics, Cliffie thought. And his father had a mediocre job. Neither of them was getting anywhere important in life. Cliffie saw it suddenly very clearly. Maybe his mother was insane, in a way. It didn't matter that she kept the furniture polished and dusted, and worked in the garden. Lots of insane people did those things. His father wore such sloppy, informal clothes, all right of course if you were a bohemian author of something, but not if you wanted to be a big-shot on a newspaper with several thousand – ten thousand? – circulation. As long as his father was playing the game at all, he ought to play it hard and well, Cliffie thought. *Win!* Cliffie sensed a crisis in both his parents just now, though he couldn't say exactly what it was.

And the way his mother's face had changed since Mildew's death two days ago, her mouth down at the corners, so preoccupied, she didn't even hear him till he'd spoken to her twice. Over a cat! Was that normal? Cliffie had heard enough about himself not being normal. He could throw it back at them.

10

11/Dec./65. Another Christmas rolls around, or at least this is the month for it. Nelson continues to thrive, enjoy life & is a darling. Sits on my lap when I type – quite often.
B. faring better, that is, he is happier, he says. That is better, for me.

Here Edith paused, her mind as muddled for a moment as if she were making a speech before an audience and had mislaid her notes. But she was alone, sitting in the semi-circle made by the bay window, facing a framed print of a Chinese figure in pink and yellow costume, which she had always found relaxing to look at. She was thinking of Brett, and trying to be realistic. He had said, or confessed, a month ago, that he thought he was in love with his secretary called Carol Junkin, but that he knew it was absurd and wanted to put an end to it. Brett called it 'a crush'. Carol was hardly twenty-five. Edith had seen her twice when she had gone to Brett's office to pick him up, when they had been going to a play or a concert in Philadelphia. Carol was shorter than Edith, sturdier, a Swarthmore graduate, a divorcée living alone in a Trenton apartment, family in Ardmore and quite well-to-do. She read German, Brett said, and liked Günter Grass and Böll in the original, and that was about all Edith knew about her. Edith assumed Brett had been to bed with her a few times – just when Edith couldn't quite imagine, but there were always times, always ways. But as of today, this morning before Brett set off, he had declared that he wanted to put an end to the 'situation' with a girl young enough to be his daughter. This was why Edith was making an entry in her diary, which she hadn't touched in some three months.

The hints Gert Johnson had dropped! Edith still winced.

'Have you met Brett's new secretary?' Gert had asked three or four months ago.

'Yes, briefly. Why?'

'Norm met her, because he was seeing about an ad in the *Standard*. She's rather attractive.' And Gert had waited in her usual way for this to sink in, or for Edith to say something, but Edith hadn't.

Edith hadn't thought Carol a knock-out. She had rather a too pretty face, the kind Edith thought uninteresting, over-sized breasts, or maybe these had been emphasized by the sweater she had been wearing. Carol wanted to be a novelist, Brett had said. Well, well, didn't a lot of people? That was no passport to success with Brett, but then he did like breasts. Cliffie had twigged it before her, Edith suspected. Cliffie had a curious intuition. But at least Brett had spoken to Edith frankly, which most men would not have done, Edith thought, at least so soon. Edith had thought things were all right with her and Brett in that department. They made love perhaps two or three times a month, if one had to gauge such things by frequency, and of course one had to. All the articles on marital problems mentioned how often, or how seldom. Were things necessarily any better, if people did it six times a week? Edith thought the atmosphere was also important in a marriage, and she had not noticed anything wrong between her and Brett. Edith had also read about the revolt of the middle-aged man, in fact there was a book with that title almost, so she supposed Brett at forty-eight or forty-nine was going through this, that a love affair might boost his ego for a while and – that he would get over it.

But Edith found that she couldn't add any more on the subject of Brett in her diary. It was a relief, it amused her to make a note on Cliffie, who was now in her imagination going to Princeton.

C. writes nice letters once a week, usually asking for an extra ten, because something has turned up like a special dance for which he has to pay admission or buy new shoes for. But his grades continue good, and his Eng. prof. is esp. pleased. Engineering isn't apple pie for C., but he is enjoying the challenge.

Edith was thinking of physics and math as she wrote that, as these had not been Cliffie's best subjects in high school. In her imagination, Cliffie was specializing in hydraulic engineering, loved the work, and was determined to stick with it. Irrigation, dams, desert pumps, water tables, all that Edith imagined in Cliffie's head as he studied in his dorm room at Princeton. Girls would write him notes, fraternities – Well, Cliffie would already have joined one by now, been invited. Edith imagined his having started in September this year, but so brilliant that he was going to finish in three years, maybe even two. Edith had been imagining a girl in Cliffie's life, two or three girls, but one who might be more important than the others, and Edith had given her a name – Deborah, Debbie. She'd be pretty, intelligent, going to Princeton also (they admitted a few girls now), though only seventeen, and so popular that Cliffie wasn't sure he was number one in her books. But all would work out in the end, and the girl was and would be a constant inspiration. to Cliffie. He had become a new boy since he had met her. But Edith decided not to begin writing about Debbie today. Debbie had come into her mind only a couple of months ago. Edith's final note was on George. Solid and real he was, and always there, for all his frailty more solid than Brett lately.

G. getting so deaf we really have to yell. He can creep to the bathroom but with much pain, he says, but he hasn't yet asked for a bedpan & I can't bring myself to propose one. Statements arrive for him from some investment company in upstate New York & I can't bring myself to look at them, though they lie around in his room. Not sure I could fathom them anyway. This company sends dividends to his N.Y. bank, and G. regularly signs us a check for $150 a month. Only a couple of times did B. have to remind him, which B. hates to do. C. is rude to G. and makes facetious remarks in G.'s presence which of course G. can't hear. C. sometimes drifts up when I clean G.'s room, as if fascinated by the moribund.

Edith closed her pen, put the diary away and stood up. She faced a fact as solid as George now, that Brett was bringing Carol for a drink tonight, or rather that Carol was coming in her car at the same time as Brett.

'I want you to meet her again,' Brett had said in his earnest way, 'and see that she's a decent, serious girl at least.'

Edith certainly hadn't wanted to make better acquaintance with Carol after what Brett had told her, but Edith had thought it might help Brett, ease his conscience somehow. His conscience clearly was bothering him. Edith looked at Nelson, coiled on the flat cushion on the bay window seat. He gazed at her with drowsy blue eyes. He was a lilac point Siamese. Melanie had sent him by special messenger last July, after writing Edith a note to tell her that a kitten was arriving. This was less than a month after Mildew's death. Last month Nelson had had his castration, which Edith had detested having to have done, but knew was necessary at six months, if she wanted to keep him home and free of battle scars.

Edith glanced into George's room before she went downstairs. Its door was ajar as usual, and lately she didn't bother knocking or calling to him, because he wouldn't have heard her. George was sleeping on his side, facing her, one arm bent under him with its bluish white hand outstretched, fingers curled, as if beseeching something. Good Christ, it was like slow death, Edith thought. She had been going to ask if George wanted his tea now, but why bother, if he was asleep? It was ten past 5 already.

Brett would be home by a quarter to 6, probably, with Carol in tow, and since there was a bit of time, Edith decided to make a brief effort with Cliffie's room. Cliffie was out. If she tidied his room slightly, having respect still for the careless way Cliffie preferred to live, he never noticed, never thanked her for vacuuming. Margaret, the black cleaning woman who came one afternoon a week for four hours, didn't or wouldn't tackle Cliffie's room, not that she and Margaret had ever had words about it. Edith could understand: there were so many clothes, shoes and magazines on the floor, it was twenty minutes' work trying to put them away somewhere so one could start cleaning.

Edith experienced the usual mild shock on entering the room, seeing the four drawers in the chest half pulled out, sweater sleeves dangling, one drawer even down on the floor – because it looked like the classic picture of a room just after a burglary.

Mechanically, Edith began folding sweaters, closing drawers, then she made the bed. Beside the bed, one damp sock. Did Cliffie have sweaty feet? Nerves? Was that why he washed his own socks so often? He'd squirm if she asked, Edith thought, so maybe it was better not to ask. She put away slightly muddy tennis shoes, gathered from among the shoes on the floor of his closet five or six more socks, obviously dirty, some even stiff. Ten or twelve comic books had slid onto the floor in front of his bookcase, ancient and creased. The top two shelves of the bookcase were reasonably neat, because he never touched them: a complete encyclopaedia for children, bound in red imitation leather, several children's books like *Winnie-the-Pooh* and *Treasure Island* (a nostalgic faded blue binding that had, and Edith recalled that it had been hers as a child), next to this *A Manual for Sexual Pleasure*, and several books by Ian Fleming. Cliffie had a desk of sorts, which was a rectangular wooden table with a big front drawer in it. He even had a typewriter, a Hermes Baby, on the table, its gray plastic cover dusty and now dented, as if something heavy had dropped on it. Edith remembered herself and Brett buying the typewriter one Christmas six or seven years ago, choosing it carefully, because they had hardly been able to afford it at the time. Had Cliffie broken the typewriter? Edith couldn't remember when he had last used it.

The table was covered with scraps of paper mostly written on by Cliffie, names and telephone numbers, Edith saw at a glance, and she had no intention of trying to sort or stack those. I HATE caught her eye, because it was in block letters, and Edith deliberately didn't read further. Had it said GEORGE, or one of the boys in town or even – herself? Cliffie blew hot and cold toward her and everyone else, Edith was well aware. She couldn't say, in fact, that she had ever had the feeling that he loved or liked her in the filial sense. She occasionally felt that he resented her, even disliked her. Edith couldn't make out Cliffie's emotions, never had been able to. She left his room with some dirty socks in her hands, with the usual feeling of being glad to leave the room, glad to close the door and pretend the room wasn't in the house.

A busty pin-up girl on a calendar in Cliffie's room (dated November 1964) stayed in Edith's mind. Was she thinking of Carol? Probably. Edith dropped the socks in the wicker basket in the kitchen, which held things for the launderette.

Edith went upstairs and had a quick bath, then dressed in a long wrap-around madras skirt of green and white floral pattern. It was not a cold day and it was sunny. She topped the skirt with a white sweater, a gold chain which bore her grandfather's signet and a couple of gold trifles including her tiny Phi Beta Kappa key. She took a little more care than usual with her make-up. Now that it was too late, she thought.

She was just bringing a plate of canapés into the living room, when the first car came up the driveway. Edith went back to the kitchen for the ice bucket, a black plastic thing. She heard Brett's voice, thought he had brought Carol, then Brett and Cliffie came in.

'Picked up our son on the –' Brett stopped, because a blue Volkswagen was turning into the drive.

'Hi, mom,' Cliffie said.

'Hello, Cliffie. And what've you been doing?'

'Taking a walk.' Cliffie looked at his mother sharply, knowingly, and unzipped his waist-length jacket.

Carol came in the front door, which was opened by Brett. She was blonde and smiling, with a bright lavender scarf at her neck, a blue suede jacket, tweed skirt, and the kind of shoes called sensible. 'Hello, Mrs Howland,' Carol said.

'Hello, good evening,' Edith replied.

'How are you, darling?' Brett said. 'I'll just go and wash – for a second.' He disappeared.

Edith offered to take Carol's jacket, but Carol kept it over her arm.

'What a lovely house!' Carol said. 'And the garden. I'm living in a cramped place in Trenton.'

'Won't you sit down? What would you like to drink? I think we've got just about everything.'

Scotch, Carol wanted. Edith was thinking that Carol's parents' house was no doubt a lot grander than theirs. The girl did have a seriousness about her eyes and brows. She wasn't silly, she had nice hands, and a general look of good family. Brett came back, smiling and pleasant, and soon they were all sitting around talking rubbish and platitudes with drinks in their hands. Edith thought, what if she should burst out with, 'You've been to bed a few times with my husband, I take it, so why the hell are we all so pleasant and smirking now?' Then Cliffie joined them, frankly smirking, which to Edith at that moment was a kind of relief.

'Have a scotch, Cliffie,' Edith said.

'Don't moind if I do,' Cliffie said with a mock English accent. 'Thenk you.' He made his own.

Edith was waiting for Carol to say, 'What a big boy you have,' from the way she was appraising him, or did she have designs on him too? Edith stifled a genuine smile.

'Carol's moving soon to New York,' Brett remarked. 'To bigger things.'

'Oh, bigger?' Carol said. 'With newspapers dying like flies there? I've got hopes for the *Post*. For a job,' Carol said to Edith. 'But frankly it's more because of a connection through my father than – my qualifications. And my father's not even in the newspaper business, he's in electronics, but somehow – too difficult to explain, he knows someone who knows someone.'

'You don't have to be *so* modest,' Brett said.

'Yuck-yuck,' said Cliffie, half a laugh, half mocking the absurd antics of the middle-aged trying to be polite.

Carol recrossed her legs and dangled a walking shoe. She had lovely dark blonde hair, cut shortish, with natural waves as Edith's had, though Carol's had not a bit of gray.

Carol accepted a second scotch, which Brett would have liked to make, but Edith was up first. Edith made a generous one. Carol looked the type that could hold it. Carol said she was going to be an assistant editor in the foreign news department, a nobody hanging on at first, she assured Edith, but she preferred that department to a better-paying job she could have got in the film and drama critics department.

'Carol will be leaving us early January,' Brett said.

Methinks they both protest too much, Edith thought. Was New York so far away? Hardly two hours in a fast car.

Five minutes later, Edith was reproaching herself for her bitchy thoughts. Carol was talking knowledgeably on the care of camellias as she stood by the front window, admiring the plant which Edith had brought in from the garden for the winter, and which now had eight buds that were going to open in January or February. Edith saw from the way Carol gently touched the sturdy leaf points that she cared about plants. Cliffie was no longer smirking, but regarded Carol with his straightforward neutral expression – observant, maybe, but maybe his mind was miles away, Edith could never tell. Edith was thinking that Carol was young, and knew little about Brett. Why fear Carol? Why worry? Brett wasn't the type to sweep a girl off her feet and never had been. He was incapable even of putting on a temporary act. And – happy thought – maybe Carol had called it off herself, and not Brett.

'She's pretty,' Cliffie said, when Carol had gone.

Carol's car had just turned to the right in the street, toward Trenton.

Brett had heaved a great sigh, and was draining his ice-watery drink. 'You look nice. I like you in that skirt.'

'Want a dividend?' Edith asked, standing by the bar cart.

Brett did. Edith made herself a short one too. Cliffie lingered, chomping ice cubes noisily. Because of Cliffie's presence, Edith couldn't talk, and yet, what would she have said anyway? She didn't feel like paying Carol a compliment, and would never have said under any circumstances, 'Well, are you sure it's really over?' So silence was inevitable.

'Am I supposed to phone Carstairs again? This week, wasn't it?' Brett asked.

Dr Francis X. Carstairs was George's doctor, who came once a month to have a look at George. Carstairs lived in Washington Crossing, and Brett usually telephoned him from Trenton to remind him, otherwise the doctor could forget.

'I don't know,' Edith said. 'It seems like a month. Phone tomorrow and ask. Or phone now.'

'I'd like to try some of that codeine,' Cliffie put in, smiling. 'Opium derivative, I see from my trusty dictionary.'

'Well, don't,' Brett said. He was walking about with his drink, and suddenly he scratched his head, which left his black and gray hair standing up in a silly way on top. 'If I catch you sampling that stuff, I'll present you with the bill for it.'

'Is it expensive?' Cliffie asked. 'Must be. Opium. Look what the junkies have to pay for it.'

'Cliffie, get *off* the subject,' Brett said.

'You've got to have a very careful prescription for that, haven't you?' Cliffie went on.

Brett nearly blew a gasket. He gasped, swung a fist in the air, but it was over in a couple of seconds. Brett became livid at what he considered Cliffie's stupid, driveling questions, his hanging onto a subject that everyone else had dropped. Edith glanced calmly at her son who was slumped in an armchair. We're all crackers, Edith thought, all insane, including old George, doped on his pain-killers. She went into the kitchen to prepare dinner.

11

It was a particularly glorious spring in 1966, not merely because of people's gardens and trees bursting into blossom (Brunswick Corner looked prettier to Edith every year), but she and Gert got the *Bugle* launched again as a semi-monthly. This was due to increased advertising, and the new price of twenty-five cents a copy. Lots of weekend tourists bought it as a souvenir. Ten or more new shops had opened in town, gift shops, two more antique shops, a pottery shop, and all these advertised. The *Bugle* now had eight pages, and was on sale in a few Phila-delphia stores such as Strawbridge and Clothier. As for Edith's duties, there was always something to report about the local fire department, the police force – the latter well-meaning boobs whom everyone laughed at and called the Keystone Kops. The local cops (two or three) often ran out of gas on a chase, lost their direction for want of a map, or were hopelessly late for emergency calls. Some Brunswick Corner residents were musicians, actors, or painters, and Edith did profiles of them. She wrote most of the editorials on such subjects as the size of shop signs, preservation of local scenery, building permits. She had written one piece in praise of the Lyndon Johnson Head-Start program, and another on LBJ's remark that the nation was not going to solve its problems by pouring money down a hole, meaning handouts to the poor.

On the Peace Corps, Edith wrote an editorial which never got printed in the *Bugle*, because Gert thought it too far out, or un-realistic.

The American Peace Corps might take with them children aged eight to ten, since children of this age mix so well with children in any country, have no racial prejudice (at least not entrenched), and pick up languages quickly. Orphanages could be solicited for willing recruits, and perhaps there would be many. The Peace Corps activities involve camping and adventure. Seeds of friendship would be planted, memories formed that will not die even at the death of those who have them, because they will pass them on to others. Lonely children, the abandoned, the illegitimate, the discouraged, will find a place in society, and instead of being the pitied, they will become the heroes, the young pioneers, if they can be adopted as junior members of the Peace Corps.

That was the way Edith's first draft went, and she showed it to Gert. Edith was briefly annoyed, out of patience with Gert for saying so emphatically, 'No. No one would ever let minors go.' But Edith didn't quarrel with Gert, and the incident was forgotten. Edith had plenty of editorial ideas in reserve. Every month, two or three people, sometimes more, whom Edith encountered on the street or in shops, stopped her and told her how much they enjoyed the *Bugle*'s editorials. Some even wrote congratulatory letters. The disapprovers were few.

And Brett was making progress on his book which he had talked about for years, *Pothole Road*, an analysis of American foreign policy since the end of the Second World War. He had re-written his outline, broken it down into chapters and given the chapters working titles, a method of structure which Edith had suggested to him. He went a couple of times to New York on Saturdays to look up things in the main Public Library and in newspaper articles.

In June Aunt Melanie paid another visit, and Edith was grateful that Cliffie had a job at that time (clerk in one of the town's haberdasheries called the Stud Box), and that he curbed his drinking during Melanie's stay. Edith had gently remarked to Cliffie that he seemed to be making inroads into the living room bar cart, and the result of this was that Cliffie cut down a bit on what he took from the living room, but kept a bottle of scotch or gin in his own room in a corner of his closet, Edith had noticed. He wasn't ever drunk, just a bit oiled all day long. She wished the Stud Box boys would call him down about it, but since the two of them were famous for being oiled themselves, it was rather vain to hope Cliffie would get a reprimand, Edith supposed.

'Let's be thankful it isn't dope,' Edith said to Brett. 'The stories Gert tells are *appalling* – right here in Brunswick Corner High School!' Kevin, their fourteen-year-old, had been recruited somehow by the police and had been on the police payroll as an informer on his schoolmates' drug purchases, a job, Gert said, that couldn't last more than a month of so, because the kids would find out who was informing and beat him up. Kevin had escaped that fate, and of course school had closed in June for summer holidays.

. Then in mid-September, when the leaves had begun to fall, though it was too early for them to have changed color – Edith's favorite season, the autumn – Brett made his big speech. Edith always thought of it as his big speech (maybe because she was sure Brett did too), though she didn't write that flippant-sounding phrase in her diary. He said he was deeply in love with Carol Junkin, that she loved him too, and that neither he nor she could repress it or hide it any longer.

'I am – bitterly sorry,' Brett said gently, firmly, and with a kind of clenched teeth desperation, 'but I don't see anything honest to do but tell you – and to hope somehow that you'll agree to a separation.'

Edith's first surprise, which was total, gave way almost instantly to a sense of impatience. She felt annoyed, as if someone had lit a firecracker under her nose. 'Are you serious?'

This conversation of a week ago, whenever she recalled it, seemed ludicrous. Brett had assured her he was serious. Then he had launched into the longer part of his speech with the same earnest, dry-mouthed determination.

'I have a right before it's too late, or at least that's the way I feel about it. Our son's grown up – for better or for worse.' A shake of his head here. 'And of course I'll see about things financially. That's my responsibility. But I have a right to be happy.'

Edith never said that he hadn't. She hadn't bothered asking if he was unhappy with her, and now it was evident that he was

96

unhappy. Or perhaps not happy enough. Not as happy as he considered he deserved to be.

'I do want to marry Carol. It's that serious,' Brett had continued.

This conversation had taken place in their bedroom upstairs, where Brett had asked her to come, Edith knew because Cliffie might have come into the house and the living room at any moment. It had been just past 6 p.m., and Cliffie was lately usually home for dinner.

'I suppose it's a shock,' Brett said. 'But I just couldn't go on like this, pretending – or seeing Carol on the sly. It's not my nature.'

Then Edith had remembered the New York research expeditions since January. He had of course been seeing Carol those Saturday afternoons. And maybe it had been three months since she and Brett had made love? Edith hadn't the faintest idea or memory, because the act of making love didn't seem terribly important. Yet, she reminded herself, what else was Brett talking about now in regard to Carol? As Cliffie would have put it, he wanted to screw a younger woman while he still could, while a younger woman would still have him. And in the midst of her confusion or speechlessness, Edith had still been able to think, she remembered, that she wasn't the first woman in the world to whom such a thing had happened, who had had to listen to the same earnest speech from an honest man who really meant what he was saying.

And now a week later, Edith hadn't been able to write a word about it in her diary. Who cared anyway whether she noted it in her diary? Certainly she didn't.

The atmosphere in the house had suffered a sea-change, Edith thought she might write, and laughed briefly and hysterically at the idea. Brett went about his usual routine like a little soldier, giving the grass what he hoped might be a final cut but probably wouldn't be, not daring to put the power mower away for the winter yet, corralling his dirty shirts for the laundry as usual.

How was he going to pay for this house as well as the establishment he and Carol would have, Edith wondered. Of course

Carol's family had money. Brett said he was sure of a job on the *Post*, he'd been making efforts there. But what if it fell through, Edith thought. Would she have to get a job? She was forty-six. She wouldn't have to get a job, legally speaking. The noose was around Brett's neck, but to be decent she might get a job, clerking in a local shop, something like that, because otherwise she didn't see where enough money would be coming from. Cliffie could get a regular job or get out, Edith thought with a surge of intent, because God knew he'd never paid his keep here. George might be asked to contribute a bit more. What was old George going to do with his capital anyway, except pass it on to Brett? Edith gathered that he and Carol wanted to move into a bigger apartment in New York than the one Carol had at the moment. They would live together for a few months, then if Edith agreed to the divorce, they would be married.

But Edith had already agreed to the separation, she remembered. She had said, 'Yes,' a word like 'I will,' when one got married, she thought. It seemed strange. Edith had sometimes the feeling she was dreaming, and when she woke up in the mornings, she would think first that it was a dream, then realize that it wasn't, because she could see at once the change in Brett, could feel that most of his mind wasn't present. Not to mention the fact that they didn't share the same bed any longer. Whose idea had that been, hers or Brett's? Maybe Edith had suggested that she sleep in her workroom, which she didn't mind at all as a sleeping place, and Brett to be courteous had said *he* would, and Edith had insisted that *she* sleep in her workroom, really because she didn't want the recollection of Brett's having been there, sleeping, so close to her desk and her typewriter, her manuscripts, notes and all the rest of it.

'What's going on here?' Cliffie asked, on noticing the new sleeping arrangements. This was at breakfast one morning.

'People have a right to sleep where they please,' Brett said, biting into toast.

'Maybe it's a new marital experiment,' Cliffie said, also biting into toast, and looking from one to the other of his parents for a reaction.

98

Edith ignored the remark, out of old habit. If Brett glanced at her, sympathetically, Edith simply didn't care. Brett would soon be out of it, she remembered.

Brett had begun his packing. Edith could see him hesitating over such things as a half dirty pair of levis, deciding to leave them. He would drive to New York with his things, he said, and return the car later.

'What do you want me to say to George?' Edith asked.

'Oh – I've already told him, tried to explain,' Brett said. 'I'm not even sure he grasped it. He's really in his dotage, poor old guy.'

'Well, it's all those pills and medicines too,' Edith said, 'making him sleepy.' She was inclined to feel sympathetic toward George just now, because George was at least polite and friendly, as civilized as he could be in his condition. Somehow Brett's behavior wasn't civilized. And yet intellectually she had to agree with Brett that he had the right. Brett had told Edith also that he had had a talk with Cliffie. Edith assumed this. Brett had asked Cliffie to come for a walk (or a beer) one evening, which Brett would never have done under ordinary circumstances.

One day that week, when Brett was at the office in Trenton, Cliffie remarked to Edith, 'My father's just an old shit like the others. An old letch – leaving you for a younger woman.'

Edith was in the kitchen then, making sandwiches for herself and Cliffie for lunch. 'I think your father thinks of it as – maybe an experiment,' Edith replied calmly. 'You're old enough to understand that. And if you want to be really grown up, don't talk about it to your chums. Or anybody.'

Cliffie nodded, his lips slightly parted.

Was he thinking, Edith wondered, that everybody knew already? Gert Johnson knew. The news spread like an invisible gas. How? Yesterday Gert had asked Edith in an unusually worried tone how she was. Gert was coming over for a drink today at 5 p.m., bringing also some checks from Washington Crossing and Hopewell Township advertisers. Edith kept the books.

When Gert arrived, Edith asked about Derek, who had been reported wounded a week ago.

'Oh, we had a letter from him yesterday!' Gert said, smiling. 'It's just a flesh wound in the calf. To tell you the truth Norm and I are delighted – *naturally* – that he's laid up. We wrote back telling him to make the most of it.' Gert laughed with genuine glee. 'Maybe the mail is censored, but *I* don't give a damn. He's my son and what the hell kind of war is *this*?'

Cliffie was vaguely watching television from an armchair and also listening to them, Edith knew. She and Gert could have gone up to her workroom, and sometimes they did with *Bugle* work, but it was time to offer Gert a rye and water, and Edith knew Gert wanted to talk to her.

'Cliffie, would you mind terribly,' Edith began. 'That's not an important program, is it?'

'It's a load of –' Instead of the final word, Cliffie brush-banged his hands together, a recent gesture to censor a dirty word, and stood up. His belly projected like an older man's, and part of his shirt was visible between trousers and the waist of his sweater.

Edith saw Gert give him a glance, as if to say, what a slob you've got hanging around the house. They took care of the *Bugle* business in a very few minutes, and Edith made a tidy heap of papers to take up to her room, then made drinks for both of them.

'By the way, I heard about Brett,' Gert said, following Edith into the kitchen. Gert wore bell-bottom pink slacks.

'How, by the way?' Edith was smiling a little.

'Oh! A friend of Kevin's. I don't know how *he* knew.'

So even Brunswick Corner High School knew. It could hardly be of interest to kids, Edith thought.

'He's really leaving – for that Carol,' Gert said in a whisper.

'Tomorrow.' Edith dropped ice cubes into their glasses, and left the rest of the ice tray on the drainboard. 'He's moving to New York tomorrow.'

'I must say you're bearing up pretty well.'

'What else can one do? I certainly don't care to make a scene. – And what good would a scene do?'

They went into the living room.

100

'Well – do you think it's going to last?'

Edith hesitated. 'Maybe. Why not?'

Gert laughed in an embarrassed way. 'I don't know the answers! You know Brett better than I do.'

Edith had faced the fact that it might be permanent. It would be stupid not to face the possibility. 'Brett doesn't do things lightly. Not something like this. He may well want to marry her. Soon.'

Gert took a swallow of her drink. Wide-eyed, she shook her head, as if she were about to say, 'The nerve of Brett!' or something like that. 'And you're stuck with his uncle – George. That's a fine thing.'

They did manage to talk of other things, until during the second drink (Gert always had two but never three in the afternoon) Gert said, 'Can I ask you something, Edie, would you take Brett back if he wanted to come back?'

That was a leap into unreality, the future, that Edith couldn't make. She shook her head with sudden impatience. 'I can't answer that now. It even bores me to think about it.'

Cliffie had drifted upstairs toward the bathroom, where in fact he didn't need to go, but he made brief use of it anyway. The house felt emptier with his father's things packed, his raincoats off the hall hooks and out on the porch, ready to be thrown into the car tomorrow. His father was coming back Sunday with the car, his mother had said, then she would drive him to the railway station in Trenton (or maybe Cliffie would do that, his mother had said), or maybe Brett would walk to the bus stop, Edith wasn't sure what he would want to do.

It was *real*, Cliffie supposed, his father's leaving, yet it made Cliffie want to laugh. Cliffie had the feeling his father might be acting, the way an actor acted in a play, not meaning it. Maybe his mother was acting, too, pretending to be unhappy – and then Brett would come back. Yet Cliffie had met Carol, and she was real, all right. She was pretty. And his father was laying her. Soon, starting tomorrow night, his father was going to be in bed with her every night in New York.

Cliffie found himself walking softly, almost on tiptoe, into

George's room, whence a gentle, wheezing snore came. George was on his back, one skinny arm flung up on the pillow as if he were warding off a blow, or maybe hailing somebody. George's mouth was open. His lower teeth were in a glass on the bedside table. Disgusting! George wore faded pink and white striped pajamas. He looked like a crazy drawing in *Mad*, Cliffie thought, or maybe a character in a horror film. Cliffie liked horror films: they made him genuinely scared for a few seconds, then they made him laugh. He could laugh *at* them, and he liked that.

'Well, what d'y'think about the *news*, George?' Cliffie asked in a soft voice, smiling. Cliffie glanced at the door, which he had left half open.

George snored on, didn't even twitch.

'Bores you, I bet. Just imagine – your nephew – Brett – running off with another woman at *his* age. Cradle-robbing!' Cliffie laughed out loud. 'Opium, George?' Cliffie sobered suddenly, and reached in his pocket for a cigarette and matches. He looked around at the half-neat, half-sloppy room, which always looked exactly the same: three or four library books stacked on the straight chair where nobody ever sat, and on the white-painted chest of drawers at least thirty little bottles of crap – pills and drops, sedatives, pain-killers, cough syrup.

'*Soo-oothing* syrups,' Cliffie said aloud in falsetto.

George stirred and snorted as he resettled his head on his pillow. His face was turned sideways now, and his skin was nearly as pale as the pillow except for a few spots of bluish-pink.

'What d'y'say, George, honestly?' Cliffie bent closer, whispering. 'Do you ever imagine –' Cliffie couldn't bring himself to utter the words. The idea, however, went through Cliffie's mind quite clearly. He imagined old George doing it with a girl, now, and Cliffie compressed his lips, and nearly exploded with a fart-like sound. Then he did laugh, heartily, on seeing that his laughter hadn't penetrated George's ears in the least!

Cliffie recalled the celebrated gang-bang or rape (his kid chums had called it by both names) years ago when Cliffie had been thirteen or fourteen. A girl called Ruthie, living in Brunswick Corner, had an empty cellar in her house and a family who were out all day, and she had been more than willing. Eight and ten boys would line themselves up around the cellar watching, getting themselves ready, and then they'd all screw her in turn. Cliffie had been ready in the way he was ready alone in bed, the way he could always do it, but that time he had suddenly conked out, although he had gone through the motions. There had been laughter and applause, as for all the boys. He had tried to pretend to the girl that he had made it, fast. It had all happened so fast, the girl had been so silly and giggling, Cliffie didn't give a damn what she had thought, anyway. Did the other guys know? Well, maybe. But now it didn't much matter, because the guys had somehow got scattered, Cliffie couldn't think even of *one* whom he knew now, and the girl had disappeared, family had moved or something. Cliffie had gone only one afternoon to the cellar, he remembered, though the cellar had continued in operation for weeks. When Cliffie saw a porn cartoon anywhere, in any magazine, he laughed, or at least smiled. As for real girls – what Cliffie saw as flesh and blood, five feet six and weighing a ton usually, he considered them a pain in the neck, demanding this, demanding that. Why did guys put up with it? Well, a lot didn't, they laid a girl for a while, then got rid of her, like Mel.

Cliffie blinked, relaxed, brought himself back to where he was, flicked cigarette ash into George's wastebasket, which was half full of revolting wadded Kleenexes. He listened for a moment to hear if his mother was possibly coming up the stairs, but he knew from past experience that Gert would stay till 6:15, the latest she could take off to get dinner at the usual time for her family. He went to the low chest of drawers, reached for the silver tablespoon that lay on a white napkin, rubbed its bowl vigorously with a corner of the napkin, stooped and made sure which of the bottles held the codeine syrup, then poured himself a tablespoonful. It tasted sweet and good, and had a base of alcohol. Cliffie liked to imagine that it gave his brain a take-off, like a rocket.

'... four – three – two – one – *Go!*' he whispered, and glanced again, unnecessarily, at George, who might have been knocked

103

out by a sledge-hammer. *'Whammo!'* Cliffie said for good measure. He thought it best to get out of the room while the coast was still clear, and went downstairs, back to the kitchen where he snared a beer from the fridge, then into his own room. He shut the door and switched on his transistor.

12

Edith had not made an entry in her diary for some four months. She wrote:

10/June/67. Awaiting a visit from dear Aunt Melanie – tomorrow. Bless her! She will do me a world of good.

The divorce is going through and would be done already but for what they call inevitable delays. I always thought people could get a divorce in a matter of days, but maybe that is only Mexico. Since we were married in N.Y. State, the only grounds are adultery and absence without tidings – first condition fulfilled, I presume. I must sue him, just to add to absurdities. I do know B. has had time (eight months or so since he left) to think things out & that he is serious.

She looked out her window at the waving tops of the willows, then wrote:

C. continues to do well and is an angel, a real bulwark, an arm to lean on. A man in my life, I might say, of the kind I need now. He is going to finish in '68 and already has two offers from companies who want him to work for them, which he modestly says every graduate engineer gets these days. Salary prob. in the $15,000 range to start. I hope he won't be sent away at once to Middle East to work. He comes home perhaps twice a month on weekends, sometimes brings Debbie. I think they are genuinely in love. That is *one* happy picture, at least, in my present life – Cliffie's success, after all our doubts.

Edith closed her diary hastily, realizing that the ink was probably not quite dry. Cliffie's pop music just now was driving her insane, as it often did in summer when the windows and doors were all open. Funny about jazz, when you were calm, it sounded great, and when you were disturbed, it made you more disturbed.

The guestroom was ready for Melanie, the bed made with Edith's prettiest percale sheets under a striped red and blue spread. Nelson was lying on the spread now, curled for sleep, eyes half closed. He was an intelligent cat, thoughtful even, or he often looked as if he were thinking, whereas Mildew had been merely wonderfully tranquil and daydreaming. Nelson's outstanding trait was his trust in her. When she got him down from trees, for instance, when he was younger, he relaxed completely in her hands and could slip through them like a piece of silk. She had learned to grip him firmly in emergencies. He did not much like Cliffie. Nelson's cool blue eyes, for all they were slightly crossed, gazed at Cliffie sometimes like the eyes of a judge too discreet to make the comment that he might.

Edith's heart gave a dip when she thought of what Melanie might say or think about Cliffie on this visit. Cliffie now had a scruffy beard, had put on a few more pounds, slept till noon often, stayed out till 3 a.m. at Mickey's, or at the house of a boy called Mel something in Lambertville. Cliffie occasionally worked as barman or waiter at the Chop House, where he made rather good money due to tips, though his contributions to the household were irregular and just enough to keep her quiet, Edith knew. Cliffie would put on reasonably good behavior for Melanie (Edith felt he nurtured dreams of inheriting some money from her), but nothing could correct his appearance.

After Brett's departure, Cliffie had felt a strain that Edith had foreseen. Now he was 'the man of the house,' a role he couldn't possibly fill, one he would run from by nature, so Edith had been cheerful, had not given a hint that she couldn't manage things herself, that she was in any way anxious. Cliffie had twice gotten rather drunk in the month after Brett had gone, got into one of his infantile tantrums and thrown a Chinese vase which had been on the mantel and which Edith had had all her life, and the pieces had been so small, Edith had at once despaired of having it mended, so had swept up the mess and tried to forget it.

Was there some hope to be taken, however, from the fact Cliffie was human enough to be disturbed by Brett's leaving? Edith liked to think so.

Edith drove alone in the brown 1964 Ford to fetch Melanie at the Trenton railway station, though Melanie in her letter had offered to take a taxi. Once more the embrace on the platform, like last summer. Edith hadn't told Melanie about Brett's wanting a divorce, only that he was living with a younger woman in New York, and had been for three or four months at the time Edith wrote the letter.

'You must tell me about everything,' Melanie said in the car, 'but maybe not when you're driving. You're looking quite well, my dear. – And how's old George?'

Edith said George was the same, but taking more pain-killers. 'Naturally this codeine stuff – probably makes people addicts.'

'Does it have to be codeine?'

'He gets used to the other things, then the doctor – it's still Carstairs – gets tired of switching them around, so he prescribes codeine – liquid. I have to sign for it at the drugstore. Then there're the sleeping tablets. I always thought codeine was sort of sleep-inducing. It's all opium, you know. In the arms of Morpheus.'

'In the arms of Murphy we used to say when I was young!' Melanie said, chuckling, 'and I think we meant bourbon. – Poor old fellow! What does George say about Brett's antics?'

'Oh – a few sympathetic words. What can he say?'

Edith made iced tea, with mint from the garden. Cliffie was not home. Edith explained that Cliffie was working in a restaurant part-time. He had said something about working lunch that day, a big birthday party with twenty people coming, but Edith didn't know whether to believe him or not. Melanie wanted to see Nelson who was in Edith's workroom now on the window seat.

Melanie bent and greeted him, not touching him. 'Nelson! What a big boy! You don't remember me, do you? – You were just – barely three month, I think.'

Nelson listened, then rather to Edith's surprise stood up,

107

arched his back in a stretch, sat and looked at Melanie attentively, as if he liked her voice. When they left the room, Nelson followed them. Downstairs, as they drank their tea, Edith told Melanie that Brett wanted a divorce.

'What? Has he lost his mind?'

Melanie was genuinely surprised, Edith saw. 'Well, no, because – he said when. he left that it was a – He said he thought he wanted to marry Carol.'

'How's he going to support two households?'

'Carol isn't poor. I might take a job of some kind. Lots of shops in town, you know, where I could get a job selling.' Edith couldn't bring herself to say Cliffie would help, too, because she knew Melanie didn't think him reliable.

'Have you agreed to the divorce?' Melanie asked.

'What else can I do?'

'Why, you've got everything on your –'

'I think it's awful, fighting these things,' Edith interrupted. 'After all, he's known the girl more than a year now. He must know what he's doing.'

'Yes. And so do I. He's indulging himself. He's walking out on a situation – you and Cliffie, not to mention George! Leaving you with *that*, it seems!' she put in, in her gentle, telling style, and continued, 'We all know about temptations like this, women have them too, but one doesn't give in to them,' Melanie gave a laugh. 'I'm sure I sound old-fashioned.'

She didn't to Edith. It was good to talk with someone besides Gert Johnson, who however had said the same thing about Brett's leaving her with George. But where did they go from here? 'I don't know,' Edith said with difficulty, 'if you expect me to fight – somehow. I just can't. It's too sordid.'

'Lots of things in life are sordid. Having a baby is sordid, but necessary.'

'I know what you mean,' Edith said, and she did, and knew that of all people Melanie could make the sordid part of life less sordid. 'But isn't making a fuss about it more sordid? You don't expect me to make a fuss, do you? I don't even want to soak Brett financially.'

Melanie leaned back on the sofa. 'I honestly don't know. I know your character, and it's not there – to fight in a case like this. I think I would, at your age. And does Brett think he's a spring chicken? Just because he's a man?' Melanie laughed again, a tolerant laugh.

Edith said nothing.

'How is Cliffie taking it? Does he know his father wants a divorce?'

'Oh yes. I think he resents the fact his father's simply run off. That more than the fact there's another woman involved. Cliffie's aware he's supposed to be the man of the house now. Naturally I don't –' Edith was finding it harder and harder to talk. 'I don't push the role on him.' Edith might have said, but didn't, that Cliffie showed signs of being worried about their finances. He did like the house and certainly wouldn't want her to have to sell it.

Edith glanced at her aunt's handsome face – Melanie was looking toward the fireplace now – and wondered if Melanie was thinking that if Cliffie did push off, it would be the best thing for him and for her? 'I do think Cliffie feels Brett is being selfish,' Edith said.

'In that respect, Cliffie is right.'

Melanie then said she would like a rest before the evening, and she would try again to say hello to George who had been sleeping a few minutes ago. Upstairs, Edith looked into George's room and found that he was awake.

'Oh, George! Aunt *Melanie* is here. Wants to say *hello* to you!' Edith thought her own voice sounded insanely cheerful, but why not?

'Oh! Oh, how nice! Tell her to come in.'

Edith made a vague gesture toward the glass that held his lower teeth, because George spoke and looked better with them. 'Melanie?' Edith said.

'Coming, dear!' Melanie came into the room. 'How're you, George?' Melanie said heartily, bending over George. 'You're looking the same as ever and it's been – oh, nearly another year, I do believe.'

·'Feeling about the same,' George assured her. He was propped on one elbow. He had not put in his teeth.

'What're you reading?' Melanie was speaking loudly, and she pointed to a closed book on George's bed.

It was not a library book, but one from the house, a biography, Edith had forgotten of whom. Anyway George didn't hear the question.

'See Brett?' George lifted his rheumy eyes to Melanie's face.

'No. No, I haven't. *Love* to see him!' Melanie shouted tactfully, and gave Edith an amused glance over her shoulder.

'We'll let you rest a while, George,' Edith said. 'Unless you'd like some tea? But it'll be dinner time in about an hour.'

'Tea? Tea, yes,' George said.

Edith had been about to open a window to air the room. Only one window was open a little. George had somehow thought it worthwhile to get out of bed and close one window, or of course he might have done it on one of his trips to the bathroom. But just now Edith thought it more urgent to get his tea and have that over with.

Melanie said to Edith in the hall, 'Poor dear!' She squeezed Edith's forearm and released it. 'I do hope he's still going to the bathroom by himself.'

'Yes. That's something,' Edith replied. Edith was not going to mention that George had wet his bed two or three times, in his sleep, perhaps. Edith knew she must acquire a rubber sheet. It had been on her mind for at least three weeks now.

Edith prepared George's tea tray and took it up.

When cocktail time arrived, a little past 7, Cliffie was still not home. Was he funking the whole evening, because he knew Melanie was here? Edith told Melanie that Cliffie sometimes had to work the dinner shift, and didn't always ring her when he had to.

Melanie was sipping a gin and tonic. The big front window was open. It was not yet warm enough for air-conditioning in the daytime, and the evening was bringing a most welcome breeze from the north.

'You know, it occurred to me just now as I was sitting in my delicious cool bath,' Melanie said, 'that if you don't fight now,

110

you may regret it. A little later will be too late and too late forever, you know.' Her voice was gentle.

'Fight how?'

'Telephone him. Tell him you love him. – You've got his telephone number, haven't you?'

Was she supposed to do that, when Carol might pick up the telephone first, be in the apartment when she spoke with Brett?

'Well, you do love him, don't you?'

'Yes. Oh yes,' Edith said.

'It's up to you, my dear, of course, but I say only that if you let the divorce go through – it's going to be so much more difficult, if Brett ever wants to come back. It seems to me you're not lifting a finger. Maybe you think it's more noble –'

'I don't feel in the least noble,' Edith said.

'It's not the time for nobleness. Brett isn't behaving nobly. All I'm saying is that if you don't act now –' Melanie let her voice trail off, then she lit one of her infrequent filtered cigarettes. She smoked perhaps three a day.

In the seconds of silence, Edith felt for the first time an abyss beneath her, around her, black and dangerous. She had a sense of empty time, lots of time, years, months, days, evenings. She was reminded more strongly, she felt more strongly than when she had written the sentence maybe twenty years ago, that life really had no meaning, for anyone, not merely herself. But if she herself were alone, was going to be alone, then the meaninglessness was going to be that much more terrifying. That was it. She felt terrified for a few seconds, as if she had had a glimpse of destiny, fate, the essence of life and even death. It had been her destiny to meet Brett Howland, for instance, to become his wife and have a son by him, and if that were taken away – Brett was obviously already taken away, and as for a son, was Cliffie of much substance? He worried her more than he comforted her.

Edith got up for no purpose except that she had grown faint and thought it best to move, to go nearer the window. Her legs felt weak, and she realized she was stooped.

'Edie, sit down!' said Melanie. Now Melanie was on her feet, extending a hand to Edith.

Edith took her hand and sat down, realized the coldness of

her own hand from the warmth of Melanie's. *I have just had a vision*, Edith wanted to say, *a vision of a valley, an abyss, worse than a cliff you walk over.* It represented the rest of her life, Edith felt, and it represented the present also. And the tragedy would not be solved by another person, not another husband, not even by Brett really, because Edith's vision had to do with her existence, quite apart from other people.

'I am not going to faint,' Edith said to her great-aunt, as if Melanie had said she was going to, and Edith sat up straighter.

'Of course you're not. I know it's a difficult time for you, darling, and I'm glad I'm here. – What does Julia say? And Bill?'

These were Edith's parents who lived in the country near Richmond. Though Edith was an only child, she and her parents were not close. Her parents were more interested in growing prize roses than in politics, and thought Edith might have married 'better,' one of the bores from a better family than Brett's who populated their district and their world. Sometimes Melanie telephoned her parents, Edith's mother being Melanie's niece, and Edith wondered if Melanie had in the past months.

'I wrote them that Brett was going to work in New York for a while and take an apartment,' Edith said, 'and that he was working also on his book, you know. I can't tell my parents everything, Aunt Melanie, I don't want to.'

Melanie patted her hand. 'All right, m'dear. Let's talk about something else.'

So they did. And Cliffie did not come home for dinner or even to sleep that night.

13

The next morning Edith shopped and was home by 10, then she and Melanie spent a pleasant hour weeding sweet peas and making an edge in the grass with the spade. Nelson followed them about, collapsing in patches of sunlight, watching them. Melanie called him their white overseer. Even at her vast age, Melanie didn't mind kneeling with a trowel, bare-legged in her longish summer skirt. The Quickmans (a name Cliffie thought hilarious, and he called them the Quickmen) were coming for drinks. They liked Melanie. And the Johnsons had invited them, including Cliffie, for dinner tomorrow night. With drives into the country, visits to antique shops, Melanie's five-day stay would be pleasantly filled. But Edith knew Melanie was going to say something more in regard to Brett before she left.

Cliffie came in before 3 that afternoon, his beard miraculously gone, his face pale, his manner chastened. Edith and Melanie were having after-lunch coffee in the living room.

'Well, Cliffie,' Melanie said. 'How are you? Give us a kiss. Um – smack!' Melanie laughed. 'I thought you had a beard!'

'Just got it shorn,' Cliffie replied. He carried a magazine rolled tightly in one nervous hand.

'You were at Mel's?' Edith asked.

'Yeah.'

'You might give me a buzz next time, Cliffie. How do I know what's happened to you, if you stay out all night? You could have been in an accident somewhere.' Edith felt false, as if she was saying what she thought she should be saying.

'Oh, if I'm in an accident, the police or the hospital always telephone home. No need to worry about that!'

'Working tonight?' Edith asked. If he worked the evening shift at the Chop House, he had to be there by 5:15 p.m.

'No,' Cliffie said. 'Well – I dunno. I can work if I want to, they said.'

'Because the Quickmans are coming for a drink at six.'

'The Quickmen,' Cliffie said, with a glance at Melanie, who was observing him with a friendly attention.

Cliffie might have slept in his shirt and trousers, Edith thought, from their look. 'Have you had lunch?' she asked.

'No.' Cliffie was walking toward the rear door of the living room, the direction of the kitchen and his own room. 'And I'm hungry.' He disappeared.

Edith said softly, 'I think he shaved his beard off for you.'

'He needn't have done,' Melanie said. 'Didn't he have one last year? Does he think I'd be shocked by a beard?'

Edith shook her head. 'I never know what's in his mind.'

'He really should get out of the house,' Melanie said gently, not for the first time. 'He's such a silly boy sometimes. He needs a few hard knocks to grow up.'

They'd been over this before. 'If you have any ideas, I'd be grateful if you told him – talked to him. One of my friends – probably Gert – said I'd be taking care of him when he was forty. I don't know what'll happen when he's forty, except maybe I'll be dead by then myself.' Edith laughed.

They were both almost whispering. Edith knew that Cliffie eavesdropped when he could, like some insane self-prisoner wondering how to escape a place from which his captors would be delighted if he did escape, or like a paranoid who thought everyone was plotting against him.

The Quickmans came, Frances pink-faced from gardening in the sun. She had red hair. Her grown-up daughter had married two years ago, and now lived in Philadelphia. Her husband Ben was manager of a car sales office in Flemington, a sturdy good-natured man with brown curly hair, balding on top. Edith had never seen Ben in other than a cheerful mood, and Edith supposed it helped to sell cars. Or was he cracked like everyone else? The Quickmans were determined Republicans, and had voted for Goldwater. They did useful favors such as cat-feeding. Now they were tactful enough not to mention Brett at all, and they hadn't asked questions even in the days after Brett's departure. Edith knew they had heard the news, not to mention that Brett's absence must have been noticed by them since they lived next door. Cliffie was not present. Was he working tonight? He had slipped out with his usual vagueness, not saying where he was going when Edith had asked him.

'We'll miss Brett,' said Ben, blinking behind his glasses at Edith. 'Hope he comes back to the homestead weekends now and then.'

Everyone was polite.

The Johnsons on the following evening were equally discreet, and Brett's name wasn't uttered. Cliffie did not come with Edith and Melanie, though he had not been working that evening. The Johnsons talked about their son Derek, who was due home for a three-week leave in August. Gert and Norm were thrilled.

'I'm gonna make shur-r,' Norm said, 'he breaks a knee in a car accident or something while he's here, so he won't have to go back.'

Derek had another five months to serve in Viet Nam.

On the fourth day of her visit, Melanie asked, 'Does Brett write to you?'

'Oh yes. I must've had – at least three letters. I can't expect him to write every week! And once in a while he phones. It just happens he hasn't phoned while you've been here.'

'And do you write him?'

'No. I don't want my letters crashing in where they're living – together.'

'But you could write him at the *Post* marked personal. You know, Edith, I think you should have a face to face talk with him in New York before the final papers are signed. Wouldn't he agree to meet you somewhere?'

They were sitting in the living room, and Cliffie's transistor again jangled Edith's nerves, but she was afraid to ask him to cut it off, lest he be sullen at dinner on Melanie's last evening.

'I can't seem to explain to you, Aunt Melanie, that Brett and

I have been over this. He spoke to me – very plainly. Seven months he knew Carol before he – sprang this thing. I think he had to wrestle with himself – though you may think that's –' Edith broke off. 'If you want me to appeal to his conscience or sense of duty, I simply don't care to. I don't think it would be right.'

'There are things in people's relationships that you can't put into words,' Melanie said. 'I don't mean to tell you do this and do that, but there's such a thing as human contact, a reminder to him that you exist. It's the years past that you've had – and it's Cliffie too. It hasn't much to do with going to bed with a younger woman, if you know what I mean.'

Edith knew. As for Cliffie, going on twenty-two, Edith knew that Brett thought Cliffie should have been on his own a couple of years ago, and if Cliffie wasn't by now, then to hell with him. *Brett's given Cliffie up as a bad job*, Edith wanted to say and couldn't. Aunt Melanie knew, anyway.

'You said Carol's twenty-six,' Melanie went on. 'More than twenty years' difference in their ages. How long will it be till she tells *him* good-bye, I wonder. Two years? I wouldn't give it that. – She's not pregnant, is she?'

'Not that I know.'

'A blessing, if it continues.'

Edith had told Melanie what she could about Carol, that she seemed intelligent, had good manners, and hadn't once telephoned Brett at the house here. And maybe, Edith thought, Carol really loved Brett.

'How long has it been now since you've seen him?'

'Oh – I think around Easter he had to come back to get something. A couple of books. Clothes.'

'By himself?'

'Oh yes.'

'How long did he stay? You didn't talk?'

'He stayed about an hour. I think I asked him if he was happy. I hope he is. Why should I bear him a grudge?'

Melanie inquired also about the financial situation. Brett was sending Edith two hundred dollars a month. Cliffie contributed between thirty and fifty dollars a month (he paid something weekly, usually, but Edith was giving statistics by the month), George more or less pulled his weight with a hundred and fifty a month, and of course his medical insurance paid for his doctor, though some of his medicines had to come out of the hundred and fifty and were rather expensive. Edith patronized the local drugstore, Stan's, and Stan would always refill the phenobarbitol or whatever prescriptions even if Edith hadn't the renewal stamp from Carstairs. Edith didn't write down the cost every time, because it was a bore and it didn't seem to matter all that much. But after the electricity, oil for the heating and hot water, gas, and the telephone bill (lots of the telephone bill had to do with the *Bugle*), the car upkeep (Ford only, as Cliffie took care of the Volks), and the house mortgage which would, thank God, be finished in another two years, and the crazy unexpecteds like the rusted boiler that had had to be replaced a few months ago, there was either nothing left at the end of the month, or Edith had to dip into the checking account at Brunswick First National. Edith and Brett kept about six hundred in the checking account, and they had around three thousand in the Brunswick Savings Bank. She told Melanie all this. Brett hadn't taken any cash with him that Edith knew of.

'I wouldn't have minded at all if he'd taken a couple of thousand. It's his right,' Edith said.

Edith went on to say that she and Brett had around fourteen thousand invested in the Dreyfus Fund in New York, and Brett hadn't said anything about this, was leaving it to her presumably.

'In an annuity?' Melanie asked.

'No, it's just invested. We let it ride. We never felt we had enough – definite money coming in to start an annuity. We were –' She had been going to say they had intended to use the money to send Cliffie to Princeton. Edith felt suddenly bewildered, as if she'd had a few drinks, though she hadn't had a drink all day. Edith realized that the sums she had mentioned must sound like peanuts to her great-aunt, and that Melanie must think she and Brett were fuzzy-minded about money, not to have straightened all this out between them. So be it, Edith thought, at least they'd never borrowed or run into debt, and they had the house here, certainly worth fifty thousand by now, more than the twenty-five they'd paid for it. This was more than one could say for people like the Johnsons who were always in the red, Gert admitted, and as Brett had said years ago had debts all over the place, and didn't own their house, only rented it.

'If I may ask, dear, what does Brett intend to do about the Dreyfus money?'

'Oh, I think he said that's mine. Yes, I'm sure he said that.' Edith was not sure. It wasn't on any paper that it was hers, and Edith felt sure Melanie was thinking this. But Brett wasn't the type to try to hang on to fourteen thousand or even part of it, under these circumstances.

Melanie had more questions. Edith told her that Brett's job on the *Post* paid nearly twice as much as the *Trenton Standard* had, and Melanie was quick to observe that Brett and Carol must be doing quite well in New York with Carol's salary plus her well-to-do-family, and Edith had to admit that this must be true.

'I don't mind taking a job as a saleswoman somewhere in town, if I have to,' Edith said. 'Might even be good for me. There're a couple of shops I know of I could try, one a gift shop and the other specializes in oriental imports – bamboo and such-like. Both the shops are always complaining about the rotten help they get from teen-aged girls. They wouldn't mind a middle-aged woman they could count on.' Edith paused and laughed. 'I know, because Gert's always telling me.'

Melanie was silent for a few moments, and Edith braced herself for Melanie to tell her to ring up Brett now, even at the office, which Edith would have been loath to do. Just then, Edith heard a car in the driveway that sounded like Cliffie's Volks, and almost at the same time the doorbell rang.

'Don't know who *this* is,' Edith said as she got up.

It was Dr Carstairs with his black bag at the door, and from the driveway came Cliffie, climbing the side steps in dirty sneakers, hands in hip pockets.

'Hello, Mrs Howland,' said the doctor. 'I think it's time for another look at our patient. Sorry I didn't have time to phone you first.' The doctor came in with the confidence of a man who knew he would be admitted. He wore a rather limp white jacket, not a doctor's jacket but an ordinary summer jacket. 'How is he?'

'Hi, mom,' Cliffie said, going into the living room.

'He had his tea today. I don't know if he's awake or not.' Edith had the feeling she had said exactly the same phrases a hundred times before.

'I'll just go up, if I may.' Dr Carstairs climbed the stairs two at a time with hardly a sound.

Had another month rolled by? Must have. 'Dr Carstairs,' Edith said to Melanie. 'He comes once a month to look at George and give him some kind of injection.'

'*Pee-eeesurr-rr! Pow!*' Cliffie put in, miming the act of giving himself an injection in the rump, wincing mightily.

Edith tried to ignore him. He'd had a few beers at very least.

'I'd like to speak with the doctor,' Melanie said. 'You don't mind, do you, Edith?'

'Of course *not*! But I've got to catch him for you, because he practically dashes out.'

'Dash, dash! *Fweet!*' said Cliffie, brushing his hands together, swinging a foot high in front of him like a football kick.

Edith wished he would go to his room, even turn his transistor on full blast, rather than this. 'Want some iced tea, Cliffie?'

'I want an iced *beer*!' Cliffie said, looking at both of them, and laughing.

He hadn't shaved in a couple of days, and was going to grow a beard again, Edith supposed.

Melanie put on a tactful smile. 'Where've you been, Cliffie?'

'Just hacking.'

This was a term, meaning to stand around talking, Edith thought, maybe a term years old, but Cliffie hung onto things in an amusing way.

'Why doesn't Carstairs give old George a real whammo and

then – *fweet!*' Cliffie gave himself the powerful injection again. '*Finito!*'

'Cliffie, on your old aunt's last day, I think you might cut the horseplay,' Edith said.

'Oh, that's all right, Edith!'

'What horseplay?' asked Cliffie.

Edith heard the doctor's light step descending the stairs, and went into the hall. He had spent scarcely five minutes with George, as usual. 'You know my great aunt, Mrs Cobb, I think,' Edith said to the doctor.

Carstairs smiled. 'Indeed! How are you, Mrs Cobb?'

'Pretty well, I think, thank you,' Melanie said. 'I don't want to delay you, but I'm leaving tomorrow, and I wanted to ask you what you think of George's condition – now?'

'Well –' Carstairs smiled again. He had declined a chair. 'He hasn't changed appreciably in years. It's just a slow decline.'

'And his back hurts him still?' asked Melanie.

'That's what gives him pain – if he moves too much.'

'And there's no new drug, no massage, I suppose, at this point –'

'He's eighty-five or -six,' Carstairs said. He had black and white straight hair, rather like Brett's, gray eyes, rimless, delicate-looking glasses. 'You don't get many changes, at his age.'

Melanie glanced at Edith, then looked back at the doctor. 'What do you think about a nursing home? I'm sorry you haven't time to sit down, doctor, but – It's that my niece has enough to do, running the house on her own now, and she's thinking of taking a part-time job. George after all could afford a nursing home.'

Dr Carstairs looked evasive, as if he were thinking of his next appointment, trying to fish up a placebo, and it came. 'That's always a personal matter – within the family.' He looked at Edith, his lips slightly parted as usual, though not in a smile. 'It's not for me to prescribe a home.'

Standing by the bar cart, Cliffie listened, rapt.

'Yes, it's for us to sound him out,' said Melanie. 'He might be quite willing.'

120

Inspired by Melanie's directness, Edith said, 'He wet the bed a couple of times recently. I really must buy a rubber sheet. Absurd that we haven't bought one yet. He's quite cognisant of what he does but – I admit it's a pain in the neck when it happens.' And Edith laughed, having tried to say it as lightly as possible, the awful, the plain fact that she was fed up. Ten, eleven or twelve *years* now.

'Maybe what you're concerned about is whether he'd go into a decline if he went into a nursing home,' said Dr Carstairs. 'I'm afraid I'm not capable of answering that. It's a personality matter. You'd have to ask George direct, see what he says.'

'He certainly spends most of his time sleeping,' Melanie said. 'How much codeine are you giving him? Would you call it a heavy dose?'

'Medium,' the doctor replied. 'Liquid form. Injections of morphine just once a month to give him a little more comfort, a little blissful sleep if you like.'

'That's right,' Edith said to Melanie. 'He probably won't wake up for dinner tonight.'

'Good!' said Cliffie.

The doctor glanced at Cliffie with no change of expression. He knew Cliffie. 'He's a grand old fellow, but his days are drawing to a close. Lots of cases like this. One has to try to make the last years as comfortable as possible.' He was drifting toward the front door. 'See you next month, Mrs Howland. Oh! Not quite true. My assistant will come instead. I'm off on vacation. You know Dr Miller. He'll come. Good afternoon to you!' Dr Carstairs let himself out.

Melanie sat down on the sofa again, her back as straight as ever. 'You know, my dear – George is just one thing too many for you right now.'

Edith looked at Cliffie, who was still standing by the bar cart listening with a blank yet attentive expression. Cliffie didn't even return George's books to the library, unless Edith prodded him to take away the stack on the hall table, and even then he'd failed her once or twice, leaving the books in his Volks, which Edith only learned when Mrs Randall, the librarian, had spoken to her about their being overdue. 'Cliffie, would you mind terribly – letting Melanie and me talk alone for a while?'

'No,' Cliffie said, moving off at once toward the kitchen.

Edith heard the inevitable plop of the fridge door, the pop of a beer can, then Cliffie's transistor blared out. The sounds of chaos, Edith thought. Melanie looked at her strangely. Was Melanie thinking *she* was strange?

'I think you ought to sound George out about a nursing home, Edith. I'd do it with you except – perhaps he'd think it was my idea, since I'm here.' Melanie smiled, then just as quickly her blue eyes became serious. 'There's a tenseness about you I don't like to see. The easier you make things for yourself – And if I may say so, George is Brett's responsibility.'

'True enough.' But Edith couldn't face or listen to any more, and she got up with the excuse that it was exactly news time, and switched on the television. The Arabs and Israelis were fighting. The noon news, which Edith had heard while making lunch, said that the Israelis were hitting Arab air bases with a startling accuracy. Melanie listened to the brief report, but not with the same interest as Edith. Edith knew Melanie's mind was more than half on her problems. The war news was followed by a beauty contest report from Florida, and Edith switched off.

'I'd like you to ring up Brett now, Edith – for your old aunt's sake. Do you mind doing me that favor?'

'Now?'

'Yes, and now he's on the way home or it's the cocktail hour, I suppose, and you're afraid of interrupting. I'll go straight up to my room so I won't hear a word. I'll close my door.'

Edith took a breath, looked at the carpet and at once looked up at her great aunt's tall figure. Melanie's blue eyes regarded Edith like the eyes of a mother-father figure – or maybe God. Could Melanie even be *right*? 'I haven't any hope.'

'Tell him that you love him, that's all, because you told me that's true. Is there any harm in that?'

'No,' Edith replied, because Melanie's tone expected an answer. After all, Melanie had been married too, and for a long time, and Edith even remembered a story of some scandal which

122

had happened when she, Edith, might have been five years old. Great-uncle Randolph had run off with another woman. Hadn't that been it? And he had come back, perhaps because Melanie had known how to handle the situation. 'All right.'

'You've got the number?'

'Not by heart. I've got it somewhere.' It was on a pad by the hall telephone, written by Brett. Edith hoped that they'd both be out, that the telephone wouldn't answer.

'Do it, my dear.' Melanie went into the hall and climbed the stairs.

Edith looked for the number and dialed it.

Brett answered on the fourth ring.

'Hello, it's Edith. How are you?'

'All right, thanks. And you?' His voice sounded the same as always, a little tense, and rather young.

'All right too. Aunt Mel'nie's here. But she just went up to her room, so I won't call her.'

'Well – give her my love. What did you want to say? – Anything the matter? Cliffie?'

'No, he's all right. I –' Edith had to swallow to make sure she could talk, and she sat forward, a bit straight, as she had used to do in classrooms when she was frightened by an exam. 'I wanted to say I love you.'

'I know you do,' said Brett in his most earnest tone. 'I love you too. But this is different. – Don't you see? I – I'm not torn between two things. This is different. I mean that, Edith. I still love you too, and I'm not going to let you down. Or even Cliffie down. If you need anything –'

'Yes, I know.' Edith tried to take comfort from the familiar firmness of his voice.

'Still there?'

'Yes.'

'Cliffie all right?'

'The same.'

'Nelson?'

'He's fine. Well –'

Edith couldn't even remember the last exchanges, once she

had hung up. She felt worse, and disliked herself for having tele-phoned. It wasn't a matter of pride, but what had she accom-plished? Her only consolation was that she had obeyed Melanie's wishes.

14

Four months later, in October, Melanie suffered a stroke. Edith's mother informed her by a telegram which said that her aunt was in a Wilmington hospital. Edith thought it might be the end. She telephoned her mother, who told her that Melanie was not in a coma, and that the doctors had some hope that she would pull through and without paralysis.

'What's the latest about you and Brett?' Her mother's accent sounded very southern on the telephone. 'You haven't written in more'n a month, Edie, and even then you didn't –'

'Nothing's changed. Didn't I tell you he wants a divorce? I signed the papers for it last week.'

'Oh! Edie!' Her mother seemed astonished, shocked – as if Edith hadn't prepared her for this for the past eight months, even a year. 'Are you doing all right? Can you manage?'

'Of course! I've been managing. – Mother, would you telephone me if there's any change in Melanie?'

Her mother promised that she would. She asked about Cliffie. Her mother had liked him, doted on him when Cliffie had been small, then her affection had cooled, Edith felt. Her mother seemed to center all her love on Edith's father and their house there, and their garden. Edith knew her mother was reluctant to use the telephone (maybe because of slight deafness), and would prefer to send another telegram if anything happened to Melanie.

Cliffie noticed Edith's tension and asked, 'Something the matter, mom?'

This was when Edith had known about Melanie's condition for two days. Edith knew Cliffie simply wouldn't care much, and an unconcerned remark from him would have made Edith furious, so she hadn't mentioned Melanie. Cliffie was sensitive to moods, but never to the reality that had caused the moods.

'Just that I failed to get some advertising in Flemington today which would've been useful for the *Bugle*.' That was true. Edith had spent more than three hours driving, waiting, then talking to the manager of a department store, but the store preferred to stick with the local paper plus their throw-away system.

'George okay?' Cliffie asked with a nervous glance at his mother. They were then having dinner.

'He's all right. Why not?'

Cliffie took a forkful of baked beans. 'When is he going into this nursing home?'

'What nursing home?' Edith waited.

'I thought you were talking about it – you and Aunt Melanie.'

Edith said calmly, 'I don't think George has said anything about it.' She suddenly had a recollection of the beige, two-story building on a hill about twelve miles from Brunswick Corner – resident apartments or some such euphemistic appellation it had, plus a real name like Sunset Lodge. Old people had apartments of their own, even with kitchens, and nurses were on hand. Gert had pointed it out to Edith years ago, when they had been driving past. Edith wondered if she should sound it out.

Cliffie soon drifted to the living room for television, Edith did the dishes, and when she was finished, Cliffie had left the house. Cliffie couldn't be upstairs with George, could he? She went into the hall to hear, if she could, any murmur of voices. Sometimes Cliffie went up to see George, or to look at him, because George was so often asleep. But Edith sensed that Cliffie was not in the house. She was quite good at sensing that (had never been wrong that she could recall), so she decided to do some *Bugle* work, type a couple of reminder letters about subscriptions, then go to bed with a book.

The next morning shortly after 8, the telephone rang, and it was Melanie herself.

'I'm phoning from the hospital, but I'm going home in two days. Isn't that nice?' Melanie said.

Edith had been awaiting a word from her mother, had been

afraid to ring the hospital. She felt she had received a charge of energy herself. 'I can't believe it! I'm so glad, Aunt Mel'nie! I was *worried*!'

Melanie chuckled. 'I think I was too! Can't talk long, m'dear, doctor's orders.'

When they hung up, Edith was smiling a broad smile, for the first time in days, she realized. Good old Melanie! How nice to have a great-aunt you could say to 'I was *worried*!' as if she were a contemporary and a pal!

Edith rang up Gert to tell her the good news, because only yesterday Edith had told Gert that she was quite braced for her great-aunt's demise. Edith breezed through her chores that morning, changed her bed and Cliffie's, and took the sheets to the launderette to be collected in the afternoon, then stopped at Stan's for cough syrup for George, because his bottle had run out. She thought of changing George's bed, but she deliberately changed his bed, usually, on a different day so she wouldn't have so many beds to do the same day. She'd best stick to that. Since she was feeling strong and optimistic, however, she thought she might approach George on the subject of rest homes.

It was around 11:30 when she went up to George's room, and she thought of telling him the good news about Melanie, then realized that George did not know Melanie had been ill. She knocked on the partly open door, and called, 'George?'

Thank goodness, he wasn't sound asleep, and he moved his head on the pillow, looking toward the door. 'Edith.'

'George, I –' Edith pulled a straight chair nearer his bed and sat down. She made sure he was reasonably alert before she went on. 'George, I'm wondering if you wouldn't be more comfortable in a place near here that has *residential apartments*. You'd have your own things around you, a nurse day and night when you push a button. Just twelve miles from here!'

George was watching her with a pink, fearful expression. Edith wished she had visited the place before talking with him.

'To go off somewhere?' George asked. 'Who?'

'I was talking about – *residents' apartments*,' Edith began

127

again somewhat louder. She was glad Cliffie had gone out. 'There's a place near here. Where you'd be more *comfortable* than here! Better service. *Other people to talk to!*'

George shook his head. 'Don't need other people!' He panted slightly. 'Me?'

Edith had taken a breath, but she released the breath, wordless. She tried again. 'But *I* do!' Now it was like a battle. And was she going to yield? 'I'm busy enough, George. If *you* wouldn't mind – If you could *think* about it –'

The front door slammed shut. Cliffie had returned. Edith got up and closed George's door, and returned to the chair.

'If you wouldn't mind too much, George – just for a *couple of months* – try it. Then you could come back here if you didn't like it.' Why hadn't she thought of this before?

'Don't want to go anywhere.'

'I'm *tired*!' Tired of the goddam trays, library books, bedpans, which she'd had to bring to him several times in the last weeks when he'd shouted for her. 'A *vacation* from each *other* for a while –' She'd go to the residential apartments place and get some information, a brochure to show him. Edith stood up, frustrated, aching, miserable.

George's brown, shiny, pink-rimmed eyes gazed at her with sadness and mistrust.

'I'll be going, George!' she shouted. 'Do you need anything now? – Lunch coming soon.' Edith went out.

Cliffie was standing in the hall, leaning against the balustrade. 'What was all *that*?' he asked with interest.

Edith was sure he knew what it was.

Cliffie was smiling.

Edith continued down the stairs, suddenly exhausted. She'd go to the damned home after lunch, she vowed to herself.

'Is he leaving?' Cliffie asked, following her.

'Not sure. Maybe,' Edith replied as matter of factly as she could. 'Are you in for lunch, by the way?'

'Oh – I dunno. It's not even twelve yet.'

Edith detested his vagueness.

'Be great if he'd leave. It'd give you an extra room.'

128

'I thought you wanted that room.' Edith spoke just to be saying something, but it was true.

'*I* don't want it! After *he's* been there so long? – Oh, well, if we got new furniture, changed it around, maybe painted the room –'

Edith would have liked a scotch before lunch, but didn't take one, because Cliffie certainly would have joined her or made a remark, because Edith almost never drank anything at noon. She decided to have a sandwich and a glass of milk and start out right away for the Sunset Lodge or whatever it was.

Cliffie hung about the kitchen, sipping from a can of beer. 'Do you think he'll leave?'

'Cliffie, *I* don't know. It's for him to decide.'

'Ha! What can that old vegetable decide?'

Edith managed to ignore it.

Just after 1 (Cliffie had gone off earlier without lunch), Edith drove to the residential apartments, which she couldn't find and had to inquire for at a gas station. She had overshot. It was called Sunset Pines, she was told. It was low and beige as she remembered it, nestled behind a green hill. Edith drove slowly toward it, alert for anything that looked like an entrance. She found it.

The hall floor was of black linoleum with a few oriental rugs here and there. There was a smell of carrots or carrot soup (nicer than medicine anyway), potted plants, a switchboard at which sat a nurse in blue and white. Edith said she wanted to inquire about accommodation for a male resident. The nurse summoned a younger nurse who was able to show Edith a typical room, the nurse told her, this one with bath, though not all the rooms had private baths. In the hall, some old people walked about, others propelled themselves in wheelchairs. The room was square, quite adequate and cheerful, Edith thought. The Sunset Pines was U-shaped. A ramp led down to a sunparlor at one end of the U, with a television set that several guests were watching. The other end of the U was a dining hall. 'For our guests who are ambulant,' said the nurse. 'Of course we serve trays, if people can't get up.' The price was two hundred dollars a week for a room with bath and full meals and monthly check-up, but did not include medicines and drugs, and a room without bath was a hundred and eighty per week. 'Of course the pension for Senior Citizens and Medicare take care of much of the expenses.'

Edith was a little stunned by the price, but after all George had it, and as Brett had said a few times, he couldn't take it with him. Edith thanked the nurse, said she would be in touch, and departed with a handful of brochures and a couple of postcards with color photographs of exterior and interior views of Sunset Pines, which looked quite attractive, though devoid of guests, even of nurses.

Since it was nearly 4 when she got home, Edith made tea for herself and George, and took the brochures up with the tray. George was asleep, and she had first to put the tray on a chair and remove from the bed his lunch tray, which she set on the hall floor. George had to creep to the bathroom as soon as he awakened. He used his cane. *Tap-tap.* When he came back and had settled himself in bed, Edith poured his tea.

'I went to the *apartment* place today,' Edith shouted freely, because Cliffie was still out. 'Brought you some pictures of it.' She showed him the postcards first, then the brochure which was printed on pale green paper.

'Where is this?' George asked, drooling a bit.

'Oh, not far! Just twelve miles away.'

Propped on one elbow, George looked through it all. 'Don't like places like this,' he remarked. 'Like hospitals!'

Edith glanced at his worn slippers, flattened at the heels because he never put them quite on, and at a crumpled handkerchief on the floor which contained God knew what but was her job to pick up.

'Expensive too,' George added.

You must be a Christian, Edith told herself, but since this didn't always work and wasn't even always to be advised, she thought with equal swiftness that she'd better hang onto the initiative she had, so she plunged ahead and said, 'Well, George, as I told you today, I have *enough* to do running this house – without Brett, you know – and I'm going to take a part-time job!

130

I thought I could make it without but –' Another deep breath and she went on, regardless of how much George could hear. 'There's a shop willing to take me on afternoons now, which is *something*, considering the summer's the most profitable for the shops here, and summer's over. The point is, George, you've got the money to take care of *yourself*!' After this, Edith felt exhausted.

George let his elbow collapse, and fell back upon his pillow with his aristocratic nose pointed toward the ceiling.

God damn it, Edith said to herself, she'd call up Brett tonight. She stood up. 'Will you consider it, George?'

'Don't want to go anywhere. No, I don't.'

Edith, feeling she had the patience of Job, gathered what she could of the clutter of dirty glasses and cups and teaspoons, a handkerchief, a napkin, and descended with the tray. Thank God, he hadn't wet the bed; one had to be thankful for small things. She thought a letter to Brett might be more forceful than a phone call.

When she had brought down the second tray and washed up she went to her workroom and began the letter. She told Brett about visiting Sunset Pines and her failure to interest George in going there.

Maybe you would have more influence if you wrote or spoke to him? I haven't mentioned it before but now and then he needs a bedpan. Or did I mention it before? Both Melanie and I think it your responsibility as well as mine ...

Edith felt a small admiration for her understatement. That day was Wednesday. The letter would go off tomorrow and Brett would have it by Friday.

15

Brett responded with a telephone call Friday evening. Frances Quickman happened to be with Edith, as Frances was returning a dozen or so glasses she had borrowed for a church bazaar.

'Suppose I catch that ten-thirty bus out tomorrow morning?' Brett said. 'I can see it's time I had a talk with the old boy.'

Edith agreed. She felt relieved. She was going to start work Monday at the Thatchery, a shop on Main Street. Six afternoons a week from 2 until 7 p.m. Edith was glad she would have something definite to tell Brett about a job.

Frances, then having a gin and tonic, looked at Edith as if she might have heard Brett's name, so Edith said:

'Brett. He's coming tomorrow morning. Going to have a word with old George. We're thinking he ought to go into a nursing home. Something nice, like Sunset Pines.'

Frances wasn't nearly so intimate a friend as Gert, but Edith didn't mind at all, just now, coming out with the truth to Frances about Brett and George. What was there to be ashamed of?

Frances said she had once visited someone at Sunset Pines, and thought it a pleasant and well-run place. 'George must be quite a strain on you – sometimes.'

'He's Brett's uncle after all,' Edith said with a smile.

'And how is Brett doing?'

Edith knew she really meant how were Brett and Carol doing. 'I think very well – likes his job,' Edith replied. 'And I think he wants to marry the girl.' Edith laughed a little. Best to come out with it. Via Gert, Edith supposed, everyone would sooner or later know that Brett and she were divorced, that it wasn't a temporary separation.

'You're taking it awfully well,' Frances said with fervor. 'I'm not sure I could do the same. And your house and yard still looks so nice – And Cliffie?'

'Oh, he's –' Edith had been about to say he was doing splendidly. But at what? Hydraulic engineering? Edith smiled at herself this time. 'Cliffie's just the same,' Edith said with equal frankness. 'Works sometimes at the Chop House as you may –'

'We've *seen* him there, yes! He waited on our table one night. Did quite well!' Frances laughed merrily.

'Your table?' Edith was startled. 'He told me he was behind the bar. Well, he'd tell me a different story just to amuse himself. Then he works sometimes at the Stud Box – God, these names!'

'Oh, sure! The nice gay boys' place. Well, I must say I've bought Ben some awfully good things there, sweaters and sports jackets. Good quality. And they don't mind taking things back if they don't fit. But *I* never saw Cliffie there.'

'I never know *when* he's there,' Edith said gaily. 'He's anything but regular – about anything.' She realized she was happy, because she was going to see Brett tomorrow.

'Tell Brett to come over and have a drink with us. Both of you, a pre-lunch drink. Think you can manage? I'll be finished shopping by noon at least, so just walk in the door. Love to see Brett again.'

Edith said they probably would.

Brett came the next morning just after 12. Edith had not gone to the bus stop to meet him, because the walk to the house was short, and she had thought meeting him might look more anxious than friendly. She had done the shopping and intended to make steak au poivre that evening, hoping Brett could stay. Brett wore his old plaid woolen jacket that he called his hunting jacket, in which he had never gone hunting however.

'So – how are you?' Brett asked.

'All right, I suppose. The Quickmans want us to come for a pre-lunch drink. But maybe you want to see George first.'

'I do – frankly.' Brett's brows drew together. Edith thought there was more gray in his hair.

'Why don't you go up alone – surprise him? Well, it won't surprise him, because I told him you were coming today. Meanwhile I'll fix his lunch tray.'

'I will. Where's Cliffie?'

'Out somewhere. I think he'll be in for lunch because I asked him to be. Told him you'd be here.'

Brett started up the stairs. 'Nelson! Hey, you've grown some more! Big boy! Don't be afraid!'

Edith heard Brett's laugh. Then she went into the kitchen to make an egg salad sandwich on toast for George, with a glass of milk. She put the finishing touches to their lunch table, wine glasses, one small red rose which was almost the last of summer, then she carried George's tray up. To her surprise, Brett was just crossing the hall to come downstairs. He had a pained expression and he shook his head at Edith. Edith went on into George's room with the tray.

George was lying back on his pillows, eyes shut, and one bony hand, a flat, rail-like wrist above it, exposed by the pushed back pajama sleeve, lay along the edge of the bed. He had covered his eyes with the back of his left hand, a frequent attitude.

'Lunch, George! How're you feeling?' Edith didn't care about George's answer, if any, set the tray as firmly as possible over his thighs just above his knees, so he could raise up and eat, then went out to speak with Brett.

Brett was downstairs in the living room, smoking a cigarette. 'Can't do a goddam thing with him. He's impenetrable.'

'Well – now you see. You mean you talked about the rest home?'

'I certainly did. I can imagine it's quite nice, from what you wrote. He just stares at me and says he doesn't want to go anywhere. How about getting someone in during the hours you're away at work? And I'll pay for it. That's the least I can do. Matter of fact, *George* could afford it.'

Edith had thought of this. But who, these days? 'I'm not sure I want just anybody prowling around my house five hours a day, Brett. Whom can you trust these days?'

'Oh, listen –'

134

'George has to have a bedpan a few times a week. If you think *that's* any fun, Brett, if you think you're going to get the average teen-aged babysitter to take care of that, you're mistaken.'

'Then we'll get a nurse.'

'That'll cost a fortune.' She laughed. 'I can hear George balking at the price already!'

'Too bad!'

'Let's have a drink at the Quickmans' and we'll talk about it later, all right?'

So they went next door to the Quickmans', where Frances greeted them warmly. Ben came in from the garden, his hands too dirty just then for him to shake Brett's hand, because he had been cleaning the power motor before putting it away for the winter.

'Great to see you, Brett! How's city life?' Ben asked.

Edith had a bloody Mary. Then she heard Brett saying to the Quickmans that he had to catch a train around 5 p.m. at the latest to get back to New York.

'My senior editor's birthday,' Brett said with a glance at Edith. 'Dinner party, and I simply can't miss it, much as I'd like to miss it.'

Edith felt a disappointment that she at once tried to conceal by a pleasant expression. After all, as far as the Quickmans were concerned, Brett might have told her earlier that he couldn't stay the evening. Brett and the Quickmans talked local news, how was Stan the pharmacist, how was the Brandywine Inn doing under its new management. The conversation was rolling along, but because time was so short, Edith suggested that they go back to the house.

'Cliffie's due soon. I didn't leave him a note about where we were,' Edith said. She finished her second drink quickly, and thanked Frances and Ben.

It was 1.20 p.m. Cliffie was in the living room. He had made himself what looked like a scotch on the rocks.

'Hi, dad!' Cliffie said.

'Well, hello! Beard again. Or still,' said Brett. 'What're you

135

doing these days? Bartending? – which bar, this one?' Brett laughed a little.

'What d'y'mean? I work at the Chop House – off and on. I work,' Cliffie said on a defensive note.

Edith went into the kitchen to serve the lunch – smoked salmon on toast, then a good camembert to follow, and fruit salad for dessert. Brett didn't like a big meal at noon. Brett and Cliffie drifted in to offer help, and Edith handed Brett the white wine from the fridge to open.

'You don't look in prime physical condition – for your age,' Brett remarked to Cliffie. 'Plain they don't work you very hard at these places.' The cork popped, and Brett set the wine on a coaster on the table.

'Why when *oy* was your age,' Cliffie began facetiously. 'What's the matter with my muscles?' He flexed an arm, and felt a bulky bicep through his sweater.

'Is that muscle hanging around your stomach there?'

Brett was freer with Cliffie, but Edith sensed a detachment also. After all, Brett was leaving the scene in a couple of hours, wouldn't see Cliffie for weeks or months. Cliffie didn't care about going to New York, wasn't even lured by porn films on 42nd Street.

With her first glass of wine, Edith felt a warm glow. She was aware that the time was racing away, and tried not to waste a minute, and at the same time not to appear hurried. 'What do you say,' she began, 'if we bundle George into the car and show him Sunset Pines, Brett? Round trip would take hardly more than an hour.'

'Just a pine at sun-*set*,' Cliffie sang, a hand at his breast. 'Cough-cough! I'm not long for this world!'

Edith and Brett ignored him smoothly, out of old habit.

Brett seemed to consider the idea for a moment, and suddenly Edith, feeling what she had drunk, exploded in laughter. 'You know, I heard the most awful story – I forgot who from, Gert, I think. A couple took their mother-in-law to an old folks' home on pretext of taking her to visit an old friend, and just dumped her and ran away. Isn't that horrible!' Edith was still laughing.

136

'Ha-ha! Hah-*hee-ee*!' Cliffie adored the story and nearly rolled off his chair. 'I like that, I really do!'

Brett gave his son a preoccupied glance. He had smiled only slightly at the story.

Brett was miles away from the problem, Edith realized. He was going to say he hadn't time to get George ready and go to Sunset Pines. He was going to leave in a couple of hours, go back to New York, to Carol, to a party tonight, then to bed with Carol. The awful reality, the present, welled up in Edith again, the bedpans, the filthy handkerchiefs. She could have screamed at Brett suddenly, but she said only, 'Honestly, I can't go on like this.'

'Nobody can!' Cliffie contributed. 'George is a *mess*. I've seen it!'

'But *you* don't do anything about it, do you?' Edith put in. 'No, that job's for *me*.'

'Edith,' Brett said soothingly.

'Me? Why I –'

'Cliffie! That's enough!' Brett showed his teeth.

Cliffie was a bit drunk, and knew his parents knew it. 'All right, I'll push off.' He got up and left the table, went into the living room, but not out of the house.

Finally Brett said, 'I'll try it again – with George.'

'If we just put on his overcoat and muffler and shoes, we could *show* him this place, which isn't –'

'I haven't got time today,' Brett said.

Just then, Cliffie was entering George's room, where George lay asleep. Cliffie smiled, then broke into a wild grin as he looked around at the customary disorder of medicine bottles, glass of water for his teeth – empty now, because he'd put the lowers in for lunch – soiled teaspoons on the napkin-covered bed-table, bedpan (clean just now) on the floor by the radiator, a couple of books on the bed. Christ, things hadn't changed in years!

'Customary disorder!' Cliffie said aloud, confident that George wasn't going to awaken. 'But old boy, you're headin' for the laist round-up, yuh know? Gettin' the boot, old fellow, and maybe today.' Cliffie leaned closer and whispered, 'Wake up! Before it's too late!'

Then abruptly Cliffie was tired of the game, disgusted and somehow ashamed of the old guy in bed, the pain in the ass who took up a room in the house and crapped in the white, blue-trimmed bedpan, the crap which his mother had to poke down the john. 'Christ!' Cliffie whispered. 'I hope the hell you fuck off today! Why not? *Why not?*' Cliffie's eyes bulged, and he spat the words out. He would have loved to give George a good solid kick in the ribs before departing, his right foot even raised itself a little from the floor, but Cliffie knew that would be going too far. Furthermore, he knew he'd better leave before his parents came up for Brett to say good-bye or some such muck, so Cliffie went out and down the stairs.

Cliffie turned right at the foot of the stairs into the hall which led back to his room, and almost at the same moment his parents came from the living room into the hall, talking, and started up the stairs. Cliffie followed them at a distance, and halfway up the stairs, stopped.

'I knew he'd be asleep,' Edith said. '*George – Brett's* here!'

George came awake not in slight jerks as he usually did, but like a tired spirit hauling itself from another land.

'Listen, George, I have to take off in about an hour,' Brett said. 'We're talking again – *still* – about this residential apartment house *not far away* from here.'

'Oh, yes,' said George.

'You've got to see the situation from Edith's point of view,' Brett said. 'And mine too. It's not as if we were trying to stick you into some awful place where there's no privacy and we'll never come to see you. You'll have an *apartment* of your own with your own things around you, like these pictures.' Brett gestured to an oil landscape and a rather good English sporting print, which years ago they had taken from George's possessions in storage in New York, at George's request. 'The place costs about two hundred dollars a week, but you can afford it.'

'A week, did you say. Two – I haven't got that.' George was on one elbow now, and looked as if he intended to rally all his strength to stand up against Brett's challenge.

On the stairway, Cliffie doubled up with mirth which he had to repress completely. Nothing less than a strait-jacket and a couple of strong men-in-white would get old George out! They should send for Bellevue! Cliffie was imagining regaling Mel with this. He and Mel broke up over the same things. Now his father was talking about seeing George's accountant in New York.

'*Yes*, Uncle George, I did go to see him. You mustn't think I'm trying to cheat you – how could I? I just wanted to know how things stood, and he says you're *making* money. If you paid two hundred dollars a week somewhere, you'd *still* be ahead of the game.'

'Is that true?' Edith said to Brett.

'Dunno,' Brett said, 'but he sure as hell won't feel any dent. He can't take it with him, can he?'

'I'll pay more *here*, if that's what it's all about!' George retorted with an air of affront, and he even looked near tears.

'That is *not* what it's all about, Uncle George!' Brett went on. 'It's that Edith is going to take a part-time job. She won't be here to make your lunch tray – or your *tea* or –'

Brett looked exhausted. His voice had gone hoarse.

'Bye-bye, George,' Brett said. And to Edith, 'I've damned well got to shove off. I'll write to him. Maybe that'll help. Meanwhile get somebody –' Brett was walking out of the room. 'Get a real nurse. George can afford it. I'll see that he pays it, and you can count on a real nurse not – not stealing stuff out of the house.'

The time had flown. It was ten past 4. They would have to hurry if they made the 5 o'clock train from Trenton, which Brett wanted to do, but Edith pulled him into her workroom for a minute to show him the last issue of the *Bugle*. It was a good issue, Edith had written an especially good editorial, she thought, on the habit of equating socialism with communism. Edith always sent Brett a copy of the *Bugle*, but somehow she had wanted him to hold this latest issue in his hands, if only for a moment. He hadn't a minute to look at it, but he smiled and made a polite remark, and folded it to take with him.

'Mind driving me to Trenton?' Brett asked. 'Otherwise I'll take a taxi, for gosh sake.'

'Of course I can drive you.'

They set out. Brett had taken two more books from the living room shelves. Edith found it hard to talk and drive, and they hardly talked at all until she saw the lights of Trenton, and entered the road to the railway station.

'I have the feeling sometimes that something's – sort of cracking in me,' Edith said.

'I'm sorry, really sorry. Believe me, my dear, if it's money – I don't want to see you even taking a part-time job. *I* can see you through. It's my responsibility.'

'Oh, a job might be good for me. It's not money.'

'Then it's Cliffie.'

'Oh, he hasn't changed. Probably never will. And – as I've said, he kicks in fifteen or twenty dollars a week.'

'Big deal.'

Edith negotiated a difficult crossing, and wished she had brought her cigarettes. They had arrived. Brett got out, and said he would buy his ticket on the train. There wasn't time for Edith to park and then go with Brett to the train. She asked him for a cigarette. He gave her three. The car had a cigarette lighter.

'What do you mean by cracking?' Brett asked.

'Mentally. Oh, there's no time to talk now. Run.'

'You have inner fortitude. Even you've said that. You have more than I have.' His hand was hardly touching the car's window-sill, and suddenly he dashed away. 'I'll write! Thanks, Edith!'

16

When Edith got home from Trenton that afternoon, she prepared George's tea tray and took it in to him (he was asleep with a book in his hands, but wakened easily, and Edith fled), made instant coffee for herself, as they had drunk the whole pot at lunch, then went to her workroom and opened her diary. Cliffie was out somewhere. She wrote after the October date:

Quite a nice afternoon, visit from B. and drinks chez the Quickmans. C. home but not Debbie. C. looks with disapproval on his father's personal life these days. 'A man abandoning his wife,' and all that. Considers B. selfish. One can see that B. is a bit ashamed of himself also. C. shows signs of being stronger in every way than B. He and D. are to be married Christmas week. Her parents

Here Edith paused for a moment's thought. Debbie Bowden's parents lived in a suburb of Princeton, and Edith pictured them in a house she had once visited near Princeton, a big two- or three-story house on generous grounds with garages, greenhouses, handsome trees, an estate that had a gate with stone pillars. She was trying to see the parents more clearly (he might be a professor on sabbatical), when she heard a call from George.

It was a familiar muffled 'Whomp! Whah! Uh – Edith!' which sounded like remote thunder or maybe a faraway car in trouble. He needed the bedpan.

'One minute, George!' Edith got it from the floor by the side window.

'All this up and down stuff today sort of – got me in the back again,' George said.

Edith assumed he meant up and down on his elbow.

'I said the *bottle* – please,' George said on seeing the bedpan.

'You said nothing,' Edith said, setting the bedpan down again and getting from underneath the bed the gadget known as a male urinal which Cliffie was always suggesting that they use as a wine carafe on the table. This, Edith recalled, as she handed it to George and tactfully left the room, she had tried leaving on the bed-table shelf within George's reach, but twice he'd spilt it, full, which was a hell of a lot more annoying than having to hand it to him and take it away again. 'Finished?' Edith called.

He wasn't.

When she had at last flushed this away and rinsed the urinal and brought it back, she was nowhere near being able to imagine Debbie's parents properly, so she left the sentence unfinished and put her diary away.

On the next Tuesday Edith received a letter from Brett dated Sunday. In the envelope besides Brett's letter was a carbon copy of his letter to George, which had come in the same post and which Edith had delivered to George before opening her own. Brett's letter to George eloquently pled for him to see his and Edith's point of view. It made more sense, Brett said, for George to go to Sunset Pines than for them to get a five-hour-a-day nurse in to look after him.

While Edith was reading Brett's letters in the living room, Cliffie came in. He had been out all night, and he looked tired and in need of a bath. Edith's first thought was that the police might have picked him up for something – he'd had his car – but she said calmly, 'Well, Cliffie. Where've you been?'

'Mel's. We were playing cards pretty late, so I thought I'd sleep there.'

Edith was relieved. 'What're your plans for today?'

'Going to have a bath and sleep some more.' Cliffie crossed the living room, coat over one shoulder, and disappeared into the dining room.

Edith heard the fridge door. She went up the stairs to speak with George. She was sure he had read the letter, because he had been awake when she brought it. She rapped on the partly open door. 'George?'

'Come in, Edith.'

142

'I had a letter from Brett too,' she said loudly and clearly. 'So I know what he wrote to you.'

'I don't want to go to any blasted nursing home!' George said. He had evidently gathered himself for a battle upon reading the letter. 'If it comes to a nurse living here, I'll pay for it!'

'Living here? *Where?*' Edith's face was suddenly warm. 'In my guestroom? I think not!'

'All right, a part-time nurse. Afternoons.'

'Quite frankly, I don't want any stranger prowling around my house!' Edith hated having to talk so loudly. She shut the door. 'Just for instance, the *Zylstras* are coming Thanksgiving week-end. Do you think I want people standing over each other in the —' She had been going to say the single bathroom they had. Granted there was a john downstairs. She seized the doorknob and opened the door.

'Won't *do* it!' George threw at her.

Edith slammed the door shut.

Downstairs in the living room, Cliffie chuckled richly. He had just ducked in from the foot of the stairs, whence he'd heard every word. A running soap opera, he thought. He could hear his mother now pounding on the typewriter, so Cliffie poured himself a generous scotch, and sipped it neat. Yummy good! Dewar's. Just what he needed along with a bath and a nap. And a little fun with a sock, maybe. Hangovers made him feel sexy.

Edith was writing to Brett. She would have preferred to telephone him, and she had his office number but was reluctant as always to ring him at work. Brett had said he and Carol were moving to a larger apartment on the 15th of November. Edith wrote in no uncertain terms that Brett must take care of his uncle himself, because his letter today had accomplished nothing.

Brett wrote by return post that he was up to his neck in work at the office, plus their moving, so could he postpone the George business for about three weeks? Edith was a bit annoyed by that. She knew he was busy, but he still had three or four hours for a New Year party here and there, so why couldn't he spend those hours in Brunswick Corner, moving George into Sunset Pines?

The following weeks passed so rapidly or so vaguely that Edith was later unable to recall details. Her job at the Thatchery went well from the start. She had known Elinor Hutchinson (a widow, a 'bit older than Edith) slightly since years. Edith was just the kind of person the shop needed, Elinor said, someone dependable who could learn the stock quickly, find what the customer wanted, and keep out of the way while people made up their minds. Edith could wear what she pleased – a skirt or slacks. Edith was punctual, and didn't mind a little overtime at the end of the day if it was necessary. The shop sold place mats, candlesticks, leather chairs and wastebaskets and tinkling mobiles. Edith got eighty dollars a week, no commission. An eighteen-year-old girl named Norma, and another older woman, Mrs Martin (Becky), were the salespeople, and all three rang up sales on the same cash register.

The Zylstras came at Thanksgiving. Edith had decorated the living room with autumn leaves, a couple of pumpkins on the floor, and dried corn ears that hung from the lintel. This traditional décor was, after all, what visiting New Yorkers expected of rural Pennsylvania. Marion, for old times' sake, brought a meringue pie, which always reminded her, she said, of the time the Howlands had departed Manhattan. Besides the pie, the Zylstras contributed a two-quart bottle of Four Roses.

'Never saw you looking better,' Ed Zylstra said to Edith.

Marion asked about Brett, and Edith told her that he was going to marry Carol.

'Maybe this minute,' Edith said, raising her eyebrows. 'Brett said around Thanksgiving, I think.'

'Maybe –' Ed stopped.

In fact, no one said anything for a moment, not even Cliffie. Edith wondered what Ed had been about to say.

In a quieter moment, Edith told Marion about her trials with George. Edith tried to make it funny and brief, and she told Marion also about Brett's procrastination.

'Of course he should go to a nursing home!' Marion said.

'Believe me, I've seen scores of cases like this. I mean *in* nursing homes, where they belong.' Marion's healthy face gave Edith courage.

'All right,' Edith said. calmly, 'but just how does one do it?'

'You force the situation via the doctor – to begin with. Doctors' orders carry a lot of –'

'Have you met Dr Carstairs? No. I'd love you to meet him.' And Edith went at once to the telephone. To her surprise, the doctor was in. Edith asked if he could come over for a few minutes either today or tomorrow. She replied to the doctor's question, with an honesty that she at once regretted, that it was not because of George, but she wanted him to meet a friend of hers who was a registered nurse. The doctor said he really hadn't the time. 'Then can my friend say a word now? Marion!'

Marion came. Marion had sized up the situation from Edith's part of the conversation, and plunged right in. 'It's up to you, Dr Carstairs, to recommend and authorize George's removal from this house . . .'

Marion talked well. Edith stayed in the living room, but she could hear most of it.

Cliffie, in a garish new plaid jacket, sat in an armchair, twisting an old-fashioned in a tumbler on his thigh.

Marion came back with a cynically amused smile. 'Well, I know his type. I'd say either prod Brett again or get another doctor who *will* do something.'

'Feel like taking a walk?' Edith asked.

They put on coats and scarves and went out into the sharp air. This was better! Marion was like a tonic. A good old friend, and yet she knew all about medicine too, quite as much as Carstairs, Edith thought. Brunswick Corner looked its best with its white or redbrick houses backgrounded by red, deep browns, patches of yellow among the trees across the river and up the hills to the south, as if a painter had dropped the colors in the right places. The air in Edith's nostrils reminded her of drinking cold water on a summer's day. Delicious! If all life could be so delicious!

'I sometimes think,' Edith began, wanting to talk and not knowing where to begin, 'maybe I'm focusing all my problems on George, and that it's not fair to him.'

'Oh, nonsense, Edith. If anybody had your problems at the moment – I mean the Brett business too –'

Edith waited for Marion to go on. They walked along Main Street westward, the river on their right. They had passed the Thatchery – open today – but Edith hadn't bothered pointing it out. Edith had begged out of working today, without much difficulty, on the grounds of having guests.

'And Cliffie. I can imagine he's not much help to you,' Marion went on. 'I mean as to your morale.'

'No. But that's no news.'

'What does he want to do with himself?'

The usual questions. Also about girl friends.

'He's not queer, is he?' Marion asked. 'Not that I care, you know. I mean – so what?'

'I really don't think so.' Edith laughed. 'Too many pin-ups in his room. Bosomy girls and all that. He just lacks – confidence, maybe. Brett's fed up with him, so you mustn't think Brett would get him into line if Brett were here. Not at all.'

I sometimes think I'm going a bit nuts, Edith wanted to say.

Then suddenly – it seemed sudden to Edith – Marion and Ed were gone. The house was empty, despite the presence of Cliffie in his room with the transistor on and of George upstairs. And Edith felt ashamed – yes, ashamed of herself. Why? And for what? She couldn't answer that. She'd been a good hostess, she thought, the food had definitely been a success, the guestroom had looked pretty. Edith sensed that Marion sensed something strange about her, and had been too polite to say so. Ed had worked on both the television set and Edith's old radio in her workroom, and both were better, the television coming in with a clearer picture now. That was proof that the Zylstras had been here, Edith thought. Then she wondered why she had needed to think that. Edith had a clear memory of Marion's rosy-cheeked, smiling face with her blue eyes and funny artificial eye-lashes which were rather becoming to her, and the only make-up (if one could call it that) she bothered with.

Brett informed Edith in a letter otherwise about their house insurance that his marriage was going to be postponed for a couple of weeks until Christmas or a few days before. She was supposed to check the house insurance sum, which 'didn't look right' to Brett, as she had the records. Edith felt Brett would avoid the actual day of Christmas or the Eve for the wedding, and found herself imagining Cliffie's wedding preceding Brett's by a few days. Edith thought of Cliffie's wedding while she washed dishes, or when she made George's trays. It was pleasant and reassuring to imagine. But Edith did admit to herself that she was postponing acting on Marion's advice: to find another doctor who would get George out. After the Christmas holidays, she would get down to it. She also nurtured a faint and probably fatuous hope that Brett would do something about it before Christmas.

Around 15th December, not having heard from Brett, she wrote the following in her diary, after a rather happy afternoon of work at the Thatchery:

The great day has arrived – at least for me. Cliffie and Debbie were married this morning at 11 a.m. at Princeton, in the university chapel. The Quickmen (as C. calls them) were present, the Johnsons of course – in merry mood! Derek with his wife Sylvia. And my parents, benign, approving, ageing. C. almost dropped the ring – a classic! – and I saw him turn pale, then try to stifle a smile – and fail. They look happy. We had a second reception at my house, the first being at Debbie's parents' & very gala with champagne, wines, cakes, even caviar. Her parents like C. & he is at ease with them. The Brunswick Corner contingent followed me to my house, C. having persuaded D. they must come to B.C., & there was more of the same, though Peace can't provide the elegance of the distaff side's estate. C. & bride departed early for Long Island, where a friend was waiting to fly them in a private plane to Nantucket for their honeymoon. C. nicely oiled, but quite sober enough to drive. Thank goodness, he's a boy who can hold his drink, even though he doesn't drink very often.

Thus C. and D. have beaten Brett to it by nearly a fortnight. Brett was not present, though of course invited. He wrote a most touching little note (and also phoned) saying he hoped I understood, but he thought it would not be appropriate if he and Carol came, and sent C. a check (how much I don't know) as a wedding present. Cool and efficient, that's Brett. And by a stretch of the imagination proper.

C. has another six months before he gets his degree, D. a year and a half, which she will very likely do. C. will continue to live in his dorm, so will D. in hers, & they meet on weekends at her house or mine, where they will have (as on occasions before) the guestroom. Neither of them likes the idea of setting up an apt. off campus, which is permitted and some couples do. 'Better for studying to live alone,' says C., 'and not worry about things like shopping.'

When Edith got up from her desk, she felt happy. She felt in another world – but a real world – in which Cliffie went from strength to strength, with his nice wife, a good job to look forward to in June, when he graduated, aged twenty-three, with a masters degree. Perhaps by next autumn, Edith could even look forward to a grand-child, but that of course was up to the young people. In her mind, Edith had already given Debbie a few family things, like the silver candelabra, which were however still downstairs on the sideboard.

Edith stared wide-eyed toward her door, and slowly realized that George was calling for something. In a flash of anger, Edith thought that in her diary she would damn well send George packing. Yes! A long car, practically an ambulance, would come from Sunset Pines and two no-nonsense young men would bundle him and his possessions up and whisk him away. Edith moved to answer George's wail.

Christmas came and went. Edith did all the right things, but she felt in a daze. She decorated a tree, entertained and was entertained, did overtime at the Thatchery and got a hundred-dollar bonus for it. The cork mats, straw place mats, Swedish candlesticks, bamboo screens disappeared, borne out the door, purchased. Elinor Hutchinson was pleased with business.

And Brett and Carol were married on the 3rd of January.

'We'd both love you to come,' Brett said on the telephone. 'There'll be people you know – like Ham Hamilton. You remem-

148

ber him!' Brett laughed a little. Ham was a boozy left-wing reporter whom Edith hadn't thought of in years, an acquaintance of the Grove Street era in New York.

Since Edith had been at that moment wordless, Brett continued:

'I don't want you to think Carol and I are unfriendly or – embarrassed. Why can't we have a nice evening in New York together? Doesn't have to be a late evening for you, so you could drive back if –'

'I don't – really feel like it.' Edith's ire had risen briefly at the word 'embarrassed' from Brett. Well, *he* certainly wasn't embarrassed, by anything. Carol was giving a celebratory party (another party) in February, because a book by her was being published with a silly-sounding title like 'How Not to Step on the Cracks' or something like that, a facetious guide for avoiding faux-pas in personal and business life. That from a woman who presumably had a brain! Edith was revolted by the idea of attending a party at the apartment of her ex-husband and his new wife, and in a vague but furious way angry with Brett for inviting her. Edith declined both invitations.

'How is George?' Brett asked.

Why don't you find out, Edith wanted to say. Suddenly she found her cool, and in a voice worthy of her great-aunt Melanie said, 'I frankly don't give a damn how George is,' and hung up.

That was true. Edith realized that her attitude had changed in the last couple of months. Brett was sitting on his duff, and had done damn-all about George. Now Edith actively detested George, or at least admitted to herself that she detested him, whereas all the years past she had not admitted it. She had to admit now that she had begun to be as subtly unpleasant and rude to him as possible.

She was happy only when she wrote in her diary of Cliffie's progress (Brett and George figured less and less in it), and when she wrote pieces for the *Bugle*. By mid-January she was working on a thousand-word article (at least that long, and not for the *Bugle*, she was going to try to sell it elsewhere) for which she hadn't a title, but her notes were headed *Pro the Third World*.

It had to do with First and Second World countries supervising all aid that went to Third World countries, and her notes ran:

Objectives and Possible Results
1) speeding up of self-sufficiency at whatever level
2) elimination of much graft and corruption in aid now being given
3) would give element of friendliness and cooperation between West and Third World
4) with important proviso that respect for Third World's values and way of life should be maintained; small industry to be encouraged; easing of tariffs
5) program above all not to be westernized, advisors and supervisors not to be para-military

Counsellors, Edith thought, might be a better word than advisors, the latter having been hopelessly tainted by Viet Nam.

17

Cliffie lay on a low couch at Mel's with an almost empty beer can in his hand. He had been up all last night and today, except for a bit of sleep around 5 a.m. and around 4 that afternoon. He knew he looked and felt a mess, but just now he enjoyed the feeling. Mel was playing records.

'Hey! – Other side? Why not?' Mel got up and turned his stack of records. He wore motorcycle gear, maybe hadn't had his boots off in twenty-four hours, Cliffie was thinking.

Sergeant Pepper roared out again. Cliffie squirmed comfortably on the couch, realizing it was dark outside (Mel's shades had been pulled down all day), and that he didn't care what time it was. Cliffie loved Mel's apartment. It was exactly what he would have liked for himself. You climbed a wooden stairway from street level, just like in an old-fashioned house (or a good film), and then you opened a door on Mel's one room which was fantastic: big posters on the walls, guys in motorcycle gear pointing pistols, naked girls. An old straw armchair hung from the ceiling for no reason, swinging when people bumped into it. Paperbacks and clothes were scattered on the floor in a way Cliffie could never achieve at home, because his mother was always straightening things a little. Mel's apartment symbolized: 'Screw everything!'

Mel was sitting on his unmade bed, working alternately with a knife and pliers, trying to get out pieces of glass imbedded in the soles of a pair of low brown boots. The boot soles were of rubber with a tread in them like that of a tire, which was why the glass had stuck.

'God damn!' Mel said. 'Musta been runnin' hard *that* night! Bugger's really in here.'

'But you got away,' Cliffie said, a little loudly because of the music.

'Sure, boy.'

Mel hadn't been wearing these boots last night. The glass was from another occasion. 'Wasn't it great last night?' Cliffie said, laughing lazily. 'Hee-haw!'

'Yeah, boy – but don't say it again, huh?' Mel gave him a glance. 'They could make it tough for me in this town. You're all right – with your mother and all that.'

Cliffie took the reprimand to heart, and at once sobered and sat up. Cliffie thought he would kill himself before he did anything to incur Mel's displeasure. Last night there had been a sudden quarrel between Mel and a fellow with a girl outside the Cascade Bar north of Brunswick Corner. Mel had swung a fist, maybe half joking, but Cliffie had plunged in and socked the fellow. The proprietor of the Cascade had suddenly appeared, then of all things one of the Keystone Kops of Brunswick C. in plainclothes. 'Cliffie! Pissed again! You're not driving, I hope?' He hadn't been driving, because they were both on Mel's motorcycle. The fellow with the girl had been lifting Mel's motorcycle – in order to get it out of the way of his car, he said – and it had been Mel, really, who had lost his temper. But as Mel later said, the fellow could have stowed his motorcycle away in the back of his station wagon, and Mel said he had had a feeling the guy had meant to do this.

'But what did we do last night – after all?' Cliffie said. The cop had drifted off, that he remembered.

'Nothing. But did you have to *sock* the guy? Buddy-o, I ain't sure you heard the last of this yet!'

Cliffie let the good music which seemed elegant, refined, expert, flood through him and soothe him. 'Okay, Mel, but the guy drove off. He didn't stay to talk to the cop there. I didn't hurt him much – a punch on the cheek.'

'How do we know what he did today?' Mel pushed his fingers through his curly black hair. He had a short beard and a droopy moustache like a nineteenth-century villain, long slender legs, and a couple of interesting scars on his knuckles.

152

Mel earned his living, paid his rent and ate, partly from carefully wangled unemployment insurance which he collected at different addresses in the vicinity (not in Lambertville, but in other towns in New Jersey and Pennsylvania), and also from part-time bar-tending here and there. A thirty-mile drive to a restaurant was nothing to Mel on his motorcycle. He also sold LSD and harder stuff, Cliffie knew. Cliffie was aware that Mel kept this drug part of his life secret from him, though maybe not from Mel's older, sometimes not older but more reliable chums, whom Mel had to use in the business. Cliffie knew Mel looked on him as a kid, a kind of apprentice maybe (Cliffie hoped that), someone Mel could ask to run out and buy cigarettes or beer at the local tavern.

The telephone rang, and Mel clumped across the wooden floor and answered.

Cliffie listened, thinking maybe it *was* the police, since they had just been talking about police action, but Mel laughed in a happy way. Cliffie stole a glance at his watch. 8 : 47, and his mother would already have had dinner. He dreaded going home, and knew Mel was going to nudge him out in a few minutes. There was nothing to eat in Mel's fridge, as they had finished the franks and a steak several hours ago, a steak Mel said he had taken from a restaurant. Cliffie heard Mel making a date to meet someone at Hopewell. Cliffie's unhappiness at having to leave coalesced, solidified somehow and he saw George Howland – the white corpse in the upstairs bedroom of his house. Revolting, stinking creature! In the last months, Cliffie had noticed that his mother also had started to loathe the old creep. His mother's voice was tense and sharp, not merely loud. His mother didn't even meet his eyes after the sick-making scenes with George, after the shitty bedpans and the disgusting snot-rags.

Cliffie forced himself to his feet as Mel hung up. 'I ought to be going home. Gotta face it.' Better that he left on his own, rather than wait for Mel to ask him to push off.

'Cliffie, you better clean up a little. Wash your face. Y'know?'

From Mel Cliffie didn't mind this. He went into Mel's tiny

153

john, and bent to wash his face without looking at himself first in the mirror. Cliffie scrubbed with reasonable diligence at his nails, too drunk to notice pain from a rather nastily broken nail. He took Mel's comb and combed his hair, touched his beard a little. He glanced with no interest at a photograph, double-page spread, of some male in full glory, then opened the door and went out. On second thought, he had to pee, so he went back. His pee was colorless. He'd had quite a lot of gin today.

Mel was tidying, hurling boots and books under his bed, even had a broom in his hand. Cliffie supposed a girl was coming.

'Don't forget, Cliffie, don't say anything about my being with you last night, in case they get onto you, will you? They just might overlook me.'

'Sure, Mel. I understand.'

'You do? Good.' Mel smiled a little. He had smallish teeth, the left front one broken at a corner. 'See you soon, Cliffie.'

Cliffie had his Volks parked round the corner. He got in and drove homeward, across the bridge into New Hope, then left along the Delaware, past Odette's. The road was good but narrowish, and Cliffie was careful, because his eyes refused to focus. The light was on in the living room, he saw as he went up the driveway. The Ford was ahead of him, parked where there might have been a garage, if his family had ever built one. Cliffie took his car keys, and when he went in the front door, put the keys on the hall table, as he usually did or should do, in case his mother had to get out with the Ford.

'That you, Cliffie?' called his mother from the kitchen.

'Yep, mom.'

'Well – well. Had a big day?' Edith was nearly finished the washing up.

'Nice day,' Cliffie replied, suddenly realizing he looked sloppy, suddenly ashamed. He lifted his head higher and asked, 'Did I have any phone calls?'

'No. Sorry.' Edith swung the dishtowel over her thumbs, folding it, and laid it over the towel rack. 'Cliffie, have something to eat and go to bed. Nothing more to drink. Promise?'

'Sure I promise. I don't even feel like a drink. What's for dinner? What was for dinner?'

'Pork chops. I stuck them in the oven. I thought you'd be home.' Edith went out.

The oven wasn't on, but the pork chops were still warm. Cliffie ate them standing, leaning against the sink, drinking the rest of a container of milk from the container. Suddenly his plate was empty, even the mashed potatoes gone. He put his plate in the sink, too tired to wash it. He heard his mother's typewriter faintly clicking upstairs.

Cliffie took a bath, moving more steadily now. His mother's door at the front of the house was closed, but a thread of light showed at the bottom, a dot at the keyhole. From George's room came snores, old reliable scraping sounds that showed the vegetable was still alive. Cliffie pushed the door wider, walked in and switched on the light, not in the least afraid the corpse would wake up – oh, no! You fairly had to kick him, stick a pin in him to wake him up! Cliffie strolled to the low chest of drawers whose top bore a white towel, and on this stood bottles of clear glass and brown glass, little jars with glass tops and plastic tops. There was also a plastic thing that was some kind of kit. Eyedroppers. Jesus! Cliffie turned around and said in a normal, normally loud voice:

'Georgie boy, what you need is exercise.'

George snored on, head awry, nose pointed at an upper corner of the room.

Edith's typewriter paused, then clicked on.

Cliffie bent and laughed silently. 'Ought to get out more!' Quite suddenly a light sweat broke over Cliffie's body. He had taken an extra hot bath. How much codeine and sleeping pills and all that would it take to kill old George? And how could he get them down him? In tea? Maybe. If the tea was sweet enough. Cliffie imagined those snores growing slower, fainter – stopping. What a blessing!

Abruptly Cliffie's daydream ended, as if he had switched off a program on TV. He detested the room, and what was he doing here? Well, there was the codeine made from opium. Cliffie liked the word opium. It sounded evil, like a Chinese den. Opium-eaters and – something was the opium of the people, an old saying. And since he was here, why not? Cliffie went to the brown bottle, pulled the rubber stopper out, and took a swig. A little second swig for good measure, to prove he could hold it. Cliffie took a swig at least every four or five days. His mother had not noticed that the tincture – another nice word – was disappearing any faster, or she would certainly have mentioned it. But he had just now drunk out of George's reserve, he realized, a new bottle. Generally Cliffie took it from the bedside bottle. Now he took the bedside bottle and poured a bit from it into the reserve, so the reserve wouldn't look as if it had been gone into, though he did not fill it quite as full as it had been, or the bedside bottle would have looked, perhaps, emptier than it should have looked. What the hell, if the bottle was by George's bedside, wasn't it conceivable that George could have taken a dose on his own?

'You're nothing but a –' Cliffie stopped, having heard a floor-board squeak in the hall.

'Cliffie, what're you doing here?' His mother stood in the hall.

'Nothing! Just –' Cliffie lifted his empty hands. 'Just taking a look before I went to bed.'

Edith drew a breath in through her teeth. 'Well, you'd better get out,' she said, still softly, as if afraid to awaken George. She turned and walked back toward her workroom, glanced once behind her and saw that Cliffie was putting out the light in George's room. Then Cliffie went down the stairs.

She knew Cliffie was sampling the codeine, but she thought if she mentioned it, it would make things worse. Cliffie would at first deny it, then having been detected would stop for a while then pilfer even more. It was a bore, one more chore, to keep fetching the stuff from the pharmacy. Dr Carstairs hadn't remarked the extra consumption, hadn't asked her if George was needing more. Edith thought Carstairs simply hadn't noticed. His visits were too brief to take in details. What did he do? He took George's blood pressure, to be sure, and his temperature. Sometimes he used his stethoscope. Edith didn't always stand in the room watching him.

Edith gasped slightly, realized she had been holding her

breath, staring at her typewriter, half her mind on getting back to where she was in her 'letter' which would have to be written again for smoothness and the ordinariness she wanted.

Where had Cliffie been last night? Mel's probably. Edith knew Mel had a telephone, because she had once looked it up, but she wasn't ever going to try to reach Cliffie there. Orgies, maybe, pop music and LSD, maybe girls. Edith imagined Cliffie chuckling on the sidelines, if there were girls. *Stop it,* she told herself. She meant to finish her final draft tonight.

Like a boat (she thought) gliding smoothly to a shore, she moved closer to her worktable and sat down. But it wasn't like that. If she wanted to think of boats, she was like a ship without a rudder now, without an anchor, turning on a dark sea, not knowing direction, unable to maneuver if it knew. It was Brett's marriage three weeks ago that had forced her to turn loose. Before that, she had had some hope that Brett would change his mind, break with the girl, come back. But he had known Carol two years now, and if he married, he meant it. It had forced a movement on Edith's part, which had been unconscious, yet still accomplished: she had turned loose of her dependence on Brett. She was alone.

She pulled her page and a half toward her and started reading through, correcting.

18

On 6th May, Edith copied into her diary a poem she had written that morning while still in bed, at dawn, with the pencil and scribbling pad she kept on the bedtable.

> At dawn, after my death hours before,
> The sunlight will spread at seven o'clock as usual
> On these trees which I know.
> Greenness will burst, dark green shadows yield
>   To the cruel-benign, indifferent sun.
> Indifferent will stand the trees in my own garden,
> Unweeping for me on the morning of my death.
> Same as ever, roots athirst,
> The trees will rest in breezeless dawn,
> Blind and uncaring,
> The trees that I knew,
> That I tended.

In June, Robert Kennedy was shot in Los Angeles at the Democratic Nomination Convention. Edith learned this when Cliffie knocked on her bedroom door and wakened her to tell her. He had heard it on his transistor. Edith got up and put her dressing gown on. Then the telephone rang, and it was Gert Johnson, who had also just heard the news.

'They're not sure he'll live,' Gert said. She wanted to come over.

Edith said, 'Sure. Come over!' Suddenly nothing mattered, the *Bugle* mailing labels she had been typing that night, the lateness of the hour. Edith absently lit the burner under the coffee pot, which still held some coffee, though Gert would probably prefer a drink. Cliffie was smiling faintly, standing in the dining room.

'Those Kennedys haven't any luck,' Cliffie said.

Edith felt jangled. She turned off the coffee, got out ice for Gert and herself. When Gert arrived, full of talk, telling Edith (who hadn't had her radio or television on) the latest news she had heard, Edith had the feeling she was hearing it through a fog, or from a distance. Cliffie lingered, fascinated, for a drink with them, saying nothing.

'It's the CIA – or it's the Mafia,' Gert said with conviction. 'Bobby had the guts, y'know, Edie, to say he was going after the Mob, d'y'know that?' (Of course Edith did.) 'And he'd already started as Attorney General – going after 'em, I mean.'

On the next hourly bulletin, Bobby Kennedy's condition was described as critical. They had got the assassin at once, and he had an Arab-sounding name, Sirhan. And who had paid *him*, Edith wondered. Like Brett, she was sure Lee Harvey Oswald had not fired any of the shots that had killed John Kennedy, that Oswald had been a fall guy, not even paid for his role, that Ruby had been a fringe employé of the CIA and had got rid of Oswald, just in case Oswald might have been able to prove his innocence.

'Any news from Brett?' Gert asked when she had calmed down a little.

Cliffie had by then left the room.

'Nothing much. He said he was going over his manuscript, retyping pages here and there.'

'Does Cliffie ever see him?'

'You mean in New York. Yes – once, I think. Cliffie went to New York to hear a pop concert and stayed the night with them. Brett invites –'

'What does Cliffie say about Carol?' Gert asked softly. Her drinks had warmed her.

Carol is pregnant, Edith thought at once. Cliffie had said that. The child was due in the autumn, either Cliffie had been told or he was venturing. 'Oh, I think – Carol's quite nice to him. So what could he say against her?'

'But still working on the *Post*?'

'Yes.'

'Convenient. They can keep an eye on each other.' Gert gave one of her big laughs.

A minute later, Gert was saying that she should get out more, see more people. Edith thought she did enough of that, all that she cared to. The Quickmans had introduced her to two couples in Tinicum. Gert sometimes played golf at a club in New Jersey. Gert had invited Edith once or twice, but Edith wasn't keen on sports and preferred to spend her spare time, if any, in other ways.

One more inch of rye, straight, for Gert, then she departed, though Edith could have sat up the rest of the night chatting, waiting for news about Bobby. Maybe. She switched her workroom radio off. Only now was Bobby Kennedy's possible death sinking in. And the insanity, the wrongness that had inspired that bullet! And Tricky Dick was the Republican candidate. What a world! What an America! California, the state with the most nuts, everyone said, full of cults, mostly destructive – they couldn't even try to conserve trees without being maniacal about it. John Kennedy, however, had been shot in Dallas. Where was the enemy? Who was it? It was right here in the house, Edith thought. Cliffie was her enemy – perhaps. He mocked the work she was trying to do, the *Bugle* or whatever. She felt also that she had lost Cliffie's respect because she had lost Brett without a fight, without protest. Cliffie, the passive observer. *He* was all right, of course, because he kept aloof from everything. If you didn't try anything, how could you fail? She remembered telling Cliffie fifteen years ago (at least) that to fail was normal, that one simply tried again. She had tried to awaken in him the joy of challenge. What a laugh!

Still later that night, Edith was awakened by the telephone ringing. She groped for the light, saw it was ten past 5, and went downstairs barefoot. Something to do with Cliffie, she felt. Hadn't he gone out? She wasn't sure, but she thought so, and she hoped it was simply that his Volks had broken down, or that he was too tight to drive home, so that she had to go and fetch him.

'Mrs Howland?' said a man's voice. 'Hopewell Township police here. Your son's had an accident.'

160

'Oh – What happened?'

'He's all right, but the car's wrecked. He hit a man walking along the edge of the road.'

'Oh, my God! You mean the man's badly hurt?'

'Both legs broken. Well, it's not a time for details. Long as you're home, we'll bring your son home ...'

From that night onward, Edith had two on her hands, George and Cliffie, because Cliffie's licence was suspended for a year. He was grounded, as he put it. This Edith had learned the same early morning, when the Brunswick Corner police plus the Hopewell Township officer delivered Cliffie. He was plainly under the influence. Edith was ashamed, though she thought she had long ago lost the capacity for that, because Cliffie was a grown man, independent of her. Cliffie looked in fact half asleep, though the half of him that wasn't asleep focused on her, as if he were trying to gauge, if he could, her reaction. Edith was concerned about the man who had been injured – a man of fifty-five, the Hopewell officer said, a plumber, married, now in a hospital in Trenton. His name was written down, at Edith's request, and left along with other papers for Cliffie to sign tomorrow, because as the police said, he was not in a condition to sign anything.

The following day, Robert Kennedy's death was announced. Cliffie was asleep when Edith left for the Thatchery at a quarter to 2. Edith worked doggedly, with more of a head-down attitude than usual. 'Don't think, keep moving,' was her frequent advice to herself, and she sometimes added, 'Don't look for a *meaning*,' because if she did look for a meaning for even half a minute, she sensed that she was lost, that she had turned loose of her real anchor which was not Brett, but a kind of firm resignation. Edith didn't know what to call it, but she knew what it was, knew the feeling. The feeling was one of security, the only security she knew now, or had now.

There was, of course, her diary. For two days after Cliffie's mishap, and Bobby Kennedy's death, Edith felt quite unsure of herself, unsure of the rails on which she moved – giving George his meals and taking sheets to the launderette and all that. So she wrote at greater length, voluptuously and voluminously, but still carefully in her big diary. As if to guard, some-how, against the future, she advanced time by four months or so, and gave Debbie and Cliffie a healthy, dark-haired baby girl (Debbie had dark-brown hair), weighing nearly eight pounds. Edith made Cliffie late (the baby having been born two hours before) in getting to the hospital in Princeton. Edith wrote:

... My parents are thrilled, telephoned Debbie, and want to come to see the new-born Josephine as soon as she is home ...

Actually Edith's parents were rather uncommunicative with her now, considering that she might be lonely and in need of morale-boosting, but Edith thought only fleetingly of that fact as she continued:

... In fact it was sheer luck that Cliffie was at home at all at the dramatic moment, because he has been based in Kuwait for two months now, since August. His company needed him in New York for consultation, he said, but I suspect he wangled a trip home ...

19

Mel Linnell dropped Cliffie, socially speaking, that summer. It was a month or so after the car wreck that the drop became definite. Cliffie had rung Mel once or twice, and Mel had said he was not free because he had a date each time. The third time, Cliffie telephoned Mel around 3 p.m. of a Thursday, when a Lambertville electrician had just finished a job on the outside garden light at the back of the house, and Cliffie could have got a ride with him, because the electrician was going straight back to Lambertville.

'Listen, Cliffie boy –' Mel began. 'I'm sorry about the car smash-up and all that. But I gotta be careful, y'know? I think you better stay clear of here for a while. No hard feelings, though.'

Cliffie mumbled something about understanding, feeling worse than he had felt when they had caught him cheating at the exams in Trenton, worse than when Aunt Melanie had caught him stealing from her purse when he was a kid. Cliffie was in a trembling tizzy of frustration, heartbreak, shock, and his first impulse was to head for the scotch bottle in the living room, but he suddenly remembered the electrician waiting in the kitchen, where Cliffie had offered him a beer.

'Sorry. I mean, thanks,' Cliffie said, 'but I won't be needing a lift after all.'

'Oh. Okay. Well, I'll push on.' The young man clumped in heavy leather boots to the garbage container by the sink, dropped the empty can in and wiped his mouth with the back of his hand. 'Tell your mother we'll send the bill. Won't be much – just rewiring.' With a smile, the fellow was gone, climbing into his little truck in the driveway, whistling.

For an instant Cliffie wished he had a job like that, well paid (electricians always were), with a truck he could drive by himself, so he would be independent, able to fool around a little here and there if he felt like it, able to wear any old clothes. This fellow had been younger than Cliffie. Then just as suddenly Cliffie realized the fellow had smiled a little, almost sneered when he said '– just rewiring,' as if it was funny Cliffie hadn't been able to do it himself. Well, he didn't like fooling with electrical stuff, because he'd once had a shock. His mother did a few little repairs since Brett went off, but for some reason she hadn't wanted to tackle the garden light.

Anyway, he could now have his drink, and Cliffie veered away from the living room toward his own room, his own bottle. He drank an inch or so neat from a tumbler. The bottle was two-thirds empty. And his pocket money was low, maybe twelve dollars. He should see about working the Chop House soon, maybe this afternoon. And how the hell would he get there by 5:30 or 7, or whenever they wanted him? If they would agree to just after 7, his mother could drop him. It was more than a mile away. Or maybe someone there knew of a waiter or a waitress who could pick him up by arrangement.

Cliffie poured a bit more for himself, remembering with warm satisfaction that he had a bank account, savings, at the Brunswick First National with over two hundred dollars in it. His mother didn't know that, Cliffie thought. She would consider it a mark in his favor, probably, if she knew he had put aside some of his earnings. However, Cliffie guarded his money jealously, didn't want anyone to know he had a bank account, and certainly not how much. The money was important to his self-esteem, and he didn't want to be asked to contribute fifty, if his mother was in some crisis, even if she promised to pay it back. He knew from the way she talked that the house was barely making it every month.

'T-chuh!' Cliffie said aloud, and set the bottle back in his closet corner. He was thinking that if his mother was *half* paid for the time she spent on articles that never sold, they'd be doing all right. Three or four evenings a week she spent typing away in her front room, making carbons, rewriting pages, a lot of them half-crumpled in her wastebasket. What a way to spend evenings! With no luck at it!

He knew he should ring the Chop House, but to delay the task, he went upstairs and strolled toward his mother's front room, whose door was always slightly open, as Nelson liked to sleep there. Cliffie disliked entering his mother's room, because even when she wasn't there, he had the feeling she was watching him from all the walls, the way he remembered as a kid people telling him that God could see everything he did at all times, a statement he had never completely believed and certainly didn't now. Cliffie moved stiffly. Nelson raised his head and gazed at Cliffie steadily from the bench under the windows.

'Hyah, Nelson,' Cliffie said.

The typewriter was more to one side than usual, and on the center of the worktable was his mother's thick brown diary. It was a wonder it wasn't filled after all these years, Cliffie thought, but on the other hand it was even thicker than a Manhattan telephone directory, though maybe not with so many pages, and it was inconceivable that anyone could fill it in a lifetime, at least with the events of one life, he thought.

Once, Cliffie remembered, years ago, he had come into this room when his mother had been out of the house, and had seen the diary open on the table, one page filled and the other half filled with his mother's neat black handwriting, and Cliffie had been seized with curiosity, but a stronger feeling had prevented him from reading it: he had imagined that he would see some awful thing written about *himself*. His mother's writing had suddenly looked like the little scribbles doctors made when they gave prescriptions, when he was sick with something, feeling awful. He didn't want to be *judged*. That was it!

'I will *not* be *judged*!' Cliffie said firmly, but not too loudly, even though he knew George wasn't going to hear him all the way down the hall.

Cliffie did bend and look at a newspaper clipping on his mother's table. It looked as if it were from the *Post*, and Cliffie thought surely the *Post* wouldn't have bothered printing anything about his silly car accident, and he was right because this item was headed *Student Uproar in Paris: the Implications for De Gaulle*. It was not of the least interest to Cliffie, indeed sent a soporific haze over his brain at once.

He turned and walked out of the room, leaving the door as he had found it. He walked down the hall toward George's room, though he was still mindful that he might ring the Chop House, ought to. After all, he'd worked there twice since the car accident. They certainly weren't boycotting him.

'Howdy, George!' Cliffie said, putting on his western accent, and debating pinching a snort of codeine, deciding not to, because sometimes the stuff tasted like Southern Comfort, which Cliffie disliked. But some for George? Cliffie laughed, happily. By God, it was time for a laugh! Cliffie poured a goodly measure of the tincture into a tumbler with a hexagonal, heavy base, like the one he had in his own room – family's best, present from Aunt Melanie – added a bit of water, added also a couple of aspirins from the bottle with cotton at the top, a bottle clearly marked ASPIRIN, then took two smaller pills from a little cardboard pillbox (red bottom, white top) with something written on it in handwriting which Cliffie could not decipher at all and didn't care to.

'Hey up, Georgie boy!' Cliffie said in the tone in which Mel addressed him.

George awakened with elaborate slowness, risible to Cliffie as ever, and Cliffie put a hand behind his bony shoulders.

'Have some *tincture*!'

'Wh-what?'

'Doctor's orders! The cup that cheers! – Doctor's orders, George, I swear!'

George was downing it. Cliffie held it carefully to his lips. George's lower lip fell in horribly because there were no teeth there at the moment.

'Good stuff, eh? Really good stuff!' Cliffie said.

George did wince, drawing his gray eyebrows together, but he said, 'Thanky, Cliff. Wha' time – time is it?'

'Ha' past three, sir,' said Cliffie, assuming his English accent.

166

Fuck it, he'd better ring the Chop House. 'Nighty night, George.' Cliffie went out, before he could be asked to reach, maybe, the bottle George peed in.

Because Cliffie did not wish to be home that evening, in case of George's unusual sleepiness, Cliffie did a good job on the telephone with Sol, the stocky, terribly-busy guy who really ran the Chop House though he was not the owner, and Sol told him to come on at 5:30 as waiter, and hung up, before Cliffie could explain that he had no transportation.

Cliffie put on black cotton trousers belonging to him – black trousers being required – and a white shirt. The Chop House offered black string ties and red and black striped vests free to their waiters. Cliffie walked three-quarters of the way, looking for a lift, getting one when he was only a hundred yards from the restaurant, but he accepted the lift anyway. He picked up thirty-two dollars in tips when the pot was divided after midnight among eight waiters and waitresses, plus his five-dollar wage. Another waiter named Phil dropped him home, right at his driveway.

'How long they suspend you for, Cliff?'

The goddam car accident had been in the *Bugle* even. 'Oh, just a year. Four months gone already.' Cliffie was exaggerating. '*I* don't care.' He got out. 'Thanks a lot, Phil.'

Cliffie saw the light in his mother's front room. He had left a note that he was working at the Chop House.

'Cliffie?' his mother called as soon as he had come in the front door.

'Yes, mom!'

'Can you come up for a moment?'

'Sure.' Cliffie climbed the stairs two at a time, hauling himself by the banister rail. Maybe old George was still asleep? Dead? Cliffie's mind didn't fathom this, refused to imagine it just now. Good. He could play it cooler that way.

Edith, in several moments of anger that evening, had thought to blast Cliffie, scare the daylights out of him by making him aware, in case he didn't know it, that he could kill someone with an overdose of codeine. George was still asleep, and she had

167

gone in at half-hour intervals to see if he was still breathing properly, or breathing at all. He was. She had been afraid to ring the doctor, afraid of what Carstairs might say – about Cliffie.

'Well?' Cliffie said, a bit defiantly.

Now with Cliffie before her, hands on his hips, Edith couldn't say the words she had prepared when she had been alone, such as *silly prank . . . criminal act . . .* even *possible murder.*

'Good evening at the Chop House?' she asked.

'Oh – nearly thirty bucks. Pretty good crowd for a Thursday night.'

Edith sponged an envelope and sealed it. *Bugle* work. 'You know, Cliffie, I think it's time you wrote a note again – or telephoned Richard Gerber's house. After all –'

'Oh, *mom!*' Cliffie raised a foot as if to stomp it, and swung his head in agony. This was the man he had hit with his car.

Edith rose to battle. She got up from her chair. 'You refused to go to the hospital!'

'Yes!' He had hated the idea. Cliffie had refused with a determination he might have shown if he had been fighting for his life.

'It's cowardly enough that you didn't face him –'

'F' Chrissake, I *wrote* him! You didn't see the letter!'

'I didn't want to see the letter, I said write it on your own!'

'Then how do you know what I said?'

'That's not the point!'

They were both talking at once, not caring how loud their voices were. Edith's anxieties had focused on Richard Gerber and she was going to see it through.

'He's just home from the hospital, lives hardly eight miles from here, and you ought to go and see him. I'll take you. I'll wait in the car.'

'The guy's got insurance. Probably enjoying a few weeks off. What's he lost?'

'Would you like to have two legs broken by some drunken idiot?'

'Sure!' Cliffie laughed, suddenly imagining having six legs, so

168

if two were broken, fine. Lie in bed and take it easy! This fellow had a wife to wait on him, the way George was waited on. How was George? In a coma? Cliffie hadn't heard any snores, but the snores were not always noisy. Cliffie knew, however, that his mother was unusually angry because George must have seemed unusually sleepy, and the bottles unusually low.

Edith knew what was going on in Cliffie's mind, knew from his faint smile. Cliffie wanted her to mention the nearly coma-tose state of old George, the plainly gone-into bottles, which Cliffie had not bothered to top up with water. She was not going to mention this. She had taken a walk, with a flashlight, around 10 p.m. that evening. She hadn't been able to awaken George for his dinner. At the same time, his breathing had been steady and strong enough to make her believe that he was not in danger of dying. And if he had been in danger? In her opinion? She would have rung Carstairs. If Carstairs hadn't been available, she might have tried to get some strong coffee down George. She supposed that would have been the correct thing to do. And yet she had taken a walk of perhaps half an hour, had come back to see if all was still well, if George had been still breathing. In her nervousness, Edith had telephoned the hospital in Trenton and inquired about Richard Gerber. That was how she had learned that he had gone home. 'I know Richard Gerber's address,' Edith said, 'and you're going to pay him a visit.'

'I will *not*!'

'You will! I'll see to *that*!'

Now it was like a flexing of muscles, a shouting bout again. Cliffie was an obdurate mountain before her – not very tall to be sure, but stubborn enough.

'You will go to see him or leave this house!' Edith said with lowered head.

That had some effect, Edith saw.

'If you refuse to see Mr Gerber, you can just ask Mel to take you in,' Edith went on. 'By the way, here's Mr Gerber's address and the phone number. If you want to call, fine. Otherwise I'll phone them tomorrow morning. All right? I'll take you in the morning, because I'm working in the afternoon.'

She was hammering the point again that he was grounded, Cliffie realized, and that he couldn't call on Mel to take him, because Mel had dropped him, a fact that his mother somehow knew, maybe through Gert Johnson, even, because that old gossip-bag managed to know everything. 'Okay,' Cliffie said, taking the paper from her hand. 'Sure, if you insist.' He turned and left the room.

What the hell could he expect from Gerber, Cliffie wondered. Anger? A cold silence? Cliffie dreaded the chore like – like what some people said about going to the dentist. He absolutely hated the idea of *facing* the guy, looking at him. He picked up a comic book from his room floor, with an idea of changing his state of mind by looking at it for a minute or two, found even this distasteful and hurled the magazine at a wall.

The next morning, just before 8, Edith took George's breakfast tray – boiled egg, two pieces of toast, butter, marmalade and tea – up to his room. It was perhaps twenty minutes earlier than his usual breakfast time.

'George?'

He awakened in small fits, stirring hands first, then his head, finally opening his eyes, emitting from his lips the fragmented words Edith knew so well. He was exactly as usual. He made no remark about the missed supper last evening. He hauled himself up a little with Edith's help, let her settle his tray. Old ship rising up, Edith thought. Old gray bones, masts, tattered sails flying, unsinkable.

'*Last of the tea!*' Edith screamed. '*Hope it's strong enough!*'

'Wha –? Oh, sure!'

Edith realized she hated him more than usually that morning. She hated also that she had to take Cliffie to the Gerbers'. More shame was due her this morning, very likely, more bad behavior from her son. At any rate, Edith did not want to give herself the consolation of a cheerful hope. Best to expect the worst. And best to pretend that all was going to be well, too. How could one do both? Deliberately, even before she left George's room, she straightened her shoulders and put on a faint smile. At least she looked all right, she thought. If only Aunt Melanie –

Edith's thoughts faltered. She had missed her great-aunt's visit this summer, because Melanie had been 'too tired' to come. And Edith hadn't been able to get away, because of the Thatchery job.

The post had come. Two bills. A bank statement. Three items addressed either to her or to 'Bugle Editor'. Nothing for George. There usually wasn't anything for George, to be sure, because since years the couple of friends who had used to write him had stopped. She would have liked to take George a letter this morning, just to cheer him up a little. Poor old vegetable! She could of course write him a letter. She smiled at the idea. Edith poured herself a cup of coffee, lit a cigarette, and went to the telephone to ring the Gerbers. She consulted the directory again for the number. Cliffie was not yet up.

This little task was over in about one minute, and Edith stood up, half-smoked cigarette still in hand, amazed that it had gone so quickly.

Mrs Gerber had sounded quite pleasant, and had said that of course her son could come by around 11 this morning, if he wished to. Richard Gerber was doing quite well. Hadn't she said that? Edith sometimes had the feeling that real things were not real – and vice versa.

She and Cliffie, both breakfasted, Cliffie decently attired in polo-neck sweater and blue blazer (it was a cool September day), set out at 10:30 for Hopewell Township. Cliffie was silent in the car, staring through the windshield, not frowning, absent.

'I think you might take him some flowers,' Edith said.

'Flowers? Flowers're something you take girls!'

'Not necessarily. I'll stop for some.'

'You could've said it – back at the house where we've got some!' Cliffie said, twitching with anger now.

Edith at that moment swung toward the curb, and said, 'Spend a dollar and a half and get some – chrysanthemums or something.' She had parked by a florist's shop.

Cliffie got out and banged the car door. He returned a moment later with chrysanthemums wrapped in thin green paper. The shop had boxes of them on the sidewalk. These were cut.

Silence.

They arrived at the Gerber's modest residential area. Edith found the street after one inquiry, and Cliffie got out with his flowers, grimly.

'I'll wait, Cliffie. Don't worry about how long it takes.'

Cliffie wanted to say that she didn't expect him to stay for lunch, did she? But he only nodded, and trudged toward the house whose number he knew from the paper his mother had given him last evening was 136. A small front porch, a two-story house, yellow and white. Cliffie rang the doorbell.

The woman was about his mother's age, and Cliffie was surprised that she smiled.

'Clifford Ho –'

'Yes. Come in, would you? Your mother –'

'Oh, she's – She'll pick me up in a few minutes. Has to do some shopping.' They knew, of course, that he was not allowed to drive now.

Cliffie climbed some stairs behind the woman who wore a pleated mauve skirt, white blouse.

Richard Gerber was in bed reading newspapers, a man with a broad head, strong brown hair growing gray, brawny forearms. He looked up at Cliffie like a perfectly healthy businessman disturbed by a visitor.

'Morning, Mr Gerber,' Cliffie said. 'I came to say I hope you're feeling better.'

'Morning.' Gerber nodded slightly.

A canary sang in a window's sunlight, oblivious of all this.

'The boy brought some flowers, Dick. I'll get a vase for them.' The woman went out.

Cliffie didn't know what to say. *Walking around a little? Going back to work soon?* No, maybe that was a bad idea. Did this guy want to go back to work? Why should he, if he was being paid his usual salary – maybe more, if one counted the insurance. 'I hope you're feeling – better,' Cliffie said.

Richard Gerber looked at him with a hard amusement, with a kind of glint. He had not completely lowered his *Trenton Standard* onto his sheet-covered lap.

Cliffie had felt the coolness of sweat on his forehead after his first words about Gerber feeling better. What the hell did Gerber expect, that he'd get down on his knees to him, beg him to use his influence to get his driving licence back? Was he supposed to promise that he wouldn't ever drive a car again, for instance? Didn't a lot of people hit people, by accident, in the dark? *What the hell were you doing, walking along the edge of the road like that?* Cliffie could have asked Gerber. *Were you pissed too, maybe? I have to pay for it the rest of my life, I suppose?*

'Hm-mph,' Gerber said, or something like that.

Gerber's eyes had not left Cliffie's. Gerber looked like an old German ham, beef, animal of some kind. There were creases across his forehead, gray hairs in his eyebrows. A strong guy, stupid too, but damned sure of himself, the way a lot of stupid people were sure of themselves. Cliffie's courage drained, but he stood up straighter, tossed his paper-wrapped chrysanthemums on the foot of the bed and put his hands on his hips.

Just then, the woman returned to the room, and moved smoothly to the bed and took the flowers. 'Won't you sit down?' she said politely to Cliffie.

Cliffie knew he had cooked it by tossing the flowers. Old Gerber's face had hardened by a couple of degrees.

'Here's our fine younger generation,' Gerber said.

'Oh-h, *Dick*!' the woman shrieked in a soprano like something out of an opera. She had an unusually high voice, anyway.

Cliffie tossed a smile at her.

'He's come to *see* you,' said the woman. 'He didn't have to do that.'

Cliffie looked for a few seconds into Gerber's steady, unfriendly eyes, and realized that they were both furious but not furious about the same thing. Their minds were on two different things.

'I'm sure the boy's *sorry* for what happened,' the woman said.

'All right, I'm *not* sorry!' Cliffie retorted at once, and turned on his heel toward the door. One false turn on the landing, then he found the stairs and dashed down, the woman behind him, but he was going much faster. Cliffie found himself smiling broadly as soon as he got into the open air. The hell with them! He saw the family car across the street, faced in the direction for home.

Edith smiled, seeing his smile. 'Went all right?'

Cliffie got in and shut the door. 'Perfectly all right. Nice guy.' Cliffie didn't look to see if Mrs Gerber was on the front porch as the car drove off.

One morning in October, Edith had a letter from Brett. It said:

Oct. 19, 1968

Dear Edith,

Carol gave birth early this morning to a baby girl. Started to telephone you or telegraph, but after all a letter is quick enough. I thought you would like to know. Both doing well.

Hope Cliffie is steadying down a bit and that you are all right, George also. I send love, as ever.

Brett

PS Check enclosed.

A check for a hundred and fifty dollars was enclosed, though it wasn't due till the first of November. Brett sent a check every month, but Edith had objected to a larger sum. Edith's first reaction to the letter was one of swift anger, a rise of warmth in her face and neck. He hoped George was 'all right', just 'hoped'. Edith stifled her anger at once: the anger was too familiar to be interesting, to accomplish anything.

She knew that it was the reality of the baby that had shaken her.

20

Edith hurried along the sidewalk in below-freezing January cold, watching out that she didn't slip on an occasional icy spot, though there wasn't any snow. She pressed a woolen muffler against her nose and cheeks with one mittened hand. She was en route to a Town Hall meeting – rather in what should have been the Town Hall, but that was enduring roof repairs, so the meeting was being held in the Unitarian church – to discuss and protest the upping of Bucks County school taxes, a protest Edith knew was doomed to fail. And God it was cold, at 6:30 p.m., and dark already, and an awful song that Cliffie had just been booming on his transistor stuck in her head:

'I'm so lonely with – *ow-chew*!'

When Edith had left the house, however, the music had been off, and Cliffie on the telephone, talking with Mel, Edith thought. She wouldn't have known this, if she hadn't come back into the house, after a few steps outside, in order to get a heavier muffler from the hall. She knew Cliffie wanted to get back into Mel's fold, the only fold Cliffie had ever known.

Her thoughts were interrupted by Charles and Mary Bell, who were getting out of their car at a corner.

'How're *you*, Edith?'

'Hello! Heading for the meeting, I suppose!' said her husband.

Edith replied pleasantly. She hardly knew them.

The white, hip-roofed church had lights in front of it, making shadows under its black roof. Lots of cars. People greeted one another, and Edith was again saying, 'Hello! How're you doing?' every few seconds as she made her way toward the door. She was thinking of Jackie Kennedy, Jackie Onassis now. The last time she'd been in a group of people – where? – everyone had been saying how shocking it was that Jackie had married a multi-millionaire tycoon after JFK. 'Imagine her living with him now!' and 'It's an insult to America!' and all that. Jackie had a taste for power and money, in Edith's opinion, and it all hung together and didn't surprise her at all. But Edith knew why the others were annoyed: they had wanted to see in Jackie a similarity to JFK, had hoped for a very American kind of idealism in her, and the disappointment in their hope upset people. Edith found a seat in one of the roomy pews. Only then did she spot Gert Johnson, behind her and to her left, because Gert happened to stand up just then to turn and greet somebody.

The chairman, a man whose name Edith had forgotten, rapped for order. He began to talk, setting the argument forth, the situation, the justifiable resentment of people who thought they were paying enough taxes already, and who furthermore might not have any children of their own. Edith removed her mittens, wriggled her toes in her boots. Her toes were beginning to hurt.

A tedious voice, a man's, came from behind Edith. Someone had stood up to speak. There was a faint ripple of laughter, very faint.

God, the church looked barren, Edith thought. In their effort to avoid painted saints, gilded columns, they had erected a well-painted barn. Emptiness. Fill it yourself with your own thoughts. Black rostrum only slightly raised, black framed windows against stark white walls.

'Where is it going to *end*?' shrieked a woman. '*My* taxes this year – I brought the records with me and I will compare them with just *one* year ago ...'

Now Edith's cold ears were aching.

'Shall we take a vote on that?' the chairman was shouting.

Take a vote on taking a vote. And considering all the gay boys, where were the kids coming from?

'Yes-s!' said a hearty, smiling voice which Edith recognized as Gert's. 'A vote on that and a vote *first* – or a show of hands –

as to how many people here right now have children of school age *going* to the schools we're talking about, because I think that's *interesting*!'

Patter of applause! Good old Gert. She was at least with it. A lot of people, not necessarily wealthy, sent their kids from thirteen to college age to a private school called Pymbroke Academy.

Edith's interest flagged after the show of hands, which looked like three-quarters of the assembled, and she found herself day-dreaming of a baby crawling around her living room floor. *Brett's* baby. Brett's and Carol's baby girl. What was she going to do with the baby girl in her diary, Edith wondered, and at once giggled. At present she was omitting her, of course, just as she had omitted Carol, at least lately. But the baby girl? Once more Edith had a vision of the pink-faced, diaper-clad lump crawling over the living room rug, much to Nelson's astonishment, the cat jumped a foot into the air, and Edith was stricken with in-controllable mirth which shook her tensed ribs.

The woman next to her looked at her.

Edith realized that she would have to leave. She couldn't stop laughing, even though her laughter was silent, so she stood up and excused herself quietly to the man on her right – taking the longer way, just because it had been the woman on her left who had glanced at her.

What was she missing anyway?

She was out, free again. She turned left on the sidewalk for the walk home. And now her giggles had gone, as mysteriously as they had arrived. Now she only smiled, anticipating the warmth of her home, thinking of dear Nelson who had in the last cold days found a nook behind the radiator handle or knob and the bench in her workroom, warmer than the bench pillow. Trust cats! And he'd never even seen the baby Edith had been thinking about and wondering what to do about in her diary. Her *diary*! Edith was again convulsed, bent over briefly then walked on. Why should it be so funny?

Cliffie met her at the door, and opened the door before she had time to touch it.

'Why, thank you! That's service!' Edith said.

'Th-they just called – from Aunt Melanie's,' Cliffie said. 'She's not feeling well.'

Edith sobered at once. 'What do you mean? Is it another stroke? – Who called?'

'A woman. I dunno.'

'Mrs Byrd?' She was a neighbor of Melanie's. 'From home, Cliffie, or was it the hospital?'

'I think it was from home. They didn't say anything about a hospital,' Cliffie replied defensively.

'How long ago?'

'Just five minutes.'

Edith went at once to the telephone, paused to get rid of her coat, then picked up the telephone and dialed.

Aunt Melanie's colored maid Bertha answered. 'Yes, Miss Edith, she's had another stroke.' Bertha seemed to have burst into tears at the first sound of Edith's voice.

'Is she at home or the hospital, Bertha?'

'She's here, Miss Edith. She don't want to go to the hospital.'

'Tell her I'll come. Tonight. I ought to be there by ten tonight.' Edith hung up, not wanting to waste a minute. She went into the living room, where Cliffie was standing blankly looking at the television screen, though the sound was now turned off. 'Cliffie, I'm going to Aunt Melanie's tonight. I – don't suppose you want to come. I have the feeling –'

Cliffie was shaking his head. 'No, I don't want to go. Do I have to?'

'Of course you don't *have* to.' Now Edith was back on the rails again, back to reality. Ring Frances Quickman first. Edith couldn't depend on Cliffie to hold the fort, feed Nelson, water the plants. The cleaning woman (Margaret, once a week) lived too far away to be expected to feed Nelson twice a day. Frances was in. Edith explained the situation, and Frances commiserated and said:

'I'll be right here, Edie, and I've still got your key, you know.'

That was comforting. 'There's some food here, but I'll leave three dollars for Nelson on the top of the fridge – under the fruit basket.'

Edith threw together an overnight bag – woolen pajamas, houseslippers, a sweater, toothbrush. She called to Nelson as she went down with the suitcase, and she gave him his evening meal in the kitchen. There were sausages and eggs for Cliffie, he was always quite happy making those for himself, and she asked him to take some up to George.

She was miles from Brunswick Corner before she realized she hadn't said good-bye to George, hadn't reminded Cliffie that he had to see that George had his meals tomorrow. Surely Cliffie would think of it. Or George would shout, if he wanted something. Old George on his rubber ring to protect him from bedsores, and the rubber sheet under the bedsheet. And now he was getting pink sore spots on the place where the rubber ring touched him!

'Good Christ!' Edith said softly, rather like Cliffie, and lifted her hands from the wheel, brought them down again gently.

It was soothing to drive. And she knew the road well. Melanie had come for one day at Christmas, only a month ago, looking as well as ever. She had given Nelson a handsome Kent hairbrush, had brought his present out last, saying, 'Surprise for you, Nelson! Merry Christmas from old great-great-great – Aunt Melanie.' And the cat had torn open the wrapping with an enthusiasm that had made all three of them laugh – because Melanie had put a piece of roast beef in with the brush.

The front porch light was on for Edith. She drove up the curving driveway between widely spaced poplars. There was a big car parked near the house. Probably Dr Phelps', Edith thought.

Bertha opened the front door as Edith's car stopped. 'Evening, Miss Edith!' she said with a big smile that was almost as usual, but not quite.

'How're you, Bertha?' Edith pressed her hand. 'The doctor's here?'

'Yes, ma'am, you'll see.' Bertha helped Edith hang her coat in the downstairs hall closet, then carried Edith's little suitcase up. Bertha wore a heavy maroon-colored bathrobe, maybe against the chill, maybe because it was late.

Melanie's bedroom door was ajar, and Edith heard a gentle chuckle, a man's. Bertha knocked gently and said:

'Miss Edith's here, ma'am – sir.'

Edith went into the room. Her aunt lay under a plastic tent – an oxygen tent. The reading light was on near the bed, but turned away from the bed, Dr Phelps had been half sitting on the arm of a big chair, and he stood up. 'Hello, Dr Phelps.'

Dr Phelps was still smiling, a neat little man in his sixties with gray hair and spectacles. 'Hello, Mrs Howland. We've been swapping stories, your aunt and I.'

Melanie had turned her head to see Edith better. She was propped up a little, smiling, but the smile looked distorted. 'Hello, Edie, dear,' she said hoarsely. 'Isn't it a fine thing – to see me like this?'

'How are you, darling?' Edith said, and pressed her aunt's hand through the plastic. The hand gave no response.

'That's the bad side – I'm afraid,' said Melanie. 'Cliffie with you?'

'No.'

'You're an angel to come.'

'Now don't you two sit up yacketing all night,' Dr Phelps said. 'I'm going home, I expect to be home – God willing – so you'll know where to find me if there's any need but – I'm not anticipating any need.' He nodded and smiled, bright-eyed.

That could mean anything. 'I'll see the doctor down and come back,' Edith said.

The doctor let her precede him down the stairs, though the stairs were wide enough for two. The brown stair-rail gleamed with polish. At the bottom it curved to make a flat, coiled newel. Edith could remember when she had had to touch the stair-rail to descend, one step at a time. Bertha had stayed upstairs in the hall, out of tact, Edith was sure. The doctor swung his muffler round his neck.

'She didn't want to go to the hospital,' he said.

'Well – how bad are things?'

180

'I'm afraid –' the doctor whispered, 'she won't pull out of this one. I'm afraid that's too much to expect. Her heart's weakening, and there's just nothing to be done about that, not at her age. But at least she's not in pain and I want you to know that. There's a nurse coming tonight, probably by one a.m. Ellie Podnanski, a nice girl. It's best to have a nurse here.'

Edith felt light in the head, airless somehow. The doctor's words seemed far away, as in a dream. Edith took a deep breath. 'She's going to die – soon, do you mean?'

He lifted his eyebrows. 'It could be tonight. She'll just – fade away in her sleep, you know. It's the way she wants it. It isn't a bad way, in her own house, with people she loves. I think another of her nieces is on the way.'

Who, Edith wondered. The doctor was speaking respectfully, but Edith was aware that he must have said the same words many times before. These words, however, were about her dear aunt, her flesh and blood.

'She's had an injection for her heart. The oxygen arrangement isn't perfect, but it helps. Don't hesitate, Edith, to call me if you want to. I've known your aunt a long, long time.' He patted Edith's arm, and went out.

Edith put her foot on the first step of the stairs, gripped the bevel of the rail. Then she started to climb the steps.

Bertha stood in Melanie's room, looking tense and a little frightened. Melanie seemed to be asleep. At least her eyes were closed.

'Would you like something to eat, Miss Edith?'

'No, not now,' Edith said, though she knew it was after 11. 'I'll get something out of the kitchen later, if I feel like it.'

'You're looking a little pale. Bet you didn't have supper.'

Edith smiled. 'I'll be all right.'

'She's sleeping now,' said Bertha.

When Bertha left, taking an empty glass and spoon with her, Edith went near the bed and made sure her aunt was breathing. A metal tank was looped over the bedpost. How long would the tank last? Edith raised the plastic and felt her aunt's fingers, which seemed to her not warm enough, but an electric heater focused on the bed, and the room was quite warm. The right corner of Melanie's mouth tipped downward now, unlike her. Edith forced herself to believe Melanie was still breathing, because she wanted her to be breathing.

Then Edith sat down in a rocking chair with a high back, sat on a turquoise-colored cushion crocheted by Melanie years ago, and the next instant, it seemed, Bertha came in silently, bearing an amber glass on a tray.

'Thought maybe you'd like this, Miss Edith. It's made the way you like it.'

Edith took it gratefully. A stiff scotch with one ice cube, now nearly melted. Edith didn't like her drinks freezing cold. She lit a cigarette, found an ashtray, a blue-and-white faience souvenir that said 'Florence', then remembered that one shouldn't smoke anywhere near an oxygen tent, and put the cigarette out. Edith looked at the leatherbound old books at the bottom of a long bookcase, at the top shelves filled with her great-aunt's current favorites, newer books in jackets. The drink helped. She felt warmer, then tired, then hungry.

She took the glass down with her, paused in the hall, then moved toward the big white door with the brass knob. She put on the light switch at once – to the left of the door – as if to protect herself from a darkness that might be hostile. This was 'the library', also the sitting room, where Melanie brought everyone for drinks before meals, for tea, just for sitting and talking. It was book-lined, but more important was the fireplace, the big low table everyone could reach from armchairs, the old piano that Melanie played sometimes. The carpet was getting threadbare. The room looked lived in. Edith went out quickly, unable to face it longer, because it was as much her aunt as her aunt herself.

In the kitchen, Edith opened the refrigerator and her gaze at once focused on a huge ham, half cut away from the bone. She took the platter out and found a knife. Ham like the old days, baked in brown sugar, browned remnants of pineapple, soft sweet gravy below, an occasional clove. Edith cut slivers with an ancient kitchen knife. She found a half pan of cornbread, poured a glass of milk and banqueted, standing, for five minutes or so.

She heard a car, looked at her watch, and saw it was almost 1. Miss – Podnanski. Edith went to let her in.

'Evening. You're Mrs Cobb's niece?' the blond girl asked, smiling, removing her coat. She had blue eyes, and cheeks pink with health. She looked barely twenty.

Edith showed the girl up to Melanie's room. The nurse took Melanie's pulse, still pleasantly smiling. She had a gentle voice. A human machine, Edith thought, and yet she was delighted that the girl was here, because she knew what to do, what had to be done. Miss Podnanski declined Edith's offer to make coffee, or to bring a sandwich, because she had just eaten, she said.

'You can sleep now,' the nurse said.

So Edith did. Without a bath, after washing only her face and brushing her teeth, Edith fell into the big bed in the room where she had always stayed at her great-aunt's.

She was awakened by a gentle knock, her name being called – by the nurse, of course. Edith got out of bed, and put a sweater on over her pajama top. She was wanted on the telephone. In the dawn light, she could just see in the hall. The nearest telephone was in Melanie's room, where the nurse had answered. Edith saw by the clock that it was ten past 7.

'Hello, *Edith*!' said a woman's voice amid crackles. 'This is Penny. I'm ringing from Ankara ...'

Another of Melanie's nieces, Edith remembered, married to a Frenchman in diplomatic service. Edith answered sleepily but efficiently. Yes, Melanie had had a second stroke and the doctor had not much hope.

'I'm leaving tomorrow – late today your time, I think. My aunt has my address ... We had a wire, you see ...'

When she hung up, Edith turned from the telephone and to her surprise Melanie was looking at her, had turned her head. 'That was Penny,' Edith said.

'Oh. Penny. – Sit down, Edie.' Those were the last words Edith could recognize.

Aunt Melanie wanted to talk. The quiet, bursting-with-health nurse touched Melanie's shoulder through the plastic, gently told her not to try to speak. Melanie's lips moved a little, but no voice came. Her eyes were almost closed. It was the first time Edith had watched a death. She did not sit down. Neither did the nurse, and after a few moments, she turned to Edith and said, still gently:

'It's over now.' And she nodded.

Edith stood another moment, as if in a trance, while it seeped into her slowly that she and the strange nurse were the only two people in the room.

Edith drove back to Pennsylvania that afternoon. She had done all she could at Aunt Melanie's house, spoken with the doctor, the undertaker, the funeral home, sent a telegram to Penny, telephoned her mother to give her the news. Her own mother was not feeling well, she said, and Edith had felt a twinge of resentment that her mother had seemed more concerned about her own health than Melanie's death. But her mother had a weak heart, so Edith supposed that was terrifying. Her mother wasn't overweight and didn't smoke, yet she had a bad heart. She was going to see the doctor tomorrow. Her mother had already suffered one stroke, maybe three years ago. Edith had even telephoned Cliffie. Cliffie had said merely, 'Oh,' at the news. Just as mechanically, Edith had asked about George. Had Cliffie given him something to eat? Cliffie replied in the affirmative, in a vague way, and Edith knew old George would be all right, nothing more certain, but she imagined the worst in regard to the bedpan, Cliffie pretending not to hear George's requests, George trying to do things himself. Then as she drove on, Edith told herself to stop it. She was always imagining the worst – naturally, so she wouldn't be surprised, and might even find things better.

Such was not the case when she got home. First, to her alarm, Cliffie's Volks was gone. He was not allowed to drive until June. The front door was not locked. Nelson came downstairs and gave Edith an affectionate 'M-wah-h!' and pressed himself against her legs, tail erect.

'Cliffie?' Edith called, thinking he might be in his room, having lent somebody his car, but there was no answer.

Edith slipped out of boots and coat, and took her suitcase up the stairs, left it on the landing and walked toward George's door, which was half open but showed no light. 'George?' she called. Then she noticed the smell.

She knew, and without a pause plunged in. It was the carpets, the hall floor and *their* scatter rugs. Edith opened George's window, and continued to work with a will, with bucket, sponges, liquid rug cleaner. George was asleep through it all, snoring gently, despite the bumps of the plastic bucket as Edith set it down again and again. Next came the bedsheets. No, first the bedpan, just for a moment's relief, because it was so much easier to clean than what she had been cleaning. Even so, she had to leave it to soak in the bath-tub in five inches of water. Amazing! In not quite twenty-four hours! She had to awaken George in order to change the sheets, which she could now do in professional fashion, rolling the patient half way across the bed and so forth. It occurred to Edith that Cliffie had played an unmentionable prank – he probably had – and Edith was *not* going to mention it, because it would only give Cliffie satisfaction if she did. She could see his innocent, well-fed face, as he said, 'But I *didn't*!'

'Tanky, Edit,' George mumbled, toothless, and turned again to sleep.

Edith glanced at the codeine bottles, realized she didn't know what their level was supposed to be, and that she didn't particularly care. She unpacked her case, went down to check the fridge and found it adequate for tonight's dinner even if Cliffie returned, had a bath and put on blue corduroy slacks and a sweater, and started preparing dinner, activities which seemed a breeze compared to cleaning George's room. She poured herself a drink, and rang up Frances Quickman to thank her.

'Well, you sound quite cheerful, considering,' Frances said.

'Why not? What else can one do? I don't suppose you know where Cliffie is? He wasn't home when I got home, and his car is gone.'

185

'His car! No, I'm afraid I don't, Edie. And the two times I went in to feed Nelson, Cliffie wasn't in.'

Cliffie did come in a little after 8, when Edith was having her second drink and listening to Fauré's *Requiem* on the record player. Because of the music, she had not heard Cliffie's car, if he had come in the car. Cliffie was pink-eyed, carrying some tabloid-sized newspaper which he had twisted into a tight roll.

'Well, hello!' Edith said. 'You're driving the Volks?'

'No, I lent it to someone. He drove it – drove me back.'

Edith knew she would have to move the Volks to get her own car out of the driveway. Suddenly she was impatient with the music, because In Paradisum was coming up, and while alone she might have liked it, with Cliffie it became a sacrilege. She switched the set off and said, 'Aunt Melanie's funeral is tomorrow morning. I'm going to get a good night's sleep and start out early. Do you want to come?'

Cliffie stared at her solemnly, almost focusing. 'No.'

Edith had expected it. 'Thanks for your help with George.'

'That *shit-ass*!' Cliffie hurled the rolled newspaper at the sofa, whence Nelson leapt down, though it hadn't come near him.

Edith put the record away in its sleeve with deliberate care. Then she took the rest of her drink into the kitchen.

She grilled two lamb chops, not wanting more than one herself. If Cliffie wanted to join her, he could, as usual. But he didn't join her. Edith ate at the kitchen table, and before she was finished, the telephone rang. It was Brett, who said he had tried earlier to reach her. Edith told him why she had rung him from Delaware, not reaching him either, to tell him that Melanie had died. She had thought he might want to know, Edith said.

'I can't make it tomorrow, Edith. I'm awfully sorry about Melanie. But my God, she was getting on, wasn't she?'

Edith when she had hung up walked away from the telephone with a bitterness, a sourness, in her heart. Brett had sounded phony. The man she had loved, lived with, whose child she had borne, had sounded as phony as a stranger trying to say the right thing.

She suddenly felt clear as ice in the head. She looked around

186

her familiar hall and stairway, at the coathooks, with different eyes – or so it seemed. She detested it all, detested Cliffie, George, even the image of her own garden. She opened the front door and let the icy air surround her, enter her nostrils where it seemed to turn to crystal. She remembered her great-aunt's face in repose, and deliberately erased from it the twist that the stroke had caused. Melanie's spirit was still with her.

21

20 March 1969. The sculpting goes on apace. Have begun a head
of C. – not that he ever has time for posing. I have to work from
photographs (as with Aunt M.) & quick sketches on the rare
occasions when he or he & D. are here. J. is one year old almost, &
C. manages to ride her on his back, if he holds one of her little
hands. The great engineer, crawling around on his knees, falling on
his face sometimes, laughing.

In her diary, Brett's little daughter had no place, had not been
mentioned, and the thought of her in the Brunswick Corner
living room no longer made Edith giggle. Cliffie and Debbie
now had a pleasant house in the country near Princeton, a comfortable number of miles from Debbie's parents, and Edith
sometimes visited them there. Brett had vanished like a shadow
that never was, never had been. Just now Cliffie commuted
once a week to New York, where he stayed overnight in the
apartment he and Debbie maintained. For a period of two
months, Cliffie was in conference with other engineers of his
company, discussing current work in Kuwait where he had just
come from, or he was at home in New Jersey working on an
invention of his own which he did not talk about to anyone
(outside of his company), even Debbie. Edith continued:

I love being busy, love the sculpting. The Zylstras both admired
Melanie. Must have her cast in the new bronze-like material which
one can polish for a highlight here and there. Then she will adorn
our living room forever.

'Our,' she thought. Who was our? But she let it stand. She
added only:

I am happy.

She wrote this with a rather defiant firmness. There was a smile on her face as she stood up from her worktable.

The floor of the room was nearly covered now by a couple of plastic sheets meant to catch the clay droppings and plaster dust from castings. She had removed the two carpets, which were rolled up in the guestroom. In February, she had found what books she could on sculpture in the Trenton library, had bought others, and bought a book about Epstein's work, which she admired. Her head of Melanie, life-size, was a bit in the style of Epstein, but there was no harm in imitating the masters, she thought, since even great artists had, at first. When she had begun her sculpting, Gert Johnson had said, 'Oh! Let's start a class! A club!' but Edith had wriggled out of that. Edith didn't fancy a bunch of semi-idle women, starting with enthusiasm, dropping out in less than a month. Anyway, who among them was equipped to teach?

Besides the head of Melanie in Plasticine, Edith had done two abstracts, each about ten inches long, six inches broad and high. One looked like a crouching horned toad, though one could see many things in it – an interesting rock, peak-roof houses, the Alps, perhaps. The other abstract was 'Four-Legged Animal,' unidentifiable as any particular animal, lying heavily on its stomach, head turned slightly with an air of alertness. Gert liked this best.

Actually, Edith was unhappy, and there were moments when she realized this, as for instance in late January, not long after Melanie's death, when she had seen jonquils pushing upward again through the still frozen ground. Pushing upward for what? She had realized that another spring was coming (it was really coming on now in March), to be followed by another summer, blossoming red roses, dahlias and all that. For what? Nature had its own rounds, and now Edith felt out, left out. She realized, when she was thinking logically (or thought she was), that this was her own doing, that her thoughts made her more depressed and unhappy. Yet the thought (that she felt left out) had its own truth and reality, so what was so wrong in thinking it? She

189

couldn't just 'deny' it, like a Christian Scientist, and derive any solace from that.

So the sculpting, amateurish, blundering though she might be as yet, took her away from the dreariness. It was a second crutch, maybe, her diary being the first. One had to live somehow. The Thatchery passed the time, brought in some money, and logically was a healthy escape, because she had to work with people, had to look presentable, had to be pleasant and efficient. Sometimes Edith saw herself quite objectively, she felt, and surely that was all to the good. Sometimes she imagined seeing herself from a great height up in the sky, trudging along Main Street toward the Thatchery at ten to 2 p.m., one more little cog in the messy human-race machine, full of proper food and vitamins, destined to die one day like everybody else.

Edith went down to check the dinner in the oven. It was Sunday. She had a pot roast, surrounded now by carrots, onions and small potatoes, gently bubbling in brown juice. It could stand another twenty minutes, she thought. Cliffie was out in the garden, rather to Edith's surprise, strolling about with a squirelike air, hands in pockets. He wore the tweed jacket with loud blue stripes which Edith didn't care for, though to be nice she had paid him a compliment on it when he had bought it. She saw him teeter a little in his slow pace, knew he was a bit drunk, and congratulated herself for not caring at all. She went upstairs again to her workroom, which she had begun to call a studio.

Her head of Cliffie showed a pleasant but determined face, looking to Cliffie's left. The strong brows scowled a bit, the closed lips, however, turned up gently at the corners. The hair on the top of the head peaked as if blown by a wind, abundant hair, with sideburns, but not long in back, certainly not the way Cliffie usually wore his. Since two months or so, Cliffie looked like an unkempt Jesus, and of course he didn't even comb or brush his hair, discouraged no doubt by the tangles.

After gazing for a while at two photographs of Cliffie propped on a conveniently near bookcase, Edith made a slight addition of Plasticine to the right cheekbone. She loved the muscular neck, which she thought a success: it had dash, and was a constant inspiration to her to make the rest of the head as good. In the dark clay head, Cliffie was emerging as a young god, the way he was in her diary, conqueror of continents, master of rivers, fine husband and provider, begetter of the angelic little Josephine.

As usual, time flew, and twenty-five minutes had passed before she knew it. Edith went into the bathroom to scrub her hands, then down the stairs. She cut off the oven, then poured herself an iceless scotch and water. She went to the back door to call Cliffie, but he wasn't there.

'Cliffie?' She directed this toward his room.

'Yep?'

'Lunch in about one minute.'

Edith had already set the table. She added a jug of inexpensive Italian red wine to the table, then carved the meat. It looked delicious, and she was hungry. Cliffie came in and sat down in silence.

'Cliffie, would you mind turning that music off?' Edith had realized it was not the transistor now, but his record player, because 'Hey, Jude' was playing over and over.

'Why? That's a good song.' Cliffie looked at her with pinkish eyes, and shoved his fork in his food.

'I know it's a good song, but this must be the sixth time –'

'It is not the sixth time.'

Edith stifled her temper, because the alternative was to go in and turn it off herself, and she didn't want a fight.

'My record player, after all,' Cliffie added in the gentle tone he sometimes assumed when he was saying something defiant. 'Got to have some rights around here.'

Edith sighed and ate slowly. 'Did something happen this morning? – Yesterday?' Cliffie had come home late, maybe 3 or 4 a.m., and Edith assumed he had been at Mickey's bar, because he never went to anyone's house, as far as she knew.

'Not at all,' Cliffie said. 'Nothing happened. Why? – Why're you picking on me?'

Edith decided to ignore it, reminded herself she had weathered many a meal like this before, that there was no use spoiling Sunday dinner with a quarrel. Better to have an imaginary conversation with an imaginary person sitting at one of the places to right and left of her. And – to make her food go down better – she reminded herself that Cliffie had been badly shocked by Melanie's death, though he had hardly said a word. He had reacted with a frozen fear, a paralysis of tongue, maybe of feeling. Melanie had been a link with Cliffie's childhood. Perhaps, Edith thought and hoped, Cliffie was capable of more normal and deep emotion than she and Brett had ever given him credit for. Edith herself, though carrying on her duties, had been also in a kind of paralysis for at least a week after Melanie's burial. She could sympathize.

'You know, Cliffie,' Edith said, 'I miss Melanie very much – shall miss her. You mustn't let the fact – that she's dead get you down too much. We all have to face death. I wanted you to know it depresses me too – upsets me.'

Cliffie threw his knife down with a clatter that sounded loud enough to have broken the plate. 'I don't give a *damn* about the *dead*! What makes you think I do? What can anybody do about it, anyway? What's the use of *talking* about it?'

'I didn't mean to be talking about it, going on about it,' Edith said quickly.

'Then shut up about it!' Now Cliffie was on his feet. He seized his wine glass and drank it off, dribbling red wine down the front of his sweater. He grabbed a napkin and gave the sweater a single wipe, wiped his mouth, dropped the napkin, and went to his room. A second later, 'Hey, Jude' boomed up louder.

Edith took her plate into the kitchen, shut the door, and finished her meal. There were baked apples for dessert, keeping warm in their pan atop the stove, but she had no appetite for anything more. For God's sake, she had wanted only to try to *join* him in whatever was troubling him, to make him feel he wasn't alone in feeling troubled, or hopeless sometimes, or discouraged. And his eyes had flashed red, it seemed to her.

She washed up halfway, so the kitchen wouldn't look like

too much to do when she faced it again. There was, of course, George's meal to be served. George was eating later, and less, but Edith had not as yet failed to give him his three meals plus, usually, tea. Edith prepared a tray, an attractive hot plate of food, a half glass of wine – surely good for him – and took it up.

She now had the old radio in her workroom, because she spent so much time there since the sculpting. She switched on to an afternoon concert. Beethoven's fourth piano concerto, she recognized, somewhere in the first movement. That was splendid. She picked up a wooden tool shaped like a spoon with a pointed tip. With this she pressed a deeper crease under the lower lids, finished them off with an upward sweep. Excellent! That was all right, and she wasn't going to touch the eyes again. She felt pleased. And now she wanted the mouth less wide, with the same puzzled, amused expression.

Edith went to work, lit a cigarette, continued. She kept a big metal ashtray on the floor now.

Into the last movement, into the full orchestra which sounded like the finale of a symphony, came a discordant roar that Edith first supposed was a car horn. But it hadn't come from the street side. She paused with the wooden instrument still held high. It had come from behind her. Cliffie was in George's room, shouting something at him, of course. Suddenly she lost the train of the music, lost pleasure in following it.

What was happening now? Curiosity made her put down the wooden thing on the square platform of the armature, go to the door and look into the hall.

Now Cliffie's tones sounded soothing. Cliffie even laughed. Then there was silence. Edith advanced farther. She could see Cliffie through the partly open door, bending over George, holding something for him.

'Ha! There we go!' Cliffie said.

Another step, and a floorboard creaked under Edith's foot.

At once, George's door went briskly shut with a familiar slam of latch. Cliffie had kicked it with his foot, Edith was sure. What was he doing?

Edith had an impulse to call out 'Cliffie!' and didn't. Maybe he was arranging the tray to bring it down, making George drain the last of the wine, but she knew Cliffie wasn't. Cliffie never did anything constructive. That was an axiom, wasn't it?

To hell with him! To hell with them both!

Edith pivoted round, faced her own room again where Beethoven played on, then turned once more to look at George's closed door. If she was so curious, she told herself, she could go and look through the keyhole. Better yet, knock once and open the door.

She didn't want to open the door. She wanted to keep standing there, looking, not even trying to listen. The music would have kept out all but quite loud sounds, anyway.

Was Cliffie just wandering about in there, whistling, tippling from a bottle of codeine? Making insulting remarks, inaudible to old George?

But Edith was imagining Cliffie bent over George with a glass of something, Cliffie grinning and ghoul-faced, laughing a little.

'A-ha! – Ha-ha!' That was Cliffie. His stage laugh, a burlesque of triumph, but with no mirth.

Edith faced her room again and walked toward it, and at that instant the brilliant music died, there were a few seconds of stunned silence from the audience, then applause began, gathered power, roared to a climax that peppered off the walls as she entered her room and closed the door. 'Bravo!' a voice from the audience cried. 'Ey!' 'Hey!' Thousands of hands proclaimed their delight. 'Bravo-o-o!'

Edith picked up the same wooden tool, lifted it to a level of the clay brow, then laid it down again. A voice had begun to announce a Schubert something-or-other. She seized the wooden stick and went to work. After a few seconds, she became absorbed, then lost. It was going to be a good session on the head. That was something. And she suddenly remembered that she was invited to the Quickmans' for a drink at 6:30. That was nice to look forward to.

Later, Edith didn't know how much later, she heard the faint boom of the front door closing. She assumed it was Cliffie going out or coming in. Her radio began to play pop music, and Edith turned it off, bent and shook the clay particles into a heap on the plastic sheet, and swept them up. She straightened her back and stretched, looked at the head in profile now, and thought it not bad. And what would Gert say? Gert was a severe critic. *Rotten* and *Kitsch* were Gert's favorite words for some of the stuff in local gift shops, *sick-making* and *phony* for the imitation peasant pottery and machine-made wooden objects.

George should be having his tea, Edith thought. In fact it was past tea time, already nearly 6. Edith took a leisurely bath, chose a madras wrap-around skirt she had not worn for months or maybe years, a white ruffled blouse, black patent leather sandals with medium heels. After all, it was only next door she was going. And the Quickmans were presenting another 'nice man', Edith remembered, and smiled a little. It wasn't for the first time. Eligible bachelors of a certain age. So far Edith had not been swept off her feet (in fact, had any of the men?), but she appreciated the Quickmans' thoughtfulness, or supposed she ought to.

'And what will you have, Admiral – Nelson?' Edith said to the cat who had followed her down. She was finishing the dishes in the kitchen, because she had five minutes to spare.

Cliffie was out, evidently. The light was off in his room, his transistor silent. She gave Nelson only a couple of cat biscuits, because he was going to want a meal when she ate later.

The Quickmans' male guest was called Lawrence Hodgeson or Hodson, Edith was not sure, a tall slender man with black hair, graying at the temples, a Philadelphia accountant. Ben and Frances had a fire going.

'You're looking awfully well tonight,' Frances said to Edith. 'Had a good day?'

'Not particularly. Well – *yes*, I suppose so. A little sculpting this afternoon. And there was a wonderful concert on the radio. Did you happen to hear it?'

Ben and Frances were not interested in the concert, but they both talked about her sculpting.

'When are you giving us a show?' Ben asked.

'I think Ben wants his portrait,' Frances said, 'or whatever you call it. His *bust*!'

Laughter.

Edith didn't mind their remarks on her new pastime.

'Cliffie didn't want to come?' Frances asked.

'I think he's out for a walk or something,' Edith said. 'I *think* he said thank you for asking him, but I wouldn't swear to it.'

Then Edith developed a chill. She felt it coming on, and sat nearer the fireplace. Lawrence was asking her if she came to Philadelphia very often, and the Quickmans were telling her about his summer house or lodge by a lake, where Ben was looking forward to fishing in the summer. Edith's teeth chattered. Frances brought a coat sweater.

'I don't know what's the matter. It isn't cold,' Edith said. She felt stupid in the white blouse, which had long sleeves but was thin. Just because she had wanted to look nice! Why? 'Silly of me to dress as if it was summer. My fault.'

'That's it, put the sweater on,' Ben said.

'We're hoping you'll stay for dinner, Edie. Can you? If we see Cliffie come in, we'll ask him too.'

'Oh, thank you, Fran, but I'd better get back. I haven't – '
She stopped, about to mention George, that she had to give him his supper.

They gave Edith a second drink. The Quickmans' old red setter lay sleeping close to the fire near Edith's feet, the picture of peace and security.

'Perhaps next time the Quickmans come to Philly, you'll come too,' Lawrence said to her. 'I happen to be Frances' and Ben's accountants – since a long time.'

The rest was a little hazy to Edith. She remembered Frances – kind old Fran with her plump, freckled face – looking at her in a concerned way as they said good-bye at the door. They were all really disappointed that she was not staying for dinner.

Edith saw a light in the front hall as she approached the door. She went in and called, 'Cliffie?'

'Yep!' His voice came from the living room.

196

Cliffie was watching television, with a glass of something.

'The Quickmans asked about you. Wanted you to come over.'

'I didn't know anything about it.'

It was true she hadn't mentioned it, because Cliffie usually didn't want to visit the Quickmans. 'It's after eight. Want something to eat or have you had something?'

His bearded face turned, showed itself round the wing of the armchair. 'I can get something later. I'm watching this.'

'I'd better take something up for George.'

'He doesn't want anything,' Cliffie said at once, looking round at her again.

'He doesn't? You asked him?'

'Yep. I asked him.' And Cliffie faced the screen again.

Edith went to the kitchen via the hall. Nelson at least would want something. Nelson joined her. She talked to him, lit the fire under the kettle, cut some heart slices into small pieces, and poured hot water over them to take the chill off. Then she poured off the water and set the plate on Nelson's plastic dining mat. Nelson set to with guzzling noises. He had always eaten in such a manner, and often Cliffie said, 'Snortin' good, eh Nelse?'

For herself Edith assembled a sliver of beef, some lettuce and shredded carrot, then realized she was not hungry. She put the plate in the fridge. She decided to polish the silver, the tea set also, Melanie's gift of long ago. The cleaning woman Margaret was not enthusiastic about doing the silver or waxing or hadn't the time, so often Edith did these things herself.

Ten o'clock.

It wasn't 10 yet, so why was she thinking of 10? She realized it was because she thought she must look in on George by 10. And why not now? She didn't want to. She was afraid to. Or was that it? Did she want to give whatever Cliffie had given him time to work? Or had Cliffie given George anything, for that matter? Of course he had. She had seen it, hadn't she? Not exactly. Not really, not closely. Could have been plain water. Why should she suspect anything? No, she wasn't going to mention that Cliffie had given George too much codeine on

197

other occasions, maybe two occasions. No. She and Cliffie were together. Yes. No. *That* was an odd sensation, if there ever was one, feeling that she and Cliffie were together.

The silver gleamed. She saw her face in the teapot, elongated, egg-shaped. She replaced the teaset on the dining room sideboard.

Cliffie came strolling in, carrying his empty glass, the other hand in his pocket. 'You're looking very elegant tonight.'

'Felt like wearing a long skirt.'

'What's the occasion?' Cliffie hiccuped in the middle of the question. He was en route to the fridge for a beer.

Edith continued with the silver, but not all of it, just the big ladle and spoon, the candlesticks. She was too tired to tackle the knives and forks. Cliffie was back in the living room.

She went upstairs. It was not quite 10. George's room was dark, the door partly open, and she walked toward it, not pausing, not listening as she almost always did for snores. 'George?' she called through the door. Then she stepped in. 'George.' She turned the gooseneck light toward her and pressed the button that lit it.

George lay on his back, mouth slightly open, pale flesh sagging under his cheekbones. There was no sound of snoring.

'*George!*' she called and touched his shoulder.

He was breathing. She thought so. But she didn't hear anything, didn't see any movement of his chest. She looked around, thinking of a mirror to hold to his nose, and found her eyes fastened on the bottles on the medicine chest – what she now called the medicine chest, the low chest of drawers. There were fewer bottles there than usual, and she saw why: they were all right beside her, by the gooseneck lamp. Tincture of codeine, the aspirins, the bottles of different kinds of sleeping pills, one type yellow, one mauve. The bottles were nearly empty. One bottle was empty.

Edith took a gasping breath, because she hadn't breathed for nearly a minute.

She made herself touch George's shoulder, and she shook it. 'George!' At least his body felt warm. '*George!*' she yelled closer to his ear. Then she held her finger under his narrow nostrils. Did she feel some warmth or didn't she? She could not bring herself to feel for a heartbeat, was revolted by the thought of pressing his wrist. His arm lay outside the bed-covers. She was afraid to, she knew.

She wanted to leave the room. She hesitated about the light, left it on, and went into the bathroom to wash her hands. Six, seven hours, she thought, since Cliffie had given him all the stuff. She ought to speak to Cliffie. She ought to phone the doctor. She was delaying. Deliberately, she felt. On the other hand, what if she was imagining all this? What if the bottles were supposed to be that empty now? Why get so excited about it?

Alarmist.

Strangely, she felt calm for the next minutes, the next many minutes. In her workroom, she changed from the long skirt into the old blue corduroys and a sweater, straightened her desk which held items for the *Bugle* that people had sent in, stuff to be turned into copy and posted to Gert, who got it to Trenton.

What was she going to say to Cliffie? How was she going to start?

Edith switched on her radio. It was jazz music and she didn't care. The head of Melanie, still in dark gray plasticine, gazed somewhat downward with a haughty, yet kindly amusement. Tonight Cliffie's clay face looked positively merry, despite the firm brows.

What was she going to say to Cliffie?

Put it off till tomorrow. Then she thought of going to bed in an hour or so, trying to sleep, lying there. That would not be possible.

Five past 11. Edith went again to George's room. He lay as before. Edith started to call his name, and couldn't. She felt his shoulder, again shook it, now with hostility. Then at once she went out and down the stairs. George had felt stiff, she thought. Cool? She wasn't sure about that. 'Cliffie?' she said, entering the living room. The television was on, but he was not there. She had the feeling Cliffie had a second before fled to his room.

She went into the dining room and across the hall. He was in his room. 'Cliffie?'

'Yep?' Pink-eyed, on his feet.

'Well.' Edith was suddenly breathless.

'Well?'

'You've done it again. Yes?'

'Done *what* again?'

Edith was breathing in a short, quick way. 'I think I'd better call the doctor, don't you?'

'Doctor? Why?' Cliffie looked at her with a stupid, animal-like defiance. 'What's the matter with him?' Cliffie swayed.

Edith turned and went to the living room. She definitely could use a drink, then at once thought she should hang on without it, then at once decided a drink was a good idea. Steadying. She poured a scotch straight, sipped half of it, while concluding ponderously that to telephone the doctor was the right and proper thing to do. She went to the telephone with the rest of her drink and dialed the number.

A strange female voice answered. 'Oh, I'm his daughter. Daddy's at a dinner in Flemington. Won't be home till midnight anyway. Is it urgent?'

'Well – yes. Could I reach him in Flemington?'

The daughter – whom Edith now recalled having met once – produced the number and Edith scribbled it down. Edith called the number. It took several minutes, while she held on. It was a restaurant. Finally Dr Carstairs came on.

'Hello, this is Edith Howland. I'm *sorry* to bother you.'

'Yes? It's –'

'George. He – he seems to be in a coma. I don't know. Could you come? Have a look?'

The doctor promised to come within half an hour, forty-five minutes at most.

Edith had a brief sense of security. She left her glass in the living room and went to Cliffie's room again, knocked quickly. Cliffie was on his back on the bed, transistor on his chest.

'Cliffie, Dr Carstairs is coming. You'd better sober up or not make an appearance at all tonight.'

'Why should I make an appearance tonight? I certainly don't want to make an appearance tonight.'

'Then put your light out – when he comes.'

'What's it got to do with *me*?' Cliffie shouted.

Edith remembered Cliffie's lying from the time he could speak. She couldn't reply. And somehow, now, she admired his falseness. It was a kind of strength. She stated the unnecessary: 'You gave him a lot of pills and God knows what else.'

'Maybe he took 'em himself,' Cliffie replied with a shrug, barely glancing at his mother.

22

Cliffie was even drunker than he looked. He knew that, and gave himself credit for doing all right so far, though he warned himself that he had better be careful. When his mother left his room, Cliffie went into the kitchen and made a cup of instant coffee, put sugar and cream in it and took it into his room.

The old bastard is dead upstairs, Cliffie thought. That was what all the fuss was about, why the doctor had to come – to make it official. Cliffie looked wide-eyed, yet directly, at his room walls, comforting himself with the familiar patches of bright red, yellow, blue – the sweaters of motorcycle racers, football players, pin-up girls with nothing on but a yellow strip, maybe a scarf, which they languidly held across their thighs. Boobies here and there did not hold his eyes just now. Yes, things seemed different with a corpse upstairs. Cliffie hoped to hell they'd get him out of the house tonight.

Cliffie wanted to wash, but didn't want to go to the bathroom upstairs next door to George's room. He washed at the kitchen sink, rubbed his face with a kitchen towel, which he tossed back on the radiator. Then he put on pajamas and his old robe, which he thought natural to be wearing after midnight.

His mother's voice, high-pitched now, extra pleasant, alerted Cliffie to the fact that Dr Carstairs had arrived. Cliffie at once put his bottle back in the closet, and went slowly down the hall. He didn't want to miss a word of this.

His mother was talking about 'a coma.'

And Dr Carstairs was in evening clothes! Black tie, anyway. Cliffie at once saw that the doctor was feeling no pain, and was smiling gaily, saying something about a friend's birthday party.

'Evening, Cliffie,' said the doctor.

'Evening, doctor,' Cliffie replied.

'Now we'll just see,' said the doctor, going up the stairs first.

Edith followed, then Cliffie. Cliffie waited in the hall outside, because his mother, by the bedside table, rather blocked his entry.

'Oh-h. Um-m,' said Dr Carstairs, and to Edith's murmured question, 'Yes, afraid so, yes.'

Cliffie saw the doctor pick up a tincture of codeine bottle – empty – from the little table.

'... nearly all gone,' the doctor mumbled. 'Yes, I can see that.'

'I was out,' Edith said, 'out for drinks. – Rather, I was working in my room there this afternoon. I did notice he was asleep at four or five, I think, but there was nothing unusual about that.'

'No,' said the doctor, picking up an aspirin bottle now, in which, Cliffie recalled clearly, one aspirin rattled around.

Edith raised her eyes slowly to Cliffie's eyes.

Cliffie looked at her steadily, wondering if she was thinking what he was, that the doctor by touching the bottles was taking off his own fingerprints or at least messing them up? *Fine*, Cliffie thought.

The doctor mumbled on. 'God knows he was getting on ... a bit fuzzy in the head, too.'

Then they were both talking at the same time about a funeral home, an undertaker, Brett, and his mother was saying shouldn't she phone him, and Carstairs was replying soothingly. Then Carstairs said it was unusual to phone something-or-other so late, but he would do it, because he knew the people there very well. At the funeral home.

Cliffie repressed his amusement: old Carstairs naturally knew the people at the funeral home very well, because he had so many dead patients! Ha-ha!

'... might've wanted to do it himself, after all,' Carstairs was saying.

Did that mean old George might have wanted to kill himself? It sounded like it.

And as Dr Carstairs, behind his mother, faced Cliffie to come out of the room, Cliffie saw a faint smile on his face – even as the doctor looked at him – that looked really like relief. *Relief.* Cliffie was sure of it. Cliffie stepped back smartly by the stairs to let them go first. In fact, they went on as if they hadn't seen him. Cliffie straightened and felt like hurling a curse at George's room, where the light was still on. *Out, damned corpse! Out! Out of the house!* Cliffie took one big stride toward the room and looked in with swift boldness.

The sheet was over the face.

- Cliffie turned and went down the stairs. Carstairs was on the telephone. Cliffie didn't try to listen, but went on to the kitchen where his mother was making fresh coffee. Cliffie felt awkward. 'He's really *dead?*'

'What did you *think?*' Edith frowned at him.

Cliffie looked away.

'Why don't you go to bed?'

'Why should I?' Cliffie replied, hands in his robe pockets. He saw his mother glance sideways at him – what did that mean? – before she prepared a tray with saucers and cups.

Dr Carstairs came back and reported that he had reached the person he wanted, and that someone should come within twenty minutes. Something more about Brett. Such banalities, Cliffie thought. Keep the conversational ball rolling, yackety-yack! Cliffie alternately stood still, or prowled about the kitchen. Nobody paid the least attention to him.

'I *will,*' his mother said, 'I *will,*' as if she were taking the marriage vows.

'Maybe the old boy wanted to die after all.' The doctor, leaning against a kitchen cupboard, lifted the coffee cup to his lips.

Then they were talking about Melanie. Corpses, corpses. Age. But his mother looked happier just talking about Melanie, even though she was dead.

'And what've you been doing with yourself lately, Cliffie?' the doctor asked, smiling at Cliffie.

Cliffie had never liked his smile. Carstairs was not a genuinely smiling type. Just then the grate of a handbrake came clearly, and that saved Cliffie from answering.

A long black car had arrived in the driveway, or at the beginning of the driveway, because the Ford and the Volks were there. Now Cliffie stayed out of the way in the half dark living room. Lots of feet and voices went up the stairs, then after about three minutes there was much shuffling down, mumbled orders. *Out*, damned corpse! Now it was really *out*! Cliffie swaggered to the bar cart and poured a straight scotch into his now empty coffee cup. This was worth a drink, if anything ever had been. He had plenty of time to drink it, while his mother bade adieu to the doctor, who was taking off in his own car. Cliffie sighed deeply.

When his mother came back, she hesitated a moment in the hall, not glancing into the living room even, then went up the stairs. Cliffie finished his cup and climbed the stairs also.

His mother was in George's room, rather slowly picking up a glass, putting a spoon in it, picking up a wadded handkerchief from the floor. 'Cliffie, could you get a tray?' she said quickly. 'Take this down with you.'

Cliffie grabbed the two glasses with spoons in them and ran down willingly. He returned with two trays. Already his mother had stripped the bed and was folding sheets and blankets, and the wastebasket was full of all kinds of débris. She had opened a window. Cliffie descended with the wastebasket plus dirty sheets and pillow-cases under his arms. He threw the dirty linen on the hall floor, wanting to get it all as near the front door as possible. Empty bottles clattered into the plastic garbage bin outside the back door. He carried the empty wastebasket back upstairs. His mother had dragged out George's suitcase, and Cliffie would have gladly flung George's clothes and stuff into it, but suddenly his mother had stopped, started to put her hands over her face, but didn't quite touch her face.

'I've really got to call Brett,' she said, and went out and down the stairs.

Frances Quickman was just opening the front door, knocking at the same time. 'Edith! You're all right? I looked out the window and saw that ambulance or something – We were worried. It's George, I suppose.'

Edith nodded. 'He's dead. Died in his sleep, it seems.'

Cliffie heard this as he came slowly down the stairs.

'Oh, dear!' said Frances. 'What a shock for you! – But maybe it's for the best, you know? If he went so peacefully.'

'I was about to phone Brett. I ought to,' Edith said. 'Don't you –'

'Oh, Edith, I'll push off – unless I can do anything.' Frances clutched a raincoat about her and had a flashlight in one hand. She wore bedroom slippers.

'I can't think what. Thank you, anyway, Fran.'

'I'm in all day tomorrow – mostly – if I can do anything, dear. Don't hesitate. – Hello, Cliffie.'

'Hello,' Cliffie replied.

Frances left, and Edith went to the telephone without even a glance at Cliffie. She dialed Brett's apartment number. There was no answer. Edith tried it again, in case she had made a mistake. Odd for them to be out so late with a six-months-old baby (otherwise a babysitter would have answered), and Edith thought they might all be at Carol's parents' house near Philadelphia for the weekend, a number she could easily get from information, but she didn't want to telephone Carol's parents' house. She would try Brett's office tomorrow morning.

'Dad's not in?' Cliffie asked.

Sometimes Cliffie called him dad, sometimes Brett. 'No. I'll try tomorrow morning. Shouldn't you go to bed?'

'No. I'll help you clean some more – upstairs.' Cliffie felt cheerful suddenly, but he added with his usual shrug, 'Why not?' as if it were as good a thing to be doing at 2 a.m. as anything else.

Before another half hour had passed, Edith had sponged the chest of drawers and the bedtable with warm water and washing-up suds, and vacuumed the carpet and floor. George's suitcases (two) had been packed with all his clothes except an ancient, limp raincoat which now lay folded on the hall floor beside the suitcases, ready to be thrown out. She and Cliffie moved the bed across the room, and now it stood at a different angle in a corner, with a window near its head and another left of its foot. Edith wanted the pictures rearranged too, but did not want to embark on that tonight.

'Come on now, that's enough,' she said finally, smiling a little. She had enjoyed the physical effort. But even Nelson had grown tired of watching them and departed.

'Do you know where they took him?' Cliffie asked, dustrag in hand. He had been wiping out the bedtable drawer, and the waste-basket was again full of junk.

Edith realized she didn't, exactly. 'A funeral home, of course. In Doylestown. Begins with a C. I'll find out from Carstairs tomorrow.'

The same morning, Edith was up by 7, feeling not in the least tired, and with her first cup of coffee went to the telephone to try to get Brett before he took off for work.

Carol answered.

'Hello, this is Edith. I'm sorry to be phoning so early, but there's something important I have to say to Brett.'

'Brett's not here just now. You see, I – Brett dropped me and the baby at the house just a few minutes ago and went on in the car to Long Island.'

'Oh? Where in Long Island? Can I reach him?'

'It's an editors' conference in Locust Valley, I *think*. International editors. I'd have to get the exact place – the phone number, I mean, from Brett's secretary. Can I give him a message?' Carol sounded most willing.

'Yes, you can. It's that his uncle George died last night – apparently in his sleep. I tried to reach Brett last night around one a.m.'

'Oh, my goodness! – I'll certainly try to reach him, Edith! We were at my parents' last night.'

Edith felt impatient, a bit silly, after they had hung up. But for God's sake she was trying to do the right thing. She poured a second cup of coffee, and telephoned Carstairs. He told her that the Doylestown funeral home was called Crighton.

'I hope to be in touch with Brett by noon or before. He'll probably have his own ideas about how things should be done.' But would he? She could also imagine Brett saying, 'Doesn't matter much now, does it?' Edith added with more conviction, 'Surely the funeral place knows what to do. I know Brett will want to come to the funeral, anyway.'

'Oh, I'm sure,' said Dr Carstairs.

By 11 that morning, Edith had not heard from Brett. She had intended to go to the supermarket that morning, so she did, in Lambertville, where the supermarket was better than that of Brunswick Corner. She bought all the usuals, including toilet paper. What a relief, she thought, not to be concerned with extra Kleenexes, sleeping pills, laxatives, boxes of cotton. It made her feel healthier herself.

Before she had unpacked the two cartons and the paper bags, the Crighton Funeral Home telephoned. They asked if she could come that afternoon to make a choice of casket?

'And there are a few other details that should be attended to,' said the gentle female voice.

'Yes. I'm hoping my husband – How late are you open to-day?'

'Oh, we're open day and night, madam. There's always some-one here.'

Brett rang at half past noon. 'Yes, Carol told me,' he said, interrupting Edith. 'Look, I'm phoning at the start of the pre-lunch cocktails here, which is the only time I'll have till – till at least five, the way things look. Conferences this after-noon –'

'The funeral home told me they're open day and night.' Like death, Edith thought. She had spoken rather coolly. 'So why don't you come any time, Brett? The funeral home – wants the casket chosen, you know, things like that.'

'Yes. At least I've got the car with me. What caused it, do you think?'

'Well – after all, Brett, he was eighty-seven, wasn't he?'

By the time they had hung up, Brett had said he should get to Brunswick Corner by 7:30 p.m. with any luck, and they could go to the funeral home in Doylestown. *They* could go. She really didn't care if Brett went by himself.

Cliffie was still asleep, but surfaced at half past 1, by which time Edith had had a bite of lunch and was about to take off for the Thatchery. Cliffie poured his usual coffee, with nothing else, to wake up on. His shoulders looked broad and sturdy, if a·bit round under a threadbare Chinese silk robe with worn out black satin lapels. Cliffie had dug the robe out from some recess in his closet, and was addicted to it lately.

'Your father rang up,' she said. 'He's coming around seven-thirty. We have to go to that funeral home in Doylestown, but you don't have to come if you don't feel like it.'

By now Cliffie was munching stale cake, dropping crumbs on the table mat. 'I don't think I want to go. Gosh – corpses, I suppose! *Corpses* all over the place? I wonder what it smells like! But I can imagine – I'm sure!'

He was nervous. Better today if he did have some drinks, Edith thought, a point about which she did not have to remind him. And she was not going to bother saying to him, as if she were instructing a child, that funeral homes displayed their corpses only to the nearest of kin, and then when the corpses were – She arrested her thoughts deliberately, yet with a feeling that today somehow signified great progress.

'Loads of food, Cliffie. I went to the supermarket. I'm off now. You going to be in this evening when Brett comes?'

'I dunno. I suppose so.'

She felt he would be.

Edith managed to tidy up her portion of the counters at the Thatchery, and to leave by 7:05. No one, today, had inquired how George was doing, though half the time one of the staff or customers did. She walked homeward, thinking that if Brett had arrived early, he probably wouldn't have a key, and Cliffie might be out.

Brett had not arrived. Edith looked up the Crighton Funeral Home to find out what street it was on. Then she washed her face, and got herself pulled together – a skirt with a white sweater, a scarf, and by then she heard Brett's step on the porch, a knock. Edith went down the stairs. The door was not locked, and Brett was coming in. He looked pale, thinner, then Edith remembered he had had a long day plus the drive from New York.

'Hello, Brett!'

'Hello. Well – what news, eh? What news!'

Edith tried to look calmer than she felt. Was Cliffie in? She hadn't looked. 'It had to come some time, Brett.'

Brett said yes to the offer of a drink, and sat down at the right end of the sofa, his old favorite place. He wore a brown tweed suit that Edith had not seen before. 'Died in his sleep,' Brett said after his first sip.

'Yes. I didn't know it till – Cliffie said he spoke with George around seven Sunday, and George didn't want any dinner. We'd had a big late Sunday lunch – you know. So I didn't know anything was wrong till around eleven.'

'Wrong?'

'I couldn't wake him up! So I rang the doctor. Carstairs was at a dinner in Flemington, so it was after midnight when he got here.'

Brett frowned, and the dry skin of his face looked more wrinkled. 'But what did Carstairs say he died *of?*'

Edith heard a creak of floorboard in the hall, then Cliffie appeared in the doorway and walked in.

'Hello, dad!' Cliffie half extended a hand and withdrew it, a gesture that suggested an awkward wave.

'Hello, Cliffe. And how are you?'

'All right, thanks.' Cliffie turned and went to the bar cart, hauled up the scotch and unscrewed its top.

'I suppose it was a kind of heart failure,' Edith said to Brett.

'Cheers, dad!' Cliffie lifted his glass. He felt well, rested, dressed presentably, slightly oiled already but not too. His father looked older and smaller than Cliffie remembered. Cliffie was not afraid of him.

Brett had squirmed with impatience at Cliffie's toast. He blinked at Edith, and rubbed his eyes as if they hurt. 'All these years. I know what a burden he was. A pain in the neck to you. I appreciate that fact.'

210

Cliffie turned toward the bottles again to hide his smile from his father.

'I'd like to hear from Carstairs,' Brett went on, 'just what the cause of death was.'

'You can ask him,' Edith said. 'I must say Carstairs didn't seem terribly surprised.'

Brett finished his glass, uncrossed his legs and stood up. 'I think I will try to get Carstairs. Now. Might be important. Have you got his number handy, Edith? I've forgotten it, if I ever knew it.'

Carstairs' number was on the well-worn top page of a writing pad by the telephone, and Edith pointed it out to Brett. Edith went back ino the living room. Cliffie was reasonably sober, but wearing the ghastly blue plaid jacket. He was in good spirits, beaming with confidence. Edith avoided looking at him, though she felt him watching her.

Brett had succeeded in getting Carstairs.

'Oh ... You're sure of that? ... Oh ... No, she didn't ... I see.' Long, long pause now. 'Yes. I understand. But shouldn't there be an autopsy then? ... No – but you didn't *order* an autopsy?'

Edith took a cigarette and moved closer to the garden window, where she could hear less well, and she tried not to hear. She turned and said to Cliffie, 'You still don't want to come with us?'

'No.' Surrounded by beard, Cliffie's well-shaped, rosy lips smiled, and his eyes were full of amusement. He swirled his glass and drank.

Brett came back and gave an exasperated sigh familiar to Edith. 'Carstairs didn't even order an autopsy. Says he thinks George might've given himself an overdose. What do you think? Doesn't sound like George – after all these years.'

'I really don't know.' Edith said it flatly, and in an honest tone – she realized. She wasn't making an effort.

'Carstairs says there were some bottles practically empty right by his – on the bedside table there.'

'I know. But quite frankly I wasn't keeping track of how much was in the bottles.'

'But who was dosing him? Was he dosing himself?'

211

'No, sometimes I did. I'd ask him if he'd had his vitamins or whatever. The stuff was there on his bedside table. He took his sleeping pills himself – according to need.' Did Brett think she was running a hospital? Edith detested talking about it. She really preferred Cliffie's what-the-hell smirk – so close to her on her left now. 'Sometimes I'd offer him his pills or that codeine syrup, and he'd say he'd already taken it.'

'I think, if it's not too late – For the sake of the insurance I – What's the name of that funeral home?'

Edith went to the directory, looked it up and pointed out to Brett the Crighton Funeral Home entry. Brett whipped out his glasses, then dialed. Edith went back into the living room.

'F'gosh sake,' Cliffie murmured, still standing near the bar cart. 'An old guy like that. Whether he took an overdose –' Cliffie was whispering.

'I agree!' Edith said.

Cliffie smiled.

Brett's voice rose from the hall. 'Because I'm not even sure that's *legal* under the circumstances. I would think also a *coroner* – Oh, the *doctor's* job!'

Edith heard him spluttering, trying to wind up in a civil manner, then he banged the telephone down.

Brett came in, saying, 'Idiots have already – He's already embalmed. Let's go, Edith.'

23

It was after 11 p.m. before Edith and Brett returned to the house. They had had dinner at the Cartwheel Inn, a roadside bar and restaurant. Cliffie was out, as Edith had expected. Brett wanted to talk with him. Brett had ordered a cremation, which he said was in accordance with George's wishes. He had asked to see George, but the attendant – a young footballer-type with crew-cut, wearing a clean white smock – had told Brett that the (what had he called it?) was not yet ready for viewing, but would be by tomorrow at 9 a.m. Brett had signed several papers, and Edith had waited on a polished wooden bench in the marble lobby, almost out of hearing of all this. Brett had sat with the young man at a desk in a far corner.

Brett was staying the night.

'You look exhausted, you *shouldn't* drive back,' Edith had said, meaning it, because even after eating dinner, Brett was gray in the face.

Now here they were, and Edith wondered where he should sleep? The guestroom, of course. Its bed was made up. Edith found some pajamas in Cliffie's room, clean but unironed because she didn't bother any more, since Cliffie didn't care. Brett liked to sleep in pajamas. Brett telephoned Carol. Then he came upstairs where Edith was turning down the bed in the guestroom.

'I've got to leave before seven tomorrow,' Brett said. 'I'd like to talk with Cliffie.' This for the second time. 'You think he's going to stay out all night? Or – I'll wake him up early. What else?' Brett looked asleep on his feet.

'I really don't know what he's doing.' Edith walked toward the door, having put the bedside lamp on for Brett.

'Can I see George's room?' Brett was already going in, flicking on the main light to the left of the door. 'So! Already – changed around.'

Edith said nothing. She could have said, 'I felt like it,' or 'After all, it was depressing,' but she felt like saying nothing.

Brett was walking about in the room, hands in his trousers pockets. 'And all those – medicines?'

'I think I threw them all out. Who wants codeine in the house?'

Brett nodded briefly, absently. 'You don't think maybe Cliffie gave him an overdose. Didn't you say –'

'Cliffie paid hardly *any* attention to George, I assure you, Brett. Never helped me – frankly.'

'Didn't you say Cliffie found out around seven that George didn't want any dinner?'

'Yes. True.' Edith went into her workroom to get a cigarette. There was usually an opened pack on her table, and one was there now.

'M-waa-ow,' Nelson said, puzzled. He lay on the curved bench seat, near the radiator.

'Oh! Sculpting,' Brett said, coming in. 'Gosh! – And there's Cliffie looking like – a Roman emperor. Better!' – Brett guffawed, as if her portrait were a rich joke, a caricature.

Edith felt resentment, even fury rise through her body to her face, her eyes, and deliberately she smiled, though Brett was not looking at her, but at Melanie's head now, then at the abstracts, to which he gave merely a glance. He still smiled, stupidly, Edith thought. 'Well. New pastime, eh? Very interesting, Edie. Not bad, really.' He strolled out again.

Edith hated that he had set foot in her room. 'Have a bath, if you like. You know where the towels are. What time shall I wake you tomorrow?'

'Best six-thirty. Can't you give me the alarm? I can grab some Nescafé when I wake up.'

She gave him the clock from the bedroom, knowing she would wake at the unaccustomed creaks in the house in the morning. And Carol was *his* new pastime. Edith was aware that the last

214

thing she wanted in the world now was to be in bed with Brett.

That night she lay a long while without sleeping, though she tried to relax, to gain energy for tomorrow. She knew Cliffie would not come home. A couple of times he had stayed the night at the house of one of the boys who worked in the Chop House, a boy whose name Edith had forgotten, because it didn't matter. She thought of the things she would never say to Brett, such as, 'So what if George took the overdose himself? So what if Cliffie gave it to him? At George's age – so what? If people have to die, and they do, isn't going to sleep the easiest way? What about *me* all these thirteen years?' Then anger, combined with shame of her petulance, made her grow tense and turn over in bed, muscles rigid again, and again she deliberately relaxed, breathed deeply. She was going to protect Cliffie, and Cliffie knew it. That was strange. Even the doctor, however, old Carstairs, was on their side. Edith laughed – but not loudly, and her door was shut, anyway.

The sound of a car door slamming, then the false start of an engine awakened Edith, because it had sounded close, right in the driveway. Brett, she thought. Taking off? Not hurrying, she pushed her feet into slippers, and walked to her workroom (the guestroom door was open), and saw Brett's car pulling away from the curb. That was a fine thing! Strange she hadn't heard him go down the stairs, but Brett could be very quiet when he wanted to be.

She went into the guestroom, where he had tossed the covers back upon the bed, to see if he had left a note. He hadn't. In the hall, Edith noticed that George's two suitcases still stood by the wall outside his room, plus the English racehorse print, which Edith had wrapped, though Edith last evening had suggested that Brett take them, that a suit might be needed for the burial, but now Brett was talking of cremation.

In sudden anger, Edith remembered Brett saying last night, 'You're getting strange, Edie. Maybe you should get out with people more.' Edith had replied that she saw about a hundred a day at the Thatchery, talked with them, had to get along with them, and she also went to dinner parties often enough.

She was also on good terms with the *Bugle* advertisers, from whom she often had to collect personally, but she hadn't said that.

It was hardly 7, but Edith didn't want to go back to bed for an hour. She went downstairs, glanced into Cliffie's room and saw that he wasn't there, though she did peer at a mound of navy blue blanket on the unmade bed, which just might have covered a human figure. She threw out what was left of the old coffee, and started afresh. While she was doing this, she heard the front door close. Cliffie, she supposed.

Then Brett appeared in the dining room. Edith was startled.

'Morning. I moved my car. If Cliffie sees my car, he'll never come in. I know my son. I want to talk to him this morning.' Brett looked stiff with purpose.

Edith said, 'Coffee will be ready in about six minutes.'

'Mind if I make a couple of phone calls?'

Edith tried not to listen, which was easy, as she could barely hear the tones of his voice from where she was. Edith poured orange juice and made toast.

Brett came back with a tense smile. 'Carstairs says he can come over around ten-thirty. Sorry I'll have to hang around, Edith, but it's worth it – to me. I rang Carol and she'll explain to my office.'

Oh, good, Edith thought. They sat at the table.

'Don't forget to take George's suitcases,' Edith said. 'Not to mention a few papers of his. They're in a couple of boxes upstairs.'

Edith had work to do too. She took a bath, put on comfortable clothes, and tackled the *Bugle* work on her table. There were five subscription reminder slips to send off (Edith kept a file, by month), and then for *Letterbox*, besides the usual gripes about the hooligan 'outsiders' invading the town on Saturdays and Sundays, thanks to the more frequent buses lately, old anti-abortionist Mrs Charlton Riggs, Tinicum, was piping up again. Last evening at the restaurant Edith had chuckled, telling Brett what she intended to reply in an editorial, a brief one of about fifteen lines. 'You sound like an extremist,' Brett had said. Edith had retorted, 'The only people who get anything done in the world are extremists.' That from *him*, she thought. How he had changed! When she had stamped all the reminder envelopes, Edith put a piece of paper in the typewriter and wrote:

The sanctity-of-life people put quantity above quality, and they have admitted this. They perhaps are the types who, when the *Titanic* sank, would have hauled everyone from the water into the too few lifeboats with the cry 'Life is sacred!' thereby sinking everybody. But we also live on a ship, Spaceship Earth, and are we going to sink that by overloading? Would the Save-the-Foetus people like to state what they would have done in the *Titanic* lifeboat situation – assuming they themselves were in a lifeboat, i.e. reasonably comfortable and lucky to survive?

It needed polishing, but the idea was there. Edith laid it aside. Brett was stooped over the suitcases in the hall. Edith went out for a breath of fresh air, and to drop her letters at the post office.

She looked around for Cliffie. Sometimes he was on foot, sometimes a friend dropped him in a car. He had not taken his Volks.

'Oh, Edie!' This was Peggy Ditson, a neighbor a bit younger than Edith, who years ago had done quite a bit of girl-Friday work for the *Bugle*. 'I heard about George! I'm so sorry dear. Another sadness, but –'

'How did you hear?'

'Gert Johnson called me last night. Frankly, Edie, it's a blessing. Don't you think?' Peggy screwed her face up in an unaccustomed frown, and turned the corners of her mouth down in an effort to look concerned, serious. Peggy was the type who smiled perpetually, if she wasn't laughing.

Edith nodded. 'He was getting on.' She wondered how Gert had found out?

'I suppose Brett – He was Brett's uncle, wasn't he?'

'Yes. Oh, I'm in touch with Brett.'

They parted.

Cliffie came in shortly after Edith had got back. It was already after 10 a.m. Cliffie looked surprisingly well, not as if he had been up all night. Upstairs, Brett was making no noise with his activities, whatever they were. Edith wanted another cup of coffee, so she heated the pot and poured some for herself and Cliffie.

'Where were you?' Edith asked casually.

'I was at the Johnsons'.'

That surprised Edith. Gert wasn't a chum of Cliffie's, wasn't anti-Cliffie either, just neutral. 'Stayed the night there? How'd you get there?'

'I saw Dinah – with a fellow in a car. They were going to her house.'

Dinah was the Johnsons' daughter. 'I gather you told them about George.'

'Yes, I did,' Cliffie said, leaning back in his chair, throwing his chest out. He was eating a second piece of toast with marmalade.

A clunk came from upstairs, a suitcase being set down.

Cliffie started, and his smile went away.

'Brett's here.'

'Oh.' Now Cliffie grew tense, dropped his toast on the plate. 'I didn't see his car. What's he doing?'

Now there was a knock at the front door. Edith went and admitted Dr Carstairs.

'Hello, Edith,' Dr Carstairs said with his thin, dry smile. 'Now what's the trouble? I've got only about fifteen minutes. Appointments this morning.'

'I think –' Edith knew what the trouble was, Brett wanted a certificate regarding the cause of death. 'Brett's upstairs. I'll call him. – Brett?'

'Yes! Coming!' He was already halfway down the stairs.

Edith let them talk. She heard Brett say:

'Just that I'd like to get some facts from you, doctor – no mincing of words, eh? You know me long enough not to, I hope.' Brett was trying to be pleasant. 'I'd like my son to be with us too.' Brett called Cliffie.

Cliffie was in his room and didn't appear for a minute or two. Now he wore a sloppy turtle-neck sweater, spotted with what

218

looked like flecks of white paint. Edith went with Cliffie into the living room via the dining room.

'Well – at that age,' Dr Carstairs was saying. 'Hello, Cliffie. At that age you could say it's heart failure, a failure of the general system.'

'You spoke of empty medicine bottles. Maybe you'd like to sit down, doctor.'

Carstairs did sit on the sofa. 'Brett, I can't say anything specific about those bottles.'

'I'm surprised you didn't order an autopsy,' Brett said.

'I didn't see any need for one. Edith didn't ask for one.'

'But the fact that you mentioned empty medicine bottles – last night, I –'

Carstairs interrupted calmly, '*I* don't happen to know if any were more empty than usual, because Edith always – Well, you know, things were going fine for George all these years with a certain amount of codeine plus an occasional morphine injection from me, which hadn't been much increased, nothing *like* a cancer case, I can assure you. I have my records. – You didn't order any extra codeine, did you, Edith?' he asked, looking at her.

'No.' Edith was leaning on the back of the armchair. 'I couldn't order extra. Stan keeps your prescriptions, you know, and I just went when a bottle of something was getting low. The prescriptions were timed, Brett.'

'Yes, but if he took all the stuff at once,' Brett said to Edith. 'How full were the bottles?'

'Brett – I wasn't keeping track of every bottle. I don't *know*,' Edith said.

Brett turned to the doctor again. 'I presume you wrote a certificate of death, doctor.'

'Yes. General systematic failure, cardiovascular failure. – Frankly, Brett, if you're thinking of an overdose, the old boy might well have given it to himself. It wouldn't have taken much in his condition.'

Here Cliffie chuckled slightly, but it sounded like a sudden exhalation or cough. He was enjoying the conversation, and

Carstairs might as well have been his chum, from the way he was talking.

Brett looked as if he could have hit Cliffie with pleasure. 'I'm sure I have to say something to the insurance people,' Brett said. 'If you –'

'Oh, no, that's for me to say,' said Carstairs, 'and I've already sent it to the State authorities. They'll send Edith a certified copy and she can send it on to you.'

Brett took a breath, but Carstairs spoke first.

'If you're thinking that possibly – old George took an overdose either by mistake or on purpose – under the circumstances, at his age, that's not going to be either here or there. It's not like a young person's suicide. I really have got to be getting along.' Carstairs glanced at his wristwatch, and slid to the edge of the sofa. 'Unless there's anything else –'

The telephone rang.

'There may be. We'll see,' Brett said. 'Thank you for looking in this morning, doctor.'

It was probably Gert phoning, Edith thought as she picked up the telephone. It was a long distance call, and a voice identified itself as that of Sarah Belleter – another grand-niece of Aunt Melanie and one of Edith's remote cousins. She said she was at Melanie's house and asked if Edith could come this week, maybe Wednesday, since the lawyers were making progress with the will, and there were a couple of things to discuss, and also Sarah would love to see her again. Sarah's voice was pleasant and friendly.

To Edith, just then, it was a lovely invitation, a welcoming to her side of the family. She had seen Sarah a few times and liked her: she was surprisingly dark of hair, with lovely brows and a voice that charmed and soothed. Sarah had been educated in England and Switzerland, and was married to a Swiss architect. 'I'd be delighted to!' Edith replied, then remembered her Thatchery afternoon which she ought not to renege on. 'Is around nine p.m. Wednesday all right? I've got an afternoon job now.'

'Oh, of course, Edith! You sound in fine form. I'm looking

220

forward. Stay the night of course. Stay a couple of nights, if you can!'

Edith went back into the living room, happier. Cliffie was standing against the breakfront, as before, but now his face was white. Cliffie was scared.

'Yes. I know my son,' Brett said to Edith.

Edith's heart beat faster. 'And what're you talking about now?' she asked in a tone Aunt Melanie might have used.

'I asked him if he possibly administered George's medicines that afternoon, Sunday,' Brett said.

'I *didn't*!' Cliffie said stoutly, but with a tremor.

'Look at him,' Brett said, shaking his head. 'Sounds the same as when he was ten years old – *five*! Denying something – like decorating the bedroom walls with your lipstick! Remember that one, Edith?'

Edith did. 'Until you can prove something, Brett – why don't you let things alone?'

'*I* wasn't *here*!' Brett said. 'Where were you – that evening, Sunday?'

'I told you – in my workroom. Nobody had a real supper that evening.'

'I don't give a damn about supper. I've got to take off.' Brett walked awkwardly bent forward, as Edith had seen him a thousand times when he was hurrying, though now he looked more bent, sillier. He went into the hall where his topcoat or raincoat hung on a hook.

Edith smiled broadly, felt like laughing even. The audacity, the absurdity, the *cruelty*, even, of accusing someone – or the same as – of something that couldn't be proven at all! Making someone miserable, just to get the petty satisfaction of –

'What's so funny?' Brett barked, coming in, straightening his coat.

'The idea of making Cliffie miserable like this! Why should you? What've *you* ever done? Done about –'

'Done? What do you mean?'

'You couldn't even get George to that – what's it called – Sunset Pines!' The name sent Edith off into genuine laughter.

Cliffie joined her with a manly guffaw. The color had returned to his face.

'I know, I know. But I think that's hardly relevant,' said Brett. 'Stop it, Edith, you're hysterical! Cool it.'

'Hah!' That was Cliffie's mocking laugh.

'The service,' Brett began, and hesitated. 'The service – I'm sure short – is tomorrow at eleven. Starting at the home. Will you be there?'

Edith hated it, as she had hated many an engagement in her life, but without pausing, she said, 'Yes.'

'Good. I'll see you there.' Brett touched her arm, then withdrew his hand almost at once. 'I know, Edie, you've had a lot to put up with and I know years ago I should've forced him to go into that rest home.'

Edith looked at him, not thinking about anything, simply wishing that he would leave.

'Bye-bye, Edith, and thank you. Bye, Cliffie.' Brett went out.

'Good – *bye*,' Cliffie said in a deep voice when the door had closed, and swung his body, arm extended, toward the scotch bottle.

'Pour me one too,' Edith said.

Cliffie did, and shot some soda into it. '*I'm* not going tomorrow,' he said as he handed the drink to his mother.

24

At half past 7 the evening of Wednesday, Edith set out in the car with an overnight bag, bound for Hollyhocks, Melanie's house. It was glorious, driving, glorious to feel free, to be moving. She was tempted to put on speed, but prudently kept within the limit, a discipline she found easy. She looked forward to Hollyhocks – a bit stripped though it might be by now – to Sarah and her husband Peter, to a civilized meal with them, to a night of sleep in her old room, maybe. Cliffie hadn't wanted to come, though Edith had said, 'Come on, why not? We'll ask Frances to feed Nelson,' and Cliffie had wavered, had almost said yes, but finally said no. Even that was progress of a sort, Edith thought. Cliffie had showed a noticeable confidence in himself since George's – removal. He had, for instance, offered to give Nelson his two meals a day, and this time Edith felt she could trust him to do it.

Edith passed familiar landmarks, looked at them with kinder, happier eyes now, she felt. God, it was amazing! Just to have George out of the house, just to feel the house somehow hers again, that room hers again to do what she wished with. Terrible to feel that way about an old man just dead, perhaps, but after all, he'd been finally a most ungrateful character, hadn't released a little extra of his money to buy her or the house, for instance, a present for the last many Christmases. And Edith would have bet her life that nothing special would come to her via George's will – not that she gave a damn. Edith assumed that Brett would be chief if not sole heir. What would a nurse's salary have been for all the meals, the time, the bedpan emptying?

She had to burst out laughing, bent over the steering wheel for two seconds, then wiped her eyes clear of tears. God, it was funny! She opened the window and let the wind blow her hair.

There was a moon that night, nearly full, and it had taken its place like something in a stage-set, it seemed to Edith, above and to the left of Melanie's milky-white house as Edith went up the driveway. Lights were on inside, not on the porch, but as she stopped her car, the front door opened and Sarah came out.

'Welcome, *Edith*!' Sarah cried. 'Cliffie with you?'

'Hello, Sarah! No, Cliffie's home – feeding the cat!'

There was Bertha in the hall, hovering to take her overnight case. A minute or so later, Edith was seated in the most comfortable chair of the sitting room, nearest the fire, with a heavy tumbler of scotch on the rocks. Peter Belleter, rosy-cheeked, with straight black hair, sat on a hassock, smiling, shy, but with a friendly manner. Edith asked about their two children, now in Zurich. The Belleters wanted to hear about the *Bugle*, about Cliffie, and since Brett was not mentioned, Edith assumed Melanie had told them about the divorce.

Sarah's dark brows drew together. She was sitting on the arm of the leather sofa, poised and graceful. 'And wasn't there – a relative of Brett's, wasn't he?'

'You mean George,' Edith said, glad Sarah had brought George up. 'I'm sorry to say he died – just last Sunday.'

'Oh!' said Peter, who was gripping a smallish beer bottle just then between his knees. 'Sunday!'

'He was awfully old – ninety or more,' Edith went on. 'He died in his sleep. The service was only today, matter of fact – this morning. Brett was there – in Doylestown.'

'Goodness!' said Sarah.

Yet in the next minutes, George faded away like a wisp of cigarette smoke – or something, and Edith was delighted that they began to talk about other things, happy things. Sarah had been 'given the task' as Sarah put it, by her mother, of seeing to Melanie's bequeathals, silver, furniture, books. Sarah told Edith that Melanie had given Edith a choice of rugs and of books, and of two settees with accompanying chairs. That was nice. Edith knew the settees, and knew her preference. But it was the atmosphere of this moment that Edith enjoyed, the ease of it, the frankness of Sarah as well as her tone of respect for Melanie.

'Of course we brought a copy, didn't we, Peter?' Sarah asked her husband, then said something else in a tongue Edith couldn't understand – Swiss dialect.

'*Of* course, *of* course!' Peter said, smiling.

'Peter thinks I forget the most important things and remember the least important,' Sarah said. 'We had photostats of the will made. You may see it, if you like.'

On her last words, there were quick steps down the staircase, not the steps of Bertha.

'Ah, Geoff!' Sarah said. 'Geoff, this is my cousin Edith – Edith Howland.'

'How do you do?' A tall man in light gray trousers and gray sweater advanced toward Edith and bowed a little. 'You've just arrived?'

'Yes,' Edith said, feeling surprised and somehow shocked that a strange man had been upstairs here. But he looked charming, polite – a crease across his forehead, two down his cheeks, like an outdoor man, or a man who worried a little too much. He had sent a whiff of after-shave lotion – or could it be pipe tobacco – toward Edith as he bowed. Edith admired his pale gray cashmere sweater. Was she falling in love – at first sight? She wasn't listening to what the others were saying, and it seemed that Sarah repeated:

'... Geoffrey Vrieland. He *is* a lawyer, but not ours! I say this so you – I mean we haven't any – what do you call it?' Sarah was smiling.

'Professional clout, maybe?' Peter put in. He had a slight accent.

Geoffrey Vrieland laughed and tossed popcorn into his mouth.

Edith was happy. She forced her thoughts away from the attractiveness of Geoffrey Vrieland, who probably had a wife – maybe even upstairs – or in Basel, where Sarah said he lived. Edith daydreamed about her settee-and-two-chairs to come. She would choose the beige satin with the tiny rosebud pattern, and get rid of the worn-out green armchair in the corner that

225

Cliffie was always flinging himself into. Brett had said, 'The upstairs needs a paint job,' and Edith had agreed, saying rather sharply, 'The whole house needs a lot,' because how did Brett think she could make vast improvements with the small amount of money that was coming in?

Bertha announced supper.

'Late supper!' Sarah said to all. 'I hope everybody's hungry.'

Melanie's Georgian silver, old pulled-thread napkins adorned the polished table. Cold fried chicken, Bertha's hot biscuits tucked into linen napkins, salad. Edith could not quite finish the hot apple pie dessert. It was only a little after 11, Sarah said, and would Edith like to have a look at some of the things upstairs?

'Or maybe you're tired,' Sarah said. 'There's tomorrow morning. You said you didn't have to leave till eleven-thirty. Is that right?'

Edith felt not only tired but sad, and deliberately sat up straighter and said she'd like to look at things upstairs. They went.

'Aunt Melanie was *very* fond of you,' Sarah said softly, and folded her hands between her knees, her hands almost lost in her full skirt.

They were both sitting on the floor on either side of a bottom drawer which Sarah had taken quite out, because the bedspreads, the hand towels were easier to look at if the drawer was out in the light.

'This last week must have been hard for you. I'm so sorry, Edith.'

'But – quite frankly George – I can't say he was close to me. An uncle of Brett's, you know.'

Sarah nodded. 'Yes, Melanie told me – about that. Edith, this can wait. Anyway the choice is all yours – here. We can talk about it tomorrow. Some of her things come in dozens, some in half dozens. Isn't it amazing how she kept all this, and in such good condition? It really is like a glimpse into – a hundred years *ago*!' Sarah smiled merrily.

Sarah was barely forty, Edith realized. And with two children already in college, and doing well, probably. Sarah had the complexion of a girl of twenty.

Edith took a hot bath. Sarah had recommended it, saying that she looked a bit tense. Edith did not feel in the least tense. She lifted the hot water in the palm of her hand and let it run down from her knees. The moonlight came strong into the bedroom, almost like an artificial light of some kind. Edith blinked, enjoying the changed atmosphere, the curved armchair wings, the fuzzy pattern of the rug that she could almost make out. She got out of bed and went to the window.

The gazebo looked enchanting, like a Japanese dream. Or should she consider it simply Victorian English?

Edith put on her slippers, a sweater over her pajama top, and went downstairs. The whole house was dark now, though a little moonlight penetrated through the hall windows. She took a coat – somebody's raincoat – from the front closet, and went out, closed the door softly, and went round to the back lawn. She had had an impulse to see Melanie's little brook – and here it was, busy, murmuring over pebbles, sleepless. She could see silvery ripples in the moonlight. Many a time Edith had waded here, when she had been four years old, maybe even smaller. In the hot summertime, after romping on the lawn, it had been bliss to cool her feet in the brook. Edith stepped out of her slippers, and cautiously set a foot in a part of the brook where she remembered there was sand. There was even the old peach tree (which had never produced well) to steady herself by.

The water was cold, numbing. She released the peach tree branch and stood up straight, would have closed her eyes completely, except that she was not sure she could have kept her balance. Her feet lost even their sensation of numbness, she looked toward her great-aunt's slumbering house – what had Goethe said, 'Kennst du das Haus? Auf Säulen ruht sein Dach.' – and she enjoyed a sense of order, of sanity. Gert Johnson, she supposed, would call Melanie's house 'snob,' out-of-date, even immoral. Edith giggled a little – maybe from chill. She climbed out of the water onto dew-damp grass, found her slippers. No use catching her death. She had almost solved the mystery of

227

existence. Almost. How often had she been on the brink of it? Maybe twenty times in her life. It had always the same elements (even on land now, she grasped them clearly, as she had in the water), and they had to do with consciousness and truth. Had it anything to do with what people *should* do, from moral ... Her thoughts were lost again, as she struggled to tighten the raincoat belt. How many individuals, or countries, did what they *should* do? No, what she meant was individual, depended on an individual honesty, on admitting facts.

Numb to the calves now, Edith trudged toward the house, looked up again at the dark windows faintly bordered by lighter curtains. In an upstairs narrow window, third from right, where the hall was, Edith saw a ghostly figure. Sarah, watching her? Edith impulsively lifted an arm and waved, and when she looked again, the pale vertical shape had gone. Had she seen it? *Yes*, Edith thought.

So Edith expected to find Sarah waiting, maybe, at the top of the stairs, when she came in. Edith was silent, hanging the raincoat back where she had found it. She climbed the stairs softly, looking for Sarah. There was no one, not even in the hall upstairs, and Edith went back to bed. She wrapped her sweater around her feet, and tired now, fell asleep quickly.

Breakfast was a staggered affair, Peter having had his very early, because he had to write letters, Sarah said. Geoffrey Vrieland looked more handsome· even than last evening, captured in a patch of sunlight at the table. Could it have been Geoff watching her last night? Hardly, unless he wore a nightshirt! Edith said to Sarah:

'I went out to see the brook last night. I thought I saw you at an upstairs window – watching me and probably thinking I was a bit dotty.'

'Me?' Sarah seemed baffled by both statements, that Edith had gone out, and that she might have been at a window. 'No, Edith.'

'Oh. A trick of the moonlight then. I wanted to see the old brook. And the moon was so bright and lovely!'

Sarah was pleasant, didn't say much of anything, but a few

minutes later (when Sarah and Geoff were talking about something quite different) Edith had the feeling Sarah had looked at her suspiciously, as if Sarah might think she was off her rocker for walking out in the moonlight.

'We've got two good hours!' Sarah said cheerfully.

She meant hours in which to look at the furniture and the other things.

Edith drove home with a bundle wrapped in a mohair steamer rug and gently tied. It contained napkins, hand towels, linen sheets, and a silver stamp box Edith had always been fond of. Sarah had said, 'Take the stamp box! I can see you like it.' It was nice to have relatives like that. The settee and armchair and two smaller chairs would come later, but within a week, Sarah said, when she could arrange a delivery.

She also had Geoffrey Vrieland's card with Zurich and Basel addresses. He had said she must come to dinner at his house, if she ever came to Zurich to visit the Belleters. He liked to cook.

Edith was home by 1:10 p.m., just time to unpack a bit and have a bite before going to the Thatchery. Cliffie's transistor was on. Edith went up the hall to say hello to him, and was surprised to see blankets and a couple of cartons outside his room door. Cliffie lay on the floor, apparently rearranging the books in his bookcase. The vacuum cleaner was also on the floor.

'What're you *doing*?'

'Oh – straightening up a little. Nothing much.' Cliffie looked embarrassed.

Edith was speechless, turned away stunned. She had seen at a glance that the two cartons in the hall contained cruddy old magazines, newspapers, even old tennis shoes. What had happened? Well, *George* was gone. Yes, that was what had happened.

Nelson came into the kitchen, tail high, and gave out a happy, prolonged cry.

'Hello, *Nelson*!' Edith picked him up, and the cat relaxed

completely, nearly slipping through her hands, purring as if she had been away for days.

Edith put the kettle on. She wanted tea now. 'Help you with anything, Cliffie?' she called.

'I'm doing all right, thanks.'

'Hungry?'

'Yep!'

Edith made tea, toast, opened a can of tuna and made sandwiches. Cliffie's transistor played 'Old Buttermilk Sky.' Edith was aware that she enjoyed it, and remembered the many times she had cursed to herself, nearly screamed at Cliffie to turn his radio off, turn *anything* off. 'Ready!' Edith called.

'Wow, that's fast.' Cliffie strolled in with a smudge of dust straight up the bridge of his nose, and a yellow dustrag hanging out of a back pocket.

'Your room's going to look nice!' Edith said cheerfully.

'Yeah.' Cliffie dove into a sandwich. 'Nice time down in Delaware?'

Edith smiled. 'Lovely. You should've been there. I went wading in the brook at midnight.'

'In this weather?'

'And your cousin Sarah asked about you. She's so nice, Cliffie. So's her husband.' And Edith talked on. Was Cliffie really listening or not? As usual, she felt he was taking in half of it. As soon as he had downed his sandwiches and milk, he went back to his room. Edith had no intention of interrupting his unprecedented effort, so she shouted a 'Bye-bye' and departed.

'Hey, mom!' Cliffie was running down the hall. 'Just that I'm – Just that a girl is coming for a drink tonight at seven-thirty. Okay? Are you home?'

'Well – do you want me to be?'

'Oh – doesn't matter.'

'I've got work to do in my room. I won't be in your way. Got to run, Cliffie.' She went on. A girl! What girl, Edith wondered. *Coming* to the house. Well, no reason why Cliffie should fetch her, she supposed. Edith was smiling.

Cliffie continued his tidying all afternoon, imbibing meanwhile two beers, in a dreamy way, as from time to time he surveyed his progress. Never before had he thrown things out, just said good-bye to them. It was like swimming for the first time, or like the time he had jumped off the bridge when he was a kid. Yet he felt like throwing things out. And it was a damned good thing, he thought. He carried two cartons of rubbish out to the back and put them beside the garbage bin for Saturday morning's collection.

The girl's name was Luce, for Lucy. Cliffie had picked her up last night at the Cartwheel Inn, in the bar part. She had short straight blond hair, streaked with brown, with bangs – not the type that usually turned him on or turned anybody on, Cliffie supposed, but she had an interesting smile, rather shy and at the same time friendly, even sexy. She had said she was eighteen, when Cliffie had asked her how old she was. She had been alone, and Cliffie had bought her a gin and tonic and sat down at the little table with her. She was from Philadelphia. *Stranger to these parts*, Cliffie had said, not a brilliant line, maybe, but it seemed to have done wonders last night. Luce had promised to come to his house at 7:30, and to go out to dinner with him afterward. Cliffie had made a trip to the bank and withdrawn forty dollars, which meant he had sixty-two on him now.

Around 5 he had a nap, exhausted by his efforts which had included going to the local grocery for fritos and potato chips. The house had gin and tonic. When he woke up, his heart gave a leap when he saw it was just after 6, and at once he thought that Luce might stand him up. That was quite possible, so he braced himself. If she did stand him up (and he would know by 8 or 8:15), and his mother said anything, he would say casually that Luce had called up and told him she couldn't make it.

His room looked rather okay, even nice, he thought. He had left one of the best pop group posters up, and there were lighter patches on the white wall where the others had been, but what the hell? No use being an old maid about a room! The funny thing was, he wasn't sure he would invite Luce even to have a look at his room. On the other hand, he *could* have the cocktail hour *in* his room. He pondered this.

When Edith came home a little after 7, she found Cliffie in the hall, looking anxious, as if she might have been his girl friend barging in. Edith was mildly surprised to see three-quarters of his beard off again, and now merely a thick hedge along his jaw-line. His hair looked as if he had just had a bath, and he had on his blue blazer which Edith thought he was a bit too plump to button now.

'Everything all right?'

'Just fine, mom.'

Edith went upstairs, and had her second bath of the day. She felt especially well, and wanted to write something in her diary. Her last entry had been about George passing away in his sleep. She wasn't going to say anything about the *cremation*, which in fact she hadn't witnessed, nor had Brett, but that service – brief, perfunctory beyond belief! And Brett had not taken the trouble to alert George's kin, if any, nor had Edith for that matter troubled to ask Gert or the Quickmans to come, which they probably would have done. Sad it had been, sad, sad. And she had sensed Brett gently smouldering throughout. For the first time in a long time, Edith had felt sympathy for poor old George, for his isolated spirit, George who had grown too deaf to enjoy radio, and had maintained to the last his contempt for television.

And now Cliffie – in a dither. It pleased Edith that he had a girl friend. Surely he'd asked a girl or two to the house before. Hadn't he? Of course she couldn't write about that in her diary, because Cliffie was married – in her diary.

Edith put on her blue corduroys, suddenly remembered the bundle on the living room floor, and went down. Cliffie was in the living room, strolling about with a scotch, and the bundle was exactly where she had left it, in front of the sofa. 'Pardon me, Cliff! I'll get this out of your way.'

'Oh. That. Yeah. Yes. Is it heavy?'

'Oh, no.' Edith carried the bundle up the stairs, and opened it on the double bed in the bedroom. Beautiful crisp linen, and

232

some other linen or cotton items quite limp with age. And the silver! And a daguerreotype that Edith had admired and Sarah had put in without Edith's knowing. Melanie's mother, Edith remembered. The picture was framed, and Sarah had remarked that the name and dates were written on the back of the picture.

She heard Cliffie opening the front door, heard voices. Edith was glad the girl hadn't stood him up. She put the linens in the bottom drawer of the big chest of drawers in her room, and laid the steamer rug over a chair to hang out. Then she went into her workroom and closed the door.

She pulled her diary toward her and opened her fountain pen.

March 30, 1969

Most pleasant visit to Hollyhocks, where Sarah & husband & friend Geoffrey something awaited. (Funeral service yesterday morning for poor George, rather grim, Brett not in good mood.)

It was her first remark concerning Brett in a long time, but she thought since this was about George, she had to mention Brett.

Can't deny I am glad he is at peace, as they say – all those comforting phrases! Eternal rest! Gathered to the bosom of. All heavenly too. I hope so. The majority, anyway.

Dear cousin Sarah, the picture of health and happiness, loaded me with goodies from Melanie's house and says there is even more to come – furniture. I now also embark on the pleasant task of re-doing G.'s old room, which I want a different color, maybe pinkish, anything but the dusty white which it's always been.

Edith hesitated, daydreamed, aware of a murmur of voices from below, but she had already decided not to try to meet the girl, lest that annoy Cliffie. She added:

Cliffie is again abroad, but Debbie dutifully came to Doylestown for G.'s service, wearing dark brown hat and veil, looking like a Currier & Ives figure, even appropriately pale, which set off her brown eyes to perfection. Brown coat with cape also. Afterward she threw off her gloom, chatting with us. Asks me always to come for a weekend, whether C. is home or not. I wonder if she is expecting again, as she seems so happy and content?

The telephone was ringing. Edith only faintly heard it, and opened her door, waiting.

'Mom?'

'Thank you!' Edith ran down. Cliffie had gone back into the living room.

'How're things, Edie?' Gert asked. 'I heard about George. I should've called you up Monday or so, but we had a crisis *here*. Norm had his tonsils out and developed the most unbelievable fever ... Oh, he's coming along now, thanks to antibiotics.' The rest was *Bugle* matters. Their printer in Trenton had appendicitis, and the next issue might be late, because there was only his apprentice to do the work, and even he (like the printer) had another job. But Edith should get her copy and *Letterbox* stuff in at the usual time anyway.

'Bet you can't wait to fix up George's room!' Gert said with one of her earthy laughs.

Chartreuse, Edith thought suddenly. With a dusty pink chest of drawers. Yes! 'You're right!' said Edith.

'Mom?'

Edith had just hung up. Cliffie was beckoning her into the living room.

'Like you to meet Lucy – Luce Beckman,' Cliffie said, gesturing toward the girl in the green armchair.

The girl sat forward, sandal-shod, in dark slacks and pink shirt. She looked about twenty, slender and almost wiry. 'How do you do, Mrs – Howland?' She had a deepish voice.

The voice sounded as if the girl might be trying to seem sophisticated. 'How do you do, Luce? – Have you folks got all you need here?'

'Oh, yes,' Cliffie said.

'Definitely,' the girl drawled.

'Have a drink, mom?'

'Not just now, thanks. Have a good time, both of you.' Edith went out and up the stairs.

234

An odd girl, Edith thought, for Cliffie to be in such a tizzy over. Not like his busty pin-up types by any means. She looked, Edith thought, like one of the youngsters labeled mixed-up. Maybe. No make-up. Trying for an air of worldly wisdom. Well, who knew? Maybe she wasn't like that at all. Edith had seen her for less than a minute.

25

Though Cliffie could drive again now, he had agreed to Luce's taking her own M-G, pretending to hesitate, though he was playing it safe in case he drank a bit too much. He ordered another round of drinks at the Cross-Keys restaurant (Luce seemed a damned good drinker for her age), and after dinner a Napoleon brandy. Not in the habit of ordering brandy, Cliffie had been almost *corrected* by the waitress, who had not known what he meant. The brandy *of* Napoleon had been the phrase in Cliffie's mind, which he had seen in advertisements. The answer seemed to be Courvoisier, according to the waitress, so Cliffie settled for that.

'You're such a kid,' Luce was saying by midnight.

Cliffie was instantly dampened. He had dredged up his best puns, and at least two good jokes. He had not tried to hold her hand, much less put an arm around her, as a lot of fellows did with a girl they were taking out to dinner. 'I'm not in the least a kid.'

Luce only laughed. She had a broadish mouth, square teeth. She laughed gently and deeply and it was rather like her voice. Cliffie wanted to tell her how much he liked that she didn't wear any make-up, not even a bit of pale lipstick.

'How come you live with your mother – at your age?'

'Because I – Why not? I'm the man of the house now that my father – pissed off.'

Luce treated him very casually, Cliffie thought. Sort of with contempt. Was that a good sign? Meaning, was she only pretending indifference?

'Music stinks, don't you agree?' Cliffie grimaced. It was piped music, coming from the walls tonight, and the orchestra sounded like a lot of old men, at least Cliffie imagined fifteen old guys, all looking like George in a nightshirt, scraping violins and blowing saxophones, and Cliffie spluttered with laughter.

'You're hysterical tonight,' Luce said loftily.

'No, I'm not. I just thought of something funny. But I won't bore you with it. – What're you doing next Saturday night? That's in – a couple of days.' Luce had said she was playing truant from her family for a while, that they'd had a disagreement about her college, which Cliffie had never heard of, near Philadelphia.

Luce sighed, and said, 'Why talk about Saturday when we're here now. Aren't we?'

'Yes,' Cliffie said, entranced. 'Is it true –' He suddenly wished he had brought a cigar, because it looked quite mature to smoke one. '– true that you're sleeping at the Cartwheel?'

'That creep joint!'

Now Cliffie laughed gaily. 'You can say that again! Okay, where?'

'Why does it matter?' She had lit a Marlboro, was shaking the match out with infinite poise and grace. 'I have friends in Brunswick Corner.'

'Who? – Where?'

'Um-um. I'm not going to tell you,' she said softly, with a smile.

Cliffie's heart thumped. He also smiled. This, he thought, *this* was what it felt like to fall in love. It wasn't like looking at boobies or some naked blonde on a poster. This was magical. Magical. Magic. Cliffie grinned like a fool.

She didn't want to go on to another place, like the Chop House or Odette's for another brandy and a change of scene. She said something about dropping him home, which depressed Cliffie, but he didn't want to be disagreeable by arguing.

'We can always have a nightcap at my place,' Cliffie said. 'My mother doesn't mind. Why should she? You haven't even seen my room.'

Luce chuckled, saying nothing. Then suddenly she swung her car off the road to the right, and they were at some crazy steakhouse, big neon sign – you had to climb steps to the door. Cliffie didn't care for the place, no atmosphere, but at least they would have a little more time together.

'Two Courvoisiers!' Cliffie said firmly to the barman.

'Plee-yuz,' said the young barman, some faggot whose face Cliffie knew. Insolent bastard. Cliffie turned his eyes away from him.

And whom should he see but Mel Linnell! 'Mel!' Cliffie cried, pleased as could be to encounter Mel, because, he, Cliffie, had a girl with him. 'Mel – like you to meet Luce Beckman.' Cliffie dragged Mel by the sleeve of his suede jacket.

'How y'do?' said Mel.

'Hello,' Luce replied huskily. She was perched like a lightweight bird on the bar stool, one slender leg dangling.

Mel was with a girl too, but didn't introduce her. They seemed to be leaving. 'How've you been, Cliffie?'

'Very fine, thank you. How's yourself, Mel?' He added with sudden confidence, 'Come over to my house some time. Mom's working afternoons and old George – just kicked the bucket.' Cliffie spoke with a smile.

'Oh?' Mel was moving on, 'Are you working?'

'Now and then,' Cliffie replied. 'That was Mel Linnell,' he said to Luce, and filled her in on Mel's interesting apartment in Lambertville, his rather mysterious work with big-shots, Cliffie said, which could mean anything, drugs, handling hot goods, though he didn't want to hammer the illegal aspects of Mel's existence, just wanted to assure Luce that he was chummy with amusing people.

When Cliffie found himself alone that night, just after he had turned the light on in his room, he was aware of a gap in his memory after seeing Mel. Luce had just said good night to him at the curb in front of his house. She hadn't wanted to come in. Cliffie saw by his corny old Mickey Mouse alarm clock (which still worked, however) that it was twenty minutes to 2.

Cliffie put his hands over his face and said, 'Jesus!' He swung around, hands still over his face, talking to himself, wincing, then experiencing a surge of pleasure, confidence, belief in the future with Luce. Then came more grimaces, snatches of recollection of things they had said that evening. This semi-agony went on for at least ten minutes, while Cliffie secured a scotch nightcap from the living room and half undressed himself.

'What a girl!' he whispered.

He had given her his address. Yes. Twice, Cliffie thought. Certainly once tonight, yes, and then of course the first time he had met her, when he had borrowed a tab and pencil from a waiter in the Cartwheel. Unfortunately he hadn't *her* address, as she had refused to give it. This thought sent Cliffie at once down the hall, in shorts and socks, for the telephone book. The directory for Philadelphia had such a number of Beckmans that Cliffie gave it up, looked in another directory which had the smaller towns, then realized that he had not asked Luce her father's first name. How could he ever reach her now? If she didn't phone him?

He was a bit too pissed to torture himself further about this, so he washed and brushed his teeth in the kitchen, then fell into bed too tired to play with a sock, though in a moment of glory earlier in the evening, he had thought of that.

Edith on Saturday morning had a call from Dr Carstairs.

'Had a funny letter from your – from Brett's lawyer,' Carstairs said. 'Seems Brett's spoken to his lawyer about the embalming of George Howland. It seems I should have asked for an autopsy, according to this Mr Gorewitz.'

'Oh?'

Carstairs' confident, smiling voice went on. 'Even a coroner. I frankly don't see it Brett's way. I've sent the letter on to *my* lawyer this morning. Now there's nothing to get excited or angry about. And don't speak to Brett about it. I'm ready to answer any and all questions.'

'Well – is he charging you with something?'

'I would say Brett or the lawyer is questioning. Well, fine, if they try to make out a case of neglect or malpractice, they'll find they have a tough row to hoe. I wanted to let you know,

239

Edith, because Brett might speak to you directly and upset you.'

Edith had looked up coroner in her dictionary to make sure: they were called in when there was reason to suppose a death was not due to natural causes. 'I know Brett didn't want the embalming, because George had something about cremation in his will, which *I* didn't know about.'

'A crematory will embalm also, if there's a delay for some reason. You find a crematory that doesn't do something along those lines these days. This Gorewitz mentions failure to do an autopsy when there might have been an overdose. Well, who knows anything definite about an overdose? I don't. Anybody can argue over this till doomsday.'

'The idea of stirring up trouble like this!' Edith had suddenly become impatient – with Brett.

'Don't you worry, Edith, because it's my concern and I'm not worried, and neither is my lawyer, because I spoke with him on the phone.'

They left it at that. Carstairs promised to telephone her in a couple of days. It ruined Edith's day. What meddling on Brett's part! Having used her as unpaid nurse for more than a decade, he was now trying to – maybe – dump an accusation of negligence on her. These days, Edith thought for the twentieth time, old people did take overdoses sometimes, or doctors gave it to them, and who made a fuss over it? The 'sanctity' of human life – surely, as long as there was someone else to change the bedpans. I'd like to see the Pope changing a bedpan, Edith thought, or even giving birth for the eighth time, maybe with a breech delivery. Eternal pregnancy for the Pope, eternal pangs! After all, that was what he wished on an awful lot of women.

Her anger, mainly against Brett, cooled down, and was at once replaced by an anxiety over Cliffie's present mood – like a downward shift of gears in her emotions. Cliffie for the first time in his life seemed to be in love, and Edith had a feeling that Luce might not bother trying to see Cliffie again, and he didn't know how to reach her. Yesterday he had gone to the Cartwheel Inn to inquire, Edith knew, though Cliffie had said he had gone there to see Luce. Cliffie had later said that Luce had not been there, had even checked out. 'I really should have insisted on getting her phone number,' Cliffie had said earlier that morning. Edith had been surprised by his frankness with her.

She went back upstairs to the spare room (she was forcing herself not to call it or think of it as George's room any longer), where Cliffie was on his knees in old levis giving the low chest of drawers its first coat of dusty pink.

'What was all that?' Cliffie asked. 'Carstairs?'

'Nothing to worry about.'

'What's the jazz about George? – Naturally I heard some of it, mom.'

'Brett didn't want the embalming. Expensive, I suppose. Something in George's will about a cremation, you know.'

Cliffie glanced at her, their eyes met, and Cliffie resumed his work. She knew Cliffie was worried, if only a little, about the overdose. But he was probably more worried about the girl called Luce. Edith was going to the Johnsons' this evening for dinner. She might ask if Gert had heard of a girl called Luce Beckman. Gert knew an amazing lot about the district.

Edith, on her knees too, brushing the wainscotting in preparation for painting, lifted her head and looked at the stark window where chartreuse curtains would soon hang, Yesterday she had found just the shade and material she wanted at a shop in Brunswick Corner, a stroke of luck which she considered a good omen. She was confident that she could mix a paint of somewhat lighter chartreuse or Cézanne yellow for the walls, and with a pair of rollers, she and Cliffie could paint the room in one morning – maybe Monday or Tuesday. Tomorrow, Sunday, Edith intended to do up the curtains on her machine. And she would make them in this room, her old sewing-and-ironing room, and pretend George had never existed.

Before heading for Washington Crossing, Edith went to Lambertville and bought a bottle of rye at the liquor shop. Rye was more welcome than French wine at the Johnsons'. She crossed the Delaware to Pennsylvania again, and drove east. Of all crazy things, she thought, Cliffie head over heels, for really the first time, at the age of twenty-four! Unfortunately, Edith thought, he had the experience of a boy of eighteen, if that. He wasn't playing it cool, he was taking it like a thunderbolt. He hadn't finished his egg or even one piece of toast this morning.

'Evening, Norm!' Edith cried as she started up the irregular stone steps to the Johnsons' house. They had a careless garden in front, which always suggested to Edith a loss of earth – straight into the gutter below – because of its extreme slope.

'Hi, Edie!' Norm's shirttails hung under his sweater. He seemed to be engaged in cutting back roses, though Edith wasn't sure.

'Hi, Edith! You're looking great!' A smack on the cheek from Gert in the steamy, noisy kitchen. Gert was frying chicken.

'Rye,' Edith said, setting the paper bag on the round cork dining table, which offered the only clear surface. 'Hello, Dinah,' she said to the dark-haired girl, who seemed engrossed in a schoolbook at the far side of the table.

'H'lo,' Dinah said. She lifted her eyes, but with an air of seeing nothing. This was the Johnsons' youngest, aged sixteen or thereabout.

Norm came in and made drinks with the new rye. The ice cubes in the drinks were mere shells, because Gert had been defrosting, and the cubes hadn't set as yet. Anti-Viet Nam war posters adorned the walls. 'I went all the way with LBJ' was not the usual pregnant Negro woman, but a photograph of an American vet in a wheelchair with his hands and feet missing.

'What're you studying?' Edith asked Dinah, over the roar of frying in Gert's two skillets.

'*Chemistry!*' Dinah looked miserable.

'Oh? Tough, I suppose!' Edith tried to look friendly, but had the feeling Dinah didn't care how she looked. Dinah seemed in a daze. Edith had forgotten if she was in last year of high school or first year of college, and didn't dare ask. Dinah was rather the runt of the litter, had twice run away from home, even had the start of a police record, for shoplifting, as Edith recalled. At least the Johnsons' two boys were doing well. A baby picture graced the sloppy bookcase top opposite Edith: a

242

pudgy thing in a diaper. Derek's, Edith thought. Derek was one year older than Cliffie. Edith started to ask about the baby, then didn't.

'Not the kind of meal,' Gert yelled from the stove, 'that y'fix when y'wanna talk to someone! Ha-ha!'

Edith laughed too. She had not sat down. 'Help you?' she asked. 'Making a salad?'

'No-o-o. Bored with salad! We got some good ice cream to finish with. *Peach*!'

The crackle and hissing abated as Gert forked out the last pieces and cut off the gas. Like a gypsy, or a leper, or a stranger, Dinah reappeared (she had gone to her room), snared some hot pieces of chicken with her fingers and dropped them on a plate, and disappeared again into the bowels of the house. Gert and Norm seemed to pay no attention. They sat and began.

'Do you know a girl called – Lucy Beckman?' Edith asked.

'Beckman? From where?' Gert bit into a wishbone.

'Around Philly. Cliffie's new girl friend. I – Yes, really!' Edith said, smiling. Gert had interrupted her with an astonished exclamation. Edith described the girl, eighteen, slender, blond-ish, and with a rather sophisticated manner.

Gert didn't know of such a girl, though she had known some people called Beckman ages ago in Flemington.

'Cliffie's *se-er*ious?' Norm asked.

'Well – as he's ever been.' Edith was a little sorry she had brought the girl up, since she didn't usually or ever talk about Cliffie's social life. There hadn't been any until now. But they were already on another subject. Lyndon Johnson again. The Vietnamese.

'People have a right,' Gert declaimed, slapping her plump fingers down on the table edge, 'to their own kind of government! If they want socialism, communism –'

'Honey, we know all that,' said Norman, picking his teeth now. The Johnsons kept toothpicks on the table in a shot glass.

The old words rolled off Edith also. There was no wine. She was finishing the last of her second rye and water. 'Socialism

is not the same as communism,' she said. 'England has socialism
– of a sort. Communism –'

'England has *mixed*,' Norm said. 'Socialism and capitalism.'

'But just the word communism means Moscow – old Stalin-
ism,' said Edith.

'Not necessarily,' Gert said.

Edith saw the hopelessness. But human voices were comfort-
ing, somehow. It was almost like reciting verses, she thought.
'The Lord is my shepherd' and 'I shall not want.' Edith said,
'Since communism is coming, all this is a delaying action – Viet
Nam –'

'Right,' said Gert, 'but it doesn't have to be Moscow communism – or socialism.'

I'm drifting to the right, Edith thought. *I'm becoming a goddam Fascist, assuming that the Right means Fascist.* 'What did
you think of my idea of observers, organizers, going into every
Third World country and – administrating food, aid of all kinds
from other countries, supervising –'

'Not bad,' said Norm.

Edith was cheered. 'To cut down graft and wastage, so that –'

'To perpetrate our way of life, you mean. *Perpetuate*, I mean.'
Gert laughed.

'No,' Edith said. 'But I admit it's another step toward authoritarianism. Didn't I write a *Bugle* editorial two years ago on
creeping authoritarianism?'

Gert tried to think.

They talked on. Edith was for 'supervision,' Gert for 'freedom
of choice.' Of course Edith meant freedom of choice also, but
how could there be freedom of choice in countries whose people
could not read, whose greedy upper classes mis-spent money
given by other countries, and food and tools were not properly
distributed?

'No use going on,' Edith said, 'until we get down to specific
countries like India, or specific cases.'

'But you're talking like –'

A minute or so later, Edith was saying, 'You can't just pour
money down a hole – as even Johnson said, and expect it to

solve problems. Look at Operation Head-Start, mainly for black kids, let's face it. It's been called a failure, but it was a wonderful idea at first, to start those kids out in school two years before kids usually go to school, start them reading.'

'Johnson said it was a failure?' Gert asked in a surprised tone.

Edith nodded. 'I read it somewhere. Well, it wasn't the hoped-for success. There *is* one way to break this damned backwardness of the blacks,' and she put backwardness in quotes by the tone of her voice, 'that's to take them away from their parents when they're two or even one year old, and bring them up among middle-class whites – you know, with books and music in the house and a stable home life. Then we'd see –'

'Wha-at? Pretty drastic,' Gert said, now bringing a big blue plastic bowl of peach ice cream to the table.

'Yes,' Edith went on in a gentle voice, thinking a soft approach might sink in better, 'but it's the only way to break the vicious circle. No matter how good schools are, kids still spend more time out of school than in. If colored kids were brought up in white households, we'd see – or prove – that environmental and economic conditions are more important than heredity.'

'Hear, hear!' said Norm.

Dinah had come in for the ice cream.

Edith wondered, however, if she really believed that environment was more important than heredity. Over the ice cream, she found herself reversing what she had said. She thought heredity was more important, had a slight edge on environment, and she said so. Then Gert got up in arms. This was racism.

'Aryan crap!' Gert said.

But Edith didn't back down. Lincoln learned his sums by writing on the back of a shovel. Nobody had been pouring money into his school.

'Cool it, girls!' Norm said, and he had to repeat it, because they were both talking at once.

'Jesus!' Gert said, exasperated.

The conflict left Edith dazed. She found herself wondering if the girl called Luce even existed? Of course. She had seen her, in her own living room, could even remember the pink shirt the

girl had been wearing. Gert served coffee. Then she showed
Edith the baby picture that Edith had noticed, and it was
Derek's baby son. Gert's voice was friendly now, but Edith
sensed that something had changed between them, maybe irre-
parably. Or was she imagining this, just because she had been
hurt by Gert's opposition? At any rate, by the time she said
good night, the atmosphere had not thawed, she felt, though
Norm seemed as usual, and Edith was for a second embarrassed
at seeing the neat, purple paper bag beside her coat on the
Johnsons' old sofa. She had brought Gert a present, and to offer
it now seemed like an appeasement, to take it home again,
worse.

'Oh, brought you something, Gert! And Norm. It's for the
house,' Edith handed the bag to Gert.

'Oh, gee!' Then Gert pulled out the square of white linen
tablecloth. 'Oh, it's gorgeous! From your old aunt, I bet!'

'Yes. Well – just for décor,' Edith said. 'Bridge table size. Or
it'll hang over the edge a bit.'

'Isn't that pretty,' said Norm, touching it carefully. 'Bet it's
a hundred years old.'

Edith smiled. 'Thank you, Gert, for a great dinner.'

Norm saw her down to her car. She drove homeward, still
feeling uneasy, without knowing exactly why. She didn't want to
lose Gert's friendship, or even see their friendship cool. Was it
Cliffie worrying her? Or Brett? The thought of Brett sent a
resentment, or anger, over her. His lawyer's letter to Carstairs
seemed merely petulant. If Brett or the lawyer wanted to accuse
somebody, why didn't they do it outright – accuse either her or
Cliffie?

On Wednesday of the following week, Edith received a typewritten letter from Brett on the *Post*'s stationery. It said:

Dear Edith,

This morning I heard by letter from the lawyer of Dr Carstairs
who dismisses my concern (about causes of George's death) as
'already clearly stated,' and he says the doctor would be willing to
answer further specific questions, should I wish.

My personal view is that Cliffie gave him an overdose. Of course –

246

who cares about fighting for the old these days? Such things are done every day, I suppose. I asked C. direct, didn't I? But what if I had questioned him for half an hour in a room alone? I can see him now, denying, like a madman. Well, never fear, my dear, I am not going to pursue the matter any further. Neither shall I turn loose of my own view. It will never be determined, probably. Certainly not after the peremptory disposal of my uncle's remains.

It goes without saying that this situation does not make me any prouder of my son or fonder of him. He is a mystery to me and I think to you.

My uncle's will is still under probate. I shall send you, however, a check for at least $10,000 when the estate comes to me.

> Yours with love and all
> good wishes,
> Brett

Edith folded the letter slowly, absently carried it up to her workroom, where she kept all her papers. The coldness, she thought, and the snideness. Couldn't he have written to Cliffie, for instance, a careful, tactful letter, if he wanted to worm the truth out of him? And she found her feelings settling once more into the groove they had been in when she had seen Brett last: the nerve of him, harping on the *cause* of George's death, when George had been for years almost too weak to get out of bed to cross his room. A current of cold air could have carried him away in the winter, a fall on the floor one of the times he tried to get up for something. And now Brett was trying to stir up a case of murder!

She was not going to say anything to Carstairs. Let him speak to her again, if he chose to.

When Edith had recovered her calm, she sat down at her worktable and opened her diary to her last entry, which had been Sunday after the Johnsons' dinner, and after she had run up the curtains for the spare room. She had written cheerfully about the progress on the room, and the coming of spring weather.

C. back on these shores again & coming with D. & baby Josephine next weekend. I have knitted a coat sweater – white with some pink. Shall give them lobster one night, squab the next, commanded in advance from the Cracker Barrel. Both are gourmets which puts me on my mettle.

Life here more cheerful since I putter around 'improving the house', painting & so forth. I am happy and feel well.

D. rings at least twice a week, says J. can say a whole sentence correctly & can read several letters of the alphabet. We shall see! She is not yet two years old.

26

Cliffie had gone several times to the Cartwheel Inn during the weeks after his date with Luce. He imagined that the plump proprietor winced or groaned silently when he saw him come in the door. Cliffie always looked around first to see if Luce might be there. He couldn't prevent himself from looking around, though he always meant to go coolly to the bar and order a beer, and then look around, or maybe Luce, if she were there, would come up to him. This had never happened.

She hadn't left her home address with the Cartwheel. That Cliffie had ascertained months ago. It was now October. Cliffie had even sounded out the waiters. He had inquired, trying to make his manner casual, if a girl named Lucy Beckman (or a girl looking like her) had possibly bought drinks or a meal and charged it to her family, leaving an address. No luck. He had asked at a couple of shops in Brunswick Corner, and one shopkeeper had asked him if he was a bill-collector. But most shopkeepers knew Cliffie, knew also that he was hung up on this girl. Cliffie didn't like it that they knew or suspected, but it couldn't be helped.

'At least,' Cliffie said to one of the shop owners – Bart Newman, gifts, candy – 'it's like having a poster up saying "wanted". A lot of people are keeping their eyes open.' That had been on a sunny morning when he had been feeling especially optimistic, friendly with everyone, even happy. Luce made him happy and unhappy too, as they said in a lot of popular songs.

His mother was sympathetic, mostly. But twice she had said to him, shaking her head nervously as she often did lately, 'I sometimes feel that girl was a dream of both of us. It's funny.'

'But you saw her, mom!' Cliffie had replied.

Then his mother, the second time, had looked away, as if she wasn't even going to admit that she had seen her.

For three days last summer Cliffie had run an item in the *Philadelphia Inquirer*: Would Luce Beckman please contact C. H., Brunswick Corner. Urgent, desperate. Plus his phone number. This had brought no result, and Cliffie had thought that to keep on with it would be money down the drain.

By October, Cliffie had lost about twenty pounds. He bought a few new trousers, rather than bunch his old ones up with a belt. He still worked off and on at the Chop House, and some of the fellows there had joked about his new slenderness, asking him if it was due to a diet or a girl. Cliffie did not appreciate that. In fact, the fellows probably knew it was a girl, probably had heard about Luce. But Cliffie was more annoyed by their subtly cynical attitude which seemed to imply that it didn't matter much if it was a girl or not, because he would never get a girl anyway.

To add to Cliffie's ill-ease in town, his mother seemed to be in increasingly hot water – or tepid maybe – because of things she wrote in the *Bugle* editorials. This fall it was something she had written about birth control. If it wasn't one thing – griping about the one thousand new houses being built on the south side of Brunswick Corner – it was something else. Cliffie hadn't read the birth control piece, but he was sure his mother had been for it, and though Cliffie was for it too and thought most intelligent people were for it, it was amazing the number of apparently bright people who weren't for it. Surely they couldn't all be Catholics. Two women, one old, one youngish, had said something to Cliffie on the street. The old one: 'How's your mother standing up against all the letters about that *child – birth* ...'

'Oh – just letting 'em blow away,' Cliffie had replied with a smile, disgusted with the old hag. It had been a windy day, and he had thought his words appropriate. Cliffie knew what his mother had written concerned abortion too, because the younger woman (pregnant), had used the word abortion. Cliffie hated the word, had never applied himself to unraveling all the fuss about it, and he had come off badly in this brief encounter, not replying anything intelligent. He wanted to ask his mother exactly what she had said (the *Bugle* issue it had appeared in now being so old, he had no idea of its date), yet the subject was so distasteful, Cliffie could not bring himself to ask a question. His mother would enlighten him, Cliffie was sure, if he asked about it, because he could see that his mother felt sure of herself, really defiant of the others. Once his mother had had quite a conversation (probably about this) on the phone with Gert Johnson, and when Cliffie had asked what it was all about, his mother had said, 'Oh, Gert thinks something I wrote was too strong. Where does one get if things aren't strong?' The way his mother had said 'too strong' might as well have been a sneer at Gert.

His mother also talked a lot against Nixon, and just as bitterly. How anyone could get so excited over those stuffed shirts in Washington, Cliffie couldn't understand. They were all alike. Years ago when he had taken more interest in professional football teams, his mother had said *they* were all alike. But he could throw it back at her in regard to presidents, governors, no matter what in politics. We all have our games, Cliffie thought, and felt it a philosophical observation. All in the mind, after all.

It had occurred to Cliffie to make a dummy of Luce for his room. He wouldn't necessarily sleep with it, of course, but what a pleasure it would be to be able to see a life-sized figure of her, pretty and slim in her dark blue slacks, pink shirt – all made of what? Straw stitched into canvas, he supposed. The problem of the materials threw him off. He perhaps wouldn't be able to hide it from his mother. But if he lived alone, he felt he would have made a dummy of Luce. Stuck it away in his closet when people came, maybe, unless he was lucky enough to know the kind of people who could laugh at it, as he would laugh, if he had people in.

Cliffie now had over six hundred dollars in his savings account, earning four-and-a-half percent interest a year, and over a hundred in his checking account. His mother didn't know these figures. It made him feel good to have some money behind him. It meant potential freedom, such as taking a trip somewhere. He saved quite a bit – maybe three-quarters – of his salary and tips from the Chop House and other odd jobs, and gave his mother at least fifteen dollars a week, sometimes twenty. She was always talking about 'just making it' or 'breaking even' at the end of a month. If she were ever in real straits, meaning if the house was, Cliffie imagined crashing through with a few hundred to bail them out, imagined being a hero for a while. But Cliffie knew he would not enjoy having to do that. Better to prod his father, Cliffie thought, if need be – earning a New York salary and married to a rich woman to boot!

Brett's promised ten-thousand-dollar check came just before Christmas that year. Brett, in a letter Edith knew he had spent some time drafting, affected a polite warmth and concern for her and Cliffie, and said that though the probate had not yet been completed (it took a year, Edith supposed), he was sending this on now, since it might be welcome at Christmas time. The check roused Edith's ire. Then she laughed a little. She had been alone when she opened Brett's letter, Cliffie being out in the driveway messing around with his Volks.

That day she had said nothing to Cliffie about the check, which she had folded and stuck under the saucer of an African violet plant in the kitchen. The cleaning woman wasn't coming that day – a new one now, Rosalie, Friday mornings – and Edith didn't care if Cliffie saw it or not. Edith had a usual day, morning at a typewriter revamping an article with *Ramparts* in mind, because the article had been rejected elsewhere. For *Ramparts* she would have to make it considerably wilder, go into fantasy really, and Brett's letter and check had put Edith just in the mood.

'You're in a good mood today,' Cliffie remarked, as they sat down to an early lunch. Cliffie had to start at the Chop House as 'extra staff' by 1 o'clock for a birthday group, one of those things that went on until 4 p.m. and meant good tips.

'Yes. And why not?' Edith said.

Her afternoon at the Thatchery went well too. She felt full of energy, intended to finish her article (which needed just a final paragraph), and go over it tonight for word changes. Tomorrow morning she would type it in triplicate, send it off to *Ramparts*, send a copy to Gert to make her laugh, and keep one copy at home.

Cliffie was home when Edith arrived at 7:15 p.m. He looked weary but content, nursing a beer can as he watched television.

'How was it?' Edith asked.

Cliffie hauled himself up and went into the kitchen, following his mother. 'Forty-eight bucks in tips.' He had not been able to refrain from saying that.

'Not – *bad*!' said Edith.

Nelson miaowed also, as if astonished, though his face had its usual calm, and Edith knew his mind was on his supper. He was always fed just before she and Cliffie ate.

Edith asked Cliffie to bring her a scotch and soda, and when he returned with it, she said, 'Did you see this?' and picked up Brett's check.

'No. A check?'

'Present from Brett.'

'Yeah? How much?'

'Ten thousand dollars.'

'*Jee* – pers! Do you mean it?' Cliffie reached for the check, which his mother had dropped on the kitchen table. 'Holy smoke! – *I* never saw a check for ten thousand dollars before!'

'You probably would if you ever bought a house,' Edith replied, and began cutting Nelson's food, which was kidney tonight, raw. 'Presumably from George. But Brett might've said so.'

'Oh – Gee-*owge*! I don't believe it. Old tightwad wouldn't leave – I bet he never left a quarter tip in his life! He'd leave a nickel!'

The clock in the living room pinged for 7:30. Somehow Edith heard it more acutely than usual.

'What I meant was,' she went on, busy preparing her and Cliffie's meal now, 'that he might have *said* it was from George, just to be nice – or courteous.' Edith laughed loudly, briefly. 'No, this presumably comes from Brett. Big present. Especially since the will isn't probated yet.'

'Oh. You mean George left us even more, maybe.'

Edith laughed again, so hard that tears came to her eyes, and she couldn't speak.

Cliffie grinned. 'No. Okay. I get it. Buying us off, sort of, in case George did leave more?'

The idea of George leaving anybody anything – least of all to her – sent Edith into near hysterics, and she bent double. 'Who knows?' she said, gasping.

'Well, hell, Brett must've seen the will. No? He's the main – He gets it all, doesn't he?'

'Yes. I think so.'

'Well –' Cliffie gestured, looking at the check on the table. 'If I were you, I'd ask to see the will myself.'

Edith went suddenly to the check, picked it up and tore it in half. '*That's* what I think of Brett's check. *And* of George.'

'Hey, mom, you're *crazy* – doing that!'

'I don't want it. It's really distasteful.' She looked at the astonished face of her son, realizing that she wanted an audience for what she had just done, vaguely ashamed that her son was her only audience, because he didn't fully understand the way she felt. She knew how she felt, could have put it into words. But it wasn't worth it with Cliffie.

'Well –' Cliffie had gone a bit pale. 'Brett can always sign you another check.'

'I don't want another check.'

'Why the hell not, if he's getting a lot from that old geezer? Why the hell not after all we – all you did for him? Mom, you're not thinking straight now. We can always patch that check up, can't we? Put some scotch tape on it, the way they do dollar bills.'

Edith set her teeth. *You are not my son*, she wanted to say. Wrong. He was her son. She wasn't going to repeat what she had said. They decided to eat in the living room, because there was something on television tonight that wasn't bad, Cliffie reminded her. He had mentioned it that morning. Cliffie said something else about the check, which Edith did not reply to, and indeed she had managed to switch off Cliffie's comments, as she might have switched off the radio or the television.

How could she really include Cliffie in her thoughts, in her reasoning, Edith thought as she ate her food (looking sightlessly at the television screen), a man of twenty-five who kept a match-book, a *match-book*, like a sacred relic of Luce Beckman, whom he hadn't seen in five or six months now? This sacred match-book from Conti's Cross-Keys Inn now lay on Cliffie's cluttered table in his room, with a little circle of space around it. Once she had reached for it to light a cigarette when she had been in his room, talking to him, and he had shouted, 'Don't touch that! – I mean, I'm saving it – want to keep the matches in it.' Cliffie knew that she knew they had gone to dinner at the Cross-Keys that night. Cliffie had gone back to the Cross-Keys to ask if Luce might have come in again. Cliffie had told Edith this in his cups and nearly weeping. In his way, Cliffie depressed Edith as much as George ever had. Edith was glad to finish her meal, pour her coffee and Cliffie's and excuse herself to go up to her workroom.

She wanted to make an entry in her diary. Edith uncapped her fountain pen and wrote:

20 Dec. 69

Splendid day. Long letter from Cliffie, with some snaps of near-by village where he goes looking around (he says) on Sundays which is one of the market days. Camels, heaps of oranges, women in – the veil. D. phoned. She considers going out to join C. when the baby is a few months older. I really think she should. C.'s every-two-months trips home are not enough. I used to think it a good idea, to keep their love fresh and all that. Now I am not so sure. They are so happy together – and who knows how long that can last? It will of course *last*, but accidents can happen, even such as death, & it would be cruel to think that they were deprived of even a week's joy and happiness together that they might have had. C. hints at another 'promotion' of some kind, says he will be home about as soon as his letter, meaning day after tomorrow latest. He will go to New Jersey first, of course, and how good it will be to hear his voice on the phone! A pity B. did not live to see C. make such a success of himself!

Edith had in the last month decided that Brett should be dead since about three years now. It didn't matter that this conflicted with George's demise and funeral service at which Brett had been present. Edith was writing her diary for pleasure, and was taking poetic licence, as she put it to herself.

Am enjoying still the lovely things, little and big, which dear Aunt M. passed on to me. The old serviettes (as she often called them), big oval tablecloth and the round one, the settee and arm-chair, the two quilts. How to describe a quilt made by someone you know? Every stitch taken with loving care (I like to imagine) by someone who loved you: that is what it means.

She could also have mentioned her gratitude for twenty thou-sand dollars, in the form of two Treasury Bonds, which Melanie had left her, generous enough considering that Melanie, though childless, had nieces and nephews and grand-nieces and so on almost beyond count, but Edith didn't like writing about money in her diary. Brett had cut his contribution from a hundred and fifty to a hundred dollars a month. What was she to deduce from this? That he thought Cliffie ought to be taking care of her? A tapering off toward zero? A gesture to ease his conscience? Edith believed it was the latter.

27

'Beer, please,' Cliffie said to the Cartwheel barman. 'Sure, Miller's is fine.' Cliffie was feeling cool that evening, standing with one leg over a bar stool, wearing a new dubonnet blazer, now unbuttoned. He hadn't even glanced around for Luce, as he usually did, for which he congratulated himself.

Tok! His beer arrived, and Cliffie's dollar bill was already on the counter. Cliffie did glance at the door, twice, as people came in. The old plump proprietor sometimes hovered near the door, greeting people. He was there tonight.

'Oh, by the way, Cliffie!' said the skinny pansy barman. 'Something in the paper today.' He pulled up a folded newspaper from somewhere. 'Here it is, yeah. Isn't this the girl you were asking about? Long time ago?' He pointed to a small item on a page Cliffie instantly recognized as the society page of the *Philadelphia Inquirer.*

Cliffie read it. *Lucy G. Beckman to Wed Kenneth L. Forbes,* said the one-column headline. Cliffie jumped slightly, but remained on the stool, 'Oh, yeah. Yeah,' he said.

'Lucy Beckman. Wasn't that the girl you were asking about?'

'Yeah, but that was a couple of *years* ago,' Cliffie said. 'Sure, I know all about this.' Cliffie pushed the paper aside.

'See-ee?' said the barman, smiling, dumping an avalanche of ice cubes into a tub with a gelid crash. 'Pretty good detective I am, eh?'

Cliffie retreated within himself, like a whole army defeated, covering its wounds, wary of the outside, the enemy on the periphery. Of course it had been a long time since he had seen Luce – two years now, a little more. Cliffie didn't like to think of the word *years.* It scared him. In a way, of course, he had given up Luce, and in a way he hadn't, because love didn't give up, according to all the songs, the poetry. He thought of the many times, beyond count, when he had imagined making love to Luce. And now he had to imagine her busy all those months, years, seeing people, meeting men, maybe making love with *them*, and finally choosing one of them to marry! Cliffie had put on a faint, casual smile, and now he lit a cigarette, shaking. He was of course paying no further attention to the barman, who hadn't a glimmer of what the news meant to him, who couldn't care less, and anyway the guy was queer, so what the hell could he know about anything? Kenneth – something – Forbes. Was he some good-looking or rich swine who had been hanging around for some time, maybe the one Luce had had a quarrel with? She had implied a quarrel somewhere, either with her parents or with a man. And now the bastard had made it – maybe. Cliffie had an impulse to look up the son of a bitch and kill him! A man to man fight. Reduce his face to a pulp. Beat him until it was impossible for him to breathe through his broken nose. Cliffie ordered a scotch.

Nothing happened that evening, absolutely nothing. Cliffie had brought his Volks, and was quite pissed by the time he drove home a little after 11 p.m., but he drove carefully and made it. When he entered the house, he heard his mother's typewriter clicking upstairs. The house felt warm. What month was it? April. Yes, of course, April. Almost three years since he had met, or seen, Luce. Cliffie had a drink on that. After all, a nightcap, no harm in a nightcap if it was safely back home.

Clickety-click. A pause. Then the spurt of clicks again. Sometimes his mother worked till nearly 2 in the morning. Cliffie shook his head indulgently. If she wasn't clicking away, she was *picking* away at the clay stuff, sculpting. Cliffie laughed a little. What was she working on now? It was an abstract-looking thing, about two feet square. Cliffie had seen his own head (though his mother didn't much like his going into her room), and had been quite startled and pleased, because he looked so handsome. Maybe his mother *did* like him, had been Cliffie's first reaction, but of course he had merely smiled, and made some com-

258

ment about its being a good job. Then his mother had sold that crazy piece to *Ramparts* or *Shove It* or some such, and had been proud of it, telling him, telling the Quickmen, though Cliffie knew damn well these were kinky-kooky publications, full of sordid exaggerations, things that could be libelous, Cliffie would have thought.

He found himself leaning heavily against the sideboard, the end of his second nightcap in his hand, staring at the tarnished silver tray with its silver teapot, sugar bowl, creamer. He had noticed before, months ago, that his mother wasn't polishing silver stuff the way she had used to, and the cleaning woman had too much to do, coming just once a week, to do it, Cliffie supposed.

Then he realized he was thinking all this crap, dreaming around like this, so that he wouldn't think of Luce. *Luce.* Gone now. Not married as yet, but just think of the people, relatives, family he would have to buck if he tried to interfere with the marriage, which was supposed to take place in mid-May, he recalled. Cliffie staggered into his own room, and once he had closed the door, gave way to tears, with hands over his eyes. He nearly fell, losing his balance, and threw himself on his bed and continued weeping.

Edith noticed the change in Cliffie, and the first indication to her was a tension which meant he was anxious about something or concealing something. 'Anything the matter?' Edith asked, not expecting Cliffie to answer frankly, and he hadn't. Nothing was the matter, he said. Edith wondered if the police had given him a warning about something.

It was Gert Johnson who enlightened Edith at the end of a telephone conversation which had begun about something else. 'That girl Luce Beckman – Remember a long time ago you asked if I knew her? I just happened to see she just got married in Philly. *Must* be the same one Cliffie was hung up on.'

'Oh. Oh.' Edith suddenly understood everything. 'Cliffie didn't mention it. Maybe he doesn't even know! Anyway – he doesn't talk about her any more.'

'Her father's a big-shot president, it seems – I forgot of what.'

'I think she's gone out of Cliffie's mind, thank goodness. Well, about Saturday elevenish, Gert, that's fine.' Gert was coming to see Edith in regard to a *Bugle* editorial Edith had written which was due to go to press next Tuesday.

Now Edith understood. Cliffie had regained long ago the pounds he had lost, had perhaps put on more, and more were due if he kept up the beer and the drink, which in fact had been upped in the last days. Gone also was the sacred match-book that had lain on his table for years. Had Cliffie thrown it away in a pet? Or was he guarding it in the back corner of a drawer? Edith thought of mentioning Luce, to offer Cliffie a word of sympathy, to show she took an interest in his life, then decided not to, as Cliffie might be more wounded if she did.

Gert was up in the air about a four-hundred-word editorial Edith had written in regard to student behavior and demonstrations at the local Brunswick School. Since Edith had backed up her article with quotes from a Brunswick Corner parent and one of the school teachers, she was sure she was not alone in her attitude. Edith sensed the old battle of tear-it-down, which was Gert, versus change-it-and-improve-it, which was Edith. Gert was on the side of the kids. Curious that Gert thought her far-out lately, while Edith felt herself ever more conservative.

The comparative calm of that week in May was broken by a telephone call at 1 : 30 a.m. one night at a moment when Edith was standing in her workroom pushing Plasticine into her abstract called 'City.' She had not been aware of the time until she glanced at her wristwatch on hearing the telephone. The downstairs hall light was still on, meaning Cliffie had not yet come in.

A voice ascertained that she was Mrs Howland, then told her that her son had a broken jaw and would be in the Doylestown hospital overnight and part of tomorrow.

'A car accident?' Edith asked.

'No, Mrs – Howland,' the voice drawled. 'Seems to have been a fistfight.'

'Can I reach him by telephone? Is he all right?'

'Oh, he's all right. No danger. But he can't talk very well, ma'am.'

Cliffie was brought home the next day around 7:30 p.m. by prearrangement with the hospital, which had again rung Edith. Edith had said she worked until 7. A hospital car came behind Cliffie's Volks, which was driven by an intern. Cliffie's entire head was swathed in a white bandage. He was dressed and walking, but could talk only with difficulty. One intern spoke to Edith about a liquid diet, the extraction of a tooth or two in lower left jaw (already done), and left her some pain-killing pills. Cliffie should see a local doctor for another penicillin shot tomorrow. Then the interns left.

Cliffie wanted a drink. Edith got a scotch for him. He didn't know what happened, he told his mother, and he was telling the truth, he said.

'Ho *bwok*-ko,' Cliffie said, frowning with pain, which Edith translated as 'black-out.' He did remember three or four fellows, some mysterious argument outside a bar or a restaurant in the parking lot, and then *whammo*! Cliffie waved a hand, meaning he didn't want to say any more tonight.

Cliffie was nearly as white as the bandage. Edith was surprised that he admitted to a black-out. What horrors! Yet curiously she felt cool and detached, rather like a professional nurse, and she behaved as one, turning Cliffie's bed down, making sure he had swallowed the right pills, that he could take on a milk-and-egg drink, and this she prepared. There was also soup for the future, and Cliffie wouldn't starve. Somehow Edith had an aversion to asking with whom he had fought, and maybe Cliffie didn't even know. How long was the bandage going to last? Hadn't the intern said a week?

When Gert Johnson came on Saturday morning, Edith had fresh coffee ready plus a delicious Sarah Lee cake – the round kind with white icing and pecans on top – and of course the bar was at hand too. Edith felt inspired to be cheerful, or perhaps she really felt cheerful. The cinnamon-and-butter smell of the warming cake roused Cliffie from his bed of pain (where he had been pleased to stay the last couple of days, reading and dozing), but the cake unfortunately couldn't go down as yet.

'Hey, I heard about Cliffie!' Gert said even before she had sat down.

'A broken jaw,' Edith said. 'Little brawl outside a – oh, I don't know, a roadside place in Tinicum, I gather.'

'Nothing with the police, I hope.'

'Haven't heard a word out of them.'

That subject was soon finished. Gert partook of coffee and cake, then she started in on the editorial which Edith had entitled *Some of Us Too.*

'Again, Edith, you're going to antagonize a lot of people.'

A few parents, of course. And 'again'? Edith waited patiently.

'Some of our readers are the parents of these kids.'

'Sure, I know that,' Edith said.

'I'm not so sure you should say – oh, "vile and vituperative," whatever it was.'

'That was a quote from an old letter I kept from the *Times*, a letter from a faculty member at Hunter.'

'Yes, but you equated ...'

Then they were off, though Edith did keep her calm. Brunswick School had just got a going over by the police for drug-pushing. At least fifty per cent of the kids aged thirteen to seventeen had admitted taking stuff 'sometimes or all the time,' according to a Bucks County survey, a clipping of which Edith had, because it had been in the *Trenton Standard*, but Gert considered that a minor matter. She was more concerned with Edith's saying that the kids were brainlessly imitating older college kids and making a game out of insubordination, insulting their elders, and demanding equal say in the running of the school.

'If the young really know as much as teachers about administration or even what they ought to study,' Edith said, 'then perhaps they don't need to go to school at all.'

'Oh, Edith!' Gert said, striking a palm gently against her hair, which had gone all salt-and-pepper in the last couple of years. 'Where'd you get your other quote from?'

'Penny Ditson. She –'

Gert interrupted, scoffing, as if Penny were brainless, but

262

Penny was observant and articulate, had a sixteen-year-old son and a seventeen-year-old daughter at Brunswick School, the son taking so much L S D, his grades had gone to hell and his mother was worried. The daughter – Edith had talked with her. Edith told Gert all this.

'It's just that the piece is a little too alarmist. We've got to tone it down a little.'

Edith yielded, hating it, hating herself for yielding. But it was that or breaking, possibly, with Gert, because Edith knew her editorials had strained their relations enough already, especially the birth-control-abortion ones of a couple of years ago. Neither she nor Gert owned the *Bugle*, and they needed each other to keep it going. Edith changed the subject finally by telling Gert about a sale she had made to *Shove It*, an underground newspaper. Edith had simply distorted an article that other magazines had rejected, thrown in some vulgarity, and sold it. Gert seemed surprised, but did not congratulate Edith very warmly.

'Oh, but that *Shove It*,' Gert said with a shake of her head. She was now on a short rye, short on water. 'They're really screwed up.'

Edith laughed gaily. 'Sure, or they wouldn't print my stuff. I have another idea – a fantastic game that I'm going to –'

'Hey! You've got the new Erich Fromm?' Gert had espied a book, a library book, on the coffee table.

Edith was annoyed by Gert's interruption. Gert had always interrupted, however, and always a bit more after a drink. How many more years, Edith wondered, would they go on meeting like this, talking, arguing, taking temporary and passing things so seriously? Maybe till they were seventy, eighty. People lived forever, these days, like old George, unless somebody put them out of their misery. Edith interrupted now with a certain defiance, 'However – wait till you see my game idea in print one day. It's called "Presidential Election," unless I think of a sprightlier title. There are masks of the president- and vice-president-elect, you see, and the people in them are immediately shot at the inauguration ceremony, but they're not the *real* president or vice-president. *They're* still alive, thus giving the American public the pleasure of four assassinations, because the real ones come on – oh, an hour later.'

'Say, how many drinks have you had?' Gert asked with a smile.

'None.' Edith spun on her toes and went to the bar cart. 'What I mean is, the security men, the gorillas, wear the masks, and *they're* shot, either at a convention like Bobby Kennedy or at the inauguration. But they could be wearing bullet-proof vests and so forth to protect them. They could even have steel armor on their faces like – knights of old, in fact, if they're wearing masks in the first place, which they are.'

Somehow Gert didn't like the idea, or took it too seriously. At any rate, she made a rather dampening remark. It was enough to shift Edith's feelings slightly but defiantly against Gert for the rest of her visit.

'How is Brett doing?' Gert asked, blowing cigarette smoke with a gentle puff. 'Ever hear anything from him?'

Edith shrugged. 'Not often. I'm sure he's busy. Baby nearly four – and maybe another for all I know.' She laughed, and thought suddenly – like a flash that came and went – of Cliffie's Josephine, a bit older and far prettier.

'Brett still sends you something toward the house, though. That's *some* kind of contact.'

Edith had forgotten that she had disclosed that to Gert. But it didn't much matter. 'Yes. I admit I need it. House taxes, you know, heating –'

'Don't I know!'

'I also need my job. And the house – it needs a complete paint job!' Edith forced a laugh.

'You're not kidding! It'd pay you, Edie. Especially the outside.'

Then Gert departed. Edith had agreed to let her re-write the editorial, and in a sense Edith washed her hands of it. It made her a bit sad and also resentful. To alleviate this feeling, which she didn't enjoy, she went upstairs to her workroom and opened her diary.

264

30 May 72. Best not to surface too often or at all. The joy of life is in the doing. Don't judge too much what is done or expect praise or thanks.

Then she re-read the *Times* article of 1 April 1970 from a Faculty Member. It began:

In view of the appalling situation at Hunter College, this correspondent, a faculty member, feels it incumbent upon him to inform the public as to how far a college of considerable distinction in this city has sunk.

A hard core of defiant students are riding roughshod over the sensibilities of their fellow students and faculty members with the malicious glee of those who know in advance that they will not be held accountable for whatever vile and vituperative utterances they choose to speak or print.

It went on:

A young lady informed the faculty with drawling insolence that if they remained intransigent to 'present student demands' for fifty-fifty representation on all faculty committees, the students might just go ahead and 'up our demands' – after all 'there are nineteen thousand students and one thousand faculty, and the Supreme Court has ruled one man, one vote – that is democracy.' Wild cheers and applause.

A fine hundredth anniversary for Hunter College.

She put the letter away in a folder marked News Clips, and turned back in her big diary, now more than three-quarters filled. Yes, the diary was four-fifths filled, she saw, and foresaw that this would make her write a bit smaller in future, so the diary might last out her life – or last a few years more anyway. She read (an entry of two years ago):

The difference between dream and reality is the true hell.

And on another page, simply:

'Dreams of hyper-acidity.'

Now what did that mean? A future title of something? It wasn't something she suffered from, anyhow. Another page held something written only five years ago, though it was a memory from her childhood:

Writing notes to Aunt Melanie on Tennessee birch-bark found in the woods, stripped carefully to give the most surface, later to be carefully folded into an envelope. What purity! The inside slightly moist, lovely tan color, so smooth, the writing surface, and on the back the crisp and curling thin white bark with brown flecks, reminding me of Indian canoes. 'Dear Aunt Melanie, we are spending the night in a motel near Birmingham tonight, we hope, if we make it that far. We had a picnic lunch on pine needles today in a huge forest. This is genuine birch-bark . . .' And how the pen glided over the tan, with a virginal squeak!

The virginal squeak struck Edith as comical, and she laughed now, but didn't change it. Maybe she had laughed when she had written it. She didn't remember.

28

Gert was of course right about painting the exterior of the house. So Edith set about this the following Monday morning. She telephoned a painting-and-lumber company named Leffingwell in Flemington, and they said they would send a man the following day to have a look and give an estimate. Meanwhile Cliffie had even on Sunday taken a look at the house and volunteered to do some scraping.

'It'll cut down on the final price, if I do a little work before,' Cliffie said. 'These guys get paid by the hour.'

Edith could never tell what chore would arouse Cliffie's enthusiasm, and sometimes she was pleasantly surprised.

Cliffie now had his bandage off – a little too soon – his jaw was still swollen, and he could just about eat hamburger and mashed potatoes. This however did not interfere with his beer and scotch consumption. Cliffie did sign checks sometimes on his own bank account for ten dollars, specifically for drink. Edith still bought liquor in New Jersey (not considered legal), and brought it back in her car over the bridge.

The estimate for the house painting was seven hundred dollars, which Edith had rather expected, but she put on a long face, talked of getting another estimate from a company whose name she mentioned, and the price was knocked down to six hundred. Edith agreed to this. The men arrived the Friday of that week, by which time Cliffie had done quite a bit of scraping and tying up of rose bushes for their protection.

The painting went on into the following Tuesday, since the men didn't work on Saturday. By this time Edith had finished the second draft of her piece called 'Shoot-the-President,' and sent it off to *Shove It* in New York. In this version the Vice-

President-elect wore the mask of the President-elect, and was shot at the inauguration ceremony on the theory (Edith wrote) that nobody knew or liked vice-presidents, anyway. This left the real president alive to display himself as a future target for public amusement. It was a game with possible variations. Presidents-elect, all in masks of the president-elect, would read the inaugural address, be shot down, and at once replaced by another man in president-elect mask, who would resume the script of the address, while among the crowd the unfortunate assassins, not in on the game, were at once jumped on by the populace or shot at and really killed by secret servicemen. Therefore the game, besides being fun for the public, was a way of weeding out and destroying real murderers in the nation. Edith was pleased with her story-game, but had no intention of showing it to Gert Johnson. Gert would think it far-out. Cliffie, so far, was Edith's only reader, and he loved it, which pleased Edith.

Tuesday evening shortly after 7, when Edith came home from work, she found the trio of painters had tied up their scaffolds and were drinking beer with Cliffie in the driveway. It was a lovely June evening, not too warm, with a refreshing breeze off the Delaware. A moon was rising, though it wasn't near dusk, and her house looked clean and proud again, really splendid with its doric columns and white shutters, its dark gray, almost black slate roof.

'Can't you do better than beer, Cliffie?' Edith said.

'Oh, this is just great!' one of the men said. 'After sweatin', y'know –'

One of his colleagues laughed loudly, and made some remark about the man's laziness.

The telephone rang, and Edith went in to answer it. It was Brett. Edith found herself stammering. Brett was like another world, another language, which she had forgotten.

'Where are you – did you say?'

'Lambertville. I said I'm with a friend, Pete Starr. Driving him to Doylestown tonight, and can we come by? Now, for a few minutes?'

'Well – all right. Yes, Brett.'

268

Edith hated it, realizing that she could have manufactured a previously made date, and hadn't had the wit. She checked that there was enough drink in case they wanted any, that the living room was reasonably clear of newspapers and magazines. Potato chips? Peanuts? Yes. 'Christ,' she whispered. She wasn't in a mood to see Brett.

A minute later the painters had left, and Cliffie came in with his hands full of empty beer cans.

'Brett's coming,' Edith said.

'What? *Really!* Really?'

'Bringing a friend for a few minutes en route to Doylestown.'

'To the mortuary, I hope.'

A car arrived. Brett came in, looking yet thinner, grayer, more anxious, or maybe she was imagining. The friend was a sturdy, boring-looking man of about sixty with gray hair, dark suit and tie, the type who might be a senator, an accountant, anything but a journalist, Edith thought.

'Pete's a writer,' Brett said as soon as they were seated, the first thing he had said besides 'Hello,' and his friend's name. 'Non-fiction. Political books.'

'Oh,' Edith replied in an interested tone. She was on her feet by the bar, waiting for orders. 'Scotch?'

Brett sprang up to help her. Scotch on the rocks, and with a splash, Brett and Mr Starr wanted.

Cliffie strolled in. His jaw was still a bit swollen, making him look, in general, fatter. 'Hello, dad.'

'Hi, Cliffie! And how're things? This is Pete Starr. My son – Cliffie.'

Cliffie gave one of his brief nods and a mumble, and stuffed his hands in his trousers pockets. He drifted across the room to get a drink.

'Who's your publisher?' Edith asked.

'Oh – um – Random House now,' said Mr Starr.

Then Brett asked about Gert, about the *Bugle*. 'You're still – writing stuff –'

'Same as usual,' said Edith. 'Don't you get it? I thought you

269

were sent a courtesy subscription.' She smiled pleasantly. She knew he was sent it.

'Can't always recognize your stuff,' said Brett, smiling also.

'Oh.' Edith glanced at Mr Starr, who was looking her up and down (she was now seated), as if appraising her for – what, at her age?

'Why're the rose bushes covered?' Brett asked.

'Oh, didn't you notice? The whole house has just been painted! Well, it's getting a bit dark outside. They've just finished.'

'Sniff-sniff!' said Cliffie, lifting his nose. 'Can't you smell the paint, Brett?'

'Why, yes!' said Mr Starr. 'Now I do.'

'Job going all right at the – What's it called?' Brett asked.

'The Hatchery,' said Cliffie. 'Or the Scratchery.'

Edith paid Cliffie no mind. 'The shop. Sure.' Edith lit a cigarette. 'Money's very useful. Also I like working. And –'

'What?' asked Brett.

'Nothing.' She had been going to mention her short story sale, but Brett wouldn't have any respect for *Ramparts* or even a sense of humor about *Shove It*. Edith really wanted to inform Brett he was dead, since about three years now. Mr Starr's arm was rising at long intervals to bring his glass to his lips, reminding Edith of toy ducking birds whose beaks absorbed liquid causing their heads to jump backwards, and Mr Starr's head did jump a bit backwards soon after his glass touched his lips. 'And how is your family?' Edith asked Brett.

'Oh, thank you, quite all right.' Now Brett chuckled for no apparent reason, almost like his old soft laugh when he was happy and relaxed, but now it came out like a habit, a social gesture, like covering a mouth when yawning. 'And Cliffie – you've put on weight, I see.'

'Thenk you,' said Cliffie with his English accent.

Edith laughed.

'Fond of the beer, my son,' said Brett to Starr. 'That's obvious.'

'Miller's, thenk you,' said Cliffie, dead-pan but enjoying himself, and lifted his scotch to the two men and drank. He was pleased to see that his father was taking the best-to-retreat tactic, and concentrating on his mother again.

'And how's your –'

'Can I freshen your drink, Mr Starr?' Edith said at the same moment, and got up, because Mr Starr was hesitating, then relenting, and presenting his empty glass. While she was making the drink, Brett said:

'How's the sculpture coming along? I'd love to show Pete. Could you possibly –'

'I don't think my workroom's in a state to be seen just –'

'Oh, come on, doesn't matter,' Brett said.

She'd be a coward if she didn't let them go up, Edith supposed. 'Very well.' She handed Mr Starr his drink. 'It's upstairs,' she said to him.

Up they went, and Cliffie remained downstairs. Edith put on the light. Her heads of Melanie and of Cliffie were exposed, uncovered, and her work-in-progress, 'City,' was on its wooden pedestal, so nearly finished that the plastic sheet was not at the moment on the floor. Mr Starr strolled around reflectively with hands behind him, looking at her abstracts, Edith noticed, not the two heads. Her work-table looked its usual semi-mess, but her diary was neatly at the left back corner, closed of course, and under the last couple of *Bugles*.

'Interesting. Yes. What's this – called?' Mr Starr asked of 'City.'

'Just "City",' Edith said.

'Like a rabbit warren,' he replied, smiling. 'How right you are. Disturbed by – overcrowding. Hm-m. Thinking of – Lorentz, maybe.'

Edith hesitated, not caring one hundred percent for Lorentz. 'I'm not a Lorentz fan. I like Fromm better, frankly.' She wasn't sure Starr understood that she didn't believe in the necessity of aggression, and didn't give a damn if Starr understood or not. She thought of asking him if he liked Daniel Bell's work, then abandoned this, too. She wanted them both out of her room.

They drifted out, Mr Starr preceding, and he went down the stairs. Brett lingered in the hall.

'How're things really, Edie?'

'Not too bad. Why?'

'Cliffie doesn't look in the pink,' Brett continued in a low tone. 'Gert phoned me. She thinks –'

Edith had suspected that Gert had telephoned. 'Well, thinks what?'

'Just that you're under a lot of strain just now. You never cashed the ten thousand, it seems.'

'No, thank you. I didn't want it. I also don't want any part of the fourteen thousand in the Dreyfus – just so there's no fuzziness in the future about that one. – I'm doing all right, Brett, if it comes to money.'

'But this silly job!' Then he seemed to give that up. 'And Cliffie boozing as usual.' Brett was whispering.

What was all this, Edith wondered, an account of her woes? 'What's silly about my job? And what're you doing about Cliffie, for instance, if you're so worried? Have you asked him to New York to have a talk with him – get him a job, something like that?'

Brett smiled a little, as if trying to get Cliffie a job was an absurdity, something that would reflect badly on him, Brett. 'I did invite him – a couple of months ago. By phone. He didn't tell you? He didn't seem interested.'

Maybe not, after you've accused him of giving George an overdose, Edith thought. She walked to the stairs and went down.

Mr Starr, who was not seated, suggested that he and Brett might be going. Edith had the feeling he had been talking with Cliffie, who was sitting in Melanie's rose-sprigged armchair.

'Your sculpture is most interesting,' Mr Starr said. 'Are you taking lessons anywhere – or did you?'

'No,' Edith replied. 'It's just a pastime.'

'No, no, it's quite good. I think you throw yourself into it!' said Mr Starr genially. 'Now if you two would like a minute in private, I'll go out to the car. Thank you very much, Mrs Howland, for the lovely drinks.' Mr Starr left.

Cliffie was watching all this from his chair.

Brett beckoned Edith into the front hall, away from Cliffie. 'The inside of the house could use a painting too. And there must be a lot of things –'

'Yes, there are a lot of things.'

Brett nodded. 'I'd like you to be comfortable, Edie.'

She said nothing.

'Well – bye-bye and thanks.' Brett leaned through the doorway of the living room. 'Bye, Cliffie!'

'G'bye, Brett.'

Brett left. The car purred away.

Cliffie wriggled as if he had insects under his shirt. 'What a prick! That old guy, I mean.'

'You think so?' Edith found the drink she had left and picked it up. She was thinking of 'Shoot-the-President,' pleased – she admitted for the tenth time – with her effort there. And there was her Democratic-Headquarters-burglary idea too, which she wanted to start on.

'Guy looks like a spy. C I A type, you know?' Cliffie said. 'Something phony about him.' And Cliffie got up to refresh his drink.

'Cliffie, did you do anything with Brett's check? That famous ten thousand?' Edith remembered that she had simply left it, torn in half, on the kitchen table.

Cliffie was embarrassed, but not seriously so. 'I did take it. It's in my room. I can't do anything *with* it, you know, because it's made out to you. *I* don't want to do anything with it.'

'I know, but you may as well destroy it. Brett asked about it.' Edith supposed that Cliffie was simply looking at it now and then, marveling at the sum.

'Well – is it serious, whether I destroy it or not?'

Edith laughed. 'Frankly no.'

She went into the kitchen to get dinner. Edith was thinking about Gert Johnson telephoning Brett and telling him about her 'strain' and what else? It had been personal, anyway, not just a business call about newspaper work. Edith had a feeling that people were ganging up on her. First signs of paranoia, Edith thought, and smiled. She was *glad* Brett had noticed that the interior of the house looked shabby, despite Melanie's new chair and settee, which Brett had not noticed, perhaps. The house was still running along, at least. Brett should have seen George's room, she thought, which looked terrific now! And Edith smiled again to herself.

Bang! She was thinking of the alternative 'wins' and 'winners' she had put at the end of her 'Shoot-the-President' piece. One winner of the game was the genuine president-elect who was *not* shot at (after so many replacements), because there were simply no more assassins left among the spectators. Then she thought of Brett, imagined his Manhattan life in a well-kept apartment with his cozy little wife, his young wife in bed every night, and maybe again pregnant. She wondered if Brett said the same things to Carol that he had used to say to her? Edith felt that she didn't care if he did.

Time for a snatch of television news while the macaroni and cheese (frozen) got its crust in the oven. Nixon was considering a trip to China, first president to make such a visit, etc. etc. and Edith's blood boiled with a wrath that she realized was irrational. Nixon was cracked. Anything to escape facing the people, to avoid answering questions that the people and the journalists asked. Even Gert had said that.

'Switch it off, Cliffie, it makes me sick. Dinner's ready.'

Edith took her head of Cliffie to a shop in Philadelphia that did casting. Bronze was out of the question because of cost, but there was a new material, a kind of plaster which could be lightened with sandpaper on surfaces such as the tip of a nose, the bulges of a forehead, and the result resembled bronze. The librarian at the Brunswick Corner library had told Edith about the shop, for which Edith was grateful. The job was going to take about three weeks, as the shop had other orders, and would cost around fifty dollars. Edith was pleased. Now the head could have *a place* in the house, a finished work like a picture, not simply remain in sticky Plasticine up in her workroom. 'City' Edith was proud of, with its fleck-like, action-filled daubs which represented people in the tiny 'rooms,' running, walking, peering out, or sleeping, brooding, collapsing. Casting this would be a horror and probably impossible, however. Edith embarked on another short story, this time straight fiction without a political slant. Her thought of speaking to Gert about telephoning Brett had vanished, which was probably all to the good. Gert called up at least twice a week on *Bugle* matters, but Edith never mentioned Brett. One morning Gert rang up to tell her their paper supplier was closing shop, retiring, and there was a choice of two other companies, both more expensive.

'Well, everything's getting more expensive,' Edith remarked patiently.

'I'm nearby. Can I pop over?'

'By all means!'

Edith was at her typewriter when Gert arrived, but she left it willingly and went downstairs. It was a little after 10. Gert wore lavender slacks, a purple sleeveless blouse bulging with bosom, as her slacks bulged, at the thighs, with flesh also. Gert was a bit knock-kneed.

'Whew! Sorta muggy today,' Gert said.

They discussed the newsprint problem, and decided, as Edith had supposed they would, to take the lower bidder between the two suppliers. The *Bugle* now had a circulation of five thousand. Lots of families sent it to their kids as far away as Australia.

In a silence, Edith said, 'I heard you phoned Brett not so long ago. He came to see me.'

'Oh, yeah. I did. Told him about your short stories – and your sculpting.'

'Do you know his friend Starr? Peter Starr?' Edith was mainly curious about him.

'No.'

'Well, what did you tell Brett?'

'What do you mean?'

Edith took a breath. 'I had the feeling he was worried about me. Somehow. And I wondered why.'

'No-o,' Gert said, smiling. 'I think I told him about some success you'd had selling a story to the underground press.'

Edith took a cigarette.

'I thought that story was fun,' Gert went on in a merry tone that Edith sensed was phony.

'Who is this Peter Starr? A psychiatrist?'

'I don't know him. Never heard of him.'

That was very likely true. 'I really had the feeling Brett and the other man were casing me. I wondered why. Then he mentioned that you'd phoned him.'

Gert looked briefly embarrassed, but perhaps was only pretending embarrassment. 'Well, yes, Edie. Matter of fact, I was worried about you, and I didn't think it would hurt – Brett knowing you so well – for him to come and see you. What's the harm in that? I don't think he sees you enough, considering you're both on good terms.'

Edith thought again of cautious Peter Starr. She had heard of a husband somewhere bringing a psychiatrist to the house suddenly, and the wife had been whisked away to a loony-bin, kidnaped more or less. 'Besides the underground press, which has the virtue of being amusing at least –'

Gert gazed into space, or at the bar cart.

'You used to be pretty far-out too, Gert,' Edith went on in a calm tone, because she wanted to learn what she could from Gert, 'yet you called me – doctrinaire or reactionary one night at your house! Potential right-winger or some such. I don't know about that. But I do believe that authoritarianism is coming because it has to. It's an historical – or anyway an objective fact, nothing to do with me personally. Society is becoming increasingly complex.'

'That's not the same as believing *in* it. Or preaching it – authoritarianism. You want to organize things, Edie, in your own way!'

'Nonsense! How could I? – One can go on believing in what one wants to believe in forever, I suppose. Isn't it more intelligent – even more interesting to see what's coming and – be braced?'

'Braced for fascism? Authoritarianism? – Nixon, that creep, for instance?'

'Why was he elected in the first place? Advertising, television. Do you expect brains, judgement from people who watch the crap on TV? Everybody in the United States watching on average four hours a day?'

Gert groaned as if she were bored, as if what she, Gert, was talking about – hope, maybe, could it be? – was something concrete and worth fighting for.

'It's galloping right-wing fascism or authoritarianism right now with Nixon,' Edith said, 'and not even the right kind, and if I write for the underground press, it's only like saying, why in hell not have some fun out of the situation? Why're you being so serious about it? I mean – what good are you doing, just saying Nixon ought to be kicked out? At least I make a mockery of Nixon's filthy methods of eliminating opponents who – who still –'

Gert rolled from side to side on the sofa, and Edith thought of Mother Earth, swinging in its course, summer, winter, tipping its axis. 'Edie, I'm worried about you,' Gert said.

Edith was – if she was frank with herself – a little worried about herself also, mentally, psychically, and yet, what was wrong? Her health was fine, the house was certainly not a shambles, she and Cliffie were making it financially, and she was holding a job, plus doing several hours a week of *Bugle* work. 'Well, tell me more,' Edith said finally.

'You've been through so much in the last three or four years – Brett, George's death, Melanie's death, Cliffie drinking too much, let's face it,' Gert said in a lower tone with a glance at Edith, though Cliffie's transistor was on at nearly full blast, playing something that sounded like 'Ring around the Rosie.' Gert went on, 'But believe me, I think you're doing *well*.'

Edith was impatient. It sounded like a word of comfort for the dying. 'To get down to brass tacks, did you tell Brett I needed a psychiatrist or something like that?'

'Well, yes, I did,' Gert said with her flat Pennsylvania accent. 'No harm in it, Edie. I really am worried and so is Norm. Just a little guidance sometimes – talking things over with someone –'

'This one didn't want to talk. Or he hasn't rung me back in the last – what is it?'

'You wouldn't object to seeing someone, would you? The way people have physical check-ups, that's all,' Gert said with a roly-poly shrug.

'No. But he might've come here in his true colors. Maybe

they're both drawing up papers now, coming to get me in a strait-jacket?' Edith smiled at her old friend Gert, feeling that Gert was not such a good friend, was not and never had been as straightforward as Edith had always given her credit for being.

'It's not like that at all, Edie. You know, if you could talk with a psychiatrist about your worries, discouragements and so forth – all those things could get straightened out. Brett said he'd pay for it, by the way. So if you're willing – It wouldn't have to be this fellow you met the –'

'I hope not. He didn't look outstandingly bright to begin with. A G.C.B. Cliffie called him, Grand Crashing Bore. Looked like a Nixon-voter. Well –' Edith tried to be cheerful, in the manner of someone who had just been told he had leukaemia, cancer or some such. 'I'm willing, I suppose.'

Gert seemed heartened. 'Dreams also – if you can remember them.'

Edith made no comment. Out of twelve dreams, she might remember one. They were weird rather than frightening, she thought, and half the time comical. Gert declined coffee, but agreed to a short rye. All they had been talking about seemed so unimportant compared to Nixon's save-my-skin tactics now, the fact that a powerful country had no leadership now. Nixon was promising a total pull-out from Viet Nam, announced figures proudly – 'Another five hundred home this week!' – because the country was full of people like the Johnsons who wanted their sons home, of course, but Nixon made no comment on the philosophy or strategy of being in Viet Nam in the first place or of pulling out now. Now that he was scared about his office, he was going to China to fill the TV screens with pictures of himself on the Great Wall, no doubt, and using chopsticks. Shades of George Orwell and *1984*. Distract the public from the real issues!

'Am I to wait for Brett to send a psychiatrist?' Edith asked as Gert was leaving. 'Or go to one myself? You seem to know more than I do.'

'Oh, Edie! *I* dunno. If you don't like this guy he brought –' Gert shrugged again, and seemed glad to take off.

A few minutes later, Edith sat at her typewriter, inspired to launch into her story of the current presidential campaign. As a working title, she headed her piece: *The World as You Would Like It, or Why Didn't We Elect McUlp?*

The piece merely touched on the Republican Party's tactics, the selling of Nixon to the American public (he still appeared odious to Edith on television, despite his new smile and make-up), and the elimination of the strongest contenders, Muskie and Humphrey, by character assassination, thus leaving the Democratic field to McGovern, the weakest candidate. That was all fact, for the American people to observe, if they would. But she let the fantasy go. McGovern was going to be defeated by a landslide, Edith felt dismally sure, but she was going to vote for him rather than for Nixon, and of course she could persuade Cliffie also. BLACKS CLEAN UP HARLEM STREETS was one of her impossible headlines under the idyllic administration of McUlp, followed by an account of the new sparkling windows and tidy streets in Harlem, a report of McUlp's 'New Joy' program, and the spontaneous movement to start spelling Harlem with two a's to remind people of the pristine Dutch village after which it had been named. Smiling, Edith reread:

PUSHERS GET THE PUSH-OFF!

New York, – The numbers runners and drug-pushers are having it tough in New York these days, especially in Harlem. President McUlp's 'New Joy' program is a great factor, and physical activity – neighborhood clean-ups and refurbishment which is going on like a house afire – is, according to some medical statistics, sweating the drugs out of thousands of adolescents. Once free of it, many are becoming holier-than-thou toward their parents, hammering at them to kick the habit or the alcohol habit, whichever they've got, and with some success. Most conclusive proof are the long faces of the few pushers left now, when their offers are met with solemn headshaking from their old customers.

Trade schools are full, attendance excellent, and the boys are getting real experience by repairing plumbing and masonry in their own houses and those of their neighbors – free, as a civic gesture. A new spirit has seized the nation. Former dole-scroungers are now handing their monthly checks *back*, causing at least one heart attack, that of a government employé at an office on 125th Street.

279

Wouldn't you like to see headlines and news items like these instead of the sordid bilge you're reading now? If so, VOTE MCULP! For instance, health. Are you interested? You should be. As soon as McUlp is elected, you'll begin to see items like this:

The nation's physical health is on the upswing. Under McUlp the government is the sole insurer of people's health, and there's no fine print in the contract. In fact, there is no contract, you just sign up the way you join the Public Library, as the American people are discovering. Nationwide coverage, not just statewide, and none of that jazz about no coverage, if you live in Pennsylvania, say, and the specialist you need happens to live in New York. We've all heard that one before. And we know who's hand in glove, or cheek by jowl, with these Blue Cross and Green Cross and Ye Olde Double-cross and all the other crosses that the American people have been bearing for decades now. It's the same organization that put the acupuncture clinic in Manhattan out of business recently on some technicality. And why? Because acupunture was actually curing quite a few people and easing the pain of a lot more, and what was worse, it didn't cost very much. No anaesthetists' fees, no blood and guts all over the place, no horrendously expensive 'after-care' in hospital beds. You guessed it – it was the American Medical Association that put an end to the acupuncture clinic. The AMA is livid for another reason these days too: they've only 60% of American MD's signed up as members in their money-grubbing outfit which wishes everyone the worst health. The other 40%, mainly young doctors, won't join. America *is* coming to its senses. Tax-payers, via the laundering by all these Crosses, are not going to continue paying double and triple for their medical care, just because so-called insurance pads their bills.

And McUlp is our leader, our man, our President!

Edith, at the end of the article, had McUlp borne out of a building (his headquarters, already burglarized by the FBI or CIA or some such, though Edith suspected Nixon's personal attention in this) by little men-in-white, because the establishment would never stand for such talk, any more than it would ever allow to be elected a president who believed in stopping tax loopholes and making low-income families exempt entirely from income tax.

And what was Gert going to say? 'Too strong'?

29

Rather strangely, there was no word from Brett in regard to a psychiatrist for the rest of the summer and even over Christmas. Only his one-hundred-dollar checks arrived monthly, accompanied by a friendly, boring little note. Gert, in their telephone conversations about *Bugle* work, sounded as she had in the old days, no coolness, no extra warmth either, thank goodness. *Rolling Stone* bought 'Shoot-the-President' after a delay caused by *Shove It*'s folding, and another underground paper having lost her manuscript, but Edith typed in triplicate, and sent in January a copy to *Rolling Stone*. The payment was not much, but it picked up Edith's spirits.

The head of Cliffie had been cast in the new material that resembled metal, and it weighed over twenty pounds. Edith had imagined putting it in the living room on its square oak base (for which she had paid twelve dollars), but she couldn't decide on a place in the living room, and thought it might look pretentious, somehow, and that it might embarrass Cliffie, so the head remained in her upstairs workroom.

In late January, Mrs Elinor Hutchinson, owner and manager of the Thatchery, told Edith in an informal and most gentle way that she could not keep Edith on. This was over mid-afternoon coffee in the little back room which had a gas burner and fridge.

'We're just a bit overstaffed,' said Elinor, peering at Edith through her slightly thick glasses, 'so I thought among the bunch of us, I'd keep the younger girls on. I don't think it'll be a catastrophe for *you*.' And she smiled, almost laughed.

Two things struck Edith, they were not overstaffed, and the two younger girls were goons. 'All right, I understand.'

'Of course work on the rest of the month if you like, even half of February,' Mrs Hutchinson continued, still eyeing Edith as sharply, Edith thought, as she sometimes surveyed the store for shoplifters, of whom there were plenty among the week-end tourists. 'It's customary to give anyone a month's notice, so you can consider it that. No hurry at all, Edith. You've been a good salesperson from the very start.'

Women's Lib, that salesperson. 'I rather like the shop,' Edith said with a genuine smile. 'There are worse in this town.'

Elinor laughed as if Edith had said something witty.

Edith wondered, as she worked on that day, if she had slipped in efficiency without knowing it, if she was too old to look presentable, to look like what shopowners wanted as a sales-person, or if Elinor had read two or three of her editorials in the *Bugle* and didn't care for them? Certainly Edith did not reproach herself for bad manners with the customers, because the other salesgirls or salespersons marveled at her patience with the dawdlers, the people who wanted to see more and more things and never bought anything, or who changed their minds when they were half out of the shop with something. All this Edith had found interesting or amusing in the human nature depart-ment. The loss of the job meant around three hundred dollars a month less, and she was going to feel it, to put it mildly.

She told Cliffie that evening. Cliffie was in for dinner, more pink-eyed than usual, Edith thought. It had been a rainy, cold and disagreeable day, and Cliffie had loafed about imbibing, Edith was sure.

'That Hatchery!' Cliffie said, picking up his pork chop to get the last bits off the bone. 'There're other shops in this – tourist town. Why's she getting so hoity-toity?' he asked, letting his voice crack.

'She's not a bit hoity-toity,' Edith said. 'There's a recession, you know. People spending less. Maybe she can do with one less, now that the Christmas rush is over.' Edith thought that Elinor might have told her before Christmas, but of course at Christmas they had all worked overtime cheerfully, and Elinor had given bonuses, twenty dollars each. 'The point is, Cliffie, it's three hundred dollars less every month. I'm going to try for something else. But you could too, you know.'

Cliffie looked up from his plate, dark eyes a little wistful, scared. 'Me?'

'Make the Chop House take you on full-time – longer hours, anyway. Something. Really, Cliffie. You're twenty-seven, prime of life, and what's the matter with a full-time job?'

'Doing what?' Cliffie demanded, as if to say for God's sake, what the hell's my family or society trained me for?

'You're got a –' She paused.

'What?'

'Nothing. No, nothing,' Edith said, waving a hand. She had been about to say a wife and child. Lots of luck! Edith smiled, then laughed suddenly. She looked at Cliffie, who simply looked puzzled. *'Nothing!'*

Edith felt disturbed. It was like a small whirlpool, she thought, small but in the core. She tidied the kitchen, expressed no interest in the television programs which Cliffie proposed to watch that evening, and went up to her workroom. There were things to attend to, *Bugle* work, the short story she was working on, half written, and the other half should come in one sitting, when she found the mood. She opened her diary. Seven days ago, she saw from the date, she had written something she had completely forgotten, and she read it with a sense of pleasure:

A cat's name should be 'You,' because that is the word a cat hears the most, if people talk to cats at all.

She turned over some preceding pages, looking for a small item that might pick her up, and found:

Why not plant dahlias by dropping them like bombs?

Edith opened her Esterbrook pen, dated the white page just below the cat entry, and wrote:

Happy news today that Debbie is *enceinte* once more. She said she cabled C. in Kuwait. She telephoned me. Sounds so happy about it. We both hope it's a boy this time ...

Edith went on for another twenty minutes or so, filling the page with her brisk, smallish script. The loss of her job – the fact of having been *fired* – crossed her mind. But good Lord, she wasn't going to write anything as sordid and depressing as that! When she had finished her entry about Cliffie's family (the new baby due next August), Edith swept her workroom floor with a straw broom which she kept in a corner. She shook the plastic sheet out, got up all the clay bits she could, brushed them up in the scoop and dumped them in her wastebasket.

Nelson watched her calmly from his old pillow on the upholstered bench, the same spot that Mildew had always favored.

'*You*,' Edith said. 'Would you like a name like You?'

Nelson made no comment.

Edith thought she must very soon take Melanie's head to be cast like Cliffie's. *That* would be nice. Two quite nice works of art, if she did say so herself. Her two favorite people. Well, Melanie was a favorite, certainly. Cliffie – at least his head was good, the head *she* had made. Yes. That was a happy idea. Except for the expense of it. Without a job now, she would have to do some figuring, see where she stood exactly. She didn't care to think about finances that evening.

Edith received a letter from Brett, dated early January, suggesting in rather stilted language that she might see a psychiatrist in Philadelphia whose name and address Brett wrote. Dr Herman L. Stetler, famous for blah-blah-blah. A real nice guy seemed to be the idea Brett wanted to convey. Edith was surprised by the date of the letter, looked again at the envelope, and saw that Brett had made a mistake and written New Brunswick first, which was a town in New Jersey.

From all I can gather, Edith, I think a consultation – or two – would do you good, would relieve your mind of strain (this is always true, when you spill out your problems to another person), and maybe Dr Stetler could see you once a week for a month or so. I know nothing of his methods, except that he is flexible, not someone who's going to sew you up with promises to see him thrice weekly if you don't want to. Quite apart from the $10,000 (which you don't seem to want) I shall be happy to pay for this professional look at you ...

The letter ended wishing her well and so forth. Brett must think it odd that she hadn't replied. Edith didn't feel like going to a psychiatrist. Was this the usual resistance of someone already in need of one, she wondered. And how about that person called Starr (was that his real name?) who Gert had said was a psychiatrist? Edith was certainly not going to mention to Brett that she had learned Starr was a psychiatrist. Hadn't Gert said that? Even though Gert professed never to have heard of him?

It was a few weeks later, when Edith had stopped working at the Thatchery, that she wrote a note to Brett at midnight. Edith had first, that evening, finished what she wanted to do – complete wiping and rearranging of kitchen cupboards and shelves, the kind of task she did better at night when time ceased to matter. Now it was mid-February, and tomorrow was St Valentine's Day, she realized.

She wrote Brett that she could not understand his preoccupation with psychoanalysis in regard to herself, and she explained that the delay in her reply was due to the fact that his letter had been sent first to New Brunswick. She wrote that she had lost her job but was trying to find another, as it was financially necessary. This was true, both facts, and Edith had considered omitting the job loss out of pride, then reflected that she preferred to be honest. 'Did your Mr Starr make such a bad report on me?' she asked in a final paragraph. 'With Allende murdered, thanks to CIA pressures and usual USA skulduggery, it seems absurd that you should concern yourself with one single woman – myself – in a small town in Pennsylvania.' When she read her letter over, and recalled the Starr evening, recalled Brett's accusation of Cliffie as administrator of the overdose to the Old Vegetable, Edith could not refrain from adding: 'Are you really trying to help me here – and Cliffie? Or are you persecuting us?' The Watergate disgrace was also making her blood boil, the fact that honest men with honest questions couldn't get *at* Nixon even for the answers, but that was so blatant now, so everywhere in the papers, it seemed unnecessary to mention that to a newspaperman as being of greater importance than herself.

Edith thought of selling some of her strawberries and raspberries that summer. Of course it wasn't summer as yet, a long way from it, but she set out her strawberry plants in neat rows in her garden, and they looked so promising! The Cracker Barrel (where once in a while, Saturdays and at holiday times, Cliffie did deliveries either on foot or in his Volks) might well buy a few boxes. Other people in town sold their produce, Edith knew – apples, cherries, raspberries. She could use the money, she and Cliffie. The Japanese shop in town (not run by Japanese but it sold Japanese goods) had not been able to take Edith on as saleswoman or salesperson: they had enough staff, they said. At least they had been pleasant about it. Not so the Sweater Shop, a new shop for women only. The woman proprietor had said in a rather crisp way, 'Well, this is a surprise. I thought you were a journalist.' Of course it could have been meant as friendly, and so Edith had chosen to take it, and had replied, smiling, 'Sometimes journalists can use some extra cash.' Had the woman said something about *Rolling Stone*? Edith had forgotten. Not many people in town knew of *Rolling Stone*, Edith supposed, and still fewer would care for it – it was not only far-out but porno as well. By the end of March, Edith had the feeling she was being boycotted. She had not wanted to feel that. But four shops had turned her down. In view of her good record at the Thatchery (if anyone cared to ask about it), she saw no reason why she should have been turned down. Younger salesgirls were always dropping out, getting married or what not. Some shop would have taken her on, unless something was wrong.

These thoughts hardened Edith against what she thought of as the community. It was annoying. To make it worse, Cliffie was in a similar boat, though for different reasons. He had a shaky reputation. People knew he was slightly oiled all the time, and probably thought it was a miracle he was still allowed to drive his Volks when he delivered groceries or went back and forth from the Chop House where he worked as waiter or barman. Cliffie was the Town Clown, plied with drink by people whose groceries he delivered, especially around holiday time, but every weekend was holiday time for a lot of Brunswick Corner people who kept apartments in Manhattan, and for the gay crowd that poured drinks with generous hands. 'They kept me in the kitchen and we were all telling *jokes*!' Cliffie would explain at 8 p.m. or so, when he came home in no condition to work at the Chop House, where he had been due at 7:30, so this meant a telephone call from him or her to the Chop House with some invented excuse. It was a wonder they still kept him on even part-time, but then he was the Town Clown, even popular, Edith suspected.

No reply came from Brett to her letter asking him to make himself clearer about psychiatrists for herself. Perhaps he had changed his mind, thought her strong enough to stand on her own feet? She hoped he thought that. She sold twelve boxes of beautiful strawberries to the Cracker Barrel, fifteen of raspberries, and repeated the performance (or her plants did) later in the season. The store provided her with the proper little wooden boxes. Old Glenn, the owner, was friendly and generous – even broadminded in putting up with Cliffie.

Gert on the other hand seemed to grow even cooler, didn't come round even during the rather awful week when Edith had to have her lower front teeth – all four of them – extracted because of progressive loosening, so she had felt hardly presentable to most people. The local dentist, Dr Payne (risible name to everyone), was insufferably slow with the permanent bridge, but Edith thought it wiser to go to him than to someone in Philadelphia, which would have taken more than two hours round trip.

The Watergate investigation dragged on, grew boring as Nixon meant it to do, but Edith followed it with an interest that did not flag. Nixon protested that the investigators were endangering national security secrets. He was like a tired jackal being harassed by – what? Dogs, maybe. But the dogs had got his scent. Edith reached a point of pitying even Nixon's lawyer. Then in August came Nixon's resignation, and a great sigh of relief across the nation. Not jubilation, as Nixon probably thought, just relief from tension and an insupportable sense of injustice.

Another Christmas. Edith used the interest on Melanie's two

bonds, plus a hundred or so from the checking account, to buy new curtains for the living room, the old flowered ones being nearly two decades old, sagging and fading.

Cliffie's room had fallen back into its old disorder, which seemed familiar and somehow homey to Edith now. For months after he had tidied it for Luce, Cliffie had kept a certain order, rather as if he expected Luce to return to see it one day, then the what-the-hell had set in, like an illustration of the fact that he had abandoned hope, Edith thought, though she didn't enjoy negative thoughts like this.

Once when his room was still looking rather attractive (Edith had put a begonia on his table, though she had to remember to water it), she said, 'Did Luce like your room?'

Cliffie's eyes flashed. 'Sure. Yes, she did like it. She said so.'

Immediately Edith was sorry, sad, because she had mentioned Luce, after all this time. She hadn't meant to hurt him, certainly. It was just that she could not think of a single other person – apart perhaps from some roustabout Cliffie brought home for a beer once in a blue moon – who had ever seen his room, or seen it when Cliffie had so expressly tidied it. Cliffie had not added any new posters. Now, again, he lived with half-pulled-out drawers in the chest, socks and shoes scattered on the floor, bed unmade, and pajamas dropped anywhere. 'It's a *nice* room,' Edith finished rather feebly, wanting to drop the subject.

Cliffie smouldered for a couple of hours after that. He *knew* that Luce hadn't seen his room, that he'd had time that evening to say, when they'd been having drinks in the house, 'Want to see my room for a minute?' but he had not said that. Cliffie sometimes pretended that Luce had been in his room, that they had sat on his bed with their drinks for a few minutes, that he had necked with her a little before they went out to dinner that night. But he knew it hadn't happened. All that work that afternoon, and some of the work was still visible, and she hadn't even glanced in from the hall! Why had his mother had to bring *Luce* up? Luce probably with two squawling kids by now, damn the swine of a husband!

It was a horrible winter. A mediocrity was in as President,

after being vetted for lack of opinion on every vital subject, Edith thought. Foreign policy, where Edith thought America was doing the worst (if one thought of the Middle East plus Chile) was unknown ground to Ford. Kissinger was foreign policy. And west of the Appalachians, people just didn't care, Edith felt. Salvador Allende had been brutally assassinated, after defending himself to the last against hoodlums in uniform. Triumph for the CIA who had spent the last months trying to cover its trail there, so it could now say to the American people 'Us? What have *we* done?' The group of countries called OPEC upped the price of oil, now reflected in fuel bills and car gas, and destined to go higher. Edith had to go to a Doylestown optician for stronger glasses (presbyopia, she had, so it was going to get worse not better), and to the dentist Payne for three lower molars – one that had been crowned, one hopeless, one that could be saved by root canal work, but she had agreed with Payne to have the three out. Then came a permanent bridge there, costing more than five hundred dollars. Her fifty-fourth birthday in October had come and gone unnoticed by Cliffie or even Gert, who most years remembered it at least by a card.

Life, joy flourished only in her diary. Debbie and Cliffie's new offspring, a boy named Mark, grew apace, laughed, astounded doctors and neighbors by his friendliness and good-humor and intelligence. 'I am not saying he is brighter or better than his sister Josie,' Edith wrote in her diary, quoting from a letter of Cliffie's, 'but Josie had better watch out.'

Edith enjoyed reading these happy entries, sometimes only faintly remembered by her, which was to be expected if she had copied them out of another person's letter, one of Cliffie's or Debbie's. Life had changed in Kuwait. No longer was Cliffie in an air-conditioned hotel, because his company had built houses for its employés. Cliffie's company, now nationalized by Kuwait, was still in operation and had built a huge training school for Arabs, and Cliffie was one of the instructors. Jet flights were free for employés and their dependents, so Debbie flew every three or four months to the States to see her parents, and of course she paid a visit to Edith too. Sometimes Cliffie came too, if he could get free. He always appeared tallish to Edith, perhaps because he held himself so straight, and he was very suntanned, thanks to his work which still called for a lot of supervising in the open fields. Edith read under the date '18 Feb. 74':

C. & D. loved the two knitted sweaters, both pale blue with white, for J. & M. They said nights could be cool in Kuwait, but maybe they were just trying to please old Gramma!

She really didn't remember writing that, but here it was! And the curious thing was that the two sweaters *existed*, done in her spare time, and they lay in the bottom drawer of the chest of drawers in her bedroom. Now that was strange! No, it wasn't. Edith knitted sometimes from 2 until 3:30 a.m. in her workroom, relaxing, thinking. Cliffie didn't know anything about her knitting, Edith thought, a minor talent (hers was minor anyway) she had acquired around fifteen and not done much with since. But she shouldn't think about the fact that the sweaters existed. *Think about the future*, she told herself, as she had always told herself, since the age of twenty, perhaps. One had to hope in order to live. Hope, of course, was nothing but an idea. So was the future. But everything that had ever counted in the world, in history, had been an idea and nothing else – at least to begin with. So as for the future, as for Josephine and her younger brother Mark, Edith would soon begin buying them shirts, blouses, dresses and trousers. Lightweight, naturally, if Cliffie continued working in the Middle East. But they would all visit here (they had, in Edith's diary, twice by now), and if it was winter, they would shiver here unless they had woollens and flannels.

Edith sat with pen poised, thinking. She saw a happy dinner party here at her house, Cliffie and Debbie and the kids, maybe the Johnsons, heard laughter, Cliffie's stories about his work on dams and irrigation projects, about models for these in the Kuwait school. Had Debbie already put the kids to bed before dinner time? Cliffie and Debbie would be staying the night, of course.

The telephone rang.

Edith went downstairs with the feeling it had rung already about eight times, and might stop before she got to it, but she was not hurrying. Maybe it was the candy shop in town, she thought, where she had gone this week, or maybe it had been last week, to ask if they needed anyone part-time, meaning Saturdays and Sundays. They had said they would think about it. She told herself she didn't care if it was the candy shop or not. That was the way to have good luck.

'Edith, I'd like to see you,' the voice said. 'I'm very near just now. Just on the edge of town. Can I come by and see you for a few minutes?'

The voice shocked her. 'Brett?'

'Of course it's me, Edie. I said it's me.'

Hesitantly, politely, she agreed to his coming by. He said in about ten minutes.

It was not quite 4 in the afternoon. A Wednesday in February. A funny time to telephone, Edith thought.

This time it was a doctor with Brett, a Dr Stetler, whose name Edith was pretty sure she recollected from Brett's letter of a year ago. Dr Stetler looked about forty, slender and dark, with a calm, preoccupied air. He seemed not to look Edith, or maybe anybody, in the face, but appeared to be daydreaming. They sat in the living room. Edith wore her usual old sweater (two sweaters because she had to economize on heat), corduroys and sneakers, and what did they expect on ten minutes' notice?

'And how's Gert now?' Brett asked.

This question, like Brett's voice on the telephone, jolted Edith, because they had just been talking about the poinsettia in the living room. 'I suppose all right. Yes. I spoke with her a couple of days ago.'

Brett glanced at Dr Stetler, who was now looking at Edith.

'And the *Bugle* work?' Dr Stetler asked with a slight accent, German or Jewish. 'The name of the newspaper here, I think.'

'Yes. That goes along as usual,' Edith replied.

Brett shifted on the sofa, sighed, with a look of wanting to say something and of repressing it. 'Not what Gert told me, Edie.'

291

'Oh? She's been making telephone calls again?' Edith forced a smile.

'Well, she said – you weren't writing so much for the *Bugle* any more.'

'No, because they don't seem to care for my editorials. I think that's it. Gert too, she's becoming an old left-wing conservative, than which there is nothing worse. I think it was mainly the birth control thing and the academic standards piece. I'm still merit-system, you know. Oh, Gert's trying to please everybody, and you know where that gets you. You've said it often enough yourself. Unless you've changed too.'

Brett smiled his uncomfortable smile, and again glanced at Dr Stetler, whose frown had tightened as he stared at some middle-distance between himself and the fireplace. 'Come on, let's not talk politics,' Brett said. 'Gert –'

'Why not?' Edith asked.

'She said you were becoming even right-wing.'

'Authoritarian, maybe. That can be extreme left too. It just means government control of things. – At any rate, I'm still doing quite a bit in the subscription and ads departments for the *Bugle*. And no complaints there either.'

'Edith – back to the point. I –' Brett seemed out of breath or out of words.

'Mr Howland believes you are not very happy,' Dr Stetler said with a gentle smile, in a gentle voice, 'and he would like you to have a talk with me. If you are willing.'

Since Edith had expected this, she remained quite calm. 'About what?'

'Your thoughts. The things you like – and don't like.'

Edith said nothing.

Brett said, 'Edith, the contrast between the outside and the inside of this house –'

All right, the inside was a mess, perhaps, needed painting, the carpet was wearing out, and for the last few months she had not waxed the furniture.

Boom! That was Cliffie coming in, and all three of them looked toward the door.

Cliffie entered, pink-eyed, wobbly, Edith saw. Of all times!

'Well, well!' said Cliffie. His dark eyes looked smaller. He was squinting at his father and the other man with eyes well embedded in fat.

'My son,' said Brett, as if he couldn't care less.

The doctor seemed to sum him up with a brief nod, and said to Edith, 'Perhaps I could see some of your sculpture, Mrs Howland. I hear you've done a couple of quite good – heads.'

Edith chose her words. 'Thank you. Just now I don't care to have my workroom looked at, however. I've some work in progress.'

'Oh, I'd be careful,' said the doctor, 'if you'd permit me – give me the honor.'

'No,' said Edith.

'No,' Cliffie repeated, and walked heavily across the room into the dining room, on to the kitchen. His buttocks looked larger than usual, to Edith, under his rather soiled cavalry twill trousers.

Edith had folded her arms. She saw the doctor nod to Brett. The doctor said :

'We both know how difficult these last years have been for you. Believe me.'

Yes, Edith thought, she had cashed one of Melanie's bonds, and would probably have to cash the other in a couple of months. It seemed to Edith that faithful Melanie was supporting her. 'Frankly, life is a bit easier since my husband's uncle is no longer with us.'

'Yes, yes,' said Dr Stetler with a smile. 'I know all about that.'

Another fainter boom indicated that Cliffie had taken a beer from the fridge.

'Gert thinks,' Brett began, and now Edith saw the doctor shake his head to make Brett stop, presumably, but Brett went on, and Edith didn't even listen, but interrupted :

'I don't care what Gert thinks. In fact I don't think she's much of a friend of mine lately.'

'Well, I gather that too from the letter you wrote her!' Brett said, laughing.

What letter, Edith wondered. But then, she had written at

least two to Gert, at least one of which she had torn up, because she had thought it too strong. Now Edith looked at Brett intently, waiting, and wary.

'However,' Brett went on, 'Gert thinks it would be good for you – *good* for you, Edith, and don't interrupt me for a moment, to talk with someone, tell them – or him – your worries, show him your short stories even if they're unfinished, your –'

'Thank you, but I hate showing unfinished things. I think it's a bit impertinent even to suggest that. No, what I can't understand,' Edith went on quickly, 'is why you're suddenly so concerned with me – after so many years now. With the world falling to pieces around us, you worry about a woman over fifty years old you've said good-bye to long ago. What about the really desperate families in Viet Nam? What do you think's happening now that we're pulling out?'

'I thought you were for our pulling out,' Brett said.

'Mr Howland,' said the doctor.

'Not the way Nixon did it,' Edith said, 'too fast, just to make a good impression back home where he'd lost his ass, as he would put it. You know *one* of the reasons he didn't want those tapes disclosed is because his language is one fuck after the other!'

'Edie, your face is all pink!' Brett said, laughing with embarrassment.

'Not from sympathy – or shame for Richard Nixon,' Edith replied. 'It's because I'm angry.'

Now Dr Stetler mouthed some platitude about priorities. Edith would have loved a good straight scotch, but did not want to extend her hospitality to these two odiously smug personages in her living room.

'Edie, you don't want to go through a breakdown, do you?' Brett asked. 'It's absurd. It's unnecessary. I want you to make an appointment to talk with Dr Stetler in Philly. Or here at home! You know quite well that's why I'm here.'

How could she doubt it? Edith said nothing.

'You've lost a little weight since I saw you. And I hear you're – antagonizing some of the people around here . . .'

Isn't that too bad, Edith thought, and continued to half-listen as Brett went on in a soothing tone. Now it was 'make friends' with Dr Stetler, or if she didn't like him, Brett would find someone else for her to talk to.

'... *not* your enemy,' Brett was repeating. 'Your friend. Trained and willing – to make life easier for you.'

Shove it, Edith thought.

Brett stood up. Was he leaving? He looked at the other man, who was standing also and shaking his head slightly.

'I'd like to see the upstairs, Edie,' Brett said.

Edith was on her feet. 'Really? Why?'

Brett had walked to the stairs. 'What's the harm? Relax, Edie, we're not going to touch a thing.' Brett climbed the stairs.

Edith followed him.

'Mr Howland,' the doctor said behind Edith.

Cliffie had wandered into the hall with his beer can. What the hell was going on? He could see his mother detested the 'doctor' who was probably a shrink. Interesting. Cliffie felt one hundred percent on his mother's side. These two – including his father – seemed to be invading the house! Now the voices were louder from upstairs. Cliffie mounted the steps, intending to linger halfway up them, where he could hear. His father was walking slowly toward his mother's workroom, preceding her, talking.

Edith managed to get in front of Brett and faced him, with her back to the open door. 'I find this extremely rude!' Her diary was open on her work table. It was somehow worse than invading a bedroom in which the bed was not made. Edith braced her hands against the door jambs.

'Edie, quite simply we want to get an idea –' Brett stopped as Edith threw off his touch on her forearm.

'Mr Howland, I think this is not the way,' Dr Stetler said.

'You will not!' Edith said.

Brett pushed off Edith's hand and walked into her room.

'Mr Howland, this is not going to accomplish –'

'Get out! *Both* of you!' Edith now had got into her room and stood between Brett and the doctor and her desk. 'Please get out.' She realized her teeth were bared, that she was panting. 'You might have given me some notice! I think this is simply awful!' She heard her own voice shrieking, as if the voice belonged to someone else.

Dr Stetler took Brett's arm, pulling him back toward the door. Edith was relieved to see that Dr Stetler, at least, had not been rude enough to stare, to gawk about at her sculpture or anything else.

They were all downstairs again. Both the men were talking. The blood sang in Edith's ears. She was not interested in what they were saying. Take it easy, she told herself, and they'll be gone in two minutes. They're in the hall now.

They were making moves of departure, thank God, tugging on coats that Edith didn't remember they had hung in the hall, pulling on mufflers.

'Mrs Howland, I am so sorry that we disturbed you,' said Dr Stetler in a tone of infinite gentleness, which made Edith think he wanted to make a 'success' of this call and collect a fee for future appointments. 'I do apologize – myself. That was your notebook, the big book on your desk?'

Edith's eyes almost closed in fury, but she kept Stetler in focus, wary of him.

'Diary, I think,' said Brett.

'I have a respect for privacy,' the doctor said to Edith in a deep, slow voice. 'It's a lovely workroom you have. I –'

'Just get out,' Edith said.

At the back of the hall, near the open door of his room, Cliffie rocked back on his heels and chuckled without making a sound. His mother was giving them the old heave-ho!

Ka-*plump*! That was the front door.

Cliffie drained his beer can, swaggered into the dining room, then into the living room. 'What swine!'

His mother had just come in from the hall. Her face looked pink and white at the same time. 'Swine. You're right.'

'Have a scotch, mom.'

'I think I could use one.' And she poured it.

Cliffie was silent, not looking at his mother, but aware of her wrath.

Edith took her drink to the telephone and dialed Gert Johnson's number. The line was busy, and Edith imagined Gert yacking away to someone else, spreading more trouble, more distorted information. As soon as Edith put the phone down, it rang. It was Gert.

'Just trying to ring you. You were busy,' Gert said.

Edith let it go by. It sounded mealy-mouthed and phony. 'Just what have you been saying to Brett – if you don't mind my asking. Your gratuitous news bureau –'

'About *what*?'

'He was just here with a doctor, a shrink. You must know. And what you –'

'Well, Edie, it's for your own good.'

'I'd be grateful, Gert, if you wouldn't talk so freely about my personal life. It's no business of Brett's who has his own life now.'

'*No*, Edie! It's abstract things, *not* personal. Objective things – like –'

'Worry about your own problems. I'm not complaining, Gert. But I don't like these invasions – into my house!'

'All right, Edie.'

Edith felt she had got the last word, when they hung up.

It had been a disturbing hour. And Cliffie had drifted out of the living room (with a glass) without further comment. Edith longed to get dinner over with, and to get back to a book she was reading in bed – still another book on the Kennedy assassination, which one was this? – unless she felt like pottering around a bit in her workroom. Yes, she would spend some time in her workroom, just to get rid of the atmosphere of those two who had been in it this afternoon.

30

The date had been set, noted in Edith's diary, for months: April 5th, a Saturday. Cliffie, Debbie, and the kids were coming to lunch. Maybe staying the night. Edith wasn't sure. Most of the time, Cliffie and Debbie preferred to sleep in their own house near Princeton, which was normal, or with Debbie's parents who, Edith had to admit, had a larger house than hers. Edith had bought champagne. Spring was definitely here, jonquils still flourishing, roses getting into stride. Edith had cut her first purple and yellow irises for the dining table.

She had said to Cliffie, whom she had wanted to be there, 'No harm in having a decent Saturday lunch now and then, is there?' when he had remarked upon the champagne chilling in the bottom of the fridge. Edith had put on a pink, short-sleeved linen dress with a green sash.

'But what's the occasion?' Cliffie asked, picking up a lobster claw in his fingers now, chewing, dripping butter.

'Spring is here!' Edith said, and returned to her own dreams. She saw the other Cliffie in a dark blue jacket (linen also) with his suntan, his strong hair, and Debbie with peaches-and-cream cheeks, and heard the low hum of their chit-chat, laughter, news.

'Mom, would you stop humming? Drives me nuts,' Cliffie said, dropping his lobster claw which made a thin, paperlike clatter. He wiped his fingers on one of Melanie's hundred-year-old napkins.

Even the coffee was a success, strong and fresh, poured from a silver pot. Then the doorbell rang.

'The doorbell!' Cliffie said, mellow indeed on champagne, scotch and other things.

'Dr Carstairs!' Edith said.

Old Carstairs smiled. 'Francis to you. How are you, Edith? My! You're looking nice today!'

Edith had thought suddenly, George isn't here. Who was sick? Had she invited Dr Carstairs for coffee? No. 'Come in,' she said. 'Have some coffee with us.'

Cliffie sat in the rose-sprigged armchair. Dr Carstairs accepted coffee. But he looked uncomfortable, and after a minute said, 'Cliffie, since I do have an appointment with your mother, I wonder would you mind if we talked alone for a minute or two?'

'An appointment?' Cliffie interrupted in the middle of Carstairs' words, but he stood up. 'Sure, sure, doc.' And he trudged out.

Edith didn't remember an appointment. No, indeed. But she sat upright, polite and attentive.

'Edith – Brett's written me a couple of times, you know, about you.'

'I didn't know.'

'Well, yes, I told you that on the phone,' Dr Carstairs said with a smile. 'Yesterday.'

His slender face looked as dry and wrinkled as Brett's, Edith thought. She listened, partly, to what he said, and he went on and on, it seemed, but she intended to be polite and not interrupt him. He was talking about her 'hardships,' while Edith thought that things were not so bad, and she did interrupt him to say so. Now Dr Carstairs was repeating:

'... Either you see someone, who can have a talk with you or – I'm afraid something might happen.'

'What?' Edith demanded.

'If you didn't like this man Stetler –'

'Oh!' Edith laughed. 'That creature!'

'I have a friend – or two I could introduce you to. One in Doylestown and that's not far away. It's a lonely life you have, Edith, and your friends –'

'I'm not lonely at all. I'm busy, to tell you the truth.'

'With no –' Dr Carstairs stopped with a shrug. 'Anyway,

Brett asked me to see you – to say what I've said. He is concerned, Edith.' Now he was fishing cards from his jacket pocket.
'Now if you're willing – and Brett said he'd pay for it –'

'He needn't bother!'

'– here are the two people *I* know. Both friends of mine, both –
here's the one in Doylestown.'

Edith only glanced at the card the doctor put on her coffee
table, and the card was illegible from where she sat.

'. . . Edith, you're losing your friends, and you don't want to
end your. days – You're not even old as yet, I mean, as a lonely
woman, living alone –'

'Lots of people live alone.'

'I'm not a psychiatrist,' Dr Carstairs continued in his patient
tone, 'but I think seeing one would do you a world of good. To
talk about your worries, grievances – Even Gert Johnson, you
know,' he went on in a brighter tone, 'rang me up last week.
Now wait a minute? She *is* your friend, friend enough to care,
it seems. I know her pretty well, too, I've been *their* doctor
for – twenty years anyway. She mentioned your writing articles
– short stories that were fantasies or near it.'

Edith laughed. 'How true! Some of them sell, at least. These
fantasies.'

'Good! Well then, fantasy is as good a description as anything, maybe. Very important and useful, if you're talking with a
psychiatrist. I'd bring a couple of stories to his office to show him,
if I were you. That's Phil in Doylestown, the one I'd recommend.' Dr Carstairs pointed to the card on the coffee table.

Edith felt a bit stunned, also bored, but quite in control of
herself. Why was Carstairs making such a to-do?

'Would you like me to make an appointment for you, Edith?
Monday? Tuesday? I know Phil so well, I can call him up
during the weekend.'

'Do you know one of my articles sold only last month?
"Under Plain Wrapper," it's called. A fantasy, of course.'

'Well – congratulations, Edith.'

'I didn't mean for you to congratulate me – but I can't understand everyone hovering over me as if I were an invalid.'

Dr Carstairs laughed his dry laugh again. ' 'Course you're not an invalid! Nobody said you were. – Now this business of sending Brett's check back, ten thousand, he said, patched up with scotch tape as if somebody's torn it –' The doctor laughed gently, as if at some old family joke.

Had she sent it back? Had Cliffie? 'If you don't use a check, the correct thing is to send it back, I believe.'

'But Brett wanted to give you a helping hand with that check. He can afford it and he still wants to do it. Wants to write you a new check if you'll accept it.'

Helping hand with stinking George all those years, Edith thought. Helping hand far away in New York, married to a woman who had his child now! 'He never helped me in the least with George!' Edith had suddenly stood up, furious. 'Brett's talking a lot of crap! He's trying to annoy me at present, if you want the truth, using my friends in fact to undermine me! Look at the Gert Johnson situation! Can't you see it? Whose side are you on – Francis?' Edith desperately wanted an honest answer to that question. And she saw Dr Francis X. Carstairs squirming under it, as he had squirmed when she had asked him if George shouldn't be put into a home. He was really twisting his neck now, and this sight reminded her of Nixon. 'This is a political world,' Edith declared. 'You're all playing rotten politics – squirming, delaying, anything to avoid stating plain truths!'

'Edie – It's not politics, it's ordinary life. It's the ABC's of life we're all talking about.'

'No! You expect me to be content with a warm house in winter, enough food to eat – television! You can all shove it! People still have brains! Even my *cat* has more brains and judgement and sense of proportion . . .'

The doctor interrupted her, standing up now too. He was producing a little round pill box from his pocket, placing the box on the table like a mystical peace offering. 'You don't have to take these, Edith. Mild sedatives. Two a day, I'd recommend. I just happen to have them with me.' A smile. 'They'd help.'

Edith felt only mild scorn for the pills, neither looked at the box nor thanked Carstairs for it. 'Now I suppose you're going to report to Gert and Brett?'

The doctor was leaving. 'Have you heard again from Dr Stetler?' he asked at the door.

Edith sought in her memory, and found him all too easily. 'That was months ago! Why should I hear from him? Of course I haven't.'

Dr Carstairs nodded. 'I'll just say good-bye to Cliffie. He's in his room?' Carstairs started walking down the hall.

Edith turned at once to go back to the living room, where she had not finished her coffee, but she was annoyed by Carstairs' lingering. There was no need to say 'good-bye' to Cliffie. She threw a pained, apologetic glance into the empty dining room, almost uttered the word 'Sorry' to Cliffie and Debbie – and maybe their two kids – who sat at the table. Or were they already in the living room? Edith couldn't think, because she was mainly thinking of Carstairs who was still in the house.

Cliffie had his room door locked, his transistor on, and was annoyed at being disturbed, surprised also to find that it was Dr Carstairs at the door. Carstairs murmured an apology, and Cliffie said it was quite all right. Cliffie was dressed but had his shoes off. He turned his radio lower.

'You know, Cliffie,' Dr Carstairs began, speaking more slowly than usual. 'Your mother's in a bad way, and I want you to do what you can to persuade her to see a doctor. Not me, a psychiatrist. I've given her two names just now. The one called Philip McElroy in Doylestown is my choice. He's a friend of mine, I know him well.'

Cliffie had anticipated this. 'Bad way how?' he asked, curious to know what the doctor would say.

'She's been under a strain for a long time, and it's showing up. You must know that. She doesn't even remember, it seems, what she's said to her friend Gert, she won't let your father – help out much.'

Cliffie waited, hands on hips, seeing the doctor a bit fuzzily. He was aware of a desire to protect his mother, to defend her

302

from Carstairs' verbal attack, and he squared his shoulders. 'I don't see that she's doing so bad.'

'She's done marvelously. But she needs a little help now – guidance.'

'Oh, fuck it,' Cliffie murmured, reacting at once to the word 'guidance,' of which he had heard enough in his time.

'Take it easy, Cliffie. When you're in a better mood – I want you to see that your mother sees my friend Phil, all right? I'm going to call him up. Brett's footing the bill, so don't let your mother worry about that.'

Cliffie hated the conversation. But fortunately the doctor was leaving.

'You're the man of the house now, Cliffie.'

Cliffie nodded slightly and coldly.

Clump-clump-clump down the hall, and the old boy was gone, letting himself out evidently, because Cliffie didn't hear any voices. Then suddenly, shrilly:

'Do *you* realize the collapse in Viet Nam? And you ask *me* to go to a psychiatrist in *Doylestown*?'

Then there was the gentle closing of the front door.

That day was not April 5th, as Edith had thought, but April 12th, still a Saturday, however. Sunday for some reason loomed like a horrible thing, like something concrete, not just a day composed of sunrise, sunlight, and dusk. Sunday seemed like a void as well as a unit, like a cube, something solid. Something was going to happen Sunday, she felt, although logically nothing ever happened on Sunday, because there was no mail, for one thing.

Cliffie had been out till all hours, and was sleeping at 11 a.m. on Sunday morning.

Edith, having had a quiet evening and a good night's sleep, spent part of the morning writing up the events of yesterday, the successful lunch of caviar, lobster and champagne, the departure of the young people at 5 p.m. for Princeton, where they would spend the next couple of days before returning to Brunswick Corner Tuesday or Wednesday to stay the night before heading for New York and the Middle East again. Edith felt happy, writing in her diary. Her black, smallish handwriting filled the page with solid information, enlivened, she felt, by remarks from Cliffie, anecdotes from Debbie about their housemaid in Kuwait who carried transistors in the pockets of her apron and on one shoulder, playing several stations at once.

These happy sentences brightened Edith's mood as she worked in the garden that afternoon. She had put horse manure around all the roses weeks ago, the manure a gift from Cliffie, who had been given it, Edith recalled, by some people to whom he had delivered groceries. Cliffie had probably told them an inane joke, or sung one of his parodies of a song. Don't look gift horse manure in the mouth, however, Edith told herself. What a shame she hadn't asked Cliffie and Debbie to stay all day yesterday and today, and go to Princeton tomorrow. But she must have asked them, she thought, because she always did. These thoughts, all these thoughts – She knew what she was trying to drive out of her mind, the awful television news pictures last evening, repeated again at noon today, of South Vietnamese refugees clinging to the bottom of helicopters, trying to get away from their own country before the Viet Cong poured in. The Communists were of course pouring in, and all this was *happening*. Now. Today. According to her latest copy of *Time*, regular South Vietnamese soldiers, in retreat and already aboard airplanes, had struck women and children with rifle butts to prevent them from boarding the overcrowded planes. *Now*, as she drove her trowel into the well-turned Pennsylvania soil, giving final touches to her flourishing rosebushes.

The telephone rang. Cliffie, she thought – maybe – wanting to tell her they were safe in Princeton, to thank her for yesterday.

No. An ache in Edith's knees as she stood up brought her back to reality. She entered the house through the back door and walked quickly down the hall.

'Hello, Edith, it's Brett. How are things?'

'Quite all right, thank you. And how are you?'

'You saw Carstairs yesterday – he said.'

'Yes.'

'Yes. Well, look, Edie, I just spoke with Carstairs, and he and his friend Philip McElroy want to pay you a visit tomorrow morning around 11. Is that all right?'

Edith was instantly annoyed, but tried to dredge up her patience. 'I don't know *why*. – I'm not going to bar the door to them, I suppose, much as I'd like to. *Brett, what is this conspiracy?*' Edith went on through something Brett was saying. '*Gert's* in on it, and *you* . . .'

'. . . *not* a conspiracy!' Brett yelled. 'Just to talk with you for, say, ten minutes! All right, Edie – as long as you're willing to see them –'

Edith had a vision of herself banging the telephone down, which she much wished to do, but found herself gripping it with all her strength. 'All *right*. I never said I was disagreeable, did I? No, I'm just a sitting *duck* here, just a target for everyone!' Her heart beat fast.

'Just take it easy. Everyone's on your side, whatever you may think.'

She gave a snort of laughter. 'But I haven't any side. I'm not against the others. Maybe that's news to you!'

Brett hung up.

And Edith hung up almost simultaneously. At once, she wished she had asked Brett if he was coming also. It wouldn't surprise her if he did. Tomorrow at 11. They hadn't asked her if she was going to be doing anything at 11 tomorrow. Edith had an impulse to ring Brett back and ask him if he intended coming, but repressed it out of pride.

She thought first of tidying her workroom for them. The snoops always wanted to see that. Then she thought, her workroom was not a mess, and why should she care what they thought about it? She had two new heads, one finished but not cast in the simulated bronze like Cliffie's, and the second she was still working on. These were Cliffie's and Debbie's two children. They had wavier hair than Cliffie's, having taken it from their mother. Josephine and Mark, one girl, one boy. The plastic sheet was worn out in a good many spots, but it served her well still. Since when was she housekeeper to a bunch of psychiatrists, strangers?

And her diary? Well, they weren't going to touch that, and there was no time like the present to do something about it. Edith went up the stairs, entered her workroom, and closed her diary, which had been open on her table with her closed fountain pen lying on it. Her first thought was to put it in the bookshelf under the window bench, on which Nelson was sleeping, to conceal it among the other books there, then she felt her workroom itself a vulnerable place. She walked to the door with the diary in her two hands (it was rather heavy), then thought that a place other than her workroom would be even more vulnerable, somehow. She'd damn well keep it in her workroom, where it had always been.

It was all very well for Brett to say people were not 'against' her, but Edith sensed that they were, and she trusted her instincts.

After a few minutes' hesitation, Edith decided to put her diary where it often was, at the bottom of a stack of stuff on the left side of her table, a stack that included a few back issues of the *Bugle*, Webster's New International, and a few old magazines she had not thrown away. Her diary had the look of an old family Bible, not something one was going to reach for, she thought, thinking of a stranger entering her workroom.

Then the doorbell rang. She wasn't expecting anyone. What time was it? Not quite 1, she saw by her watch.

Gert and Norm were at the door downstairs.

'*Hello*, Edie!' Gert said with a big smile. 'Can we invite ourselves for a pre-lunch nip? We brought the booze!'

Norm lifted a brown sack with a sleepy air, though his hands looked as if he held a short rifle.

'Come in!' Edith said, but she put on a cool air which she maintained.

Ice, glasses, drinks. And platitudes. Edith cut through it by asking:

'Did Brett speak to you today? By any chance?'

'No,' Gert said, and Edith felt she was lying.

306

'No,' Norm said, sitting spraddle-legged in the armchair, wobbling his glass on his thigh.

'Why?' asked Gert.

'Oh – nothing. Just wondered,' Edith said.

There was conversation, of a sort, but the talk and the atmosphere was phony and dreadful, Edith felt. They asked about Cliffie. Well, Cliffie was still asleep. And so what? She and Gert had had their showdown on the telephone, a couple of times, Edith thought. She knew that Gert knew that she considered Gert her enemy, so why any pretense any longer? Edith also knew that Gert knew about tomorrow's appointment at 11, but hadn't the guts to mention it or admit it. Oh, no, not Gert! Were they checking to see if she looked as if she would run out on the appointment? Out of fear? Or boredom? Edith sat up straighter, and asked if anyone wanted a dividend.

'*I* think we'd better be pushing on,' Gert said.

Edith couldn't recall a time when Gert had refused a second drink.

'You're looking *well*, Edie,' Gert said with another smile.

They were gone. Their voices kept on in Edith's ears like echoes. Edith had asked about their kids, how they were doing, all the usual questions. Something about the *Bugle*. Had Edith reminded the Lambertville Cinema (a struggling movie house) that their advertising rates had to go up fifteen percent this year? Edith said she had reminded them, which was true.

She made a late lunch for Cliffie and herself, then awakened him. He was unusually jolly and talkative, but Edith barely listened.

'... Then we shot some pool in Trenton,' Cliffie said, grinning, winding up his account of the night until 3 or 4 a.m. He had mentioned Mel, seeing Mel, who Edith thought had long ago dropped out of the picture. Cliffie was cheerful because Mel had taken him up again, it seemed.

Edith was thinking of Marion and Ed Zylstra, wishing they were around, as in the old days. But they had moved to Dallas five, maybe seven years ago, and Ed had been killed in a terrible car crash. Marion had remarried, and was living in New

Orleans – wasn't it? No, of course not, *Houston*. She had married an electronics scientist or engineer.

'Houston? What about Houston?' Cliffie asked, sopping up gravy with a corner of bread.

Edith had not realized that she was thinking out loud, daydreaming. 'Oh, I was thinking of – Marion. You know. You remember Marion and Ed Zylstra.'

Cliffie shook his head, not because he didn't remember, but because his mother was in such a fog lately. 'Sure, I remember. – Mom, what's the matter today?'

'Nothing,' she said in a cheerful voice, shaking her head also.

Then she was in the kitchen, and thinking of the afternoon concert (it was just after 3) which she would switch on in a couple of minutes, after she had given the kitchen a lick and a promise, as Aunt Melanie had used to say. She put the butter back in the fridge, and Nelson stuck his head in, pale head and dark ears, and Edith almost closed the door but didn't, thinking of old Mildew – poor creature! But that of course *hadn't* happened, Mildew's neck severed, her head in the fridge, eating. That had been a dream, really only a dream.

Edith bent toward Nelson, smiling. 'Nelse, old pal! Didn't I feed you this morning?'

Anyway, she fed him now, and Nelson was in no danger of starving. Nor was he fat. He looked perfect.

That afternoon, listening to César Franck and Bartók on her radio, Edith worked on Mark's head. She felt secure standing on her feet, metaphorically and literally.

Cliffie, in his room, felt restless, though he flopped again on his unmade bed. What the hell was the matter with his mother? She was a bit cracked, he had realized since a long time, but today she seemed worse. Had some people come in this morning while he was asleep? Cliffie was not sure. Lately his mother talked to herself, and if he had been asleep, hearing or imagining voices –

'... Danang since ...' said the voice on Cliffie's transistor, 'is in chaos as South Vietnamese soldiers and civilians flee southwards, deserting their p –'

Cliffie switched off. He had a dark blue sock in his hand. His room door was locked. Now he could faintly hear music from the upstairs. The news every hour on the hour lasted only two minutes or so, but because his mother talked so much about the collapse of Saigon, Kwan Tuck, Muck Tuck or whatever the hell it was, Cliffie was sick of it, and couldn't even endure the news until the music came back on again. Cliffie turned over on his stomach and thought of Luce, remembered Luce with her tantalizing, joking smile, her slim dark trousers which he would soon take off, her scream of pleasure and laughter as her eyes looked upward. *Luce!* Her bastard husband could never give her the pleasure that he could. And Luce knew that.

31

Dawn and the chirps of birds, sparrows, the wanted and the unwanted birds. April! And Monday. As soon as Edith was out of bed, Nelson appeared – where from? – and addressed her with a firm, questioning 'Mi-wow-ow-ow?' as if his brows frowned, as if his query were too important for him to waste time with a 'Good morning.'

'I *know*,' Edith said. Nelson wanted his breakfast.

She put the coffee on, fed Nelson, went to see if Cliffie was awake at a quarter to 9, knocked on his door. No answer, and she opened the door gently. Cliffie looked sound asleep, face to the wall. She closed the door again.

The post brought a telephone bill of nearly a hundred dollars, and Edith signed a check for it. She had already had a bath and was dressed, and now she went out to drop the envelope with the check in the corner box, and to buy milk and eggs at the Cracker Barrel – certainly an expensive store compared to the supermarket, but after all they employed Cliffie part-time, and it behooved her to patronize them now and then. They also carried an especially good brand of tomato juice, of which Edith bought a bottle.

'Hi-i, Mrs Howland – Edith! How're you today?' asked the skinny fellow with Rudyard Kipling mustache (except that this rather young man was blond) at the check-out counter.

'All right, thank you,' Edith said with a smile. She had forgotten his name. Sam? 'And so should you be with these atrocious prices!'

The mouth under the mustache chuckled richly. 'And how's Cliffie?' *Bing-bing* went the cash register, *clunk* went the tomato juice into a sturdy brown bag. 'Our star boy, y'know. People like him. People say he ought to go on the stage!'

Was he joking? Pulling her leg? All the world's a stage, Edith thought, and hated herself for thinking of it. 'A born entertainer,' Edith said with gentle scorn, and took her leave with the brown bag, smoothly, swiftly.

At 11, she was straightening her workroom a bit, sweeping (after having addressed a few envelopes in advance for *Bugle* subscriptions), and in fact she succeeded, as she had meant to do, in not being aware of the exact time, when the doorbell rang. She glanced at her wrist watch and saw that it was 11:25. She went down the stairs and opened the front door.

Carstairs was with a tall man in a tweed jacket, sweater, a shirt open at the neck.

'Morning, Edith,' Carstairs said. 'Sorry we're a little late. This is Phil McElroy – doctor.' He smiled. 'Old friend of mine.'

'How d'y'do?' said McElroy with a broad smile.

McElroy reminded Edith a little of Jack Kennedy. 'Brett not with you?' she asked. 'Come in.'

'No, no. He's working, I suppose,' said Carstairs.

They went into the living room. 'Nice house you've got here,' said Philip McElroy. 'I was admiring your roses – just now. All around the pillars like that.'

'Thank you,' said Edith, her voice frail suddenly. She waited for them to get on with it, and finally Carstairs said:

'We were wondering, Edith, if you'd be willing to come to Doylestown to have a talk with Phil or for him to come here – I can take off in a few minutes – to have a talk about life, you know. Everything.'

'I'm rather busy,' Edith said, and shook her shoulders, almost shuddered with sudden impatience. 'Why I command all this attention when – I'm sure you've heard the news, doctor,' she went on, addressing Carstairs. 'Not to mention *Time* magazine right there,' and she pointed to an issue with a large photograph of a Vietnamese child, mouth open, wailing. The black band across the corner said COLLAPSE IN VIET NAM.

'Of course I've heard it. It's tragic,' said Carstairs.

'Yes, and the TV shots,' McElroy put in, glancing at Carstairs. 'Yes – the American pull-out.' McElroy shook his head.

'At least it shows the power of the people in the streets,' Edith continued, 'the ordinary protesters finally stopped Congress from voting more money for the war. But we might've made better provision for helping refugees *out*. That wasn't right, on our part.'

'No,' McElroy agreed.

Edith's heart beat as if she were arguing violently with someone who disagreed. But McElroy and Carstairs were not disagreeing, and Viet Nam would now go Communist, which Edith had never wished. She tried to say some of this, and found herself stammering. 'It's such a mess. I was for pulling out, but *now* look!' Then for an awful few seconds Edith realized she did not know what side she was on in regard to the Viet Nam débâcle, and felt like someone who had just fallen backward on the ice. Ludicrous.

'Well, Edith, what do you think?' asked Carstairs. 'Phil has helped an awful lot of people right around here, people you might even know. But of course they might not tell you – any more than Phil would ever tell you that he's talked with them, helped them out of tough spots. You'll feel worlds better after yacking away to –'

'About what?' Edith was pleased that her question seemed to silence them. 'Sounds quite boring to me and for anyone else, I should think.'

'How about showing Phil some of your nice sculpture, Edith?' Carstairs stood up.

Edith had a sickening déjà-vu feeling. The same old rubbish! Were they all *acting*, like players on a stage? Her mind fastened on her diary upstairs, visible on the corner of the desk, under those papers. 'I don't – if you don't mind, don't like people I don't know very well going into my workroom.'

'I do understand,' said McElroy. 'So never mind that. It's more important that you talk with me – about your daydreams, what's on –'

'If you think I've got time for daydreaming!'

McElroy laughed. 'Who has? But you write short stories, I've heard. Bring one or two when you come to see me. Or read from them yourself, just the parts you want to read.'

'That I would never do,' Edith said with an effort at pleasantness. 'Anyway, several are published.'

'Exactly,' said McElroy. 'That's why I propose that you read to me from them.' He opened his hands with an air of innocence.

Edith shook her head.

'Edith,' Carstairs said, 'if things get worse –'

'What things?' Edith interrupted, now with all her guards up. She was imagining little robot medical men-in-white invading her house, carrying her out, plus her diary – unless she burnt it.

'Edith, do you realize that you've lost a few friends lately? You must have realized that people aren't visiting as much as they used to.'

'Oh – little neighborly tiffs now and then. If you mean my editorials – and published stories – Who reads around here, anyway?' But she thought of the Quickmans. What had that been about? A little argument four months or so ago. Maybe she'd called them idiots. Something political, as Edith remembered. Now they were being a bit cool. So what?

'If you don't make an effort now on your own,' Dr Carstairs said, 'you may soon have to be under real surveillance, Edith.'

'What?' Edith pretended an amused surprise. Without debating it, she decided to try a slight appeasement. 'Listen, if you want to take a look at my workroom, come ahead.' She stood up. 'Just give me two minutes – one minute – to make sure it's presentable. All right?'

'Of course!' said the affable Dr McElroy.

Edith went up the stairs as Cliffie came into the hall.

'Hey, what's up?' Cliffie asked.

'Nothing!' Edith was in a hurry.

She took her diary from the table corner and carried it to her chest of drawers in the bedroom. She opened the bottom drawer, which held folded old white sheets, clean but worn-out tablecloths, and stuck the diary all the way back in the right-hand corner, had to pull something out to make it lie reasonably flat, and found a cluster of old Christmas cards. The one uppermost said 'Love from Brett' and below it in a different handwriting 'and Carol.' She disliked having found it. It seemed a bad omen, and she thought of dropping it in a wastebasket now, and yet didn't want it even *that* visible when the two men came upstairs, so she left the card where it had been, but pulled the whole batch (she must throw them out) forward so they would not touch her diary.

Her workroom was quite all right, table even neater than usual, the head of Cliffie looking particularly handsome with the sunlight glowing golden on one polished lobe of his forehead. People in fact said, 'Why don't you put it in the living-room, Edie?' But Edith somehow didn't want it down there. One of the kids – maybe. Or Melanie even, but Cliffie no. Edith started for the stairs to call the men up, when she changed her mind about the diary. Why not in its *usual* place, which certainly didn't catch the eye, and which seemed safer somehow than the drawer? And anyway, why should she take pains to hide her rightful possessions? Edith went into her bedroom again, got the diary from the bottom drawer, and was hurrying out with it to replace it under the stack of papers on the corner of the worktable, when she saw that Carstairs and McElroy were halfway up the stairs, Carstairs coming into the hall.

'Edie?' he said.

'Sorry. I'm a little slow.' Trembling, Edith carried the diary in both hands to her worktable, calling, 'Wait, please!' and got it back where it had been, straightened the papers atop it with a shove of her palms. The men were at the threshold. 'I'm sorry. I've changed my mind. I don't want you to come in. Do you mind?' She was walking toward the door. 'What's there to see anyway?' With feeble gestures she was backing them out of her room, feeble only because she was still trying to be polite, and resented that she had to be, because both Carstairs *and* McElroy might have realized that she damned well didn't want them or anybody setting foot in her workroom or even looking in.

314

Somehow – she succeeded. Murmuring, smiling, they were all descending the stairs again, and Edith relaxed proportionately.

'So, Edith,' Carstairs said when they were all sitting down again, having taken their former places like well-trained school-children, 'how about making a date now with Phil? Some time this week?'

'No,' Edith said, tired of even saying 'thank you.'

'Edith – I have a request from Brett to order you to see a psychiatrist, whether you want to or not.'

'From Brett. I like that! What's he got to do with me? He's no longer my husband, and even if he were –'

'Edith, Edith, listen for a minute. I'm a doctor, and I've known you and your family a long time. Phil's a doctor too. Now both of us . . .'

The rest of it Edith switched off. And Dr Carstairs went on mumbling, making gentle gestures, for quite a long time. She again imagined the little men-in-white dashing up the stairs, invading her workroom – finding the diary. The Paul Prys! Barbaric snoops! Why weren't they content with porn? No, just because they were *doctors*, they claimed the right to intrude on other people's privacy!

Edith drew herself up in her chair – the rose-sprigged arm-chair – and said, 'Would you like to see my head of Cliffie? A piece of my sculpture? I'll bring it down for you.' She was almost in tears, but she thought of Melanie. Melanie would some-how maintain her politeness in the face of anything, *anything*.

'Love to!' said Carstairs.

'Can I help you?' McElroy was on his feet.

'Oh, no, thank you. Doesn't weigh much.' Edith went out. Appease them a little, she thought. Make a gesture of goodwill!

Upstairs, she lifted the head, which was now fastened to its square oak base. A fine head. They would give her a word of praise for this, and it would even be genuine, Edith believed.

But what came next, she wondered, as she walked with the head toward the stairs. The date with McElroy – or someone – sponsored by Brett, the swine. Edith hated Brett at that moment. Hadn't he done enough damage? Smug, self-righteous, inflicting unhappiness on other people, grabbing everything for himself. A tear zipped down her cheek, and she tried to wipe it with a movement of her shoulder. Then her heel caught on the third step – Damn it, of all the awkwardness! Flat shoes too, sandals, not due to bell-bottoms either, because her corduroys were rather narrow.

She was falling, the head in her hands weighing a ton, suddenly, pulling her forward, and she had no hand to catch the banister rail.

She was aware that she didn't scream, although she was terrified. It seemed a slow motion fall, she saw herself slanting head downward now at the same angle as the stairs, and she thought of Cliffie as a small boy of eight and ten, potentially handsome as he was now potentially handsome, like the statue she held in her two hands. She thought of injustice, felt her personal sense of injustice combined now with the crazy, complex injustice of the Viet Nam situation – a country in which corruption, as everyone knew, was a way of life, normal. Tom Paine. *The summer soldier and the sunshine patriot* ... Her head struck hard, yet gracefully (she believed) on one of the bottom steps or the floor, and the light went out for her.

A little more than an hour later, Cliffie stood in the silent living room, alone. They had taken his mother away in a long car, maybe an ambulance, maybe a hearse, Cliffie hadn't looked closely, but the same kind of car they had taken old George away in. *Dead.* Cliffie couldn't believe it. His mother dead. Old Carstairs had said he would tell Brett. Hadn't he said that?

And Norm Johnson was coming in about half an hour to pick him up to take him to dinner at their place, and he was to spend the night there. Even Frances Quickman – yes – had come over a few minutes ago, and she was feeding the cat tomorrow morning.

His mother *dead*. It wasn't sinking in, as yet, even though the police – two of the old Keystone Kops – had been standing right in the downstairs hall, staring at his mother and making notes, just a few minutes ago. Cliffie had had a bracing straight scotch just five minutes ago. It hadn't helped much. Now the house was his. Hadn't somebody said that? Carstairs? Of course it might be partly his father's too, Cliffie wasn't sure how those things worked, but maybe his father wasn't or wouldn't be interested in the house. Cliffie was in no mood to think of the fact that the house was now his responsibility.

He found himself leaping up the stairs with the objective of taking a look at his mother's room. Best to do it now, best not to be afraid of it. Cliffie stood up straight and walked in. The sculptures. Those two little kids' heads. Why had she wanted to do something like that? Boring little beasties, Cliffie thought. And the typewriter, its blue paint and part of the metal worn away at the bottom corners, typewritten pages everywhere. Gosh! She would never touch the keys again. And it looked like she'd just got up from there.

'All right, all right!' Cliffie said aloud. 'It's not true!' But his own voice frightened him, rather than helped. And what he had said was false. He knew that. His mother was gone, forever.

And the dictionary. And the diary. He saw the diary, the big brown thing on the corner of the desk, as usual. She had had that since before he was born, Cliffie thought, and he thought he remembered his mother saying so. His own birthdate would be there – all the stories, the things that had happened, the judgement of him would be there, written for all to see. Who *was* going to see it? Brett? Yes, maybe. His father was the type. His father would hold it against him, the little details his mother might have put down, the little bad things. Cliffie decided to keep that diary himself. Yes, dammit! And get it out now, he thought.

Cliffie pulled the diary carefully from under the stack of papers. The leather binding was starting to crumble at the top and bottom. It weighed more than he had thought it would.

He carried it down, carefully down the stairs, up the hall to his room. He had decided to put it in a back corner of his closet, the drawers in his chest of drawers being so weak now, they probably wouldn't hold the weight without collapsing. Cliffie thought, as he pulled away a pair of sneakers, old socks, to make room on his closet floor, that he would never open this diary, never read anything in it. The idea shocked him, scared him. It would be worse than seeing his mother naked suddenly – something he certainly never had wanted to do, and never had done, even by accident. He realized that he had a respect for the diary and a fear of it also. He would take care of the diary, he decided, and this thought gave him comfort. He wouldn't let anyone else look at it, ever. He had thought, a minute or so ago, that he could burn it now in the fireplace, maybe finish burning it before Norm arrived, at least finish burning it tomorrow. But even that took or would take a courage that he knew he hadn't. No, much better to keep it hidden, to keep it from the others, other people. Maybe always. Maybe for all his life. He would never tell anyone that he had it. He would carry it around with him, hidden. Yes, even if he got married, his wife would never know. Somehow, he would manage that. Unless in some moment of extraordinary courage he would rip it to pieces and burn it.

There was a knock on the door, sound of the front door opening, a step. 'Cliffie? – It's Norm!'

Cliffie straightened up, half closed his closet door. Norm had arrived to take him to Washington Crossing. Cliffie opened a drawer and found pajama pants, couldn't find the top, and snatched from the floor a different colored top he was currently wearing. 'Right there, Norm!'

Uniform editions of Patricia Highsmith's books available from Atlantic Monthly Press:

____ *The Cry of the Owl*   *$8.95*

____ *Edith's Diary*   *$8.95*

____ *Eleven*   *$8.95*

____ *Found in the Street*   *$8.95*

____ *A Game for the Living*   *$7.95*

____ *Tales of Natural and Unnatural Catastrophes*   *$8.95*

____ *Those Who Walk Away*   *$7.95*

____ *The Tremor of Forgery*   *$7.95*

____ *The Two Faces of January*   *$7.95*

You can find all of these books at your local bookstore; to order directly, mail this coupon to:

Atlantic Monthly Press
19 Union Square West
New York, NY 10003

Please send me the titles checked above. I am enclosing $_____. (Please add $1.50 per book for postage and handling. Send check or money order: no cash or CODs.)

NAME _____

ADDRESS _____

CITY _____ STATE _____ ZIP_____

We cannot ship to post office boxes or to addresses outside the United States. Prices are subject to change without notice.